Simon Parke has been a scriptwriter for *Spitting Image*, a Sony award-winning radio writer and a weekly columnist for the *Daily Mail*. An Oxford graduate in history and a former priest in the Church of England, he is now CEO of the Mind Clinic and author of many books including the Abbot Peter murder mysteries, set in Seaford on the Sussex coast, where Simon now lives with the seagulls and his running shoes.

the *Soldier* the *Gaoler* the *Spy* and her *Lover*

SIMON PARKE

Marylebone House

First published in Great Britain in 2017

Marylebone House
36 Causton Street
London SW1P 4ST
www.marylebonehousebooks.co.uk

Copyright © Simon Parke 2017

British Library Cataloguing-in-Publication Data
A catalogue record for this book is available from the British Library

ISBN 978–1–910674–46–8
eBook ISBN 978–1–910674–47–5

Typeset by Graphicraft Limited, Hong Kong
Manufacture managed by Jellyfish
First printed in Great Britain by CPI
Subsequently digitally printed in Great Britain

eBook by Graphicraft Limited, Hong Kong

Produced on paper from sustainable forests

Acknowledgements

My hearty thanks to Blair Worden, my tutor at Oxford many moons ago, when this era was my special subject. We met again for lunch at the beginning of this labour, and I'm grateful for his unnecessary kindness, his unparalleled knowledge – and his wise disdain for historical fiction. To Jack D. Jones for his detailed information about Charles' stay at Carisbrooke; to John Fox for his ground-breaking research into the life of Jane Whorwood; to Karl French, my excellent editor; to Simon Jenkins, Paul Carter, Shellie Wright and Elizabeth Spradbery, who kindly read and commented on various sections of the manuscript; and to Alison Barr at Marylebone House for her entrepreneurial sense that here was a very good story that really should be published. I hope, in time, you agree with her.

This work is dedicated to Clive Williams

This is a true story in the fiction section.

The characters and events are real, as is some of the dialogue.

The oddest scenes are those most likely to be true; the past is hugely unpredictable.

The story charts the final eighteen months in the life of Charles I, mostly spent in captivity of one sort or another.

During this time he ate well, lied well, caused a war, tried to escape (endlessly), had an affair with one of his most tireless and inventive subjects . . . and died magnificently.

He is the only English king to have been executed, when few in the country wished him dead, including his nemesis Cromwell, whose wife Elizabeth was a fervent royalist.

But history is forged by personality, and here they are – the convinced, the conniving and the confused – wrestling with themselves and each other to create an impossible killing.

And here is a nation stumbling on the rocky question: 'What now?'

Main characters

Oliver Cromwell	From gentry farmer stock, more recently soldier and politician
Robert Hammond	Former soldier and king's gaoler at Carisbrooke
Jane Whorwood	Organizer of royal support network and king's mistress
Charles I	King of England, recently defeated in (un)civil war
Elizabeth Cromwell	Daughter of merchant, wife of Oliver Cromwell
Henrietta Maria	Queen and French wife of Charles I
Henry Ireton	Political ally and son-in-law of Oliver Cromwell
William Lilly	Astrologer, poor boy made good
Anthony Wood	Intelligencer
Henry Firebrace	King's servant, lively
Abraham Dowcett	King's servant, depressed
Cornet Joyce	Son of a tailor, the soldier who took Charles from Holdenby
Brome Whorwood	Husband of Jane Whorwood
Edmund Ludlow	Republican, lawyer, cushion-thrower, ex-Baptist minister
Ruth Hammond	Mother of Robert Hammond
Major Edmund Rolphe	Former shoemaker and Hammond's deputy at Carisbrooke

November 1647

I make my way through the London crowd and in some haste.

I'm always in haste, I know – it's how I live, there's so much to do, and people always in my way, holding me up, which is most tiresome. To be stuck behind another is torture, so I do push a little, particularly the loiterers or the infirm who so slow me down – but politely, I hope. I push politely, wishing only that they step aside and leave my path clear.

'Less haste, ginger lady,' says a man with a barrel, whose ankle I touch with my shoe. He looks at me as if I have done him wrong, but really, what does he expect, holding everyone up like that? I do not have the time or will to argue. I ignore the man, and then I look up . . . and Lilly's house appears before me: the Corner House on the Strand.

It is a grand affair – his wife's money, but that's another story. Fine beams and large windows, opposite the Strand Bridge; and a dwelling much visited in these troubled times. Even good Christians seek the opinion of the stars these days – though what I believe, or expect from the wizard, I'm far from sure.

I know a little of Mr Lilly. I'm warned he is more of the parliamentary persuasion. I do not care. As if I care! My belief is that the stars do not have favourites, so neither can an astrologer – or else he's a fraud. And perhaps he is a fraud, I know not. And what truth ever came from the mouth of a parliamentarian anyway?

But the king needs help; it's really most pressing, with escape from the palace uppermost in his mind. We need him away from Hampton Court, and he mentions the Scots as a safe haven – but I do wonder. Did they not sell him to the English in February as if he were an old shirt? They could sell him again, they're like that. I know them, believe me.

Charles does not encourage this visit of mine; he makes that quietly clear. He doesn't like the stars, they offend his religion . . .

though his religion does stretch its permission in other areas; he likes it enough when I suck his royal treasure. And in this matter, I care not what he says anyway. The plain truth is, he needs the instruction of the stars, so I will bring it to him.

And I'm now knocking on Lilly's door; and I'm knocking hard for he seems to take an age to answer. And I call out, 'Mr Lilly, Mr Lilly!' It's a name known well by those with dilemmas to settle. He seems quite the fashion among those with the money to worry; and his new book *Christian Astrology* is much purchased, I hear. Perhaps I should become a writer! The money seems easy enough. And I'm told the rogue adds 'Christian' to the title to find more readers, since the Presbyterians declare astrology to be of the devil. But it makes no odds to me. I would dance with Satan if it helped the king's cause and I will not pretend otherwise.

Where is Mr Lilly? Does the wizard sicken?

*

The door was opened with reluctance. A face peered through the crack to gaze on a tall, well-fashioned woman, with a round visage, a little scarred by small pox. And while ginger hair was not best for marriage, a truth well known, it seemed to suit her well. Such things could be seen before words began.

'William Lilly?' asked Jane, looking on a boyish man, easy on the eye and hair with the edge of grey.

'I would suggest another day, madam. I am indisposed.'

He pushed the door closed and Jane pushed it open again.

'I have travelled a distance and will be heard.'

'If it's a consultation about a relationship that you seek—'

'I wrote to you.'

'I receive many letters, many requests—'

'About the king's private matter.'

A pause.

'Jane Whorgood?'

'Whor*wood*.'

'Whorwood.'

'It doesn't matter who I am.'

2

'It matters to me; the nature of the visitor becomes the nature of my work.'

'I do not come about myself, as you well know.'

'But you bring yourself, so you are part of the story.'

Why doesn't he just open the door? she wondered. She had pressing concerns and he was wasting her time. She did not like her time wasted.

'This is a most urgent matter,' she said.

'I appreciate your haste, but another day would be best, Mrs Whorwood.'

'I do not have another day, Mr Lilly.' As if she was leaving here now! 'But I do have the payment we agreed.'

Money usually spoke well; yet the door on the Strand remained closed.

'I should warn you,' he said through the crack, 'that I have just buried a maidservant, taken by the plague.'

'I do not fear the plague, sir – though maybe the pox.'

'We are clear of that, I believe.'

A forward lady, he noted, and one not to be eased from his entrance.

'Then let me enter your house,' she said.

The door on the Strand was opened, and Mr Lilly, nimble of foot, was climbing the small stairs, dark and creaking, to his consulting room. Jane followed him up, glad to be free from the bustle outside.

'They say you are for parliament,' she said.

'I'm sorry?'

He stopped on the stairs and as she continued up; they collided.

'They say you are for parliament.'

'And you a Scot, perhaps?'

He continued upstairs.

'My father is a Scot. Why do you ask? Do you have feelings about the Scots?'

'Your fiery hair betrays you, that is all.'

'I hardly think it a betrayal. Scots rule the country, do they not?'

'Ah, so your hair is power.'

'Does it have power over you, Mr Lilly?'

Lilly smiled politely. They were standing in a low-hung space, with a drawing table, parchments, almanacs in tottering piles, the dry smell of chalk and strange instruments of metal; she recognized a sextant. It reminded her of the captain's quarters on a ship she'd once had cause to visit in the London docks. The captain had been eager to show her his quarters – too eager, as it transpired. His intentions were most clear, after many days at sea, when she'd wished only to see his cargo of gold, destined for the king. And here in the Strand were the same bare boards, the restrained sunlight, the decanter of port and the male desire to find order and meaning. She picked up the sextant.

'The trinketry of your trade?'

'Jacob's staff.'

'How do you mean?'

'It is what we call the instrument you hold.'

She put it down, looking now at a chart for the twelve months of the year.

'An ephemeris,' he said. 'It gives the positions of the astrological aspects as they're found today. Is that why you've come – to learn my trade?'

It was popular knowledge that during the civil war Lilly had been consulted by both sides.

'Well, are you for parliament?' she asked.

'Remind me why I should tell you such private things.'

'It shall become plain.'

'Then I am for the wisdom of the heavens, Mrs Whorwood.'

He was for truth; but also for business.

'Fine enough,' said Jane, keen to move matters along.

'And I ask ten gold pieces for its discovery.'

'We have agreed the sum.'

'I just remind you.'

'There is no need. I am not forgetful of numbers and have good credit.' The London merchants provided that.

'I received your letter concerning the king's ... predicament,' said Lilly.

'And I hope it is now burnt?'

'Ashes to ashes, dust to dust.'

4

'But is it burnt?' He had not answered the question.

'Ashes to ashes, as I say.'

'The letter is in ashes?'

'As one day we shall all be, Mrs Whorwood.'

Jane put down her bag and took a stool. Lilly did not wish his visitors to stay long; though often they did, pouring out their hearts and the difficulties of their lives.

'Mr Wood has not approached you?' she asked casually, as Lilly disappeared into a dusty room full of more books. Jane had never seen so many. It was a rabbit warren, one door leading to another, one room to another – and all full of parchment.

'Mr Wood?'

'He keeps a kestrel's watch over royal letters; he likes to snoop and swoop. You know of him?'

'I know of no Mr Wood.' How did she know about Mr Wood?

He returned to the room with a large tome, opened it on the table and began to set up his equipment. Jane watched.

'You are certain of your craft?'

Jane had money, but expected good return on her investment. Which businesswoman didn't?

'The wise men followed the star, did they not?' said Lilly. He was glad of the Christmas story and told it throughout the year.

'Astrology is an ancient gift but disreputable now – that's what some say.'

Lilly smiled wearily at Jane's assault. 'Until they *need* me, Mrs Whorwood – and then they cease from their sniping. This I have noticed. Indeed, they beg me . . . as you do today.'

'So how do you come by this knowledge?'

'I'm sorry?'

'Who taught you this knowledge of the stars?' She remembered the king's warnings in this matter.

'A Welshman called John Evans of Gunpowder Alley, if you're interested – formerly a clergyman in Staffordshire. He was my first tutor.'

'But also a rascal.'

'Who says so?'

5

'The king says so,' said Jane firmly and Lilly was surprised at this royal interest. 'He was forced to flee to London when his occult activities attracted the attention of the church authorities.'

'He did experience some awkwardness with the authorities, as have many good men, the king included. But he taught me the rudiments of astrology well enough.'

'And he was caught giving false astrological judgements to please a paying client! That was the same Mr Evans, was it not? I am aware of these things, you see.'

Lilly took a deep breath. 'Then you will also be aware that I dissociated myself from him as soon as his dissembling was discovered.'

'I imagine you did; but perhaps the deceiving disease was passed on?'

'I have no interest in deception, Mrs Whorwood. But if you would like to leave, I will quite understand.'

He did not need her business, for gold coins came and went these days. And while he was familiar with suspicion in his clients, and happy to calm it, this woman would not be calmed . . . and began to irritate, if he was honest.

'I will not be leaving,' she said.

'Then shall we to business?'

But Jane had further questions. 'They call it a parlour game,' she said.

'They call what a parlour game?'

'This!' She indicated his tools spread out before her. Lilly's eyebrows declared disbelief at this woman. 'I'm not saying so myself,' added Jane. 'Just reporting what people say.'

Lilly felt that there was something vulnerable about her – and something desperate. His irritation calmed.

'The horary astrology, in the hands of a master, is no parlour game,' he said firmly. Jane thought she might have angered him a little, though discerning another's mood was not her gift. 'It is demanding and precise, combining science and art.'

He pointed at the chart he'd prepared, laid out on the table before her. She could see he had not been careless in the matter.

'Properly used,' he added with a sniff, 'it will give answer to any well-defined question.'

'And mine is this: Where should the king seek refuge?'

Jane could hold back no longer. She needed to believe . . . and became a convert to the stars in that moment.

'He has refuge at Hampton Court,' said Lilly. 'A good refuge, I'm told. He is imprisoned there, but well served and lacking cause for distress.'

Jane would ignore the idea that an imprisoned king might lack cause for distress; they must proceed. 'But if he were to seek another refuge?' she asked.

'Another refuge?' Lilly's face could not hide surprise.

'Where would he go? That's my question. Do the stars suggest a better home for the king?'

Lilly nodded slowly, and pondered the heavens laid out before him, a grid of twelve squares. He drew some lines and looked puzzled.

'It is Jane Whorwood?'

'Yes.'

'And are you married?'

'Why do you ask?'

'It is a holy estate, Mrs Whorwood.'

'That depends on who you marry.'

'I was fortunate enough to marry well,' he said. 'I merely wondered if it were so for you, as there is some confusion in the stars—'

'What sort of confusion?'

'Perhaps too strong a word. A slight mist, possibly . . .'

He now regretted this path; he did not enjoy talk of feelings and sensed their approach.

'My marriage would confuse anyone,' said Jane. 'Well, anyone who looked for love and kindness, for both have been absent.' She looked him plain in the face.

'I see.'

'Can the stars understand that sometimes marriage resembles a lodging in hell, Mr Lilly? The priests struggle with that.'

'It was just a thought,' he said, easing back. 'There was some resistance among the planets . . . it need not detain us.'

'I don't mind being detained. For if we are to speak of marriage, Mr Lilly, where to start?' She seemed keen to begin.

'I understand if you do not wish to speak of it,' said Lilly kindly – and in hope. But Jane was eager, for she could speak of it nowhere else.

'Matters did not begin well,' she said, getting up off her stool. 'My father-in-law dropped dead on the morning of my wedding. Can you believe such a thing?'

Lilly put down his pencil. 'Unfortunate.'

'I think it was deliberate.'

'An inauspicious start, I grant you.' And, Lilly wished to add, rather selfish.

'One might say so, sir.'

'I did see some tension in the stars—'

'My tension was much nearer home.'

'His death must have dampened the gaiety of the day somewhat.'

'There was an atmosphere after the news spread, which lingered a little. But life must go on, Mr Lilly, this is what I said to the priest – and Brome didn't care a great deal. His father lacked warmth, and whatever pain there was during the service, was later drowned in wine, which sadly made many to vomit.'

'An inspiring story,' said Lilly, deploying irony to hide his shock.

'Though had I known what awaited me,' said Jane, 'I too would have chosen death that day.'

She returned to her stool and Lilly to his charts. Enough had been said . . . though not for Jane.

'And then the authorities fined Brome – who was below consenting age – for consummating the marriage without his father's consent.'

'Ah.'

'Or indeed mine, for that matter . . . but that was not the crime, in law, at least.' This was not territory he wished to explore. 'A ghastly night. And the matter is still with the courts.'

William took no pleasure in gossip, and desired a return to the stars – more wholesome company.

'Then during the civil war, Mr Lilly, my dear husband left us all and fled to Holland. He felt he was safer there.'

This man did appear to lack grace.

'And you?'

'I stayed – with my two surviving children.'

'There had been loss?'

'Two others died young.'

'I am sorry for your grief.'

'No, they were the lucky ones, believe me.'

Jane felt some discomfort. She had not been a good mother to her children Brome and Diana – or not in the conventional sense, not in the sense that she loved them. She couldn't say she loved them. Her strongest feelings were always the feelings to leave the family home, and she'd done that often enough. Children might please from a distance; they played in the street beneath her now and looked charming. But she had not liked her own too close or dependent, had not warmed to responsibility – too much restraint on her life. They gave her headaches and tension in her neck. She had not liked them as people, and this didn't help. So all in all, she'd been an appalling mother, and Lady Ursula, her mother-in-law, had removed her from the will in disgust.

'You were never a mother to your children!' she'd railed.

'And unfortunately you *were* a mother to yours!' screamed Jane in reply. 'Your footprint is heavy on all your offspring – and I had the misfortune to marry one of them!'

Lady Ursula was without obvious virtue, and she and Jane did not get on, nor pretend to. Some said Jane shouldn't burn her bridges with the woman who held the family purse strings – but that was a bridge that would have to be built before it could be burnt.

Jane's husband – the hag's son – was a waster and woman-worrier; she knew this now. He'd bullied and abused her for years. No, worse, he'd humiliated and ignored her, chasing the servant girls and catching them in the most intimate of ways – and all well known in the area. Thin wainscoting, noisy beds, wooden partitions, creaking stairs, ill-fitted planks, large keyholes and the servants' hungry eyes and ears – these things removed the privacy of a home and trumpeted Brome's behaviour widely. So the guilt should not be hers alone.

'He should never have wed you,' was the mother-in-law's chant, like a dull choir in a cathedral – endless. Jane could not disagree;

it would have been a fortunate escape had he not. She was nineteen when they married and Brome fifteen, with barely a bristle on his chin.

'But with land enough to make up for the years,' her grasping father told her.

The land was his best feature, there was no doubt of that; but you do not share a bed with the land.

William Lilly smoothed out his charts. He looked forward to returning to the stars.

'So I do not know if that is a holy estate or not,' concluded Jane.

'There's much we do not know.'

'But much that we'd like to, Mr Lilly. I'm sure your marriage is quite perfect.'

William had married rather well, in the world's eyes. A penniless employee of Gilbert Wright, William had married his widow Ellen on the old man's death – after she had declared herself in favour of a different way. She was quite clear that having twice married for money, she now looked for love, regardless of either status or income.

'I am finished with these things, Master William!' she said. 'Quite finished!'

'So what is it that you seek, ma'am?' he asked. 'It is sometimes an easier calling to declare what one does not want than what one does.'

'I seek a man who will love me, Master William!'

'I see.'

'I want love.'

'And that will be no great test for any man of substance, ma'am, for you are full of kindness.'

'But not in the first flush of youth.' This was true. She was in her stately fifties and could not pretend or look other. And then suddenly it had all appeared plain to William.

'Would you consider my young hand in marriage, ma'am?'

'You, William?' she said, laughing, for he was a country boy without family, prospects or income. The idea was ridiculous ... though eventually she agreed and they were married in secret at

St George's church in Southwark, telling neither family nor friends for two years.

'And I was content with her,' he journalled, 'content in marriage for six years, when, upon her death, she left all monies and considerable property to me – near to the value of one thousand pounds,' which enabled this bumpkin to buy a share in thirteen houses in the Strand and to lease the Corner House for himself – which is where he now sat with Jane Whorwood and the king's matter.

Was the king really planning to escape?

'I am pleased to say my marriage has been a fortunate affair,' he said, with tightness in his throat. He did not like to speak of himself on these occasions; while Jane decided not to mention Sir Thomas Bendish, her recent lover. She didn't wish to confuse the stars with her lovers, though they probably already knew. And if they didn't know, where was the value in telling them?

*

William Lilly, who had other matters to attend to this morning, offered Jane a planetary reflection. It concerned the movement of Mercury 'lately separated from the sextile of Jupiter and the Moon by a quadrate'. She heard the words but not the meaning. And then suddenly, from the claptrap and gobbledygook, Jane discerned a line of significance.

'Twenty miles from London there is a place of safety.'

'For the king?' she asked and he nodded. 'Twenty miles from London?'

'Twenty miles, or thereabouts. This is what the planets suggest by their leanings.'

'Anything else?'

'This place of safety lies in Essex.'

'Essex?!' She could not help the exclamation; almost a squeal. The county of Essex was already in her plans; before she had stepped through his door, she had thought of Essex – and now it was confirmed by the stars. Perhaps she could have saved her gold pieces; she did think this. But then again, the bigger picture had been revealed: the stars and Jane agreed, and she knew what she

11

must do. She knew a house there, about twenty miles from London, and suitable for the king and his hiding, while other plans were made. He could sail to France from Harwich . . . there was no need for her to stay now.

'Thank you for your time,' she said, gathering her effects and crossing the room. She placed the bag of coins on the table. 'It is a matter of some urgency.' She then turned to him with her darting eyes. 'I can assume your confidence in these endeavours? I would not wish this news to spill.'

Lilly's smile said that such instructions were quite unnecessary as he guided her down the dark stairs and out into the street. Brief goodbyes followed, the door closed and Jane was back in the bustling Strand, from where she made her way down to the river. Her boatman would take her to Hampton Court, for both she and the stars knew what the king must do.

He would be safe in Essex; and then it started to rain.

Earlier in the year

'There's no light,' Elizabeth had said the first day after their move that summer from airy Ely to cramping London and their house on dark and dubious Drury Lane.

'We shall bring light,' said Oliver cheerily. But the shadows remained and the ceilings were low.

Cromwell loved his wife, but didn't know her. How could he after so much absence, first in parliament, then at war? He'd always written to her from the battlefields, from one tent or another, and she had written still more in reply. He told her of military advances and exploding throats; she told him of the housekeeping, the boiled beef and the children. But the merchant's daughter he'd married all those years ago – marrying money from the fur trade – was still, more than he cared to admit, a stranger to him.

And he to her, of course; Oliver had been of solid stock when they wed, a gentleman farmer, and few progressed from there. Elizabeth had never dreamt he was destined for eminence. Yet now their home was visited by every officer and sectary in the land, all with a cause and a prayer to lay before their victorious general.

Listen. There was another of them, rapping at the door. Brisk. Impatient – this was an impatient time, when God was on everyone's side.

'It will be Cornet Joyce,' he said, rising from his chair. 'I'll greet him.'

But Elizabeth was quicker. This was her home; she would not be usurped.

'Cornet Joyce?' she said, opening the door.

'Ma'am,' replied the soldier, bowing, 'and here to see the lieutenant-general.'

He felt uncomfortable on the doorstep and a little judged by the lady . . . no, much judged. He knew who faced him, of course, Elizabeth Cromwell, and he'd heard talk of her. She wished for

13

the king to be restored to the throne, they said; which was not the view of the soldiers. Whether the rumour was true was not for him to say. Nor did it matter, for it would not alter his course. He was a man under authority and would pursue his cause with due order.

'You had better come inside,' said Mrs Cromwell. 'The lieutenant-general is expecting you – though the hour is late and perhaps your boots could do with some cleaning.'

'Why, thank you, ma'am.'

'I shall not be doing it,' she said sharply. 'I simply observe.'

Joyce almost blushed.

Drury Lane smelt worse than Ely . . . rotting fowl and fish in the kitchen, excrement everywhere else – horse, rat and human. The cesspit had shocked her even more than the absence of light; a solid stench unredeemed by fresh air. And forty shillings for the night men to empty it! Forty shillings!

'They took away eighteen barrels,' said Oliver when they left – an attempt to placate her. The men had worked hard, if noisily, throughout the night, with only a little spillage. But she was a trader's daughter, with a disapproving nose for cost – especially the cost of shit. The house was convenient for power, of course, closer to the clamour of Westminster, where Oliver could go, shout and still be back for tea. But it was only four doors down from The Cockpit, Drury Lane's finest stew-house – a brothel so busy that their alehouse never closed.

'It does not much scent the moral air,' Elizabeth had said, shocked at the periwigs and lipstick that daily sauntered past her window. And then, of course, there were people like Joyce, knocking end-lessly at their door in their grubby London boots. Some said they should be more finely housed; after all, Oliver was now an eminent figure, a leader among men. But where was the money for such a move?

Mrs Cromwell closed the door and pointed Joyce towards the parlour, where the lieutenant-general waited. The new arrival had not seen his commander since Naseby, the battle that had sealed the king's demise and proved again what prayer – and a disciplined cavalry – can achieve. Cromwell had created a wonderful army, but

14

had he also created a political monster? The thought troubled him more and more these days. He would need to harness them, bring them into line.

Joyce remembered Naseby and his general before the battle ... that quiet time of mist and wondering that precedes the thud and groan of engagement. There had been drizzle that morning. He could feel it still, inside his collar, trickling down his back ... and faltering morning fires. In the dry of the tent, he'd asked his general about plans for the day.

'We shall not trust in plans, Cornet Joyce,' said Cromwell, 'but in the providence of God, a better trust by far.'

'Indeed we shall, sir,' he'd said, returning to his regiment, happy to be on God's side and knowing Cromwell did have plans. He always had plans, though from where they emerged was hard to say. He would sit, ruminate, and then stir ... and when he stirred he could be a volcano. He'd been a disciplinarian with his troops. If they smoked, they were fined; if drunk, it was the stocks; and if they deserted, they were whipped. But in battle, these soldiers did what they were told, unlike the royalist rabble who imagined it all a game and chased after loot. Naseby was a victory for discipline ... and prayer.

But that was two years ago and a very different time. Away from the battlefield, with candles for cannon, Joyce must speak candidly with his commander about the king. Charles was presently held prisoner at Holdenby House, where he'd been taken after the Scots sold him to the English for £200,000.

'Both a pig and a king have their price,' Cromwell had said.

But the issue now was this: was the king safe? Or rather, was he secure? It was parliament who held him there, but with some laxity. Charles maintained his own household, receiving visitors unchecked, and talk of escape plots abounded, stretching the patience of some – for if they lost the king, they lost everything. And while the providence of God was a wonderful thing, placing the king in their hands, it now needed a little help. This was the belief of the soldiers ... and their representative today, Cornet Joyce.

'Cornet Joyce!' said Cromwell in welcome.

'Lieutenant-General.'

Joyce found himself bowing as Cromwell – sturdy but not tall – moved forward to embrace this faithful soldier. There was some awkwardness in the low-roofed parlour: a clash of physical styles. You cannot hug a head bowed and Joyce's head hit him midriff; but Cromwell made light of it.

'Life was easier at war than at peace!' he said and Joyce agreed. Life *was* easier at war. Men were more comfortable in battle; they knew where they stood in a fight and what they had to do. No one knew what they had to do these days, and trust died a little every day. 'Now, you will have a seat.'

Elizabeth arrived and put a small glass of beer in front of Joyce, with bread and butter. He'd been told that Mrs Cromwell's hospitality was reliable but frugal, and he'd eaten a pasty on Long Acre before arriving.

'You have concerns for the king,' said Oliver, sipping at his sherry. He liked a smoke and he liked a sherry; and he knew people's minds, even when miles away. Whether by spy or intuition, he seemed to know why Cornet Joyce had come.

'I wonder about the wisdom of Presbyterian officers guarding the king at Holdenby House,' said Joyce.

'You fear they may be in parliament's pocket?' enquired Cromwell gently, as though the thought was fresh, when all knew that it was so. They were deep in parliament's pocket.

'I believe we could find more reliable officers, sir.'

'Or perhaps a more reliable parliament?'

Cromwell laughed. It was a joke – though not a joke. Joyce didn't laugh. Parliament was as bad as the king in his army eyes, possibly worse. And he was not a man of laughter, tending more to the earnest way, full of zeal for the Lord's instructions and discomforted by merriment. He would not say so here, but he believed merriment to be the royalist way and the way of Babylon.

'I do not believe we should speak with parliament now,' said Joyce. 'Holles plans to take Charles from Holdenby and return him to London and his throne; that is the rumour.'

Cromwell knew the rumour; and knew Holles, the Presbyterian leader in parliament, as an overbearing and army-hating windbag.

They'd started as friends and ended as enemies, the Presbyterians holding there to be but one way to worship and quite insistent it was theirs.

'Forget Christ! Intolerance is the principal Presbyterian belief,' a raging Oliver had once said to Elizabeth.

Cromwell came from the independent tradition that believed in religious tolerance for all – except blasphemers and the Catholic sort; and his army felt the same as he. So as war had become peace, and the need for soldiery less pressing, most MPs now hated Cromwell and his army, with the antipathy generously returned. Cromwell had defeated the king for parliament . . . but there the friendship finished. Oliver retained his seat in the House and was dutiful in attendance, but while they debated with words, in truth this was war by another name.

'You say I should vacate my seat in the House and stop being an honourable member for Huntingdon?' asked Cromwell.

'What authority lies in that dung pit now?' said Joyce. 'God spoke at Marston Moor and Naseby. God never spoke at Whitehall.'

It was good to hear soldiers' talk again.

'Cornet Joyce, you speak with spirit.' He spoke with impertinence as well, mind you. 'But we must beware of dismantling parliament too hastily; for if that authority falls to nothing, then nothing can follow but confusion.'

'But confusion is what we have, sir. We are there already, and these parliamentary men, they do not understand sacrifice – sir.' That was true. 'Or what must be done for good to prevail.'

'And what must be done?' asked Cromwell. This conversation was like speaking with himself.

'These men, sir, who sit in their rows and make their votes – they avert their eyes now from the rough justice of war.' This was the talk of the army camp. 'They look away from the harsh transactions of requisitioned supplies, from the spirit of untutored men seeking redress – un-monied souls with no status. They do not want to hear of such things or know of such things, now their precious war is won! Can I speak plainly, sir?'

'You can.'

'This war and this army embarrass them! That's what we do; we embarrass them! They want only their Presbyterian prayer book and the king back on the throne!'

Cromwell felt the stirrings of a time lost, when battle lines had been more clearly drawn. And he felt the change in his army, no longer that rough but obedient unit, drilled and unquestioning. The child had grown up and now thought for itself – however wild their thoughts might be. Though nothing here was new. He'd known this truth a while, and said it to Fairfax: 'Never were the spirits of good men more embittered than now.'

Joyce leaned forward. 'How can men such as these – these soft parliamentary men – bring liberty to this nation? They know only cowardly talk and secret negotiation with the author of our woes. They press for a uniform religion, imposed like a blacksmith's clamp on every human soul.'

Cromwell agreed with each word, but feared their pace. There must be unity in this matter. They must all move as one, with people courted and cajoled into compliance.

'Have what you will, Cornet – but what you have by force, I look upon as nothing.'

'Are we not the Lord's army victorious by force?'

'We are . . . but the Lord's army now awaiting fresh providence.'

'I have a thousand horse, Lieutenant-General—'

'Mr Cromwell, please. I no longer fight.'

'And almost two regiments.'

'That is a good crowd.'

'And with those horse and regiments, I might surprise Colonel Graves and his hundred men at Holdenby.'

'You plan an attack on one of our own?'

'No, sir.'

'Then what?'

'This is no attack. I will merely propose to the colonel a different keeping for the king.'

'A different keeping?'

'A safer keeping.'

'And you will propose that with your soldiers lined up behind you.'

'You know the value of an army, sir,' said Joyce.

Cromwell contemplated anger; it came to the surface on occasion, as did his tears.

'A cornet to humiliate a colonel?' he asked.

'I desire to humiliate no one, sir. I am quite content to serve under another in this project, one of higher rank.' Cromwell nodded. 'My only desire is to make the king more secure.'

'You will fit better locks?'

'They say Colonel Graves couldn't secure a donkey that is lame.'

'That is the soldiers' view?'

'It is well known.' Cromwell smiled ... but the cornet was concerned. 'There are those who would have the king free, Mr Cromwell. When many good men have died to make him captive.'

Joyce had lost his brother and uncle at the battle of Marston Moor. Terrible things had been done in the war, awful murder – an uncivil civil war, fracturing families and nation, while the king played bowls and read romances in Oxford.

'You speak plainly,' said Cromwell.

'We fought a war that we might, sir; speak plainly and believe plainly.'

Had he said too much? But what else could he say? The lieutenant-general appeared indecisive, as if uncertain of the way – when he'd always been sure in battle. Joyce had a plan that demanded immediate enactment. It was simple, necessary and pressing, yet the response in this parlour was slow and unformed, like drifting fog.

*

Charles had spoken with Colonel Graves about his desire to explore the landscape of Northamptonshire on foot.

'Holdenby is a fine house, Colonel Graves.'

'I'm glad your majesty finds it so.'

'I knew it as a boy, of course, as a prince, and have many happy memories of this place. Better times than now ... much better times.'

'Indeed, sire.'

'Such grand parties my father had here – festivities quite envied by the French!'

The king did go on about the parties, but Colonel Graves nodded with deference, for his Presbyterian childhood in King's Norton had known nothing of such luxuriance. And while one should not applaud the lavish and the lewd, excess did encourage a certain respect.

'And I wish now to explore the estate,' said Charles, as if the parties demanded it.

Graves nodded once again. He could hardly say no to such an innocent and natural request from the king.

'And a little walking might do my physic some good,' added Charles, noting the colonel's acceptance of the scheme.

'I commend your majesty on such wise self-regard,' said Graves. 'Though you will understand if I send some soldiers with you – to ensure only that you do not get lost, sire. You would not be the first in these parts.'

'Lost – or escape, Colonel?' He looked hard at Graves. 'I am saddened by your poor trust; that you imagine I might escape this brief custody, which you manage with such courtesy.'

'I imagined no such thing, your majesty!' Though he had imagined this, and felt a little restraint might be wise. He did not wish to lose the king for parliament, for he was their best – and only – card. They were friends, the king and parliament, Charles assured them of this ... but they still needed it in writing.

'Then I will enjoy the company!' said Charles.

And shortly after, the king set out to explore the land around Holdenby, accompanied by two young guards who were much in awe of their companion, being carpenters by trade and not given to walking with kings.

'Have you ever walked with a king before?' asked Charles as they climbed a hill, leaving Holdenby behind.

'I have not, your majesty, it is an honour,' one of the guards replied.

'It *is* an honour, yes – and one I cheerfully grant you.' They walked on. 'You shall tell your parents of it, no doubt,' continued Charles. 'You walked today with the king!'

'I shall tell my mother, sir – my father was killed at—'

'I have sons of my own, you know, and you are like them – in some ways.' The young men blushed. 'I miss them greatly, of course, and when you are fathers you will understand. Still, we shall be together again soon, with the help of my dear friends in parliament.'

'I hope that very much, sire.'

They walked further still, along a little-travelled track over a carpet of early summer daisies, and then Charles spoke again.

'I must now let you return to Holdenby, my children, while I walk on a little, alone.'

'Sire?'

'I need solitude; his majesty desires to be alone and will make his own way back shortly.'

He indicated that they should now turn around, this instant, without discussion, and leave him – though they hesitated.

'It is the king's command, soldiers. A command the wise heed.'

'Yes, your majesty.'

They did not know what to do as they stood amid the cowslips, but he was the king and God's anointed . . . and so they obeyed. They turned round and walked back to Holdenby, debating among themselves what Colonel Graves would say, while the king carried on down the track, glancing back only to ensure his privacy. It was good to be free, simpler than he'd expected. Jane had provided him with a local map, brought on her last visit – though quite where he was now he couldn't be sure. He should have asked the young soldiers before they left, but they were a distance now.

Charles, alone with the breeze and a bee, looked around for assistance.

*

Perhaps they were right, those Leveller fellows. This is what Cornet Joyce now considered beneath the low ceilings of Drury Lane, glad of the steady fire.

Many in the army said Cromwell was the present difficulty: a hero in war, but a disappointment in peace. It was common talk in the regiments that the army leadership had become too grand for their own leather boots. They said the search for power had gone to their heads, had severed their bonds with the common soldier, when it was the soldiers who'd got them here . . . and having come this far, they would not now be denied.

'You seek my authority in this matter, Mr Joyce?' said Cromwell.

Joyce looked at him through the pipe smoke. He had not seen his commander in this manner – a man grown weary, restless and perhaps caged in this small, damp dwelling, where his wife cleaned and altered constantly. She took his plate as soon as he was done with his bread. And Cromwell seemed to read his mind.

'You notice the damp, Joyce?'

'There is something in the air, perhaps, sir.'

This was not a conversation they'd shared on the battlefield.

'My wife has tried a house perfume to make the air better,' said Cromwell and Joyce nodded. 'The place was left too long before our arrival, you see. I'm not sure about the perfume,' he said, lowering his voice. 'I tell her we just need the chimneys smoked and heated again … and the rooms aired. Though whether London air is the best—'

'About your authority—'

'Yes.'

'I believe your orders would add weight and legitimacy to my business, sir,' he said.

'And your business is to remove the king from his Presbyterian gaolers and secure him in some manner for the army.'

'It is, sir.'

'And I commend you in your work, Cornet Joyce, whatever it may be.' Joyce wondered what he meant. 'You appear to have God's wind in your sails,' he continued, after sipping a little more sherry, as if toasting the scheme. 'A sure sign of the providential hand.'

He got up as he spoke, and walked towards the door.

'So I must detain you no longer. You have a long journey ahead and much to do. I understand you must act with speed, if you are to proceed as described. Give my best to Colonel Graves, should you meet. Solid soldier, Graves, Regiment of Horse, I believe.'

Joyce was standing in Drury Lane with his own horse, unable to remember how he'd got there, and unsure as to what Cromwell had meant. Did he commend Joyce in his endeavours, or command him? Did he now proceed with Cromwell's authority or not? No matter, he would ride north to Holdenby House, to ensure the king was securely held.

This was the Lord's work – but Joyce would help, by God!

The track, promising at first, had narrowed and become a path overgrown with forget-me-not and weed. Charles stumbled and then stopped, gazing at the map, which helped little if you did not know where you were; Holdenby was a large estate, he remembered his father saying. Ahead, he saw a cart proceeding slowly, which suggested a road – perhaps the road to London, or Oxford, where he had safe houses. Jane would have things ready for him . . . and his splice hardened a little at the thought of her.

He struggled through a hedge, climbed over a wall and found himself, after a little toil, on the road he sought – surely it was so? He felt as tired and dusty as the summer, his skin a garment of sweat, but wiping his eyes he saw a woman on a horse, and was now waving her down. He would use his charm; the people had always loved him.

'I seek the best path to London, good lady,' he said. He had no fear of recognition, having tied his thick hair back in a tail.

'Your majesty!' she exclaimed. 'Are you lost?'

'I appear to be,' said Charles, looking up to the surprised rider, a most attractive lady in her bonnet. 'I seek the road south; and you must not speak of this meeting, never. Do you understand?'

'You seek the road south?'

'I do, good lady, but it is not something you must speak of.'

'But that is away from Holdenby.'

'I flee evil men.'

'Which evil men?'

'The worst of sorts.'

'But my husband said nothing of this.'

'Your husband, madam?'

'Colonel Graves, your devoted and admiring servant.'

'Colonel Graves is your husband?'

'He rides with me, but a little way behind. Here he is now!'

The colonel appeared over the brow of the hill and rode up alongside the country conversation.

'Your majesty, I had not expected to see you here, regaling my wife with pleasantries.'

'A little lost,' said Charles.

'As is your escort,' said Graves and the king shrugged. 'And despite the fresh map you carry?' The king had neglected to return it to its pouch. 'So well equipped for the journey home, your majesty.'

*

With the Thames seagulls arguing overhead, Jane stopped in the street and felt ill. A man was scolding his children, ill-language flowing from his mouth, and he reminded her of Brome – not his face but his manner; she couldn't escape her husband.

And then she was walking again and thinking again that if she'd been a poor mother, Brome had been a monstrous father. A good father might have made her a good mother, as one candle lights another. Had Brome shown even a little goodness to her, then perhaps her disposition would have altered, with more tender habits to the fore, more kindness in the kitchen, more joining in bed? Perhaps then she would have liked her son instead of being repulsed. It didn't help that the little fellow shared his father's name – a name passed on like the plague. It had been hard to separate the two sometimes.

But what excuse for her daughter Diana? Why had she not cared for her? Perhaps, quite simply, she was not a motherly woman. Such people must exist; it was no crime. And anyway, there was always her grandmother and servants to play the parent at home. If one must live with one's mother-in-law – never a choice – at least let them serve you! And this is what she told herself again and again as she rode the wet lanes of England in the king's cause. Especially when war broke out, that terrible war, when the king had replaced all others in her affections . . . for wasn't this every patriot's duty?

She had left her children for Charles, this was her reasoning. And she was good at her work, there was no one better. With his queen in exile, how necessary she became in so many ways, and she did it all for his majesty: raised money, smuggled gold, handled intelligence, linked loyalists. She was a go-between, a carrier of secret ciphers, coded messages – 'a lady worthy of extended notice',

24

as one opponent declared, and much to her delight, for Brome could manage no such words.

To support her dear king, she'd created a network of contacts extending from London to Edinburgh, from Grimsby to Cardiff, covertly relaying news among the royalist supporters, via laundresses, merchants, latrine emptiers . . . there was no one she wouldn't use. For good reasons, those who emptied latrines were rarely stopped and never searched.

But her real work began when the greedy Scots, for a Judas fee, sold the king into English hands in February 1647, after which he was held at Holdenby. And there he remained, 'a bird in a gilded cage, a golden ball thrown between parliament and the army'. The king needed friends, and would find one in her. Contact became daily at Holdenby, with compliant guards and the kind Colonel Graves.

And escape would be easy; she had left him a map on her last visit . . .

*

'It is the story of a country boy who walked to London and there found fame and fortune,' wrote William Lilly in his diary. 'And it is my story! The story of a Leicestershire lad who – with his father languishing in the debtors' gaol – took his penniless self to the capital, worked hard, married well . . . and discovered the stars.'

William enjoyed reviewing his life – a life lived beneath the kind guidance of the heavens. He found pleasure in discerning again the golden thread of fortune through the difficult years. And as a carriage halted noisily on the street outside, with some disagreement about payment, he remembered his own carriage journey south, less fine than the one he noted now.

He'd left his home village of Diseworth on 4 April 1620. It was a cold, stormy week of rain and late spring snow, smacking his cheeks and soaking his shoes. He'd walked to London alongside the carrier's wagon – he had never been carried himself. 'I footed it all along,' he wrote, 'arriving at half past three in the afternoon on Palm Sunday, 9 April, praise be to God,' whereupon he made his tired way to the residence of Gilbert Wright, Master of the

25

Salters' Company, who lived at the Corner House on the Strand. And for the next seven years – had it been that long? – he worked as Wright's servant and secretary. It was a secure enough post, but menial for one of his intelligence ... and here regrets lingered.

For sometimes he looked north – he did on occasion – to the university at Cambridge where his fellow students had gone to study ... students not as bright as he, for he outshone them all in Latin and should have joined them there. But his father could not pay the fees, and so it was the long walk south for the scholar denied – and the household chores of Mr Wright.

But how circumstances change! Marriage, money and the discovery of astrology altered everything. 'For it was at this time,' he wrote, 'shortly before Ellen's death, that I appreciated a hidden and stupendous truth: that all sublunary affairs depend on superior causes. This opened to me the possibility of discovering these causes in some manner; of discerning the shape of events before they occurred by the configurations of the superior bodies, the stars – even events between parliament and the king!'

He was permitted one more entry before interruption on this particular morning.

'My family for generations were yeoman farmers; but I had not that inclination or gift. And so I walked south with six shillings in my pocket which I've turned into a thousand or more! And now I sit with wealth and fame, while my friends call me the "English Merlin", and my enemies, "the juggling wizard and imposter". And maybe both are true.'

The knocking was loud. People rarely arrived at his door with a sense of calm.

'I need to know if he's the right one,' said the distraught woman at the door. 'If he's the right one for my Lucy.'

'I see.'

'They speak of marriage – but do the stars speak of marriage? I have my doubts.'

'Do you have coin?'

'I have coin,' she said sticking a sovereign in his face before withdrawing it back inside her tight clench. 'And his name's Matthew.'

26

'And you know Matthew's birth date.'

'I know every dark crevice in the wretch's soul.'

'Would you like to come up?'

*

'Your attempt at escape was not well received, your majesty.'

Your majesty? Perhaps it was the building, the fine windows and hangings. But Cornet Joyce regretted the subservient tone in his voice; like some butler to his master, when he was no servant to this man, this bringer of death.

'I'm not sure a king *can* escape, Mr Joyce. You cannot imprison a monarch.'

Joyce disagreed ... and this was hardly a prison anyway – little like Newgate or 'Little Ease' by the Tower, where the poorer crooks rotted. Holdenby had been the largest private house in Elizabethan England, that's what they said, built by Hatton and visited by the queen herself, who had gazed on it with some astonishment.

'You have many windows, Hatton.'

'Through which to gaze on you, your majesty!'

The old charmer. In fact, Holdenby had one hundred and twenty-three large glass windows, set around two fine courtyards, and became a favourite haunt of Charles' father, King James, who'd used it to entertain in his wild and some said wayward manner. Young Charles had heard his father grow very loud in this place, and not always sober. Dear man that he was, he could discover a very foul mouth inside him and a rage that sent many people running.

And somewhere inside, in a locked-away place, Charles remembered other less wholesome affairs – things he'd never told his mother. His father with his favourite men, behaving as they did, naked and naughty with each other ...

But thirty years on, the rolling countryside of Northamptonshire held a quieter jewel, no riotous parties now. Instead, Charles found himself detained here, a prisoner at Holdenby and facing an abrupt young man – the sort he'd never had to meet, let alone speak with, until these useless days.

'I'm not sure a king *can* escape, Mr Joyce. You cannot imprison a monarch.'

'I believe we have, sire.' To imprison the monarch was Cornet Joyce's purpose.

'No, believe me, I remain the king and you my subject, wherever I take my rest. These things do not change with a battle or two.'

It was the all-knowing smile that stirred the soldier's fury.

'Whether you are king or not, sire, I do not know and do not much care, but I come here now to secure your person.'

'Secure it for whom? For myself, I feel quite secure here at Holdenby. It is a place with a rich royal heritage.'

'Secure in the providence of God.'

Charles raised his eyebrows a little. 'So you even organize our Lord now, Cornet? Promotion indeed for the son of a tailor.'

Joyce had no answer except the army at his back. He looked behind him, with deliberation, through the window, to where his troops had gathered. He was feeling the press of time and the fear that Colonel Graves would return from London with additional forces. He had not expected Graves to act as he had; but a change of plan was necessary and Charles seemed to read his mind.

'I will miss Colonel Graves,' he said. 'But perhaps he goes to get help, and will come back to save me!'

Graves had fled Holdenby . . . and this changed everything. Cornet Joyce had arrived peaceably enough, yet without intention had put terror in the heart of the man. Graves had gazed on the new arrival as if Joyce were some avenging angel, here to punish and take revenge. Did he feel guilt at his collusion with the king? One might surmise that. Joyce had spoken briskly to him, this was true; and perhaps in a manner ill-fitting a cornet addressing a colonel. But he'd merely explained the need for a change in the king's keeping, a securer kind; and if Graves heard insurrection in that, then it was not from Joyce's mouth.

'And you come with some authority behind you?' asked Charles. 'Beyond an ability with clothes?'

'They are my authority,' said Joyce, indicating his troops. 'A note written in steel and signed in blood.'

'A persuasive authority indeed,' Charles said with a smile.

28

And later that day, Cornet Joyce, the proud son of a tailor, marched the king of England to army headquarters at Newmarket. The king was truly imprisoned now.

*

'I must leave, my love,' said Oliver. And she was his love; he had loved no other, nor would he.

'Do not forget Bridget is coming this evening . . . your daughter.'

'I know my daughter.' Elizabeth shrugged her shoulders. 'I'll not be here, though,' admitted Oliver.

'Another war?'

'There will be no more of those; for the cause of the war is caged.'

'So where?'

'Army headquarters.'

'Newmarket?'

'Newmarket.' He still held the courier's note. 'The king has been seized,' he added, and then regretted his remark.

'Seized? By whom?'

Oliver paused. Why had he spoken? 'Cornet Joyce.'

'The little man here last week?'

Oliver nodded. 'I don't remember him as small,' he said. 'A fine soldier.'

'He seemed small to me,' said Elizabeth. 'And dirty shoes.'

'I don't imagine the apostles' feet were clean.'

Oliver walked over to the window and peered through the glass, much smeared with London and in need of a vinegar scrub. He heard Elizabeth busy behind him, finding work . . . but remaining close by, for she wasn't finished.

'And the king's abduction – this is your work, is it?'

'It is not abduction, Elizabeth.' He was aware that it was . . . so he'd continue to ponder their grubby street and the tarted women flouncing by, a far cry from Ely indeed. 'And not my work, in any manner. I have not lately left London, as far as I know.'

Elizabeth smiled at her devious husband. 'But he told you what he was about?'

'He spoke of his concerns; and they were proper concerns – as far as they went.'

'As far as they went? They seem to have gone to Newmarket.'

'The king is safer there.'

'You mean you are safer.'

'Cornet Joyce is a good man.'

'And are you, Oliver?'

*

'I do not *retire*, Mother.'

'How can a man retire at the age of twenty-six?' she asked, ignoring him.

'I did not say I was retiring.'

'You used the word, I heard you.'

'I used it inadvisedly.' Why had he used the word retire?

'Twenty-six is no age to sit under the lazy tree,' she observed.

Robert Hammond – former commander in the New Model Army and friend of Cromwell – was in Chertsey. He stood in his mother's kitchen, where she could always be found, preparing some meal or other for herself, or for a neighbour, whether they wished it or not. He regretted mentioning retirement, but merely spoke his mind, concerned at republican feeling in the army, where Levellers and their democratical brood held sway. When all that England needed was quiet agreement with the king, these fellows discovered only injustice to debate and pamphlet about, with their fierce and militant pens.

'I am not retiring from work, mother – I merely seek another way, apart from the army.'

His mother was carrying a boiling saucepan of udders, tongues and turnips to the table. 'Apart from the army?' she said, thumping it down. 'But what is to be done in this land apart from the army?'

'Plenty, I hope! The army will be at war with itself soon.'

*

'You spoke of seizing the king,' said Elizabeth, wishing to pin him down with her words. 'When you spoke with the cornet, the matter was discussed?'

'We wondered about his safety.'

'And did you authorize him in this action?'

30

'I'm not sure this is your affair, wife.'

He was a rage inside but held it back, for Elizabeth did not like his anger; this he had learned. She would turn on him with abuse, go silent for days, or bang plates in the kitchen and harden her manner, as if locked inside a shell.

'Well, did you?'

Cromwell sat down and picked up his pipe. He knew better than to stop her; she could not be stopped . . . but he could ignore her.

'I commended his spirit.'

'You commended his spirit?' Elizabeth polished a pewter jug with fury. 'And you think it wise to seize the king from parliament's grasp?'

'Is it wise? I do not know if it's wise, but parliament can no longer be trusted to keep him safe, that is clear – and the soldiers would not be keen to see him slip away.'

A pause.

'So the army rules now?'

'They have a voice, I think.'

'They have a sword.'

'They felt the heat of battle, Elizabeth. Do you not think that gives them a voice?'

Elizabeth polished some more. 'And you think the king will be pleased?'

Cromwell laughed. 'We are not here to please the king.'

'So why are we here, Oliver?'

*

'Who is Robert Hammond?' asked the king. 'And why should I care?'

'He was a soldier, your majesty,' said Firebrace, who still wondered that he spoke with the king, when he used to sell offal in Swindon.

'With us?'

'With Cromwell.'

'He was a Roundhead?'

Charles rolled his eyes. Why would he wish to see one of Cromwell's wretched soldiers? Did he come to gloat? And anyway, all was well at the moment, with no need for interruption. Hampton

Court was a good dwelling, a fine staging post for his purposes. Eighteen of his staff served him here, in this most genteel of imprisonments. He had kept both his cook and his dogs, though not his wife, and woke up every day in a palace, as a king should.

He'd always liked Hampton Court, and had come here often with Henrietta, just ten miles up the Thames from Whitehall. So the reasons for wasting time with this Hammond fellow were not immediately apparent . . . though Firebrace remained insistent.

'Was he a real soldier?' asked Charles. He did not mind a little conversation with Firebrace – containment could be dull without Jane – and Firebrace understood his meaning. Not all soldiers were real soldiers. Some had been more famous for looking dashing on a horse than bloodying their hands with the fight; and sadly, such men had tended to be fighting – or posing – for Charles. No one posed in Cromwell's New Model Army. They would have been struck by divine lightning after a long night of prayer.

'Hammond distinguished himself at the capture of Tewkesbury, your majesty.'

He had done his homework. Eager and meticulous in the king's service, he did not wish to return to Swindon.

'Then I wish he'd been on my side; that was a sad day.'

'Though he is not without a temper, it seems.'

'I do not need to know,' said Charles with a sigh. 'I tire of this Hammond already, so put him aside from our conversation. I think I will go for a walk. Have my shoes made ready.'

*

'So why encourage the little cornet?' asked Elizabeth.

'I did not encourage him.'

'You did not forbid him.'

'I merely understood his reasons. And in truth, my dear, I don't believe he intended to take the king. That is not the appearance of the matter.'

'He travelled across England with the king by accident?' *Really, Oliver – do better than that!*

'My understanding – what I am told – is that he panicked a little in the heated moment, something easily done.'

'What heated moment could there be, with an army behind him and little in front?'

Why was his home such a bear pit sometimes? Oliver did wonder . . . as if parliament had decamped to Drury Lane.

'Colonel Graves ran away,' said Oliver firmly. 'When he saw Joyce and his troops.'

'But why did he run, when Joyce was on his side?'

'Men panic; it is a weakness. In women as well . . . I have known it in women.'

Elizabeth sensed Oliver's slow withdrawal of information, like one holding back logs from a fire.

'So where is the king now?' she asked.

'He'll be taken to Hampton Court. And there we will talk and find a way to return him to the throne. Enough? I have had quieter days in battle.'

There he could rage and feel God's fury in the charge; but he could not rage here. They never spoke angrily to one another. It was not seemly in marriage.

'I simply do not understand what passed through Joyce's mind,' said Elizabeth. She couldn't put the matter down, and Cromwell stood up, too stirred to remain seated.

'Then let me tell you, good wife, about the mind of these soldiers!'

'There's no need to shout.'

'I am not shouting.'

'You raise your voice.'

'But still more peaceful than the cannons these men heard . . . men who have seen and smelt the fight, watched friends and brothers lose legs, lose heads, lose uncles, lose fathers – and now they ask themselves, "Why was it so?" This is what they wonder; they wonder why those things were done, if we are simply to put the king back on the throne as if no war occurred.'

'Because he is the king,' said Elizabeth, flatly.

'As if they had not endured the drowning rain of the campaigns; the disease and the cold, which killed more than the fighting; family against family, the destruction of the suburbs – thousands upon thousands of homes pulled down in order to starve a town; the execution and lynching of prisoners—'

'Both sides, I hear.'

'And no holier for that.' After Naseby, more than a hundred women who followed the royalists were massacred; the rumour was they were Irish. 'But it's no surprise – can anyone venture surprise? – that the army question a little! That the army asks why the author and perpetuator of this war should be so hastily and happily returned to power.'

'Because he is the king,' said Elizabeth again. 'Your anger does not make him any less our monarch.'

Silence.

'And now parliament, driven by Holles, refuses to pay them,' said Oliver. 'They fought for parliament but now parliament refuses them money on which to live. They rely on free quarter from those around. This is not as God intended.'

'They plunder the helpless – it is well reported.'

'They are God's soldiers who seek some reward, Elizabeth. I believe this to be fair!'

'You're shouting again.'

'I do not shout.'

'Why can you not admit that you shout?'

'A raised voice is not a shout.'

Silence.

'I merely believe it fair that they demand some reward, some recompense for such sacrifices made.'

'The king would look after them better than parliament,' said Elizabeth, and her husband grimaced. Neither would help the army now. 'But you abduct the king, and make him an enemy again.'

'It is unlikely any soldier will trust the king after the Naseby letters, wife.'

It was delivered quietly but with power and now Elizabeth hushed. The discovery of Charles' private correspondence after the battle had not served his cause well. He was exposed as a man governed by his Catholic queen, Henrietta Maria, and particularly damned by evidence that he conspired with the Irish rebels: the English king in league with Catholic traitors against his own people! It was a long way back from such revelations.

'The king must help us to trust him,' said Oliver. 'We seek trustworthiness. Is that too much to ask?'

There would be no peace in Drury Lane tonight.

*

'He shot a Major Grey in a duel,' said Firebrace, keen that Hammond should not be forgot. He felt a meeting with Hammond would well serve the king's cause. Hammond could help him.

'Duels?' said Charles, some way away. 'I never understood them.'

The duel was too specific for this king, too decisive, not his way at all. The imprisoned king, as both friend and enemy declared, 'was a master of determined hesitation and silent prevarication'. A duel was uncomfortably forward.

'He was then tried by court-martial, sire.'

'Who was?' Charles' mind had wandered again. He'd forgotten his walk and thought now of Jane, who would be visiting later.

'Hammond, sire.'

'Hammond, yes.'

'Robert Hammond.'

'And why are we talking about Hammond?'

'He wishes to see you.'

'I need to speak with the Scots; I think that might advance our cause further. I may escape north.'

He spoke mainly with himself, while stroking Bishop, his cocker spaniel who gave much delight, a faithful friend in unfaithful times. And the wall hangings gave pleasure, friends to the royal gaze. The army had lately brought them from Whitehall to give comfort to the king in his unfortunate captivity.

'Hammond then fought at Naseby, your majesty, took part in the storming of Bristol and Dartmouth, and was present also at the battle of Torrington.'

'Is this the best you can do to cheer me?'

'Before capturing both Powderham Castle and St Michael's Mount.'

Two further royalist disasters.

'Quite the busy bee,' said Charles, who had avoided the civil war as best he could. He had settled in Oxford and found it a pretty city; and he'd first met sweet Jane there, of course.

'And Cromwell trusts him, sire. He sends Hammond to parliament to negotiate on behalf of the army.'

Charles remained a distant figure to Firebrace. The person of the king seemed never quite there.

'Different people pass through him,' he once said to Dowcett, a kitchen servant.

'And not one of them great,' came the reply.

'But still divine,' Firebrace had said reprovingly. 'Still divine.'

'I'm expecting a guest,' said Charles.

'Hammond seeks also to be your guest.'

'I do not warm to him.'

'But perhaps he warms to you.'

There was a short pause.

'I am hardly his best friend,' said Charles, laughing a little. 'It seems he has spent his life fighting me!'

'But he changes.'

'Does anyone change? I doubt that very much. I don't see anyone changing.' He would not be changing.

'I'm told that he now doubts the army.'

'A little late for that – the cavalry are back in their stables.'

'And wonders whether it is justified in using force against parliament.'

'Against parliament? And what about the force it uses against the king? Is that a matter of no consequence?'

'We merely notice, your majesty – and take one step at a time.' Firebrace heard himself being magisterial and was rather pleased . . . Swindon left so far behind. 'He does not like the noise the Levellers make in the army, this is what I hear.'

'They are all quite mad.'

'Then you share that with him at least.'

'Are we done?' Charles offered a vague smile as he spoke.

'Hammond has sought and obtained retirement from active military service. A bold move, I'm sure you'd agree.'

'If you say so.'

'And wishes to meet you and pay his respects.'

'Wishes to meet me? He has stolen all my goods, but wishes now to give up a life of burglary and become my companion?'

'These are difficult days, your majesty, and any friend—'

'You really do not see my offence!' Charles was amazed. 'He falls out of love with the army, becomes a nobody on earth, boasting neither status nor power – and now wishes to kiss my ring!'

'He is also the nephew of Henry, your chaplain, your majesty.'

Charles sighed. Why was he talking to this half-wit Firebrace? What had brought him to this? He wished for the old days, before the war ruined everything.

He looked around him . . . and thought of the Banqueting Hall. Why would he not be there tonight?

'Have you ever seen the Banqueting Hall in Whitehall, Firebrace?'

'No, sir.' How could he ever have seen that? 'I have not been to London.'

Charles just smiled; he would not be speaking further on the matter. It was a building close to his heart – and not for discussing with servants, who simply wouldn't understand. Built by Inigo Jones for his father, it was the finest building in Britain, there could be little doubt, in contrast to the chaotic and shambling structures around it that comprised his Whitehall residence. It was a jewel, without question. But a jewel which held inside another jewel . . . for inside the Banqueting Hall was dear Rubens' masterpiece – and the greatest Baroque ceiling north of the Alps! Charles was near moved to tears at the thought of it, for there in that painting was all that was good: kingship, honour and the benefits of Stuart rule. Such art! On one canvas, a cherubic Charles held aloft by England and Scotland, while Wisdom holds the joined crowns of the two nations over his head. Magnificent! In another, his dear father is carried on the back of an eagle to join the gods in heaven. Could anything be more beautiful? And how could his subjects be so blind of eye as not to discern the truth of all this?

His predicament struck him again. Tonight, he would play cards with unimportant fellows and perhaps gamble a coin or two – when he should be in the Banqueting Hall! Charles and Henrietta Maria, how they had excelled at the theatre of it all! The masques, the public displays, the magnificent hospitality of Whitehall. And how wonderfully such events, such excess, had declared due status – Charles' God-given kingship! This is how he felt. He had ruled by masques rather than parliament, by theatre rather than debate, an altogether better way. 'Britannia Triumphans' – now that had been a spectacle! A heroic allegory of Britain's naval might on the high seas, and such was the scenery in the hall, one might have imagined one truly was at sea. Here was theatricality, nobility and virtue!

And his Henrietta played her part. She came alive amid revelry, it was where she was best. Dear Henrietta. And the two of them, they were good together, despite the difficult years, the early ones ... and yes, they were difficult, almost intolerably so. He had been crowned at Westminster Abbey without his wife at his side, because she refused to participate in a Protestant ceremony. Really! It did not go down well with him or the lords.

And that was merely the start, for they'd quarrelled about everything that year. In the end, he'd expelled most of her French attendants, and such was her pique, she withdrew her services – those of the body – from August through autumn and Advent. The seasonal words, 'How long must we wait, O Lord?' had been spoken with feeling by Charles.

But then she'd had no English, poor girl, written or spoken, not when they'd first met – except the Catholic creed, which is not the language of love. She set herself apart in that regard – always French and always a Catholic and therefore much scorned, for the English did hate the French ... and Catholics.

And all so different from their first meeting. Ah, that was a night of almost unbearable happiness, when they shared discreet looks across the colour and lust of the French court. Had Charles ever felt so fine? She was a bright fifteen when they married, a good age for sacred union and with such vivacity. Charles loved that vivacity, so merry and gay – his little flittermouse, he called her, my flittermouse! And she adored him, he felt this every day of their courtship, the handsome prince from across the water, such good days ... though perhaps her ageing had proved unfortunate. It was not for a husband to say, of course – for better or for worse, as the marriage service declared. But these days her teeth stuck out from her mouth, a little like tusks, though such pretty eyes above the tusks and a good enough complexion. Her arms were long, of course, perhaps longer than her body required, and her shoulders uneven. And Henrietta was a spendthrift little minx, no question about that! She drained the treasury daily with her dress buying. But she was kind to her court dwarves, particularly Little Sara. More considerate than some, anyway; she was almost always kind to the dwarves. And yes, the masques had been so fine beneath the Rubens sky ... and he would swive with her in costume when all the guests had left. They had been good together, Charles and Henrietta.

But now she was gone, taking refuge at the French court these past two years. They wrote, of course, such sweet messages; but one could not grind with a letter; and neither could it not hold you on a cold night or handle the king's treasure.

'Jane Whorwood is here to see you, sir,' said Firebrace.

September 1647

Col. Robert Hammond
Governor of the Isle of Wight

Carisbrooke Castle
September 1647

Dear Aunt Margaret,
I have arrived at Carisbrooke Castle and feel better already for
the sea air.

Can you hear the seagulls? They make more noise than the
Levellers at Putney!

You ask about my appointment to this post, which I must
explain. It has happened swiftly but well; and I write optimistic
for the future. You will know that Philip Herbert, governor of the
Isle of Wight, resigned on 3 September. I confess I did not think
on it greatly, believing it no concern of mine; but then found
myself approached by Thomas Fairfax. He is well known to
me, commander-in-chief of the army and a good man; and he
asked me to consider succeeding Herbert as governor.

I did not need to consider long! After all, I have left the army
now and seek a different path. In particular, I tire of political
stirrings there, with the soldiery much disturbed by malcontents,
who complain that dear Oliver and his friends visit the king at
Hampton Court 'and kneel, kiss and fawn upon him'. They do
not believe the king should be talked to, it seems; they call him
'the man of blood', and there is little the army leadership
can do.

Oliver tried to bring order at Putney, tried to hold them
together: 'Let us be doing but let us be united in our doing!' he
pleaded. But the contrary voices were many. Edward Sexby –
the madman – claimed they were trying to heal Babylon when
Babylon did not wish to be healed; though the worst offender,

I have no doubt, was the revolting John Lilburne – always revolting in my estimation, I will not hide my feelings. He singles out Cromwell and Ireton with especial relish, accusing them of 'vaulting ambition, Machiavellianism, hypocrisy and insincerity'.

You will understand, dear aunt, why I seek a quieter life on this isle of solitude.

And so here I am, at my desk, installed in the castle, governor of the Isle of Wight – a windy venue for retirement but also bracing. And I hope you are proud of your nephew. I am commissioned to my post by Fairfax, with the ordinance passed in the House of Lords. So whether I am the army's man or parliament's, I know not; but it is of little consequence, for while determined to fulfil the duties before me, I have left the national stage and gladly so. My greatest challenge is to find a new cook, and improve the table in this place!

And yes, as you intimated to me in your letter, it was indeed a great honour to meet with the king in person, shortly before my departure. Uncle Henry brought me to him at Hampton Court, where he is held in a gracious manner, and I was keen to profess my loyalty, after our differences on the battlefield. I do believe he looked on me with some sympathy and warmth, for he is a most magnanimous man and no enemy of mine. Uncle Henry commended me as a penitent convert, which the king took well and he gave me his hand to kiss, which was a signal honour. In that moment, I felt the war to be quite over.

And now I lay my quill down. But I look forward to seeing you soon at Wolverton Hall, which holds such happy memories for me.

With the deepest and best of wishes,

Your nephew, and new governor,

Robert

*

They met at Hampton Court just as they'd met at Holdenby House. Jane's energy knew no bounds in the cause of the king, whose needs were many.

'No compromise,' she would say to Charles. She always said that: 'No compromise.'

Her own life was full of compromise – one laid on top of the other and stacked in a large pile. But she'd insist on another path for the king. 'Who do they think they are?' she would ask. And as one imprisonment became another, Charles liked to hear such words, for he felt the same about the little people who opposed him. Who do they think they are? And why do they busy themselves in ridiculous opposition?

'I like your spirit, Jane,' he would say in his gentle Scots brogue and with the stammer she found so winning; sometimes he was like a little boy. 'You are my sm-m-mooth-thighed flittermouse, my red-haired Henrietta!' and Jane was happy to be so, for she had great respect for Henrietta, in her absence across the sea.

And then he took her hand, pulled her towards him and kissed her bared arm from wrist to shoulder, licking as he went. She laughed a little and when he'd finished, he looked like a guilty dog. He had never before licked her arm.

'You have exquisite arms, Jane,' he said and she laughed a little more. 'They please the king.'

'I'm glad they please the king,' she said, for she wanted to please him, but was surprised to please in this manner. He had previously kissed her forehead and touched the soft skin beneath her neck and above her breasts. And twice he had placed her hand on his trousered cock ... and once matters had proceeded further. A man has needs, and the king, while divine, was also a man. And he would not remain in this gilded cage; Jane would ensure he was free. Jane Whorwood would release him, like a dove of peace, for this, and only this, would bring calm to this troubled nation.

'I go to see William Lilly,' she said.

'William Lilly?'

'You know of him.'

'I know he's a charlatan. I would not waste your time.'

'I will not stay long – but who knows what wisdom he may offer us?'

'The so-called "oracle man".' Charles spoke with disdain.

'And perhaps we need an oracle.'

'I would call him "the cunning man".'

'He answers two thousand questions a year, so I am told, and is paid half a crown for each one. There are many who believe.'

'And many ways to part a fool from his coins.'

'He does see the future, in a wide degree of matters.'

'Farmers asking about their crops, old men about their illness ... and mothers enquiring after their daughters' young men. I would not wish to join that dismal crowd.' And then to further make his point: 'He is an occultist, Jane, who learned his craft from that appalling Welshman Evans. The Presbyterians accuse him of witchcraft, and on that single matter, I agree with them.'

'The Independents treat him more kindly.'

'He says what they wish to hear.'

'He was much visited by the army during the war, they say – and they were victorious, we cannot deny that.'

Jane had no opinion of the stupid men employed by Charles to lead his armies in the war, apart from Prince Rupert, who was rather dashing.

'I think their cavalry was more telling than the stars,' said Charles.

'I will see him, though,' said Jane. She was set on it. 'Perhaps God does speak through the stars. We must weigh and consider all.'

'I do not wish to know,' said Charles, turning away, cold to this conversation; and that was the end of the matter.

'Then I will be gone, sire, and return soon.'

Jane could be in the Strand in less than three hours, if the tide was kind.

'You must stay a little longer, Jane,' he said. Charles did not wish to be abandoned now. 'Please sit.'

Jane sat down across from the king. She did not wish for another lick or stroke, thinking of Henrietta, who was her dearest ally in the king's cause.

'How was Cromwell today?' she asked, aware of his visit that morning.

'He becomes easier by the day,' said Charles, amused. 'We laugh together. I believe he likes to laugh with a king. He had only a little land in Huntingdon – so to speak with a king does give him some excitement.'

And then a concern crossed Jane's mind. 'I trust you will not agree with him on any matter, your majesty, be it the smallest thing?'

'I shall perhaps *appear* to agree, and draw him in that manner. Appearance – everything is appearance, my dear.'

'As long as it is artifice and not collusion. You must remember who you are. No compromise.'

'I hardly need dissemble, Jane.' He did not wish to talk about such things with her; they should not concern a subject, this was the king's business ... but he would calm her. 'I believe he desires me on the throne as much as I desire it myself, but he would tie me with parliament, which clearly cannot be.'

'It cannot be, no.'

'And he would have them appoint my advisors too!'

'That most certainly cannot be!'

'I confess to secret laughter when we meet, behind my earnest face.'

'It would be no throne with such an arrangement.'

'No throne at all. Now, come over and sit with me, Jane.'

'I should be on my way, your majesty.'

'You will place yourself here on my lap that I may take better notice of you.'

'I have a journey—'

'And that is a royal command.'

'I have spoken with Firebrace about destinations,' she said.

Charles paused his desires. 'I think I shall escape to Scotland,' he replied. 'Now please, you must come over here for I swell a little and need comfort. I think we should be merry for ten minutes before we must be parted again.'

*

A scarce believable scene was emerging in Corkbush Fields near the Hertfordshire town of Ware. There was mutiny in the air and incredulity in those who beheld it.

After all, this was the New Model Army, famous for discipline, prayer and fasting – yet here it was in revolt. They were waving muskets, with shouts and slogans, and stones were thrown at commanding officers. It had not been like this at Naseby.

'England's freedom, soldiers' rights! England's freedom, soldiers' rights!' they shouted.

There was the sense that day that anything could happen. Battle-hardened men felt unpaid and unvoiced and were no longer prepared to stand for it; no longer prepared to listen to their leaders, who spent their time sweet-talking with the king and sharing his anchovies and wine. So they came to Corkbush Fields to say, 'No more!'

And now Cromwell was riding hard at them. He was riding into the troops, as if at war, riding alone into the waving muskets of his own soldiers, shouting in prayer, shouting God's fury and swinging his sword, like one deranged. He was attacking his own men, the saints who'd marched by his side down the years. And he knew the regiment he tilted at: that of Robert Lilburne, brother of Leveller John.

'Who will fight with me?' yelled Cromwell, as he rode into the ranks. 'Who will fight with me?'

This was not as it should be. The army had gathered here to sign a declaration of loyalty to Fairfax and the army leadership, who for their part had promised to take this show of unity to parliament to demand the payment owed. And most were content with this, loyal to their godly boots; but not Lilburne's regiment, they had more political airs. They'd arrived with their own 'Agreement of the People' stuck on their heads – paper fliers of insurrection wedged in their hatbands. Cromwell admired neither their manner nor their dress.

'They have paper fliers in their hats, like children at a party,' he said to Ireton.

'They seek to be seen.'

'Then they have my attention; but shall not enjoy it.'

They'd chanted the Leveller slogan, 'England's freedom, soldiers' rights!' And after shouting a while, the stone-throwing began – aimed at one of Fairfax's officers who'd approached them to reason and discuss.

'I come in peace,' he said.

'He brings false peace!' one shouted back and cast the first rock.

Fairfax was in shock. He wanted reason to rule, but Cromwell chose force – quick and determined, like in battle. And off he went, springing forward on his horse, riding straight at them, aiming at the ranks of the mutineers.

'Oliver!' shouted Ireton, a cavalry man himself but left stationary by the speed of Cromwell's movement. The mutineers saw him coming and backed off, pulled away; they even broke lines to allow him through. Cromwell slowed his sweating horse and shouted at them to surrender.

'And remove those strange agreements from your hats, you prick lice! Such frippery in your hair, you look like girls after school!'

'We will not do so,' shouted a leader. 'We stand for the agreement!'

'And I stand *on* the agreement! I stamp its nonsense in the mud!'

Jumping down from his horse, he seized the papers from two or three heads, held them up and then threw them down, trampling them into the Corkbush soil.

'You speak too much with the king!' shouted another, but it was a voice lost in the wind.

Cromwell was moving among the men, close to their faces, looking each in the eye. These were his sort, honest folk, but no matter now – like old fruit they'd gone rotten. With the officers who'd followed him, he seized eight or nine of their leaders and had them taken away under arrest.

He looked around at the remaining soldiers. Some removed the paper agreements from their hats themselves, others just stared. No one had disobeyed the general before; these were different days. Cromwell mounted his horse and returned to Fairfax.

'This must be stopped,' he said, by way of explanation.

'But whether you calm them, I don't know,' replied Fairfax.

'I calm them.'

And he had. The uprising was sunk like a spinning top with no spin. A sullen quiet prevailed and Cromwell acted without delay. There, in the fields of Corkbush, a court-martial trial was held in the open air, with all nine found guilty of mutiny and the three ringleaders sentenced to death.

'We will execute only one,' said Cromwell.

'Only one?' queried Ireton.

'Just one.'

'I see three ringleaders.'

'Only one; let mercy reign.'

Ireton raised his eyebrows. 'And which of them will choose their death? We may not find a volunteer.'

'An honest man would volunteer. But if there is not one of those, then let them cast lots, as they did in the scriptures.'

The condemned men were taken to the edge of the encampment and there each selected a stone from a table. It was Private Richard Arnold who chose first, civil war veteran, Leveller agitator and former Baptist minister. He turned his stone over to discover the scratch mark none wished to see. He looked up in shock, and then defiance, while his friends were asked to leave his side.

They didn't move at first, and Cromwell warned them: 'Stay and you die; which is a waste not wished by God.'

With a nod of the head, Arnold let them leave. He was alone with his stone, so poorly chosen. Cromwell ordered the musketeers to raise their arms, then spoke.

'Richard Arnold, you have been found guilty of mutiny and have chosen the marked stone. You will die by musket fire. Do you have anything to say?'

'Charles is a man of blood and you speak with him.'

Silence. The army wanted an answer.

'When I speak with the king, I speak not for myself but for the army and for England.'

'What do you know of the army now, Mr Cromwell? You lord it over us these days and laugh with the king.'

'I laugh, do I?'

'We hear that you laugh.'

'I did not know laughter was a sin. But I do know we are better together, Mr Arnold, whether we laugh or not. I know that only our unity will bring God's will.'

'There can be no peace in the land while the king lives, no peace!' And then he started again, looking around him for support. 'England's freedom, soldiers' rights! England's freedom, soldiers' rights! Death to the man of blood and death to all who parley with him!'

But none joined in, resolve having left the place. Richard Arnold was alone in Corkbush Fields.

'No one wishes to fire on you,' said Cromwell, walking a little towards him. He'd been a brave soldier and deserved an honest death. 'But they will fire, because it is better that they do.'

'Better for who? They kill an honest Englishman!'

'Honest Englishmen must stand together at this time.'

'Honest Englishmen stand for the godly and the downtrodden, for persecuted sectaries and virtuous tenants exposed to the malice of royalist landlords!'

He sounded like a pamphlet and shouted on: 'And if only the propertied are to have the vote, then why did we fight? Why did the common soldier fight? For we return from battle with nothing but our wounds and more slavery!'

'There must be order in the land,' said Cromwell.

'Without the army, these people are undone!' shouted Arnold, shivering a little now. 'England's freedom, soldiers'—'

'Fire!' shouted Cromwell, his patience dismantled. The marked stone hit the earth before Arnold's tortured body, which fell twisting against the table.

'Fire!' shouted Cromwell again, more shots aimed at the groaning man, the table pushed over and Arnold rolling back . . . until still.

Silence. Only the call of the birds and a westerly wind; but there was no more mutiny among the soldiers that year.

*

Robert Hammond was counting his blessings, like a child with an orange. How delighted he was to be away from the army and not debating politics with the wide-eyed loons now in residence there. He could not understand why Cromwell even spoke with them; you do not remove rats by feeding them. The army was changing, this was clear to Hammond: no longer the honest fellows they once were. The Levellers had too much influence, republicans and democrats all, and four-square against all that true Englishmen held dear. And Robert would not countenance any of it. His days of conflict were done, and he delighted in the weight eased from his back. Instead, he listened to the seagulls, breathed in the untroubled air of the Isle of Wight . . . and remembered the old hag.

'I see a new life beckoning,' she'd said, after taking hold of his hand outside parliament and feeling his palm. 'I see a new life beckoning!' He'd made light of it, laughed at her even – she probably said it to everyone . . . but he could not help notice the truth of her words. A new life had beckoned.

He would write to his mother; he should do this more often. He'd tell her how glad he was to have retired – no, how glad he was to have acquired a civil post, away from politics, 'for which I am not made, Mother. I fear the army will break their promises to the king and I am not so averse to his majesty – if I may confess this – for he is a good man, I believe so.'

He chose his words carefully. His mother was an Independent and no lover of Charles. Her favourites came and went, she fell out with everybody, but the king had never been admired.

I remain an Independent, as you would wish; but in favour of both the king and liberty of conscience; and certainly not of the extreme party, who batter the ears of Cromwell these days.

And generally, I seem to make a good impression on the Isle. Even Oglander, a famous royalist, yesterday called me a 'gentleman and also the son to a gentlemen'. I do try to get on with all people.

In the meantime, Aunt Margaret sends her best wishes. I have visited her at Wolverton Hall, which is barely four miles from Carisbrooke, and I hope to see more of her in my time here; the slow life will suit me for a while.

From your dear son, of whom I trust you are proud,
Robert

He did wish her to be proud of her son.

*

The rain did not concern Charles. After three months of captivity in the palace, he was finally free from Hampton Court – a move achieved with surprising ease. He was imprecise about his destination, though he sensed that Cromwell was right.

In truth, he would have preferred to stay where he was. Hampton Court was a comfortable setting, more suited to a king than Holdenby, and he had planned to remain while his adversaries squabbled and begged for the honour of a royal smile. But then came the rumours of murder; strong rumours that could not be ignored. They'd been passed to him from more than one source – and, significantly, not denied by Mr Cromwell, who was plain and straight, if nothing else. He didn't dislike the man.

'We will do all we can to protect you, your majesty,' he'd said.

'And is that sufficient?' asked Charles.

The rumours spoke of agitators in the army. These were common men with sudden voice and power, men who sought 'summary justice' against the king.

'I cannot say,' said Cromwell.

'Do you know these men?'

'We do know these men; but we perhaps do not know all their friends – or where they might be.'

'And your meaning made plain?'

'We will do all we can to protect your majesty. I have spoken this morning to Colonel Whalley, who commands the guard.'

'And you were clear to him about these threats to my life?'

'Clear as the gospel, sire. "Have care of your guard, sir," I said, "for if such a thing were done it would be a most horrid act!"' Charles nodded ... more horrid for him than for Cromwell, he felt. 'But the army that guards you here is an angry army, sire, stirred by agitators.' Cromwell must make this clear. 'Many feel badly towards you; I cannot dissemble. Who knows what plots exist in the minds of men?'

And that was enough; it was clearly time to take his leave, with certain plans in place. But due to haste – Firebrace was particularly flustered – no actual destination was settled upon as the king set off. He thought briefly of the whimpering Bishop, whose large eyes had looked bereft as Charles left his rooms. He had shooed him away, a little angrily perhaps, and closed the door on his pleading paws, for needs must – a cocker spaniel could hardly accompany the king on this venture. He'd be looked after when he was gone, and not punished; this was the king's hope. They'd be kind to Bishop. Charles had never harmed anything, apart from some rabbits and deer, and he hoped that other humans were as decent as he.

These had been his thoughts as he crept down the back stairs, stairs that had never been guarded – a kind omission – and then out into the wind-thrown rain of this September evening. He was a free man for the first time in eighteen months ... even if it was the uncertain freedom of the fugitive.

'The king is somewhat free!' he said to the rain, 'though unsure as to his way.'

*

He'd get back to the palace in Whitehall, Charles was quite sure of that – back to Whitehall with his head held high. When all this silliness and nonsense was over, he would once again take walks in St James's Park with Henrietta on his arm, king and queen together, like the old days. She plotted wonderfully from her Parisian exile, pressing Mazarin on the matter, selling the crown jewels to raise funds. She would continue the fight on his behalf ... and then there was Jane, sweet Jane. He could always rely on her. Henrietta would like Jane.

'Your majesty, let me cover you,' said Legge, one of the grooms of the bedchamber and helper in the escape. He appeared out of the squall and walked alongside his majesty, trying awkwardly to cover him with his coat. But it was a wilful wind and Charles told him he was not obliged to continue.

'I have walked in the rain before,' he said. 'The king is not made of clay.'

'Certainly not of clay, sire. More like gold.'

'They say creation sickens for the return of the king; that these days, it rains in sadness.'

'The sadness at least masks our escape,' said Legge, feeling that sadness must have a reason.

There were search parties behind them, no doubt. Charles thought he could hear their shouts. But Legge was a colonel in the war and moved with determination, a better soldier than housemaid and glad now of the adventure. And while the rain was severe, it did make a good shield, as Legge observed – a wet curtain as they advanced towards the village of Thames Ditton; and there, a boat was waiting on the rising water to take them across the river. Legge held it as best he could as Charles tried to climb in, but the wood was wet, not kind to the grip, and twice the boat moved just as the king's leg was lifted, causing him to slip and curse with frustration. On one occasion Legge himself fell into the water, apologizing loudly.

'It would help if you held the boat,' Charles said to Legge.

'Yes, sire,' said Legge, in much discomfort, for the water was cold and the mud clinging. There were no shouts in the distance, though, which reassured, but no time for delay – the army would be consumed by fury. Finally they were afloat, Legge rowing hard across a strong current, carrying them upstream.

'We're drifting!' said Charles. 'You are not an oarsman, I fear.'

And then the pleasing sight – appearing through the rain on the other side – of Firebrace and Dowcett with horses.

'God bless your majesty!' hailed Firebrace as Legge aimed the boat towards the shore.

'We have a journey ahead of us,' said Charles, once he was landed. He did not like his feet being wet.

'You spoke of Bishops Sutton in Hampshire, sire.'

'That is certainly a consideration.'

'Fresh horses await us there,' said Firebrace. 'A ride of eight hours.'

He had done his best to research the king's wishes, but it had all been so hasty. If only he'd been given more time; he'd only received the message after luncheon, this very day.

'Do we have a path, sire?'

Charles surveyed his damp companions. Legge, Firebrace and Dowcett were keen fellows all, but none was Columbus. And so he himself would be the guide – and he was the king, so why not?

'We shall ride to Bishops Sutton,' he said decisively. 'And be away from there before the dawn's exposing light.'

'We were not able to obtain maps, sire.'

'Follow me, Firebrace.' A king did not need a map.

*

They were now quite lost, passing through a forest, soaked and uncertain. Charles rode a little ahead, with the distance between monarch and servants allowing for some grievances to be aired.

'I said this would happen,' said Dowcett.

'You say nothing else,' replied Firebrace, who was dismayed by Dowcett's lack of spirit, when he had enough energy for five.

Charles, on returning to parley with them, believed the failure lay with them rather than himself. They'd travelled too far west, this was apparent; so when dawn broke, the king and his companions were not leaving Bishops Sutton with food in their bellies and fresh horses beneath them. Instead, they were in Windsor Forest – or so Charles thought.

'I have ridden here before,' he said. 'In merrier times.'

'So what are we to do?' asked Legge, seeking an order, for he was a soldier.

At least the rain had eased a little and there was the hint of light in the east.

*

'The search parties have found nothing, Lieutenant-General.'

The courier was in a state and Cromwell made to put the young man at ease.

'Mr Cromwell will do. I am no longer a soldier.'

'Mr Cromwell.'

'And your name?'

'Scratching, sir. Mark Scratching.'

He and Henry Ireton had heard the news at army headquarters at Windsor.

'I imagine the search has not been helped by the rain, Soldier Scratching?'

'Not helped by the rain, sir, no.' ·

Silence.

'So, the king is truly gone?' asked Henry, still shocked, contemplating the awfulness of this news. The courier nodded.

'And how did that occur, Scratching? How exactly did the king dance out of our care?'

Henry Ireton was Cromwell's right-hand man, his harder edge. He had a square head, famously square, and piercing eyes that saw with more clarity than kindness and suspected even the innocent. You could sweet-talk Oliver but not Henry, that's what they said.

That he was also Cromwell's son-in-law – married to his eldest daughter Bridget – was strangely unimportant.

The nervous courier continued: 'Colonel Edward Whalley arrived at the king's bedchamber at five o'clock to accompany the royal prisoner to the chapel – as usual, sir.'

'And the king wasn't there?'

'No, the king was there – he was inside the bedchamber writing letters, that's what the colonel was told, and couldn't be disturbed.'

'A prisoner who cannot be disturbed? I desire such imprisonment myself.'

'And then the same thing happened at six o'clock, sir.'

'Whalley was turned away again at six o'clock?'

'They said the king was still at his letters; he does like his letters.'

'And the colonel did not wonder a little?' asked Ireton. Was Whalley an idiot?

'I don't know, sir.' He had not wished to be the messenger today. 'He wondered at seven o'clock, though, because when there was still no sign of the king, he did suspect the king's servants of subterfuge, and looked through the keyhole and banged on the door. But getting no answer – the door was locked – he insisted on being taken round the back way, through the privy gardens and up the privy stairs.'

'And on entering?'

'The king's cloak was lying on the dressing-room floor.'

'But not the king.'

'No, the king was gone. They reckon he had a head start of five hours, your grace.'

'Mr Ireton will do. I am not yet a bishop.'

Cromwell laughed; a more unlikely bishop would be hard to find. Like himself, Ireton was from Independent stock and not for dressing up in popish finery. All you needed was faith and a Bible. Scratching looked down at his shoes, as if he personally had led the king to freedom.

'We do not hold you responsible, Scratching,' said Cromwell.

'Thank you, sir.'

'Now go and find yourself some food, and consider your work for the evening done.'

'Work for the evening done, sir,' said Scratching, nodding vigorously in relief.

'You have been a faithful messenger, which is all that is asked of us.'

'All that's asked of us, sir.'

'Isn't that so, Mr Ireton?'

'Quite.'

'That we be faithful messengers ... now be on your way.'

'Yes, your grace.'

'Mr Cromwell, if you please! No pretensions of status here! I do not like the pretensions of status!'

Scratching backed out, begging their pardon once again. Cromwell broke the silence that hung heavy for a while.

'So where does he travel, Henry?' He looked wearily at the sword that lay calm and sheathed on the table. 'And how deep is the dung in which we stand?'

*

Dowcett had said all along that there was no forest on their route; Firebrace was too enthusiastic about everything. He was much too busy with his plans to see that most things did not go well, not in the end. This was Dowcett's wisdom: that life was endlessly unfair and frustrating.

'There's no forest on the way,' he'd said to himself – but audibly enough, for even kings must listen sometimes, particularly when lost on a wet night with the army giving chase. They'd all be dead by sunrise.

Charles never listened, though, and certainly not to servants. They needed to look to themselves, this was Charles' view, and to their lack of preparation – for how could the king discern the way, when he had been captive for eighteen months? It was his servants who should have provided maps of the route. Why were there no maps? Did he have to do everything himself?

'I am disappointed in you,' he said, in a manner as chill as the rain. Servants should serve; but these servants judged him! He was oppressed by the journey and by the company of his companions.

55

Servants came and went as bidden; but these ones loitered and not in a helpful manner.

'I need you to dismount and walk your horses,' he said.

Legge, Firebrace and Dowcett looked confused. 'Dismount, sire?'

'I need to think a while,' said Charles, who could not think while they remained in their saddles alongside him. 'You will walk your horses down the next hill, while I decide what to do.'

'We must go to the West Country, your majesty,' said Firebrace. Why were they telling him where to go?

'The West Country is with you. They will rise in support.'

'I asked you to dismount, not make comment.'

He didn't use names, not to his staff; it seemed beneath him and might discomfort them. They must simply do as they were told or he'd become angry – and he didn't wish to be angry. That was the last thing he wished, for he was a man of peace.

Legge, Firebrace and Dowcett dismounted. They plodded down the hill, pulling their horses, while Charles reflected on his movements; and it was then that he realized where he should go.

'The Isle of Wight!' He said it out loud. 'Carisbrooke. I shall go to Carisbrooke on the Isle of Wight.'

Hammond was the man he could work with now. He had felt the young man's admiration when they'd met at Hampton Court, and he liked admiration. And Charles was no stranger to the Isle. He had such happy memories of his visit there as a prince in the summer of 1618. Easier times, halcyon days. It had been a warm summer and he'd dined at the castle and found solitude in the well-house, watching the treadmill donkey . . . good memories indeed.

He would ride forth and tell his servants where they were going; after providential guidance, they were going to the Isle of Wight to reclaim his youth and his future!

*

'To France, I imagine, via Jersey,' said Henry. Where else would the king go? He'd be off to find Henrietta – and a Catholic army. 'An unfortunate loss, wouldn't you say?' He was angry at the fool Whalley for allowing such escape, and angry with his father-in-law who'd appointed Whalley and his regiment to guard the king. 'I had heard Whalley was a most courteous host to Charles,' he continued. 'But this was surely a courtesy too far.'

'Edward is an honourable man,' said Oliver, 'and a fine soldier.'

Whalley had been one of his own regimental commanders, brave at both Gainsborough and Naseby. He would not easily criticize.

'But a piss-poor gaoler,' said Henry, not given to such language.

'There was rumour he'd choose the custody of the Scots,' said Oliver, wishing to speak of Charles rather than Whalley.

'And in the face of such rumour, we chose to leave the back stairs unguarded?'

'Jersey is possible as well. I've heard that Henrietta has kept a boat there for some weeks.'

There was further silence between them which grew tense.

'We should not have lost him,' said Henry, the sense of blame apparent.

'I felt him to be a man we might work with,' said Cromwell. 'A man of honour. He is the king, Henry.'

'But never a man to trust, Oliver – this was quite clear from the start.'

'Clearer now than then; hindsight speaks with an easy clarity.'

'Clearer now he is gone to France, in search of an army larger than ours. Clearer now that everything we have worked for is sunk!'

He had never liked Oliver's happy talks with the king, but then Oliver could never hold a grudge. He'd wished only to bring the king round to a new way. Cromwell liked peace; few knew this ... but Henry did.

'You cannot stay angry for long, Oliver.' Cromwell looked vacant for a moment. 'It is a weakness of yours. You were angry in war, but forgot your wrath in peace.'

*

Charles had come to the house of the Earl of Southampton, where he dried slowly in front of the large log fire. He had told the earl he was staying the night, which was a shock to his host.

'You catch me unawares, your majesty.'

'They say the second coming of our Lord will not be much heralded.'

But the earl would have preferred the second coming; it would have been less upheaval. And the day had started so well, with a fine breakfast of beer and fish, until Jeffrey had approached the table, bowed, and announced news of a royal arrival. He had not himself been convinced it was a king, inclining to scepticism. 'He says he is the king, sire – but whether he is so?' Jeffrey made a doubtful face.

'Yet he claims to be the king?' said the earl, putting down his beer. What was this?

'He says he is the king and says it with force – but does not resemble a king.'

'And have you ever seen the king, Jeffrey?'

'I've never seen him, no, sir.'

'Is he short?'

'He is short.'

'The king is short.'

'But he's damp and, well, dirty, sire . . . not monarchical, is what Sarah said.'

The earl said, 'Thank you, Jeffrey,' and shared his doubts. After all, he'd spoken with Charles at Hampton Court only last week, and he'd been peaceful enough then; in some luxury and ease, in fact, with paintings by Dürer and Rembrandt recently delivered from Whitehall. Why would he leave such a place? But on his arrival at the front door, it was the king, standing bedraggled in his porchway, and he couldn't hide his surprise.

'I hope my subjects are always glad to see their king,' said Charles, a little reprovingly.

Some more so than others, thought the earl, and none when the visit is unannounced or at this time of the day. But then the king did not live in the world inhabited by others. He lived in a world that happened on his behalf, with no other cause considered.

'It is an honour, of course, your majesty, but an unexpected one. You have left your lodging—'

'My imprisonment—'

58

'At Hampton Court.' The earl was considering the implications, both for the king and for himself. 'And the army?'

'They will be looking for me, no doubt; I hardly think they are pleased that his majesty has left their care. But I had no choice, no choice.' There was always a choice, thought the earl. 'They would have murdered me, the soldiers. There were plots.'

'Then you must come inside, with your—'

'My manservants have travelled with me.'

Legge, Firebrace and Dowcett looked like three wet hunting dogs, who'd been hunted themselves.

*

Hammond was feeling in splendid spirits. The Isle of Wight was a most invigorating setting: a taste of heaven, if one could say such a thing. He might well retire here – this was his thought as he set out this morning for a meeting with some local gentlemen in Newport. It was the island capital, a mile to the east of the castle, and it would be a pleasant ride. The sea air was good for him; he felt this.

'To be free of England's politics is a wonderful thing,' he had told Captain Rolphe that very morning, and the pleasure could not be chased from his bones. He would visit Aunt Margaret tomorrow, and with the help of these local dignitaries improve the table at Carisbrooke Castle. He did keep a very good table, as Sir John Oglander had himself acknowledged, and he was eyeing the Isle's fowl when waylaid by two weather-beaten riders.

The smaller man spoke. 'Do you know who is very near you, sir?' he asked.

'I beg your pardon?' said Hammond. 'Do I know you?'

He should have had an escort. He had grown a little casual on this holiday isle.

'Do you know who is near you?' said Firebrace again, more pressing.

'Come no closer, rascal, until you have declared your business,' replied Hammond, who had once been a soldier.

'You have heard of the king, I believe; met him even ... he says so.'

'What would you know of the king?' The men were vagabonds.

'He is near.'

'Who is near?'

'Even good King Charles, who is come from Hampton Court.'

'He is imprisoned there; he cannot be here. Now be on your way!' Hammond nudged his horse and began to move on.

'He was imprisoned there,' said the man. 'But left – for fear of being murdered privately.'

Hammond paused his horse and felt the shadow of dread across his day. 'He is come from Hampton Court?'

'He is.'

'And come here?'

'Escaped the army's clutches, with cleverness and guile, and now seeks refuge with you, while he considers matters.'

'Who are you?' Hammond was disturbed.

'It matters not. What matters is the one who sent us.'

'You have authorization?' He dearly hoped they did not.

'Here is the letter . . . with the king's seal.'

Firebrace rode towards Hammond, handed over the parchment and withdrew while Hammond broke the seal and read.

'He seeks refuge on the island?' said Hammond, beginning to feel faint.

'He is close by, Mr Hammond, and we have little time.'

Dowcett looked at his friend with disquiet. Firebrace had said too much, though it was Hammond who grew pale and started to tremble. He was in danger of falling off his horse.

'He is much discomposed,' thought Dowcett and moved slowly towards him. Hammond waved him away.

'Where is the king?' he asked, regaining himself. He was sure there had been a mistake, a misunderstanding.

'All will be revealed,' said Firebrace.

'Is he on the island? Because if he is, I am undone, I tell you that quite plainly. And if he is not on the Isle, which I sincerely hope is the case, he must be kept away. He must be kept away at all costs. Do you hear me?'

'He cannot be kept away, Colonel. He is the king—'

'And I his loyal subject, of course, but ... but here in the trust of the army and parliament.'

'Your king needs you.'

'And I am greatly honoured.' Dowcett thought he looked more haunted than honoured. 'And, of course, I will act with honour, in any way I can,' Hammond added.

'Then no harm done,' said Firebrace, cheerfully, though he had not slept for thirty-six hours and was wet through to the marrow of his Swindon bones. Hammond, however, was thinking only of harm: of the consequences of turning the king away, a terrible dilemma before him. For if the king were to escape his attentions now, how would the army take that? And how would the nation take it, on hearing that he, Robert Hammond, had refused to receive him in his hour of need? The two horsemen drew closer.

'We need your assurance, Colonel, of safe-keeping for the king.'

'He comes here to save his life, you say?'

'Evil plots – he would not have lasted another night at Hampton.'

'Then I assure you that if the king puts himself in my hands, I will do all that can be expected of a man of honour.'

Firebrace looked to Dowcett. Was this reassurance enough? Dowcett offered nothing and Firebrace realized the decision was his. They'd risked their lives to bring the king south and now the future of England lay in the balance. He looked at Hammond ... yet Hammond still wasn't sure.

'I have a mind to take one of you as a hostage,' he said. Firebrace and Dowcett looked at him bemused, as if he was a child – or worse, a loon. 'An insurance against any tomfoolery,' he added. 'The other will then take a message to the king – if he is indeed here.'

Neither Dowcett nor Firebrace would be held as hostage.

'We have not travelled here to be made hostages, sir,' said Firebrace.

'No,' said Hammond, who then changed his mind. He didn't like those looks, and agreed to ride with them to see the king.

'Let us all go to the king and acquaint him with our plan,' he said.

'With all my heart,' said Firebrace, who thought this was the way to proceed, though Dowcett was less certain.

'You mean to carry this man to the king?' whispered Dowcett. 'Before you even know whether the king will approve of his undertaking or no?'

'Approve of it? It was the king's idea, surely?' muttered Firebrace, who longed for a little human enthusiasm from his colleague. 'This isle was his idea.'

'But he did not ask that Hammond be brought to him.'

'What else can we do?'

'We do not know his intentions, which are probably bad. He might be coming to make an arrest.'

'I think not.'

'Well, sadly, the king is not made secure by your thoughts, Firebrace.'

'He is an honourable man, with an honourable bearing.'

'They said the same of Pilate.'

'And what choice do we have?'

'We will surprise his majesty, that is for sure. And perhaps feel his wrath.'

But Firebrace didn't care. He had been a long time in this saddle, and for most of that time, damp, underappreciated and hungry.

'Let us to the king!' he said cheerfully.

*

Jane paid the boatman three ha'pennies, which she was happy to do. She enjoyed travel, even travel in the rain on a wet boat bench without cover. She liked to be carried, by horse or boat, and for a moment to be quite powerless in the world, with nothing to do, nothing which she could do ... but sit and be carried. Some found travel tiring, but this had never been so for Jane; it was here – and perhaps only here – that she found rest, reliant on another to do their work and nothing to be done while they did. Though today there was anticipation as well, for she was eager to see the king and, with the advice of the stars from Mr Lilly, to organize his escape to Essex.

But on her arrival at Hampton Court she was aware of dissonance in the air. There were more soldiers than usual and no peace. Instead, there was the dull sense of rage and a heavy cloud of blame.

'And who are you?' asked a soldier, accusingly.

'A servant of the king,' said Jane.

'A servant who travels to and fro at will? Are you sure you're not the queen?'

He was mocking her, and she blushed.

'I do what I can. The king has many needs.'

'I'm sure he does, miss, but the king is not here. Your deceitful master has moved on.'

'Then where is he?'

'Not for me to say; nor you to know.' He seized his moment of power.

'Has he been moved by the army?' asked Jane. 'We really should be told! A king needs his household!'

'He's not where he was, that's all I can reveal. Best find another master, one more reliable.'

The army had clearly moved him, thought Jane. But then came a question from the soldier that made her think again . . . and filled her with hope.

'Perhaps you can tell us where he might go?' said the soldier.

'Where he might go? Has he escaped?' She was both concerned and excited. Had he made for Essex, where he'd be safe?

'When did you last see him, lady?'

'Just two days ago.'

'And of what did you speak?'

'I bring only messages of love and support from his wife and family abroad, Captain. He misses them greatly.'

'He said nothing of this?' The soldier waved his hand vaguely.

'There was no talk of his leaving, no. He wanted only friendship with the army – and thought Cromwell the best of men.'

How did she say that? Jane needed to be away from this place; she needed information. She felt unsettled when she didn't know where the king was.

'If I hear anything, I will assuredly let you know,' said Jane.

She would not flirt with this man to find out more. It would be like flirting with a wall.

*

The king had chosen his refuge wisely. The earl had always been solicitous for his welfare and a supporter of his cause. Here was a subject with no time for new voices in government, whether parliament or the army. What sort of chaos would that lead to? No, the sooner Charles was returned to the throne, the better it was for everyone – this was the earl's belief.

But while he spoke of honour at this royal epiphany, he was thinking mainly of money, for a king was nothing but trouble and cost. Monarchs do not understand the world, how finances work, how an income needs to be earned, how bills need paying, how bankruptcy strikes. They imagine their large travelling entourage and endless meals round another's table a return to the simple life and no imposition on anyone.

So while the earl wished the king safe travel, he wished it to be in another direction, away from his home ... and as soon as could be arranged. And his best hope lay with the man now sitting downstairs: Robert Hammond, the new governor of the Isle of Wight.

Hammond had arrived mid-afternoon with Firebrace and Dowcett, who both looked shattered. He had also brought Captain Basket, the commander of Cowes Castle, and his odd servant, Edward, who appeared to do little serving and called the captain 'Jonathan'. Hammond regarded it as all very strange and asked why he was not in the kitchen with the others.

'Edward does not react well to pepper,' said Basket, by way of explanation.

'A servant who cannot enter a kitchen must limit his worth, surely?'

'He is a boy of many talents, Colonel, if we can look beyond our stomachs for a moment!'

It was a clever parry by the captain, and Hammond pursued the matter no more; especially as Edward now stared at him in a disturbing manner. And where was Firebrace? He'd told Hammond he'd go upstairs and warn the king of his arrival, but that was an hour ago.

*

64

Charles, meanwhile, had changed his mind again. He'd decided against the Isle of Wight and asked now for a boat to France, unaware that the ports had been closed in response to his escape. Firebrace told him that theirs was the last boat through, on account of the governor, Colonel Hammond, being on board. Charles was not pleased.

'Have you brought Hammond with you?'

'Yes, sire.'

'You've brought him here?'

'It was your desire to place yourself under his—'

'I have changed my plan.'

'We did not know, your majesty.'

'You have quite undone me!'

Firebrace was confused. 'You said in the wood, your majesty, that you wished to go to the Isle of Wight and the care of Colonel Hammond.'

'And Henrietta?' asked Charles, pointedly. Firebrace looked blank. 'If Hammond is here now, how may I go from this place? Answer me that.'

'Well, sire—'

'How may I now travel to see her in France? You take me from my wife, kind sir!'

Firebrace was a resourceful fellow, with a plan for every need, but he wilted in the ever-changing wind of circumstance . . . and felt spliced by royal irony.

'If you will give direction, sire, and hold to that opinion a moment, Hammond need not interrupt us.'

'And how might that be?'

Firebrace looked with deliberation at the knife tucked into his belt. He would kill a man for the king; even a governor. This is what he imagined, at least; he'd killed many a pig and it couldn't be so different.

The king was walking up and down the room, pondering the violence. 'The world would not excuse me, no,' he said, shaking his head.

'Really, sire?'

'If I should follow this counsel, it would be said and believed that Hammond had ventured his life for me, and that I had

65

unworthily taken it from him. I could not have that charge laid at my feet.'

Firebrace felt numb. Thousands had died in war, awful deaths – one couldn't pretend otherwise – without bothering the king's conscience. Yet now he baulked at one more . . . and would instead blame Firebrace, from this day on, for the dark unfolding.

'No,' said the king, 'it is too late to do anything other than to walk the path you have forced me down, and leave all else to God. Let us travel to the Isle of Wight, gentlemen – and may God smile on our endeavours.'

Firebrace wished for the same. He had not seen that smile for a while.

*

Downstairs, Hammond, Basket and Edward were having supper in the earl's parlour. They'd made small talk, comparing cooks and such like, but as Edward's eyes continued to stare, Hammond was suspicious at the delay. What was going on upstairs? When conversation stilled, Dowcett – a miserable presence – was sent to remind the king that these officers were still waiting. But another half-hour passed before Dowcett returned for them; and soon they were climbing the stairs.

'Your majesty,' said Dowcett, leading them in. 'May I introduce Governor Hammond and Captain Basket.'

Edward had not been allowed upstairs to see the king, which caused a tantrum. Captain Basket would have relented, but Hammond did not.

'He shall not see the king,' said Hammond, after taking Basket aside. 'For I do wonder if he might be a man better suited to the molly house.'

'I refute your inference!' said Basket.

'He looks at me strangely,' said Hammond. 'And asked whether I was of the marrying persuasion!'

'A polite enquiry.'

'It did not feel polite to me – which makes me wonder why he is quite so close to you.'

Basket breathed deeply. 'We shall not fall out over this boy, Hammond. These times need bigger men than that.'

'Indeed they do,' said Hammond. He had no wish to fall out with Basket, who could be a necessary ally in the days to come, however he lay in his bed.

'But let us be mindful of the rumours,' said Basket.

'What rumours?' said Hammond.

'The king's father, of course.'

'King James?'

'King James of blessed memory . . . and a fine man.'

'A very fine man – with a wife and two fine sons,' said Hammond, sensing what was to come.

'Yet with a preference for men; which we will not judge in a king.'

'We will not judge indeed,' said Hammond firmly.

'Nor speak again of Edward and the molly house,' said Basket.

'Quite so,' said Hammond. 'Quite so.'

*

'This has been a most mismanaged day,' Charles said.

The king's small frame was rigid with rage, though when Hammond entered and kissed the king's hand, Charles received him cheerfully enough. He explained the death threats that had forced his hand, and asked to be kept safe until an agreement with parliament could be reached. There was no trusting the army now, he said; he wished only for an agreement with parliament and an end to all this unpleasantness.

Hammond said, 'I will do all that I can, sire, to give you your desires.'

'My good and faithful servant!'

'In relation to the orders and directions parliament may supply,' he added, still angry at the delay. Charles raised his royal eyebrows. 'It is to parliament that I answer,' explained Hammond.

'Though I am your king,' said Charles with a smile.

'You are my king, sire.'

It was a qualified assurance from Hammond, and not quite to the royal liking, but accepted. Charles could manage this affair. Two hours later, and much to the relief of the earl, they were on the water again, crossing to Cowes, where they left Captain Basket and Edward. Charles would spend his first night on the island in the Plume and Feathers – an adequate inn, though the carving on the oak bed headboard was unfortunate. 'Remember thy end,' it said, which Charles took as a bad omen and knelt in fervent prayer.

*

'So what now of the Essex homecoming?' wondered Jane Whorwood, in some panic.

Her head still chewed on the question. She was behind events when she should be in front of them – and foresaw several dreadful unfoldings. She must stop the king from travelling any further. He'd mentioned Hammond, but surely he would not go there? Hammond was not to be trusted, this she knew. Her courier was waiting as she wrote; he would ride straightway, and Charles could be reading it by the evening candle.

Mrs Jane Whorwood

London
11 November 1647

Your majesty,
Greetings from your fervent well-wisher, Jane, amid changing circumstances.

I hear you have left the ghastly restraint of Hampton Court, fleeing for your precious life. I celebrate this freedom you have made for yourself, but urge you to be careful of your destination; and please – I'm sure you shall – hold yourself back from the Isle of Wight. For what seems like gold may not be so; and consider whether Cromwell might have you snared in his evil net?

You may question me – but has he not carefully lured you south and given you eyes for the Isle? My reasoning is clear. He fears those in the army who would attack your majesty, and wishes for you a safer and more secure keeping. Where better than the Isle of Wight, where extremists cannot come, the Solent in between?

You know he puts Hammond there, a trusted associate, appointed by the army; but, we note, sent to visit you on his

*way to the Isle, to smile and speak of loyalty to your royal person.
And all the while, Cromwell sows fear in your noble soul, feeds you
with stories about murderous intent, and then entices you south to
a most convenient imprisonment over the water, safe in his hands,
with his monkey Hammond as the keeper of the king!*

*Did not the ease of your escape surprise you? The Venetian
ambassador speaks of foot and horse guards being set to watch
over your person, but we must wonder where they were on the
afternoon of your bold escape?*

*How clever to free yourself from their designs, your majesty, and
yes, all now is set fair! You will cross the water to France. There is
a boat in Sandwich, all is ready, you will travel in disguise; these
matters are being arranged. But stay clear of the Isle if you would
avoid the army's net.*

With a devoted admirer's love,

Jane

*

'He is on the Isle of Wight,' said Henry, walking towards Oliver.
They were at Hampton Court together, surveying the fateful scene
and raging at Colonel Whalley – though Ireton raged more than
Oliver, who seemed a relaxed figure as they paced the gardens.
'He was taken there by two men called Firebrace and Dowcett,
according to Wood.'

'Then I am sure it is reliable, Henry. Wood is sound on the
whereabouts of people; he knows where I am whenever he
needs to.'

Wood was the best intelligencer currently serving parliament
and the army, though some felt he mainly served himself. He knew
when Henrietta changed her mind, not by reading her mind but
by reading her mail – and if royalist couriers were dedicated souls
and busy across the kingdom, then so was Wood.

'You seem unusually gay, Oliver,' said Henry, who couldn't help
but notice.

'Really?'

'Unusually gay.'

'I can scarce be in mourning.'

'We have lost the king.'

'He could not stay here, Henry. There were dark schemes, we know that.'

'How dark?'

'And is it so bad he now has his back to the sea? Perhaps he will retire himself to France and save us the trouble. One of his children can reign.'

'You imagine our problem drifting quietly away?'

'And in the meantime, while he gathers himself, where safer for the king than in young Robert's hands?'

'Robert drifts, Oliver. Robert Hammond is a drifter, a pleaser. He will need watching.' Ireton was not happy with these outcomes.

'Then we shall watch him with keen eyes, Henry, but the king has chosen an army holding.'

They walked the courtyard silently for a while, as if in meditation, watching their feet on the flagstones.

'Did you tell the king to go there, Father?' asked Henry. 'Or have you just been fortunate?'

*

It was Sunday morning and a blustery sea air wreaked salty havoc with the oiled royal hair.

Charles, under escort, was preparing to leave Cowes for his new home in Carisbrooke Castle. It was not a traditional royal procession. There were six elderly guards from the local militia and Firebrace, Dowcett and Legge, rather enjoying the pomp of it all, as they were not usually accorded such interest. Other members of the king's household should have been with them, making it a grander affair, but they'd been held up by choppy water in the Solent and so temporarily remained in Portsmouth. Also waiting there, with several cooks and a laundry lady, was the king's barber who was much missed.

In the meantime, the king would travel via Newport, where news had travelled fast. Groups of bystanders watched the royal journey – though he was also a prisoner, in some manner. And it was not quite in the style Charles would like. He did not yet have his royal coach; he would ask for this to be brought across the water. But he rode his stallion in regal style and was not a prisoner in chains, not at all. He was a king on an island throne for a while, before making his sure and certain way to France ... or London.

And as it transpired, Newport was a most favourable experience, confirming Charles in his decision to come here, despite opposition from some. Yes, he'd read sweet Jane's letter that morning, advising him against these things. But she could get too anxious, really she could, and become rather wild in her declarations. She would see sense soon enough, for here he would set up court, be separate again and parley with his supplicants on his own terms. And perhaps he would travel to France. Henrietta desired this, longed for his body beside her again; this she had made clear.

A king leaves his kingdom only in the last resort, however. The people do not like a king who leaves. And while he longed to be with Henrietta − as a husband must long for his wife − he felt better able to manage affairs of state here. And even as he thought of Henrietta and then of Jane − Henrietta in English form, one might say − a woman approached him through the crowd. She was bright-faced and bonny among the Newport faithful and he waved her through the elderly line of island militia around him.

'Come!' he declared. She carried a rose and reached up to offer it to his majesty, to place in his hands.

'This is a blessed rose, your majesty, which survived the autumn frost. And that shall be you! You too shall survive the frost of these bitter times!'

Others warmed to her confidence, and told him he was most fortunate, more fortunate than he could imagine, for the whole island was for him − apart from the governors of the castles, perhaps. But everyone else, they were unanimous in their support, even the castle guards, twelve old men who'd been there for years! They were the king's men through and through − and surely Hammond would be, if he had sense?

'Be of good heart, your majesty!' they shouted and other similar lines. 'You too shall survive the frost!'

Though seven miles away, at Nunwell Park, there was a different feeling.

There, on the east of the island, the royalist Sir John Oglander held his head in his hands at the latest news. His understanding was different from the Newport crowds, less excitable. Once deputy-lieutenant of the Isle, he now sat in his study, looked out across the fields, and watched the sea wind bend and billow in the long grass. With sadness, he wrote in his diary, 'I can do nothing but sigh and weep. And the reason for my grief is that verily I believe the king could not have come into a worse place for himself; or a place where he can be more securely kept. Once this place was wholly for the king, yes indeed; but there are few honest men here now, that is my experience.'

He watched the dark ink sink into the parchment and wondered what lay in store for his king and country.

*

Hammond too held a quill. He was back in the castle, placed behind his desk, ink on parchment to parliament, writing of the latest events to befall him on this once quiet isle. Cromwell would not smile on him for writing to parliament, he knew that. Oliver didn't like parliament. But parliament must hear of these recent events first and give him instruction. He could hardly manage this affair without such guidance.

'I await instructions,' he wrote, feeling sick at the circumstances that closed round him.

When he took this post, he had not expected to be the king of England's gaoler.

*

'The stars did not mention the Isle of Wight?' said Jane.

'Not to my knowledge.'

Lilly continued with his sextant, in the cause of another client. Mrs Whorwood was neither invited nor welcome.

'Perhaps they become a little forgetful,' she said, to prod him a little. 'Do stars grow old and forget things, Mr Lilly – like an old man wondering where he left his slippers?'

'Stars are eternal,' he replied, studying his work. He wished to offer no encouragement to this woman, who seemed to have taken some perverse fancy to him ... one could imagine that.

'Eternally wrong, it seems, for they spoke to you of Essex, some way from the Isle of Wight. How foolish can ten gold coins be?'

Lilly put down his pencil and pondered her face. This woman was stiff with frustration and would not be gone without some attention given, some calming offered. 'It appeared a safe place, Mrs Whorwood.'

'Not to the king, it transpires.'

Lilly smiled wearily. 'So the king's unparalleled wilfulness is on display again. Do you wish me to pretend surprise?'

He could not hold that in, but Jane was equally stern. 'Or is it rather the immeasurable pride of the parliament and army who imagine they can contain a king?'

Jane had given no warning of her arrival; she did not like to give warning. She'd been passing, near enough, and felt it only right that Lilly be confronted with this matter. She had no plan here ... but things needed to be spoken.

'You may share a morning draught with me, if you wish,' he said. 'And I have some pickled oysters.'

He fetched refreshments and they sat across the table from each other. She wondered if he approached her in some manner – men did this, she found – but couldn't be sure. She was not certain if Lilly had sex in him or what stirred his fancy.

'On what do you work?' she asked.

'I work privately.'

'I saw the name of Charles.'

'You did?'

'While you were out, in the other room, my eyes could not help but wander to your parchments.'

'You pry?'

'I do not pry – I merely have eyes.'

'And busy ones, Mrs Whorwood.'

'My eyes must always be busy on behalf of the king.'

'There are many called Charles in the world. You saw nothing of consequence.'

'But only one who is the king's son, Prince Charles – which is more exactly what I saw.'

Lilly sighed. 'He is safe with his mother in France and need not concern us.'

'He is the king's son and most definitely concerns us.' Lilly gave up the fight, sinking back in his chair. 'Is it true what they say?'

'What do they say?' he asked. Who had this woman been listening to?

'That when he was born, Venus was the presiding presence in the sky.'

'She was.'

This was the only astrological story she knew . . . apart from the Christmas story.

'Some said it was like the star that guided the wise men to Bethlehem,' she added.

'Those seeking royal preferment, perhaps.'

'Yet it was true! The guiding star was there at his birth!' Jane pressed Lilly like no other.

'It is true,' he said, 'that Prince Charles was born with the sun in Gemini, Virgo on the ascendant, and the moon in Taurus.'

'And of what future does that speak for the king's son?' She leaned forward, like one sensing a great discovery.

'The celestial picture is thus dominated by Mercury, which might – and I only say might – suggest a quick intelligence.'

'Like his father, Mr Lilly, like his father. People do not always see this, but the king, he has such intelligence.' Lilly pondered her again. Was this monarch worth her devotion? And of what substance was this devotion comprised? 'You were telling me of his son,' she said.

'I believe you were telling me.'

'Please. And you must have another oyster, or I may eat them all!' Jane did like oysters.

'We can expect a restless spirit in the prince,' he said. 'Though this latter trait may be the gift of his mother, rather than a star. I'm told Henrietta can be more remote than any planet.'

'You will not speak of the queen in this way!'

'I will speak as I wish, Mrs Whorwood – and not be ruled by your guilt.'

A pause.

'And Prince Charles?' She wished to return to the prince.

'What of him?'

'Is there anything else to be said . . . with regard to his character?'

'We note that with Mars in Leo, here is a young man who can draw from the well of physical courage.'

'Again, like his father.'

'Not a well-established perception.'

'The king is a fine horseman, if you didn't know, Mr Lilly, quite fearless in the saddle.'

'I'm aware he rides – but heard it was usually away from battle.'

'A youth who excelled at both tournament sports and hunting.'

'He was a weak and sickly child, Mrs Whorwood. They thought he would die.'

'But a child who did *not* die, Mr Lilly, that is the point. One who would not give up, who worked hard to strengthen his body. Such determination in one so young!'

'You speak as though you were there.'

'So of course his son will have physical courage. He falls not far from the tree.'

Jane was elated, felt hope once again. So intelligence and courage were there in the prince? The king's son had a bright future; how could it not be so? And if the son, then the father also, her dear king. She had lost hope, become desolate and confused – but no more.

'I will take my leave, Mr Lilly,' she said, seizing one last oyster.

Lilly smiled. 'You are converted afresh to the wisdom of the stars now they speak to your longings, Mrs Whorwood.'

'I do not need the stars to know these things, Mr Lilly. I have always known them . . . always.'

*

'There used to be a donkey in the well-house,' said Charles, enjoying the sea air – perhaps the only thing lacking at Hampton Court.

The king and Hammond walked and talked on the first day of his confinement; though Hammond preferred to speak of hospitality. He had woken in shock and then terror on remembering the events of the previous day. But might he now become a close confidant of the king? This thought had arrived at breakfast, and calmed him a little. Perhaps even a man the king came to rely on?

'I came here as a prince, you know, nearly thirty years ago,' said Charles. 'I remember the donkey well.'

'How the years pass, your majesty,' said Hammond, wondering how one spoke to a king beyond deference and gratitude, which could not be sustained beyond a brief encounter. And yes, perhaps these memories explained much. Perhaps here lay the reason for the king's surprising arrival. A return to an innocence lost? A return to simpler times, before he turned a nation against itself in war? Was this an act of repentance, even?

'And there is still a donkey in the well-house,' said Robert, cheerfully. 'Though perhaps not the same one.'

'I doubt it.'

'Maybe father is replaced by son on the treadmill.'

'One hopes so.'

'Unless the son would prefer to be free.' The thought did strike him.

'That is not a choice, I'm afraid,' said Charles. 'There is only the treadmill; like father, like son.'

They walked with apparent gaiety, but Hammond felt discomfort. Loyal subject and gaoler was a difficult blend – the two did not marry. He would describe himself as the king's guardian; this had been his thought after writing to parliament. If any should ask, he was the king's guardian, ensuring his monarch's safety. He offered protective confinement while the future shape of the kingdom became clear. The king would return to the throne, this was certain, and it would not harm Robert if he was remembered as the king's man in his time of crisis.

'It has gone a little to ruin, I am told,' said Hammond, surveying the castle.

'I think we all have,' said Charles.

Hammond felt sudden pity for this small man. He had traumatized the land, there was no doubting that, yet now he looked weak, like the newest child in the school yard, ripe for the bully boys.

'And I will need to journey a little every day,' said Charles, looking east. 'I cannot be ensnared here in the castle.' He was testing the water.

'Your desires are my desires,' said Hammond, though he did worry a little as he said it. That was the deference of a servant, and he was not a servant. He did not wish to dishonour the king, in any manner, but neither did he wish to lose him; and ensnarement was in some degree Hammond's task. It would not look well if he mislaid him, that was for sure, and to that end the castle would not be his friend. It was a Norman edifice, set on a chalk plateau, with defences built at the end of the sixteenth century in the face of Spanish threat. So while it was primed and ready to keep naval enemies out, it was not equipped to keep restless prisoners in.

Hammond still had the eye of a soldier, if not the heart. The porous chalk made the moat – traversed by a long stone bridge – quite dry, so there was no need for a swim to escape, while the low outer walls could easily be climbed, even by a small king. And how to patrol the great length of the perimeter with twelve old men as guards – twelve men who were staunch royalists and could only climb stairs with difficulty?

The inner walls were good, however, and the walls surrounding the courtyard; they were a proper height, as Charles observed.

'The Normans built tall walls and walls to last,' he said, with a prisoner's regret.

'Trust is the highest wall,' said Hammond, looking into royal eyes which offered little in return.

'Indeed,' said Charles, looking away. 'One must always trust the king. It is the duty and the joy of the subject to trust the king.'

*

In the end, Cromwell threw a cushion at Edmund, such was his frustration at the words said and the accusation made.

'Crush the Levellers, Oliver, and you crush the soul of this revolution,' Edmund had claimed.

'But there is no revolution, Edmund!'

Oliver did not believe in a revolution; that had never been his wish. He had no desire to oversee revolution.

'Not after Corkbush Fields, there isn't! You shot your own, Oliver, gunned him down while all a-chatter with the king. How things have changed since the war is gone. I quite forget who is with who these days!'

They had met at Ireton's house, the three of them. Henry warmed more and more to Edmund Ludlow's republican company; Oliver had noticed this. And so they pondered the vexed unfolding of events now the king had bolted and shifted matters south. And they gathered as companions round the table, or so Oliver thought, until Ludlow – never one to hold back – remembered himself a lawyer and forgot himself a friend, and started accusing and accusing. He would not let up . . . and Cromwell was throwing the cushion, for what else could he do, then retreating fast down the stairs to the kitchen, chased by Ludlow.

'If the flinging of soft pillows is your only answer, Oliver, then I appear to have found your marrow!'

And Edmund pursued Oliver around the table, the cushion still in hand. Being the quicker man, he was soon beating the soldier with it, and between the blows Cromwell was laughing but Edmund more serious, though trying to smile.

'My counter-argument!' he declared, with a final bash . . . and now the feathers were leaking and the two men exhausted, when Ireton arrived and called a halt.

'You damage a wedding gift, Edmund!'

'And this man damages my country!' he replied, pointing across the room to Oliver, the heavier man and still out of breath.

*

The king and Robert walked back towards the inner courtyard, across the stone bridge to the gatehouse and guardrooms. And Hammond's heart sank as he looked again on his new home: a crumbling castle and a run-down garrison, maintained by a hobbling staff – this was his kingdom! Yesterday, it had seemed quite heavenly – but today? The only consolation was the officers' house, where Hammond quartered in his bachelor way, a fine residence built in the 1580s.

And there was other good in the place. The food had improved since his arrival, and now the king was their guest it would need to improve further still. For this reason, his first instruction had not been for more guards, but that his mother should come quickly from Chertsey. She was to be hostess at the castle; she would sort things out.

'I have written to parliament,' said Hammond, as they reached the gatehouse.

'Of course.'

'It was about the conditions of your confinement.'

'I desire very much to speak with my dear friends in parliament,' said Charles. 'It is time this kingdom was restored to peace, and together we can make it so.'

Charles had no desire to speak with parliament. They'd need cosseting for now, polite and hopeful words, for they did run the country in a way. But his heart was set on the Scots, and their army coming south . . . a fact not for public mention. The truth was, agreement with the Scots was close to completion, much of it achieved by covert correspondence while at Hampton Court. They too needed sweet words, for they had not been pleased by his arrival on the Isle, after they'd offered him refuge in Berwick. But then perhaps they shouldn't have sold him back to the English – then he might trust them more! In the meantime, he told them to ignore all his public utterances, made simply for effect; and he knew the value of smoke for blinding eyes.

'You must prepare your forces for invasion and leave the rest to me,' he'd said, and he smiled now at the memory.

Hammond noted the king's cheer and was glad that he was happy here.

'I believe parliament wants only the peace of this kingdom and yourself on the throne,' he said. 'Something conciliatory from your majesty would move this matter forward.'

Charles eyed him with pity. 'So parliament is your master now, Robert – and not the army?'

It was a casual question, though not casual at all.

'Honour shall be my master,' said Robert.

'But who funds your honour?'

*

'We will pay more attention to a woman,' said Wood, the intelligencer. He had a dry voice, like dead sticks after a long summer.

'A woman?' said Cromwell.

'Indeed. She serves the king rather well.'

'You mean like Adam, we may be toppled by Eve?' Cromwell smiled as he spoke, imagining this to be the prelude to more serious learning. He looked for sharper intelligence from Wood, not talk of women.

'Your mocking spirit may be her greatest disguise, Mr Cromwell.'

'I do not mock. I—'

'You mock the idea of a woman wielding power.'

'I have daughters myself, Mr Wood, and know their power. They handle me more cleverly than the king.' He was too soft with them; they made him so. 'Elizabeth is perhaps less susceptible to their charms.'

'And yet still you giggle?'

Wood was unmemorable but unforgettable. You would not remember the bland face beneath thinning grey hair, but you would remember the meeting. No one straightened Cromwell like Wood, and he continued: 'I do not speak of homely play and parlour games, Mr Cromwell, I note our national stage and the poisoning of power.'

'Then you will give me the substance of this, Mr Wood. I am not aware of this mystery woman's power.'

'She is not your friend, that is for sure, and she encourages the king in similar disdain.'

'She is the king's friend?'

'And busy in that friendship . . . very busy across the land.'

'Is she not a wife to someone – or a mother?'

'Both, but unhappy at home and so blessed with a great energy for travel.'

Oliver's mind wandered. He had never wondered what Elizabeth performed while he was away; she ran the home, of course, scolded the children . . . perhaps a little too much.

'And what does this woman do with her travel?' he asked.

Wood extracted some notes from a bag and placed them on the table. 'This is only what we know,' he said. 'But it's enough to stir interest.'

'Tell me.'

'She has the web of a spider in autumn, Oliver, delicately spun but strong – merchants, laundresses and God knows who else.'

'He does, yes – God knows all things.' Like the writer of Ecclesiastes, Wood did stray from the divine path sometimes.

'Webs of intrigue established at first by her stepfather, James Maxwell, once groom of the bedchamber for both Henry and Charles.'

'I know of Maxwell: a self-important Scot.' He had no time for Maxwell. 'And Henry would have been the better king,' said Oliver, drifting a little.

'He would have preferred your religion, if that's your meaning, and been a more assured leader of men.'

'And taller.'

'But weak against typhoid, Oliver, and so a passer-by in our history. It's not the dead who disturb us today.'

'You were saying,' said Cromwell, feeling put in his place.

'As Black Rod, Maxwell is Charles' private money man, a fat rat in the sewer of royal finances. Suffice to say his stepdaughter will be well versed in double-accounting and commercial trickery.'

'Not such feminine traits, perhaps.'

'He worked closely with merchants, as does she.' Oliver did not warm to this talk. He liked battles between men. 'And she laughed at you in Oxford.'

'Laughed at me?'

'During the war, she smuggled gold into the city, while you besieged the place! All given by London merchants.'

'How?'

'I'm sorry?'

'How was it done?'

Wood was enjoying this. 'She had it hidden in bars of soap and then taken into the city via the laundress, an Elizabeth Wheeler. Perhaps she walked past you and waved, for who gives a woman a second glance? And it was gold well spent – used to effect the transportation of the queen and the Prince of Wales to France.'

'I was only there at the end,' said Cromwell, defensively. 'At the siege, I mean, and somewhat distracted by family affairs – the marriage of my daughter Bridget and Henry at nearby Holton Hall.'

'Holton, you say?' Now Wood looked surprised.

'The Whorwood home, yes. You did not know?' He liked it when Wood didn't know. 'And I remember Lady Ursula as a most forceful woman.'

'Then remember also her daughter-in-law, Jane Whorwood.'

'I do remember her – a rather distant girl, there but not there.'

'It is Jane I speak of, Oliver.'

A pause.

'Jane Whorwood, a spy for the king?' Wood nodded. 'But she was at Henry and Bridget's wedding!'

*

Wood held back amid Oliver's confusion.

'Always important to get the oldest married first, Oliver. Bridget is your oldest, isn't she?'

It was offered as a kindness, to ease the sting, a chance to speak of family – but Cromwell sat in silence. He felt foolish . . . made foolish by a woman with gold hidden in soap, walking past him with a smile and a wedding invitation in her hand, when all the time, she'd been . . .

Wood continued, angling his eyeglass towards his notes, like an advocate in court. 'They say other things.'

'And what do they say?'

'Jane made money for the king by defrauding parliament's revenue committee and corrupting its chairman.'

'I see.'

'You see only a little.' Cromwell was angry now, angry that a woman whose family he knew should behave in this way. 'And she is a most busy postal service,' added Wood. 'She has couriers of her own – good men, not vermin – relaying intelligence between the king and his followers, and between the followers themselves. They reach as far as Edinburgh.'

'Edinburgh? Well, we will deal with Scotland.' The Scots would be a good vessel for his rage.

'And her sister – Elizabeth, Countess Lanark, you will know of her – she intrigues with Jane. It is a family affair – and then—'

'And then what?'

'An affair of a different hue . . . Sir Thomas Bendish.'

'What of Sir Thomas?'

Sir Thomas was presently in Istanbul. He'd been sent there by the House of Lords earlier in the year, ambassador to the Ottoman Empire. What had he to do with this awful woman? Bendish was a royalist to his belt buckle, but not a bad man. His lands in Essex had been confiscated after his support for the king in the civil war, but there was a sense he'd paid his dues – £1,000 to get out of prison. It was now felt he was ready for service again.

'He had relations with Mrs Whorwood.'

'Had relations, Mr Wood? Sir Thomas is married.'

'So is Mrs Whorwood. Such things occur, Mr Cromwell.' He was aware they occurred, but they puzzled him. 'The two of them were part of the royalist ring in Oxford; lust and politics walk hand in hand.'

'This is the same Jane Whorwood of Holton Hall, you're quite sure.'

'The same. They make jokes about her name.'

'Jane?'

'Whorwood.'

'What jokes? And is the king made aware?'

Wood removed his glasses. That was enough for today.

'The king drinks from the same trough, Oliver.' Did Oliver understand? 'Jane is now the king's watering hole; and her name, in the king's ciphered love letters, is seven–one–five.'

'Seven–one–five?'

'Seven–one–five is the king's naughty number.'

*

They met together again, sooner than expected. Hammond had gathered the gentlemen of the island to explain the situation, now much altered.

'The king has arrived among us,' he said, and knew he had their attention; they looked like a circle of surprised frogs. The king had been scared away from Hampton Court by extremists, he said . . . no, not scared, but ever mindful of the danger to his royal person, he'd felt it best to leave. There was no need for alarm, he assured them, thus causing alarm – but certain security measures had been taken, given the fear of a Leveller presence on the island.

'Levellers?' No one liked to hear that word.

'They may secretly be plotting his assassination,' said Hammond, adding that his majesty must be kept safe, this was paramount: 'For posterity would be unforgiving if harm came to him while among us.'

So the gentlemen of Newport had been warned. Colonel Robert Hammond, governor of the island, would do his best, but he would not take sole responsibility for the welfare and whereabouts of the king. They must sweat a little too – though excitement trumped sweat today. And when the meeting was over, Sir Robert Dillington was the first to ask Hammond if he might be allowed to see the king after dinner.

'By all means, Sir Robert,' said Hammond, who then had a good idea. 'Of course, I would invite you all to dinner with the king, had I fit entertainment and some fowl for his majesty!'

He was soon overwhelmed with culinary offers, generous in the extreme, with many birds and several fish made available; after which Hammond returned to the castle in good spirits, buoyed by the promise of provisions from the local gentry.

His mother would be pleased . . . perhaps even proud of her boy.

*

The gentry arrived at the castle with various forms of fowl. Charles kept them waiting, writing in his room. Charles always kept people waiting, finally appearing two hours after the agreed time. After they had kissed his hand – the gentlemen of Newport unanimous in their kneeling – the king made a short speech. He used this moment to outline his reason for leaving Hampton Court and to speak of his future hopes. They were eager to hear him, and Charles expanded a little in the light of their adoration. They would not only kiss his hands. The gentlemen of Newport would eat from them.

'Gentlemen,' he said, 'I must inform you that for the preservation of my life, I was forced from Hampton Court, for there were bad people, agitator fellows, who had both voted for and resolved upon my death, so I could no longer dwell there in safety.'

There were outraged grunts of support, though cautious, as none wished to interrupt his majesty.

'And desiring to be somewhere secure, until happy accommodation may be made between myself and my parliament, I have put the royal person in this place, for I desire not a drop more Christian blood to be spilt.'

Hear, hear! He had touched a nerve there. The civil war had been brutal, as nations are when they turn on themselves.

'Nor do I desire to be chargeable to your good selves, really not; so I shall not ask so much as a capon from any of you. My desire in coming here is simply the security of my person until the river of sweet resolution flows in our midst.'

'I toast the end of the king's retirement!' said Hammond, caught up in this most moving of moments.

'Let me be heard with freedom, honour and safety,' declared Charles, 'and this cloudy path shall become clear!'

With his personal safety assured, he was now ready to reassure parliament, the army and the Scots of his undiluted loyalty to their cause.

*

Robert Hammond came to the Isle of Wight for a quiet life, after the madness of war and the insane peace that followed. There was agitation and confusion everywhere, and of course the king must be protected from the ghastly Levellers. All this was self-evident.

But should the king take a degree of responsibility as well? There was something of this unformed thought lingering in Hammond. If the king had chosen the army when they entered London at the end of August, he'd be back on the throne by now and all would be well with the world. A king was the natural shape of things, after all, and Charles was a decent man. But he hadn't sided with the army; he'd merely strung them along. He'd preferred genteel captivity to reasonable compromise because as well as being decent, he was also a slippery fellow.

'He muddles the clearness of any argument,' as Oliver once said to him. 'I offer him what he desires and it somehow becomes a confusion.'

Cromwell and Charles, a most unlikely couple, had conversed favourably at Hampton Court, as Hammond knew – too favourably for some. The king had even made an impression on Elizabeth Cromwell, who was introduced to him that summer, in the palace gardens.

'May I introduce my wife Elizabeth, your majesty,' Cromwell had said with pride.

Elizabeth curtsied in the August sun and walked forward towards the king, holding court beneath the oak tree. She curtsied again on arrival at his side. 'A great honour, your majesty.'

'The honour is mine, Elizabeth. I do believe your husband has been hiding you from me!'

Elizabeth blushed a little, for Charles was a handsome man, if small, and Oliver smiled uncomfortably at the flirtatious comedy of the moment.

'My family keeps me busy enough, your majesty,' she said brightly.

'Indeed, Elizabeth, and what great credit that sentiment bestows on you. Where would we be without our families?'

'Quite so, your majesty.'

'I long for peace in this land. Your husband knows this better than any man.' He looked at Oliver, who nodded gravely.

'But, dare I say, that I long even more to see my children, and to delight in their growing ways.'

Elizabeth felt much moved. She was not one for tears – that was her husband – but her frame heaved a little. 'Then I hope both your longings are fulfilled, your majesty, for they do you equal honour.'

They talked a little more before Charles withdrew, leaving Elizabeth in a state of some euphoria.

'I wish there were more like him,' she said. 'Men who cared about their families. He is a true king.'

In the months that followed this garden encounter, summer into autumn, Charles had done everything asked of him by Cromwell – except come to an agreement. And then parliament quibbled about paying the army the money they were owed; a foolish move, ruinous really, in Hammond's eyes, for now the army distrusted both parliament and the king, who already distrusted each other . . . a country governed by distrust.

And into this discontent there stepped the leafleting Levellers.

They weren't army people, these agitators; they were London people, theorists from the city, with no place for a king. They claimed the people were the ultimate source of political authority. Hah! And they spoke wildly of 'free-born Englishmen' who would decide for themselves who should sit on the throne. As if you could choose a king! And then Harrison, a man much listened to, referred to Charles as 'a man of blood' and suddenly everyone was calling him so. It was hardly a surprise when these mad fellows started calling for the trial of the king. But could you really bring a king to trial? What in the constitution allowed for that? The whole idea was entirely mad. In the circumstances, Oliver had been most restrained. Hammond would have shot more than one mutineer in Corkbush Fields.

So the Levellers were a scandal; all right-minded people knew this. Charles was correct to remove himself from danger. But . . . well, if only he could take a little responsibility for these outcomes. This thought did nag a little in Hammond.

And then suddenly, and without warning, his study door opened.

*

It was his mother, standing in the doorway of his study – like she'd stood in the doorway of his childhood bedroom.

There had been no knock; but then, why did he imagine there would be? Mothers don't knock, especially when ruffled by the king's dietary demands, and she arrived early at her point.

'No larder could satisfy that man's cravings!'

Hammond hoped they would not fall out during her stay on the island. He would need patience, of course. He had become used to her absence, even fond of it; it had been one of the blessings of the battlefield.

'This is not the king's court, where he can demand as he will,' she continued. 'He is a prisoner here.'

'He is a prisoner, I know – no one knows this better than I, Mother. But—'

'There is no "but".'

'But he is also the king, and we must feed him well; which is why I brought you here, for you are a fine cook.'

He risked a compliment. She normally got angry when praised, as if it was quite misplaced. And in truth she wasn't a fine cook, no one would call her that, but she was competent around the kitchen and worked hard . . . just what he needed.

'I won't be flattered, Robert.'

'I do not flatter you.'

'He is a feckless waster, who insists on fourteen courses! What would the Lord say to that?'

Hammond had no idea of what the Lord would say but opened his mouth anyway: 'Surely our Lord said that it is not what goes into our body that is sinful, but what comes out of it?'

'You've quite lost me, Robert.'

'I believe he was saying that no food is unclean in itself, mother. It's about the words we speak rather than the food we eat – however many courses.'

Robert was pleased with this reply, for he too liked his food; though his mother was unmoved.

'Fourteen courses go into his mouth, and dissimulation comes out of it! I don't see St Paul applauding.'

Robert should never argue scripture with his mother, for she paid more attention to it than he did. She could always find a fitting piece, especially a judgement, and he had endured a great deal of that down the years. One day he would please her.

'Perhaps we can reduce the number of royal courses a little,' he said, willing her to be gone. 'I could have a word.'

'You speak as if it is a polite discussion.'

'He is king, Mother.'

'He is King Ahab, sure enough.'

'Hardly.'

'In the thrall of his very own Jezebel, Henrietta Maria, the Roman whore.'

'Charles is no Catholic. Absolutely not; he's Anglican to the prayer book in his pocket, it is well known.'

But Ruth hated Anglicans as well. 'Ahab was a man judged by God in battle: felled by an arrow and the dogs licked his blood. Kings come and go, Robert, and the worst kings find judgement awaits them.'

'I will speak to his majesty about his food.'

'Tell him not to turn away from the eel merely because the sauce has no garlic.'

'He may have been turning to speak with someone.'

'He could have twenty courses and still be a dissembler.'

And with that, she was gone, returning to her duties in the kitchen, while Hammond pondered the wisdom of inviting his mother to Carisbrooke.

December 1647

'Charles tries to calm the Scots,' said Wood.

'No one has ever managed that,' replied Cromwell. 'They don't have a calm bone in their bodies.'

'In negotiations, I find people believe what it suits them to believe, do they not, Oliver?'

Cromwell felt the words like a scrape of ice on the heart. Was Wood mocking his talks with Charles as naive? He'd undertaken them with an honest will, a will for reconciliation . . . and Wood could be scorn incarnate. Elizabeth hated the man, wouldn't allow him in the house. She said he liked information because it gave him the power to mock; he delighted in 'spring flowers and ridicule. He could make everyone a fool,' she said.

She did have a tongue, Elizabeth. Sometimes Oliver would not enter the kitchen if he knew her to be there, and she was there a great deal. The kitchen was her domain: the large pots on chains hanging over the open fire, the long family table down the centre, the water pump with its large brass tap, always dripping, the mangler for the washing, the smell of meat and soap – here she made the rules and most freely spoke her mind on Wood and other matters. In the parlour, it was Oliver who had the final word; but in the kitchen, his wife.

'How does the king calm the Scots?' asked Oliver. 'I know only cavalry.'

'He writes smooth words,' said the spymaster.

'And you have seen these words?'

'I possess an interesting letter.' He always possessed an interesting letter. 'A copy . . . a copy is taken before it continues its journey.'

'You have a long reach, Mr Wood.'

'He tells them not to concern themselves with anything he might or might not have said to parliament.'

Cromwell looked blank.

'The Scots are to know that his heart lies with them, he says; that he is a man of his word and that – how does he put it? – "many things may be fitly offered to obtain a treaty, that may then be altered when one comes to treat". The Scottish commissioners in London were much smoothed by that.'

Cromwell sat in silence.

'This is a winding road, Mr Cromwell, a twisting thing. We see only our journey to now and note it well.'

Oliver felt a passing sense of despair, liking journeys that were plain and clear to the eye some miles ahead.

'You do not bring me good news, Mr Wood.'

'That is not my job, Oliver. I simply tell you the truth.'

'And you tell me we deal with a dissembler.'

*

'You can't let them push you about, Robert! You always get pushed about.'

'No one is pushing me about, Mother.'

Ruth Hammond was in his doorway again, making all things public when his study should be a private place.

'They're pushing you about, anyone can see that. The scullery maid, Josephine, she says it!' Mrs Hammond indicated down the corridor. 'You're the governor, Robert! You do as you will, not what that parliament wills.' She spat the 'parliament' word. 'That shower want only for us all to become Presbyterians, that's their plan – which would be worse than the king of Spain!'

'I am simply in their employ, Mother, not some despot from the east.'

'You'll never be mistaken for one of them. Despots are not so lily-livered.'

He wished his mother would stay with the cakes and gooseberry creams and keep away from politics and loud references to himself.

'So what do they say?' she continued.

'Who?'

'And hurry, Robert, don't flannel, because I need to get back to the kitchen.'

He would like to help her there. 'They're just tightening the net a little,' he said. 'Some new orders to make the Isle more secure.'

'What manner of orders?'

'It needn't concern you.'

'I am a member of staff.' Hammond sighed. 'And your mother.' She paused for a moment as Hammond shrugged. 'Be wary of those who never held a sword against the king, Robert, that's all I say. They will be the ones snuggling inside his royal pocket.'

'Parliament is some way from the king's pocket, Mother. They wish the king safe; but kept here.'

'You need your old regiment with you, that's what you need.'

'Mother, this is not army business.'

'Not army business? It was General Fairfax who sent you here.'

'Yes – and parliament who authorized my arrival . . . and pay me.'

'You will have to decide, Robert, that's all I say: is it parliament or the army? As our Lord said, you cannot serve two masters.'

And Charles makes it three, thought Hammond gloomily.

*

Meanwhile, Charles is writing to Jane. Her spirit so reminds him of his dear wife Henrietta, some years in France now. Had the two women met, he fancies they would have been like sisters; he is quite certain of that.

I am daily more and more satisfied with this governor, sweet Jane. Everything is being done to ensure my comfort, which gladdens me. My furniture from Hampton Court has arrived, with only minor damage in the move. I have also been free to choose my servants, so the lively Firebrace is here with the melancholic Dowcett, as well as my barber Michael and many Scottish voices round about me, beautiful to my ears; and correspondence can continue, through our established channels, so do write.

God has also blessed me with the arrival of my royal coach, shipped, I am told, with some difficulty. So now I travel more freely on this fine island, observing much, if you understand my meaning. I wave to my subjects from the coach window, as I make a circuit of the place, and many look on with much wonder. I do not believe they have seen a king in his coach before, and it's a fine coach, as well you know. This warms my heart, to be among my people. They say I look most handsome in my coach; I trust you would say so too.

I have been deer hunting and hawking, of course, and visited the chalk columns called the Needles on the western tip. These quite stir the spirit. They say it once linked this island with the county of Dorset, which is a wonder I can scarce comprehend. While on another day, I travelled to Yarmouth to be entertained at a banquet given by Mrs Urry, and the food was most passable. Truly, the people here are gladdened to see me, and kneel often before me in joy and reverence.

I should also make mention of my visit to the church at Bonchurch on the south of the island, where I discovered a funeral party. When I enquired who had died, I was told that it was Sir Ralph Chamberlain. During his life, they said, he had fought and bled for my cause. I then discovered that he carried wounds from my service in his body – wounds he could not survive, causing death. When I heard it was so, I stepped out of my carriage and joined those mourning. They beheld this act of humility and gentleness in a king, and it gave them consolation, I believe.

You must come to this isle, Jane, when the time is propitious. This is a royal command. I have privacy for the warmth of friendship and I will seek to make it so. You can bring me much comfort.

From your grateful and sore celibate majesty,
Charles

January 1648

'His flight was less innocent than we thought, Oliver.'

'Oh? It felt all so innocent to me, Mr Wood! '

'Sarcasm, Mr Cromwell? It suits you as well as a dress.' Cromwell shrugged. 'And means your anger grows,' added Wood.

'I am not angry.'

'Sarcasm is anger's bastard son, Oliver. It announces a silenced rage.'

Perhaps his anger did grow ... for a man he'd trusted had clearly lied about his intentions. Oliver had entreated with the fellow in honest discourse – and been made a fool of. The army had mocked his negotiations, and clearly Charles had laughed with them.

'It suited you to believe it good,' said Wood. 'And when something suits, we notice not its wiles.'

That jibe again.

'I learn slowly of the man's dishonesty. Others race ahead in that discovery.'

They sat together in his damp parlour at Drury Lane, with its thin green rug and large Bible on the side.

'The fires deal slowly with the damp,' he'd said when Wood commented on the musty air. 'It is a great deal more favourable than it was.'

Elizabeth did not allow Wood in their home; but she was away, helping the needy spinsters of Southwark, with whom she spent considerable time these days, sewing clothes for the poor south of the river. Cromwell had returned here from the army camp at Newmarket, to listen better to the converse of parliament. Archbishop Laud – that awful man so loved by Charles – had called parliament 'that noise', and Cromwell understood the sentiment. It was clear the Presbyterians were talking to the king without reference to the army, their faces drenched in smug.

'What have you uncovered, Wood?'

'Me?' He posed as the innocent schoolboy.

'You are restless as a bear who waits on the dogs.'

'We have a letter, Oliver.'

'You always have a letter. What sort of letter?'

'Left behind by the king in Hampton Court.'

'And we hear of it only now?'

'It was found only when his furniture was removed, to be taken to the island. He has his royal coach now and travels extensively.'

'And what do we learn from the letter?' He asked without wishing to know.

'We learn, to speak his words, that when he left, he was "retiring himself for some time from the public view both of my friends and of my enemies".'

'He did not intend the Isle of Wight.'

'It appears not.'

'So where did he intend?' Wood shrugged. 'Is he Elijah, flying in his chariot to heaven?'

'I have informed Hammond,' said Wood.

'A man busier than he would have liked, I fear. I am told he looks quite ill and now regrets his retirement to the Isle.'

'I have relayed the simple facts to him, Oliver: that the island was not the king's first choice, nor the care of the army his desire. The letter he left behind, as he sneaked down the unguarded stairs' – he paused for a moment to allow time for shame – 'indicates other intentions, another purpose. He would like to have got more cleanly away.'

The terrible significance of that occurrence hung between them.

'Perhaps no ships arrived to take him,' said Oliver.

'They say Henrietta is presently off Jersey. A boat has lingered there a while, declaring itself bound for the Americas when the wind changes; but the wind has changed several times to my knowledge and the boat still remains.'

'Then you need to find out.'

'He is well served by ciphers at present. Many different codes, the royal bedroom must be awash with secret lists. And lemon juice.'

'Lemon juice?'

'He writes a great deal in lemon juice . . . not the ink of those with nothing to hide.'

'Hell's bells! Does the man do anything straight?'

'But his codes we will crack like eggs; and we have a friend there.'

'Where?'

'Close to the king.' Like a magician, Wood liked his revelations.

'How close?'

'Is it true you threw a cushion at Ludlow?' How did Wood know that? 'Many have wished to, of course.'

'It is time to go, Mr Wood.' He did not wish to speak of the cushion – but did wish to go to the theatre. He was going to the theatre this evening, to see a play by Mr Shakespeare.

*

'The king has made a secret agreement,' said Jane.

Why had she come back to the Strand? She had no wish for a continued relationship with Mr Lilly, no desire at all. An irritating fellow and somewhat cold . . . though intriguing, and she had to tell someone. She held too much inside, too many secrets and it made her ill; some suggested this. She suffered headaches, sometimes monstrous in their power and never once helped by leeches fixed on her neck, and found occasional release in speaking of the matter.

'An agreement?' said Lilly, apparently bored.

'It is secret,' said Jane, 'and need not detain us.'

He had offered her wine and she'd turned him down but accepted some elderflower cordial and sipped like a sparrow.

'With whom is this secretive agreement made?' asked Lilly.

'I cannot say.'

'But it is a secret that you know.'

'I am included, yes.'

Of course she knew. She was an important person, after all; this was not always appreciated by some of the king's more lordly supporters.

'Then it is not so secret.'

'It is completely secret!'

'Known by the king, the king's mystery bedfellows – and you. That's quite a crowd.'

'But no one else knows, and I will tell no one.'

Lilly poured a little more wine into his glass and more cordial into Jane's.

'It is hard to hold a secret; this is my experience. I always tell someone.'

'It is not hard for me.'

'Perhaps you flatter yourself, Mrs Whorwood.'

'Even the king's advisors left the room,' she boasted. 'No one must know.'

'Yet you know.'

'And there the story ends. Do you find that so hard to believe? Is my sex so talkative?'

She mocked him. Did he not realize that she was more loyal than any man and would never betray the king?

'Though as I say, you speak of it now,' said Lilly, sipping his wine.

'Speak of what?'

'The secret.'

'I speak *of* it ... but I do not speak it.'

'You edge round its circumference,' said Lilly with a smile. He grew fond of this woman; sympathetic at least. Her appearance deteriorated with the months, her skin pasty, her eyes more hollow ... attractive all the same through the scarring.

'I need to know where this secret will lead,' she said.

'The stars don't deal with secrets.'

'So the stars need secrets unravelled? They know the future – yet need the present explained?'

'The stars like facts, Mrs Whorwood. Without facts, they can only mumble like an old man, incoherent.'

'You have clearly met my husband.'

Jane sipped her elderflower cordial. She wished to keep the matter to herself, and she would; yet this afternoon, she could discover everything. The truth of future things lay at her feet. Imagine if she could give that to the king!

'There will be war,' she said.

97

She would say nothing else.

'Another war?'

'There is no other possible path.'

'There is always another path.'

'Not now.'

'Then he has not made agreement with parliament,' said Lilly, more stirred than his demeanour showed. 'I do not need the stars to tell me that.'

What was Charles planning? His mind was busy; he must calm himself.

'There shall be a second war,' said Jane. 'They will invade from the north and sweep down to London.'

She looked him in the eyes, testing him. Lilly only sighed.

'And it is signed and sealed?' he asked.

'Two copies. One is kept by the king, hidden in his writing desk.' She had to speak, to affirm the facts, to give the stars the facts – and to reveal the full cleverness of the king to this sneering man. 'The king has done all this, while his captors thought him servile and silenced!'

'You know your way round the king's bedroom.'

Jane looked at him with blank surprise. 'And what if I do?'

'I am concerned only with your safety, Mrs Whorwood. People can be unkind.'

'My safety does not matter.'

'Perhaps it should.'

He did fear for her; he foresaw a woman badly used.

'And anyway, many servants know their way round his bedroom. He is the king; they serve him as I serve him.'

'And the other copy?'

Jane paused, but only briefly. It was good to speak of these things – she felt better.

'Encased in lead and buried in the castle garden. It will be collected later by their agents.'

'By the Scottish agents?' Who else was there? 'I suppose they could not have been discovered with it, when leaving.'

'I believe that would be awkward.' She smiled mischievously. 'And it was signed on Christmas Day, Mr Lilly: a good omen surely? Signed on the birthday of our Lord! What do the stars think of that? Shall the Scots reach London, Mr Lilly?'

*

Oliver returned home after an evening with the Drury Lane Players, and their performance of *Macbeth*. He walked now in some wonder at the telling; and noted a writer not much mistaken about the Scots! He liked the theatre and would attend when Elizabeth was absent, for she was not a stage-lover herself.

'Theatre is the chapel of Satan, Oliver, and the sanctuary of harlots.'

'You overstate, wife.'

'Do you not see what goes on around you?' she'd said. 'Are you so blind?'

'I see the play.'

'Few others do. It is little more than a pit of assignation. It attracts that sort, common strumpets waiting only for the play's closing line – and some not even until then! And then it's back to The Cockpit.'

'Men take their wives, Elizabeth, I see them. You describe a fiction in your head.'

'No man takes his wife to the theatre, Oliver. He takes his mistress.'

'You do not wish to join me then?'

They had not spoken again on the matter; he went to the theatre when she was away.

But the play disturbed his sleep, waking him in the early hours, dark forebodings of future gain, the complicity of king and queen and the evil that spilled from them. In the deep dark of the pre-dawn, he wrote two letters.

The first was to Hammond, in which he called the king's flight and subsequent events 'a mighty providence to this poor kingdom and to us all'. He closed with this exhortation:

We shall prevent the king's dark visions of the future and calm his ambition with steel. More soldiery shall soon arrive on the island – proper soldiery, fit for the fight. In the meantime, I urge you to search out any juggling undertaken by his majesty. He is a clever juggler and has ciphers in his room, with which to disguise his correspondence. We ask that you make a visit to his lodgings privately, and see if this list might be discovered?

He wrote also to his son-in-law Henry Ireton, at army headquarters, with unusual brevity:

We close the net around the wild bird and send extra guards. We tell Hammond to have the king's bedroom locked every night, with the keys taken to him and him alone. Parliament may speak with the king – but we can hold him. We do not wish him sailing in his sleep to France.

February 1648

'I can assure you, Mr Hammond, I am here at Carisbrooke out of choice rather than necessity.'

The king seemed most certain in the courtyard at Carisbrooke, where Hammond had waylaid him.

'I pray that is so, your majesty, and that you speak plain; for we are both men of honour and must deal with each other as honour dictates.'

'And this suspicion is not necessary, really not.'

'Only I believe it is.'

A brave remark from Hammond, placing a marker in the sand. Hammond would not be the king's stooge. But Charles would explain. He could always explain.

'When I left Hampton Court, as I had to do, I had no other intention but to come here. Indeed I would prefer this place to any in all three kingdoms – excepting perhaps Whitehall – to conclude a treaty with my friends in parliament.'

'I trust you, your majesty, let us be clear,' said Hammond, backing down, 'but there are some who do not.'

'Suspicion suits no one. It can make you ill, I am told.'

'They wish me to sack Legge and certain other members of your household.'

'Who wishes this?'

'Parliament. They call them delinquents for helping you to escape.'

'You are no delinquent for saving the life of the king; you should be knighted!'

The thought had crossed Hammond's mind. 'I have told them as much, your majesty – without talk of a knighthood – and resisted their call.'

'Then that is the end of the matter.'

A pause.

'It is not quite the end, your majesty.'

'It is surely the end, for you are the governor of this island; and I am the king.'

'Only now the army demand the same; Fairfax and Ireton press me on the matter.'

'Fairfax and Ireton? Now there is an ill-matched pair . . . in agreement only on the size of Cromwell's wart!'

It was true they were cut from a different cloth. Both had been soldiers against the king in war; but Fairfax the gentler towards him in peace, wanting no more trouble now – just a return to how things were, with due compromise all round.

'Even so . . .' This was difficult for Hammond.

'You buckle like a coward at their request.'

'No, again I stand firm.'

Charles' eyebrows rose in surprise. 'Good man, good man. And you will be rewarded, of course, this goes without saying. I can quite see you as an earl of the realm.'

And with the conversation concluded, Charles withdrew to make plans for his escape. Now he had reached agreement with the Scots, he must make his way to France and await developments. The French and the Scots would work together to restore him to his throne.

*

Meanwhile, Firebrace waited for him in his quarters.

'The boat is ready, your majesty. And there is no time to be wasted.'

Matters were proceeding at great pace, and providentially so. Charles had written to Henrietta, asking that she arrange a French ship to be ready at Southampton. Firebrace informed him that the ship was now ready, so he must leave tonight.

'I will leave the castle in a relaxed fashion, as if taking an evening stroll,' he said.

'Yes, sire.'

'I'll need my riding boots.'

'They are here, sire.'

Firebrace knelt down to ease them on to the sweating royal feet. He was excited to be part of such momentous events – the release

102

of the king from captivity. He had thought of nothing else all day, but had chopped logs for the king's fireplace, to pretend normality. He always felt better for chopping logs, it calmed his mind. He'd even taken to chopping logs for Colonel Hammond, who'd asked him one day to fill his grate as well. Firebrace believed that only good could come from keeping well with the governor, that such connection would serve the king's cause. And so he chopped wood for both, and found Hammond an easy man to like, despite being the enemy. They discovered a shared interest in the art of duelling, particularly with the fine-bladed Italian rapier. And so sometimes, as Firebrace stacked logs in Hammond's study, they would discuss footwork, guards, attacks, defences and counter-attacks, which was a pleasing way to pass the time.

The soldiers, however, were less kind and would sometimes mock his chopping.

'It'll be the king's head next!' they shouted amiably and Firebrace would laugh. Little did they know how soon the king would be away from their clumsy care, and would not need these logs where he was going. He'd heard it was warmer in France.

'And now we must hurry,' said Charles – as if Firebrace didn't know this, for he'd been hurrying all day in his mind. With the king leading, they walked together down the worn stone stairs, making for the gatehouse, from where they would proceed towards the sea. But before entering the courtyard, Charles glanced out through the narrow window at the weathervane.

'The wind is not kind,' he said, pausing.

'Please hurry, sire.' He did not understand why Charles was delaying.

'But the wind,' said Charles. 'It is unfavourable.'

'The wind can turn.'

'This wind will not take us to France.'

'The wind can change, sire. A westerly is more usual; there will be a westerly tonight when you need it. This wind need not detain us now.'

'No, we must perhaps wait awhile. I sense this.'

'We must leave, your majesty.'

'We will calm ourselves for a moment; this is the wiser path.'

Firebrace was not for calming, for the king knew nothing about wise paths.

'There can be no calm until you are safe in France, sire. Then we shall be calm, and find the peace that eludes us now.'

'We will wait . . . wait, watch and allow the weathervane to change. Walk with me in a casual fashion in the courtyard, where we will take the evening air.'

'This is no time for strolling, sire, I really think—'

'There is a season for everything.'

And so they arrived in the courtyard, pretending calm . . . but stepped into unusual activity around the castle gate, where Hammond could be seen dismounting and hurling orders, like the soldier he'd once been. He was a disturbed man and not the one Charles had left just an hour ago. And then the wooden gates across the inner entrance to the courtyard swung heavily shut and a doubled guard appeared – younger men he had not seen before, men who did not hobble and wheeze.

'I will not need my riding boots,' said the king. 'France must wait. There will be another time.'

March 1648

A few weeks later — time slowed, accelerated and slowed here — Hammond sat alone in his study. The candles flickered as he wrote in the hand of a broken man. Disappointed hope is a terrible thing and this day he had seen it die; seen the laughing and smug faces of the departing Scottish commissioners — an inscrutable triumph writ across their bearded chops. He had seen also the resigned weariness of the negotiators of parliament. There would be no agreement with the Commons of England. Parliament had been tricked, sent away with nothing; there was no question about that.

And so he picked up his quill, dipped it in black ink and began to write to the speaker of the House of Lords.

Col. Robert Hammond
Governor of the Isle of Wight

Carisbrooke Castle
13 March 1648

My lord, this day I was in the presence of the king when he communicated to the commissioners of parliament his answer to the bills and propositions lately presented to him; and for which we had such high hopes. But these are now a deflated thing, and finding matters contrary to my wishes and expectations, I believe it my duty to take stricter care of the king's person, who daily becomes less plain in his dealings with us.

In particular, I have decided to remove all from about him — his excessive household — that are not here by authority of parliament. Let him feel the chill of our resolve in this and other matters.

By the blessing of God, I shall omit nothing in my service of parliament, in relation to this dangerous trust. But yet, my lord, I must humbly beg of you — for I know it is impossible to secure the king here for long — that his person may be removed from this island as soon as is possible. It does not go well with us to have him here. And if this be not possible, I ask then that I may be discharged from my employment, it being a great burden upon my soul and quite insupportable to me.

Yours in faithful trust,
Robert Hammond

*

The king was furious when Hammond told him on their morning walk.

'Ten of your household are to go, your majesty. It has been decided.'

Charles looked at the list of departures. 'You appear not to like servants with a Scots accent.'

'It is not the accent that offends, but those who imagine themselves to be postmen.'

'Is it you they trouble? Or Farmer Cromwell?'

Hammond thought this impertinent. 'They trouble us all.'

'The Venetian ambassador says Mr Cromwell can produce tears at a moment's notice. I merely wondered if he'd been crying in your ear?'

'It has been decided, sire.' Hammond would not be drawn.

'And such a plain man, don't you think?' continued Charles. 'In the manner of his dress, I mean – which appears the creation of a poor country tailor. No signs of a meeting with elegance in that man.'

Charles looked out to sea, small but imperious.

'You seem not to like the lieutenant-general today, sire.'

'I like him well enough . . . for a farmer.'

'And lately a soldier, who defeated your armies soundly.'

Charles ignored that. 'No, I merely question what has changed, Colonel? For I thought we agreed my household would remain as it was.'

'We did not agree, your majesty. I stated my intention that it would.'

'When you imagined yourself in charge of this castle.'

'I am in charge of this castle.' Now Hammond was bristling.

'And is it true that he loses his temper quite horribly?' asked Charles. 'I hear Mr Cromwell has an exceedingly fiery temper, which is most unsuitable – to have no control over one's temper. Wouldn't you agree?'

'This path leads nowhere, your majesty.'

'I suppose with seven sisters – he had seven sisters, I believe – one would learn to cry ... otherwise one might stand out rather.'

Charles could not countenance crying. His brother Henry laughed at him if he cried – just as he'd laugh now at the tears of the farmer.

'You seem too interested in this man, sire. Does he haunt you?'

'I think rather he haunts you, Colonel, with dark messages.'

'My intention has altered, that is all; and that is the end of the matter.'

Charles smiled with mockery. 'Your intentions change like the weathervane.'

'As do your own, sire. Is it the wind from the north we should most fear now? I hear you like it the best.'

They walked a little in silence along the castle's outer wall. Hammond felt strangely calm in this contest ... a surprising equal to this man who had once brought on nerves and deference; and Charles walked with a little difficulty up the hills, his legs not strong.

'I did not regard you as a weak man, Hammond,' he said, pausing to look out towards the sea. 'Really I did not, quite the opposite in fact; I spoke highly of you. But this is a monstrous violation of the king's prerogative. I do not believe that too strong a wording.'

But the decision was made. Hammond could be stubborn as well, and later that day, Legge – one of those destined to leave – bid farewell to his master.

'My work goes on, sire,' he said with a solemn bow. He did not know what work that was or what future awaited him, for he had no employment – a king's man since the war, and a soldier during it. He had lost touch with the civil life, though he'd worked for the Wilshere family when younger. They might take him back.

'You will not go unrewarded,' said Charles solemnly, king to subject, though he hardly meant it. He would not think much of Legge or his well-being in the coming months.

*

The evicted servants, a disgruntled band, travelled to Newport by horse; there they settled down in an inn and ordered ale, and rabbit and carrot pie. They spoke much of injustice and their fears for the king's safety, with little regard for who overheard them ... which may not have served the king's cause.

For in the same inn that night was Captain John Burley, formerly of the navy (before it turned traitor and Roundhead), and before that, a royalist soldier. With much grievance stored in his soul, he was not a man to be pushed around, and when he heard the stories of these servants, evicted so harshly, he was much stirred. How dare they sack the king's household? And when, dear God, would these intolerable behaviours cease? He, for one, would not tolerate such treatment of Good King Charles. It was time to act, and he called a young servant.

'Go fetch the town drum, boy! And let us save the king!'

On receiving the drum, quickly acquired from the mayor's lodgings, he had it beaten loudly in the streets of Newport, shouting, 'For God, the king and the people!' And he gained a following, though mainly of women and children with little else to do. No men in Newport followed him – a disappointment, for he desired the overthrow of all forces against the king and he needed the men. The mayor, however, was horrified and asked him to give the drum back.

'What are you doing with my drum?' he asked when he caught up with Captain Burley.

'Calling the town to arms, Mayor!'

'Are you mad in the head, sir?'

'For God, the king and the people!' shouted Burley.

'I want my drum back.'

'When the king is free from bondage, and only then, shall the drum be returned!'

Captain Burley was done with this appeasing of evil. And rumours of insurrection were quick to take wing, causing panic

108

among the king's gaolers. Captain Basket of Cowes Castle took time away from Edward to alert the navy in the Solent to be watchful.

'Watch for those damn Dutch ships!'

There were Dutch ships anchored nearby and they'd been causing concern; but while nothing came of it and the drum beat stopped, two hundred additional soldiers of the New Model Army arrived on the island soon after.

'Burley tried for treason and hanged in Winchester,' was printed on a flier and distributed around Newport to deter others. Hammond felt this to be an overreaction. The man was an idiot only, but you couldn't be too careful these days. 'Every wedge is thin at its beginning,' was the wisdom of the court.

'The only man to be executed for beating a drum,' Hammond said to Captain Basket.

But the captain had no qualms with the punishment. 'You do not beat a drum for God and the king, when God and the king are opposed.'

Hammond did not mention Edward.

April 1648

'When did it change, Oliver?'

'I have known in my soul since Putney; but sometimes I have forgotten, for perhaps I wished it were not so. This is what Wood thinks.'

'What does it matter what Wood thinks? He is a louse.'

'A louse with keen eyes.'

Elizabeth and Oliver lay in the four-poster, with the curtains up, winter now passed. It was the time before sleep, for musing and reflection, when the candle flickers and the day is done. Such moments took Oliver back to the battlefield tents, scattered across England, when the guns quietened and the horses grazed, and he would write letters to Elizabeth by candlelight: 'You are dearer to me than any creature, let that suffice,' he'd said. And he didn't know it, but Elizabeth had kept that one, somewhere in a drawer. For a long time, he'd even carried a line of hers, written to him before Marston Moor: 'Truly my life is but half a life in your absence.' In that moment, he had wanted to walk from Yorkshire to Ely to be with her; and yes, he was angry that the king had kept him from his wife . . . though he could be angry with her when she pressed, as she did now.

'And what did you forget?'

'That the king deceives; that the king always deceives. He is bloody and inconstant in word.'

Elizabeth snorted. 'He fights for his life, Oliver. It is what any man would do . . . it's what you have done.'

'His life is not in danger, Elizabeth, it never has been.' He was so weary of this conversation. 'But his integrity is; he does not deserve restoration.'

'You think you deserve more reverence from the king?'

It was not really an answer. They lay in silence a while.

'I have not told you,' said Oliver, sitting up. He was hurt by her words and now pushed the pillow behind him as a cushion against the headboard.

'You have not told me what?'

'Though no doubt you will brush it away as if nothing, and find in it a new way to praise Charles.'

'Of what do you speak, Oliver?'

'We were close to agreement last November, the king and I.'

'I am aware.'

'Very close. We offered him religious toleration, unlike either the Scots or parliament. So he could have kept his beloved bishops; and really, that is the most of what he wishes. He clings to his bishops most of all . . . and then we received news.'

'What sort of news? You tell a slow story and I will soon be asleep.'

'An army spy in the king's bedchamber told us that on the same day the king spoke with Henry and me, he wrote also to Henrietta.'

'So?'

'We were informed that the letter would be sewn into a saddle; and that this saddle would be brought to the Blue Boar Inn at Holborn at ten o'clock that night. The messenger would then ride on the saddle to Dover, where people waited, who knew what to do.'

'And you believed this?'

'Henry and I travelled to the Blue Boar, dressed as troopers.'

'I should like to have seen that.'

'And on arrival at the inn, we went inside and sat with our beer; it was Morning Dew, a sweet ale, as I remember.' He remembered good ale. 'But we left a watch outside, to give warning of the courier's arrival.'

'And no one recognized these two "troopers"?'

'A busy place does not question. And then, at ten, the man with the saddle arrived, so we rose, went out with drawn swords and approached the courier. We told him everyone was being searched, to put him at ease; but told him that as he looked honest, we'd just search his saddle. And this we did, taking it inside and cutting it open.'

'And?'

'We found the letter, which we returned to the saddle and then to the courier, who, unsuspecting, set off for Dover. But the letter was—'

'Was what? You grow tense, dear; you make the sheets tense.'

'Charles explained to Henrietta that he was being courted by both factions – army and parliament, and that he'd go with the best offer for the time being, but ultimately he would choose the Scots.'

Elizabeth felt the shock. 'The Scots?'

'Henry and I took horse and went to Fairfax at Windsor, aware that there were no tolerable terms for the king, apart from his own terms; and from that time forward, we were resolved upon his ruin.'

'Mmm . . . well, I hardly think one letter proves a case,' said Elizabeth. 'Unless you wish it to, Oliver.'

She extinguished the wick-lamp and lay still. Cromwell stayed upright for a while, like he had in the battle tents, trying to read the darkness and prepare for tomorrow's struggles.

*

Charles was absolutely furious – incandescent that his diplomacy was stifled in this manner. Parliament had declared it treason to speak with the king without their permission, which had not pleased the Scots; for they'd been speaking with him a great deal.

'They presume to dictate who I may, and may not, speak with!' declared Charles in derisory fashion. Jane calmed him, saying it would make no difference.

'How will parliament enforce their rules?' she said. 'Invade Scotland with rhetoric and a sharp turn of phrase?' Charles laughed a little; she could amuse him as well as stir him. 'They used to have an army, of course,' she said, 'but not now – the two do not speak.'

'This is much to our advantage,' he agreed. Her presence and her words, they calmed him; and he liked her dress, which he found most comely.

'Such fracture among your opponents, sire . . . and each wound crying for the healing touch of the king. We only have to wait.'

Cromwell harangued parliament when he could, sometimes rattling his sword as he spoke, to better make his point. He did get angry and it had rattled in its scabbard in January when he told them they should not 'suffer a hypocrite to reign' and that they could expect 'neither safety nor government from an obstinate man whose heart God has hardened'.

Charles told Jane that, for a farmer, 'Cromwell is a clever man – he manages to ride two horses, the army and parliament. But we all know his favourite mare.'

Parliament, fearful of the Scots, ensured closer detention of the king. His wanderings were now confined to the castle. He was to be kept in check somewhat – no more adventures round the island in his royal coach, which for Charles was most disappointing.

'You deny a king his coach, Colonel? I am surprised you leave me my legs!'

'Your legs remain, your majesty. They are just fenced in a little; you will not need your coach around the castle.'

Hammond had become ever more suspicious, and less respect-ful, of the king's privacy. And he did wonder what to do about the king's laundrywoman, Mrs Elizabeth Wheeler of Westminster. There was clear evidence from parliament's informers that Charles was receiving messages via this lady who daily brought in his clean linen. But how could the king be denied fresh laundry? Hammond would certainly not be providing it.

*

And now – ye gods! – yet another royal escape plan, here on his desk, 'designed and quite ready' according to the Derby House Committee. They even told him the 'how' of it all in their clever London ink.

'The king is to be drawn up out of his bedchamber into the room over it; the ceiling will be broken in places for this purpose. He will then be conveyed from one room to another, through the ceiling, until he be past all the rooms where the guards stand at the doors or windows. After this, he will be lowered and make his exit.'

Hammond sighed and pushed the text away ... to a more distant part of the desk. It was all very well receiving such news, but what was he to do with it? Reinforce the ceiling? Place guards in the loft? Sleep with the king himself?

And in the same post, a letter from Cromwell, which he had no desire to read. It filled him with gloom, like a missive from a former love – one who won't let go and writes only to harass his new life. Thankfully, it made no mention of the ceiling, but did inform him that three boats were arriving from Jersey to collect the king and then take him back there. So three boats were to land on the island ... but where? And when? And how exactly was the king to be collected? Hammond could not close down the sea.

He did his best to respond to these endless rumours of escape. He asked parliament for money to strengthen the castle defences, and they agreed money for the building of some higher walls ... and also sent twelve brass guns from Poole. With the arrival of the two hundred extra troops – a more practical help – external security was certainly better, but internal security still suspect. As far as Hammond could see, Charles' twenty remaining staff comprised one large escape committee.

*

Meanwhile, Jane is writing to Henrietta Maria, who in many ways is now like a sister to her, though they had never quite met.

Mrs Jane Whorwood
Servant to His Majesty the King

London
5 April 1648

To your majesty in sad exile and true queen of England,
I write of recent events at the castle, minded to keep you informed
of all that occurs at Carisbrooke until the king is freed to be with
you once again.
That will be a happy day indeed!
We have lost a little ground of late. I understand that Colonel
Hammond – a weak and suspicious soul – has now appointed

four conservators to guard his majesty. This does not help our noble cause, but should neither panic nor dismay. The king shall escape before England sees summer; this will happen without question.

The traitors appointed are Thomas Herbert, Captain Anthony Mildmay, Silas Titus and Robert Preston. Dull fellows all, but they must intrigue us now, for they circle the sun, employed in constant attendance upon the person of the king. They are to work in pairs, I am told, loitering by his side, except when he retires to his bedchamber, after which they are each to guard a door, with their beds laid across it, until he comes forth again. They were chosen as the severest of the king's household and most trustworthy. This we must work on, for no one is trustworthy when money or privilege is offered.

They sleep with their beds against the king's doors at night, though for how long they tolerate this inconvenience, we will see. These men do not imagine themselves as bed-shunting gaolers. They have higher thoughts of their status and can no doubt be turned.

Meanwhile, the king's household in the castle has been reduced to twenty, both harsh and unnecessary. How a king can survive with fewer than forty servants, I don't know. Many of his old servants did survive, praise God, including Firebrace, who grows in use; but Napier and dear Mrs Wheeler are among those now leaving his employment. The loss of Mrs Wheeler is keenly felt for she was a resourceful woman. I have known her many years and she and her assistant, the sub-laundress Mary, handled all of the king's correspondence; by the grace of God, young Mary had access to the king's bedchamber during the day, while empty and unguarded.

Letters would arrive – yours among them, and always the most keenly read – via brave couriers coming to the island. They travelled by night, skirting the patrols – yes, there are more of these now, extra troops in all places. Mary would hide letters beneath the bedroom carpet for his majesty to collect, so she shall certainly be missed. We've kept Dowcett, though whether this is good, I wonder – slow-witted, I fear. He helped get letters to Mary and *will need fresh guidance now. Men are a duller breed, they lack imagination; excepting his majesty, of course, whose grace overwhelms the whole island.*

In his most royal service, and in yours,
Your sister Jane

*

The king had now said goodbye not only to faithful friends but also to a decent laundry service.

'I have need of linen,' he complained to Hammond as they sat together in his study. It felt strange to be behind a desk, conversing with a king, who had the less comfortable chair and came as a supplicant. Though the strangeness was lessening; Hammond grew in confidence.

'Then perhaps you should walk around the castle less,' he said. 'It is the walking that makes you sweat and smell.'

'The king does not wish to walk less. He merely wishes to have due regard paid to his linen. Do you not find this room a little dark, Colonel?'

'But your majesty has made unfair use of his laundry,' said Hammond.

'I miss your meaning.'

'The laundry was offered to manage your clothes, not your correspondence.'

'The king must continue to rule and find the means to do so; you forget this, Hammond.'

'We have an agreement.'

'There is no agreement that can bind a king.'

'There is a man's word, on which trust is built.'

'Dear Colonel, you must remember that kings are different and not like you at all. To sit behind your desk bestows no authority on your person, when a king sits opposite you. Wherever I sit is a throne.' Charles smiled. 'I jest, of course.'

He did not jest.

'I myself have need of only two shirts a week,' said Hammond, primly. 'Enough surely for any honest man.'

116

Hammond remained angry that his search of the king's desk for ciphers had revealed nothing. Where did he keep them? Everyone knew he was receiving them; yet no one knew where they were kept.

A prisoner, royal or otherwise, should not run such rings around him.

May 1648

And as summer dawned, the healing evenings were causing Hammond further irritation. They certainly weren't healing for him.

'Stop this blaspheming nonsense,' said Rolphe, who found the idea of them quite deplorable.

'How can I stop the king's healing?' said Hammond. 'It would be like stopping Jesus!'

'I have never mistaken the one for the other.'

Apart from individual visitors, who were difficult enough to watch, large numbers of supplicants traipsed to the castle, through all sorts of weather, to be touched for the King's Evil. The sovereign had the power, so tradition had it, to cure those suffering from the scrofula by the royal touch. And so patients with this or other illnesses – the boundaries were ill defined – would be admitted in groups to be blessed by the king's holy hands; and despite the stricter care, this remained easy access to the king for any of his subjects. Why put beds against his doors at night, when any could walk in and be healed? People arrived from near and far – there were three from Yorkshire tonight. They'd lodge in Newport or the surrounding villages, and wait to catch the king on his way to supper or when out walking.

And whatever Rolphe said, Hammond could not stop the healings. That would hardly be fair to the ill, though he did wonder if those who saw the king were quite the invalids they purported to be. Recently Lord Rich had claimed to be afflicted by the King's Evil, which was possible; but it later turned out his other business was to consult the king about the royalist uprising in Surrey.

There was too much shiftiness for Hammond's liking. He'd disliked duplicity in the agitators, but now found their deceit outstripped by that of the king; and a chasm formed between them, between the king and his gaoler, and growing wider with each lying day that passed.

'A relationship cannot live on hollow words,' wrote Hammond in his diary one evening, the ink heavy with self-pity. And there before him on his desk was an old letter from Ireton, written the previous November. He'd spoken then of 'the great charge and burden brought upon you, Robert, even in that place where you had, I believe, promised yourself nothing but peace and quiet'.

Hah! Some peace and quiet this had turned out to be.

*

Jane had a particular need; a most secret requirement. And Mr Lilly could help – though could he be trusted? And had he been right about Essex? She would never know now, for things had moved on. Or rather the king had moved on, quite against her wishes – and was now marooned on that wretched island, when he should be in France, this was quite clear . . . and so she needed some acid.

'Do you have feelings for the king, Mrs Whorwood?' William Lilly was pondering his dispensary.

'Surely every subject has feelings for the king?' said Jane.

'There are different sorts of feelings.'

'But only one king, and it is his safety we consider now.'

'I consider the stars.'

'And what do they say today? Grilled fish for tea?' She hadn't intended to sound disbelieving – or impatient. But she had no time for pomposity.

'They do not speak much of aqua fortis, that's for sure,' said Lilly. 'Or of its corrosive powers on prison bars.'

She'd had to tell him what the acid was for. It was hardly a normal request for anyone other than a murderer, which she definitely wasn't; and anyway, she needed to take someone into her confidence.

'It's how things must now be done,' she said.

'Do be careful of your feelings, Mrs Whorwood.'

'I'm careful about the king's freedom; that is the only "care" I know.'

'Your feelings – they haunt you, like a gaunt-eyed ghost.'

'And you are a fine reader of women, are you? Would your wife say so?' She had not met his wife, or knew if he had one now; she did not see one around. 'Or are you more for the theory of other people's lives?'

Lilly pondered his books. He made his charts, this was his calling, but no chart could be separate from the flesh and blood of the client. There were days when he wondered if their eyes told him more than the stars.

'I do have concern for your feelings.'

'I came here for a name, not a sermon, Mr Lilly.' Jane was tense in her speech. 'Sermons pass me by these days.'

'You must be a lonely woman.' Lilly watched tears fill her eyes, wiped quickly away and removed from her cheek. 'And tired, I imagine. I know a little of your activity.'

'I have strength, Mr Lilly, if people do not make me sad.'

It was an instruction, like his father's had been. 'Now don't make me sad!' he'd say, trapped in the debtors' gaol, sad his life was this way . . . a big man made sad . . . and Lilly thought of him now.

'Sadness progresses nothing,' added Jane. 'Unlike aqua fortis.'

There was a pause.

'And Queen Henrietta?' he asked, gazing out on the street. 'Do you serve her as well?'

'The king says we are like sisters.'

She had not meant to say that; those had been private words at Hampton Court. But Lilly showed no particular interest, watching the thoroughfare below, which had no hour of quiet. Perhaps he would move to the country and become a country squire? He had heard of others doing this, buying a manor and some heraldry. But what would sheep make of an astrologer? And what would he make of them? He would not make money, that was for sure, there being no better shopfront in the world than a shopfront in the Strand.

'I do have a name for you,' he said, turning back inside.

'How do you mean?'

Was he about to insult her? Jane would not stand for it.

'Someone who will provide what you seek,' he said.

'The acid?'

'They can supply you.'

'And files?'

120

'He is a locksmith and well stocked. He will serve you well.'

Was it her imagination or was he being coarse? You never quite knew with Mr Lilly. He gave her a name and address, a locksmith in Bermondsey, and having committed both to memory she stepped out into the street with a plan in her mind and a king to serve. Why would she be sad? She was too busy to be sad; while upstairs, William Lilly took up his quill. The stars may be impartial – but he was not and knew who'd be interested in the news just revealed.

*

Dowcett was a large man, steady and slow like the elephant on display in London – and as much born to espionage, this was quite clear. So the king was tender in encouragement, for he needed him; this was how far he had fallen. King Charles now needed the melancholic Abraham Dowcett.

'Be confident,' said the king.

'Yes, sire.'

'Appear confident in what you do.'

'Yes, sire.'

'And nothing can go wrong.'

'Unless I'm caught – sire.'

'I will, of course, be as careful as I can be,' said the king, 'so there is no suspicion cast.'

'Yes, your majesty. And if I am caught?'

'Your discovery will prejudice me quite as much as it will you.'

'Not quite, your majesty. They hanged Captain Burley for banging a drum; they have not hanged you for a war.'

It had to be said, though Charles perceived it as a fine nonsense.

'Ah, Abraham, you are a true Englishman, the most noble sort!' Dowcett did irritate him. 'And now we are both servants of this country; we merely serve in different ways.'

Very different, thought Dowcett, and said, 'Yes, your majesty.'

And Abraham Dowcett was proud to be a true Englishman, and happy to be named as such by the king. But he knew there were spies everywhere in this household, informing and counter-informing. Quite simply, he wished to keep his head down.

'Let not cautiousness beget fear, Abraham, this is the thing . . . and be, er, confident of me. Yes?' Charles touched his arm, something he avoided with servants – but needs must, and Dowcett noticed. He noticed that the king both touched him and used his name. He could not but feel the force; who wouldn't? So he determined to do as he was told: he would attend the king at meals.

'If there is a letter to pick up, a secret sign will be given.'

'Yes, your majesty.'

'You will then go and collect the letter from my bedroom.'

'And will I know the secret sign?'

'Of course; it cannot be secret from you!' Here was a very stupid man. 'If there is to be a collection made, I will let fall my handkerchief. Like this.'

Charles let his handkerchief fall to the ground. Dowcett watched.

'This will be a sign that a letter from me is ready to leave the island.'

'Yes, sire.'

'And if I have safely received a packet, and wish to make this known, I will let fall one of my gloves. Like this.'

Charles dropped one of his gloves, and again, Dowcett watched.

'Yes, sire.'

'I will be curt with you, though, in my manner.'

'Curt, your majesty?'

'I will be curt, a little surly in my manner towards you.' Dowcett nodded. 'But you must not take it ill in any way. If I look sourly on you in public, it is your best disguise; you will appear as one outside my circle, someone not cared for or respected.'

So, little acting required, thought Dowcett.

Maybe he did this for Firebrace more than for the king, because they were friends in a manner, though different to their core. Firebrace was forlorn without a scheme in the air, and delighted in finding ways.

'The king gives me a problem, Abraham – and I find ways!' he'd say.

As page of the bedchamber, Henry Firebrace had access to the king's bedroom during the day, and so replaced Mary when she was removed, checking beneath the carpet for correspondence in and out. And sometimes he and the king spoke, direct to one another, Firebrace having found a way. He would ask one of the guards if they wished to be relieved. He'd tell them to go downstairs and enjoy some supper and a pipe; they never turned him down.

And once they were gone, and happily feeding their faces, Firebrace would speak with the king through the partially open door to his room – partially open because the guard's bed blocked it.

'I do believe we out-fox the colonel,' said Charles through the door on one occasion, which made Firebrace feel splendidly proud, as he knelt on the guard's shifted bed.

And after a while, he became yet more confident. Not content with speaking through a half-opened door, he pierced a hole in the stone wall, behind a tapestry, so he could talk to the king without moving anyone's bed to open the door. This was less of a risk, if someone approached: no door to close and no heavy bed to push back. And in these hole-in-the-wall conversations, the second royal escape attempt took shape.

'This is the plan, your majesty, and I believe it possible.'

'Tell me your plan.'

'I have noticed that the inner courtyard is not well patrolled at night.'

'Indeed. I too have observed this.'

The conversation was slow. There was only one hole through which to listen and speak, so ear and mouth needed time to adjust. Sometimes two mouths spoke and sometimes two ears listened.

'So if you were to lower yourself from the window to the courtyard below, the two of us could make our way to the battlements on the south side. This is remote from the officers' quarters on the north side and from the gatehouse and guardrooms in the west.'

Had he finished? The king felt he should speak. 'Quite. And what th-th-then?'

Ear to the hole again.

'John Newland, a merchant of Newport and one of our own, has made a ship available to us. And Richard Osborne will also help.'

123

'We trust Mr Osborne?'

'We do, yes.'

'I have my doubts.'

'As Gentleman Usher and holder of your gloves during meals—'

'Mr Osborne holds my gloves limply. It speaks of disdain.'

'That is his manner, your majesty.' Why were they discussing this?

'It is an unfortunate manner.'

Had the king finished?

'The holding of gloves is a personal matter, your majesty – the manner of it, I mean. We all hold gloves in different ways.'

'It should be done confidently and with swagger . . . especially the king's gloves.'

'Mr Osborne is both trustworthy and invaluable, sire, I can assure you. And he will pass notes to you, by placing them in the fingers of the gloves.'

'He could be a parliament man.'

'I do not believe so, sire.'

The king was wearing him down. Firebrace had this entirely planned and simply needed a 'yes' from the king. Was that too much to expect?

'And if he is on parliament's side,' added Firebrace, 'which he isn't, but if he is, then I am more lost than you.'

'And when we get to the battlements?'

'A rope will take us to the base of the curtain wall, where Osborne and Edward Worsley – another trusted servant of the king – will be waiting to help you down the bank. They will have with them a spare horse saddled, with pistols and riding boots; and from there, we will make our way to the boat. Everyone is well instructed in their part.'

It was their best chance to date. Without a doubt, the king would soon be free.

*

In his parlour at Drury Lane, across from the almshouses and the goldsmith – and four doors down from The Cockpit – Oliver drew on his pipe: both pleasure and relief, with neither so common these days. Opposite him was his son-in-law Henry, as clear-eyed and square-headed as ever. On the battlefield, Oliver was the more compelling, energized by the grand vision and big movements of men and beasts. He struck opposition flanks with discipline and power.

But in the cold pursuit of a civil matter, you wanted Henry in command; Oliver knew this. He admired – no, he envied his son-in-law's clarity of thought and ease with decisions, no cloudy thoughts. Cromwell changed his mind four times a day, and under duress (this was well known) would become becalmed, decision-less for days. 'Oliver without Henry is like a man without an arm,' he'd heard it said.

'The king puts himself up for auction,' said Ireton, waving away the smoke. 'We bid, as do the Scots, as do parliament; and it is intolerable. This is all I say.'

'You have little time for Charles,' said Elizabeth, who was stoking the fire – a task she saved for Henry's visits; this Oliver had noticed. But 'Henry is family' was Elizabeth's view ... and why shouldn't she be with family in her parlour?

'He will take the highest bid,' said Ireton, who did not regard this as personal. Whether he had time for Charles was not relevant; the king's political whoring was simple fact. 'And if our bids do not much impress him – and I cannot imagine one that would, other than a bid penned entirely by Henrietta while astride him – then he will take himself to France.'

Let Elizabeth be upset at his coarse tongue; he cared not.

'Oliver remains a monarchist,' replied Elizabeth coldly, still hovering, still busy at the grate. 'You are aware of that?'

'And I remain a monarchist,' said Henry, light-heartedly. 'We seem a gathering of royals!'

'You do not sound like a monarchist.'

'Perhaps I do not sound like a monarchist at any cost. It is a distinction worth drawing. We all draw a line; we just differ in where we draw it.'

'But not Charles,' said Oliver, quietly but firmly.

'I beg your pardon?' said Elizabeth, her face turning from the heat.

'Not Charles.'

There was some silence.

'You have not said this before,' said Henry. He did not wish to assume, but ...

'In the present storm,' said Cromwell, 'we must make the best of the anchors we have.'

Elizabeth laughed in mockery. 'And where are the anchors if Charles goes?' she asked. 'No one knows whether you are monarchical, democratical or aristocratical, Oliver! Perhaps you should float to the Americas and start all over again!' He had thought of it, when younger. 'So which are you?'

'Perhaps I am all of those, Elizabeth – and none.'

This does not bode well for a decision, thought Henry.

'Did not the Jews have patriarchs, judges and kings at different times?' asked Cromwell and it was a telling hit. 'Their anchorage changed, and perhaps ours does too.'

'Strange words from the man once so impressed by the king.' Elizabeth was angry. 'Who came back to me from Hampton Court with stories of his "grace" – that was your word – and "kind fatherhood" to his children.'

'And it was so, I do not dispute it; and you thought the same, and have loved him ever since.'

She would ignore that. 'No one would guess you'd fought a war against him, Oliver. "Charles is a good man, Elizabeth," you would say, "I warm to him greatly".'

Ireton felt awkward. Though a strong woman in her household, he had not expected Elizabeth's intervention.

'I was taken in,' said Oliver. 'I acknowledge my mistake. Does that improve your spirit?' Elizabeth's face did not suggest so. How was life improved by apology, with the mistake already made? 'The glories of this world so dazzled my eyes that I could not clearly see the great works God is doing.' There were tears in his eyes, the water of remorse and repentance. But Elizabeth stood with her hands on her hips.

'Sometimes, Oliver, I have no idea what you're saying,' she said, with the sigh of one too busy to stand here wasting her time. 'In the past year, you have been for parliament over the army, then for the army over parliament, then for the king over both and now for the parliament and army against the king! They say you drift and slither like an eel in grease!'

It was only later that they sat alone, Oliver and Henry. The fire had near burned itself out, unvisited by Elizabeth and unnoticed by them in their solitude.

'She doesn't believe we should disturb the throne . . . never has,' said Cromwell.

'But would you keep a throne?' Ireton looked vainly for precision.

'There is always a throne, Henry. The question is only how many sit on it.'

'But Charles shall not sit there?'

'He is an obstinate man whose heart God has hardened.'

Those words again. Ireton had known this truth for a while and was pleased Cromwell had now joined him.

'I will write to Hammond to be aware of any deception going on at Carisbrooke,' said Ireton.

'If that is what we must do,' said Cromwell. Melancholy brought caution and there'd been much in his spleen of late. It came like a fog, bringing doubt to the path. God had been in his victories, this was quite clear. But where was God in this confusion . . . and had he withdrawn his blessing? Oliver looked in vain for a sign; every day he looked for a sign.

'Perhaps I will draft the letter,' said Henry, 'and you write it. It will be better from you.'

'I was not put on this earth to be your secretary, Henry.'

'You must decide for yourself why you were put on this earth, Father.'

And for the first time, Oliver was not sure. The beacons by which he had steered his life had all been destroyed, lost in the miasma of move and counter-move. Cromwell felt hated by republicans, hated by the king, hated by parliament and hated by the Scots. Was this a sign of godliness – to be hated by all? Some did preach that. Certainly, there was little joy here . . . only the scream of Christ on the cross, 'My God, my God, why have you forsaken me?'

'You're doing well, Oliver,' said Henry, with a kindness that surprised them both.

*

'And how *is* the king's health these days?' asked Brome.

After some angry searching, he'd found his hopeless wife Jane in the gardens of their country estate in Sandwell – well, his country estate. There was nothing here that was hers. And he did not object to Sandwell; it gave him status and a little income. One day he would reclaim his family manor at Holton – a grander holding. But this would suffice for now; and he'd been looking for his adulterous wife all morning.

'He keeps his spirits up,' said Jane, cautiously. She'd hoped not to see her husband this morning. She'd hoped not to see him since their marriage day, but the longing was particular today. They had rowed last night; he'd been drunk and had shouted. She'd wished him back in Holland, he'd taken offence . . . and she'd slept in the guest bedroom. Where Brome had slept, she could not be sure. She'd heard him on the step to Kate's room, one of their maids who he liked to visit. But she found him in the morning on the divan in the parlour. She'd left the curtains closed, but in the half-light gazed on the snoring figure, shorter than her, turning a little to fat and his curly hair thinning, she noticed . . . no longer a boy.

But now she was discovered by the rhododendrons and could not escape.

'It must be hard for him without his wifely comforts,' said Brome. 'Very hard. You know how men can be, when left alone in the world.'

She did not like to hear him speak of the king. It was an aspect of her life where he had no place, no claim – territory free from his sneering, grasping presence.

'I don't know what you imply,' she said primly – though she did know what he implied. He rubbed his cock to make it plain.

'They love each other, Brome – is that so strange?'

'They love each other across the sea? His prick must be longer than I thought.'

'It's a feeling you might struggle to understand.'

'Oh, *I* might struggle – but not you?' He moved towards her. 'So you now are all love ... and I am none?'

Jane did not have time for this. He seemed bent on confrontation, and really Jane wished only to withdraw.

'I loved you once,' she said, quietly.

'You tell me now! I did not know it!'

'I loved you once.'

'You *tried* to love me once.'

'And what else did you want? Is trying not enough?'

'I think ... I think I wish for it to be less *trying*, perhaps. I think I wanted to be loved and swived without the trying, Jane – such beggarly portions offered. I was only a boy after all.'

And you still are, she thought. This was clear to Jane, a boy who could think of no one but himself.

'Perhaps I froze in your care, Jane, what do you think?' Jane shrugged. 'But no matter, no matter, for others unfreeze me now ... and I own everything – even this flower!' He snatched at the rhododendron bush, wrenching a small branch free. 'While you have nothing bar the king's swivelling stick – and that will be a brief ride, for sure.'

'I have a cause, Brome, that's what I have, a noble cause. And I wish to return to it now.'

'So is that what we are to call it?' He was sneering, circling her. 'You open your legs and call it a cause?'

'I see no purpose in this communication. I wish to leave.'

'And leaving is your habit, Jane, is it not? Is it not you who keeps leaving, leaving our home? You leave a great deal.'

'Our home? Is that what you imagine – that this is a home?' She could not let that pass.

'You leave a great deal,' said Brome again – and now both finger and fist were close to her face. She pulled away.

'How would you know anyway? You've been neutral in Holland these past two years, frightened for your life, while I and the children took care of ourselves. I've never had a home here.'

'And that's been your choice! *Your* choice! You left home long before I did, Jane, with your meetings and your travels and your conspiracies.'

There was a pause. Jane breathed in, halted for a moment.

'I do it for the king and the nation.'

'You do it for yourself, you harlot. What does he promise you?' Again his face closed in. 'Or is it simply enough to be free of your children?'

'He promises me nothing.'

'He uses you for free? I did imagine as much . . . a vaulter for the king, a convenient whore, bitch and jade!'

'I will leave this afternoon,' she said.

'It is what you do best, Jane. And on your return – whenever that might be, I care not – you shall sleep in the attic. That shall be your place now.'

Jane was shocked. 'It's where the maids sleep,' she said. 'It's where—'

'We shall move Kate, give her a different role in this household, as "governess", I think – yes, she deserves that for the manner of her performance.'

'You cannot do such a thing. I am your wife.'

'And I am master of this estate, Jane,' he said, walking away, gesticulating at the surrounds, 'owned by my family for centuries – while you are a late arrival and without authority here.' And now he turned, spun round, advanced upon her, grabbed her face, pressing his fingers into her cheeks. 'And Kate – she keeps a warmer bed than yours – I'm sometimes quite amazed how warm.'

Kate now appeared close by, with some agitation.

'Begging your pardon, sir, but Reverend Wainwright is here, seeking to speak with you.'

'Then I will come, thank you.' He swung free of Jane, pushing her away. 'I would not keep a holy man waiting.' Jane stumbled and half fell, tripping on her dress. 'There is certainly nothing to keep me here,' he said to Kate, patting her bottom, as he strode back towards the house. 'Mrs Whorwood was just leaving. She's always just leaving.'

And she was, even as she got up from the ground, already on the road in her mind, on her way to London. She had money; she would be on her way. She would find Mr Wallace, a wily merchant fresh from the sea, and she'd celebrate his recent good fortune ... in person.

*

The king's escape drew nearer.

In response to Firebrace's plan, the king started taking daily walks round the castle, surveying the escape route. He felt confident and predicted success for the scheme; Firebrace felt the same, pleased with his careful planning. The king thought Dowcett might be a weak link and shared this privately with Firebrace, who nodded and tutted, though in his estimation the break in the chain was more likely to be the king.

'Only the king can upset a good outcome,' he told Dowcett. 'All else is well in hand.'

'Is he worth the trouble?'

'Hush now, Abraham. Those are not good words when we have work to do. I will flush the king from this place!'

*

It was the night of the escape and the stars were bright with excitement. With the boat in place, moored not far away, Worsley and Osborne approached the castle walls with the horses. Firebrace was in the courtyard below Charles' window, taking an evening stroll. He had not spoken with the king today, but they had communicated yesterday through the wall, and all was in hand. There was alcoholic laughter from the guardrooms, which was all to the good.

'Drink well tonight,' muttered Firebrace. 'And you will wake with very sore heads indeed!'

The king's window was thirteen feet above the courtyard. There was no light from there, as arranged, and the rope was ready, smuggled into his bedroom by Dowcett, using the back stairs. It was time.

Firebrace looked around and threw a stone towards the window, to indicate it was safe for the king to make his move, to begin his descent. The king was waiting, standing in the darkness of his bedroom. He crossed himself briefly and the escape from Carisbrooke was under way.

131

The window opened, a figure appeared in the frame ... it was Charles, moving awkwardly. Firebrace watched. There was a scuffling noise as Charles twisted his body to the shape, forcing it through the narrow portal between the bars. Firebrace peered into the courtyard gloom for any guard on patrol, but saw none. They seemed well set in revelry for the night – it could hardly be more propitious. And then above his head, a groan; the king, despite rigorous struggle, was stuck.

Firebrace had told him he'd need to remove one of the bars. The king said he could get his head through without removing them; he felt the opening was quite wide enough. Firebrace said he should dislodge the bar, by chipping away beneath; it could easily be done. But the king said such work would be noticed, that they would notice the damage to the cement work. He then encouraged Firebrace to concentrate on his part in the escape ... which he had, and now regretted. Everything he had planned was in place, but the king was stuck between the bars, beneath a bright starlit sky.

He willed the king through, as one giving birth, but heard only struggle, more groans and then silence. Firebrace thought for a moment that he might have fallen, difficult to explain, but no; for now candlelight appeared from the king's window, which was some relief. The king was safely back inside. The guardroom merriment continued, his escape attempt unfulfilled – but also undiscovered.

'Where is the king?' asked Worsley, nervous at their hazardous predicament beyond the castle, with a spare horse. This was not the place to be exposed.

'He will not be coming,' said Firebrace, in a shouted whisper.

'What?'

'He will not be coming!'

'Why not?'

'He just will not. There is mischief.'

'Mischief?'

'I cannot perform miracles. Now go!'

'But Mr Newland is ready.'

'And the king is not, which leaves us nowhere! Now ride – or we'll be seen!'

He wouldn't tell them about the window; they might curse the king, which they would regret in the morning. And so Osborne and Worsley rode away, complaining about the incompetence of Firebrace, who turned back towards the castle and retired to bed.

Dowcett was waiting outside his room. 'A good night?' he asked.

'I have known preferable evenings.'

'The king remains?'

'He remains.' Dowcett left a pause which Firebrace filled. 'He became lodged in the window,' he explained, looking around to ensure no one listened in. There was always a soldier somewhere.

'Lodged?'

'Stuck – stuck between the bars.'

'Which you asked him to remove.'

'I did make that suggestion. He had to fall back into his room in the end. He may be a little sore in the morning.'

'Much wasted time,' said Dowcett as he turned and walked away, leaving Firebrace alone in the corridor, glad only that their tracks were covered and that none need ever know what had been planned this night.

Only in time, they would; because there were no secrets at Carisbrooke.

June 1648

June found the king unsettled. The rain would not stop, quite merciless in its persistence, and thoroughly removing the joy of the month. In his youth, pink/red roses had grown in the Spring Gardens of St James's Palace; he remembered them well, forerunners of summer. But none grew here, perhaps frightened by the rain. It beat against his window like a mad beggar and spoke despair and hopelessness.

Until now, he had felt a man in control of his affairs. He was king, after all, and no one could govern without him, this was common knowledge, and of course his enemies were divided, increasing his value. He could escape when he wished; this had been his sense. And he would escape, if it served his cause. There were plenty of loyal subjects waiting only for his nod.

But should a king have his cabinet broken into? That was treason, surely?

'You search my rooms?' he had said to Hammond, with understandable shock.

'What if I do?' Hammond replied, flustered.

'An invasion of the king's person. I can hardly believe it of you, Colonel.'

'I'm afraid you're a prisoner here, your majesty, and one can search a prison cell. It is not the king's residence in Whitehall.'

Hammond was furious that he had been caught. He had met Thomas Herbert just as he was leaving the king's rooms, while his majesty ate. It was the best time for a search, when the king was enjoying his food, but his majesty had sent Herbert upstairs to fetch his coat, hence the unfortunate meeting; and Herbert would tell the king . . . because the wretch told the king everything.

'You do not trust me?' said Charles.

Hammond smiled in despair. 'You rise early, sire, and retire late to bed; but there are those who wonder what you do with your time in between ... and your ink.'

No one wondered – everyone knew. Much of the royal correspondence was being intercepted, once it had left the island.

'He might as well address it to Cromwell!' they said.

*

It was in 1635 that the institution of the post office was created. Wood remembered the date and sneered at the man behind it: Thomas Witherings, an unsavoury London merchant, and not a man for the history books. He'd proposed to Charles' council 'to settle a packet post between London and all parts of his majesty's dominions for the carrying and re-carrying of his subjects' letters'. It would require the building of six great roads, he'd explained, the expense of which did choke them a little; but he'd justified the outlay with some cunning, claiming speed of internal communication was vital to the country's defences against the darkly evil Spaniards. Wood smiled bleakly at the thought: this new-fangled post service at once elevated from a business to a cause! It was for the defence of the realm, long live the king! Witherings was nothing but a chancer, of course; yet from such talk emerged a service required to run night and day, and with stipulations – many stipulations – about speed of delivery. Post between London and Edinburgh, for instance, was to travel there and back within six days.

'He is a man of dubious integrity, Oliver, a slippery fellow,' said Wood.

'Witherings? I am well aware. Parliament sacked him often, I recall.'

'And each time, they'd bring him back.'

'I know.' It hadn't been Cromwell's doing.

'He's like a bouncing ball in a field of shit – he does return a great deal, and each time a little more coated.'

'A king's man, I'm afraid.'

'But we must applaud his creation, Oliver: staging posts at an interval of twenty miles in the south parts of England. I confess to being impressed.'

It was rare that Wood gave credit to an intelligence other than his own.

'And the north?' Cromwell knew of its deficiencies beyond Ware.

'The north is less well served, I grant you ... unless you travel to Edinburgh.'

'And soon I might,' said Cromwell. 'But with an army rather than a packet. There is growing malignancy north of the border.'

*

Hammond would use the postal service for regular letters; this was his habit. They took a day to reach London, unless the Solent was choppy. And on occasion, the king himself took advantage of the service he'd sanctioned, for there was no faster delivery. But out of discretion he generally favoured his own couriers, including 'the plain fat man', a relentless carrier of royal post.

The king's letters were less secret than he imagined, however; for parliament's Derby House Committee heard everything. They employed a spider's web of agents, and at the centre of the web sat the largest spider of all – Secretary Walter Frost, who guarded the names of informers so closely that not even the committee knew who they were. They were 'Walter's Ears', anonymous and everywhere, listening to the nation – in streets, taverns, army bases, post-houses ... and in Carisbrooke Castle itself. The enemies of Charles, they knew what Charles was doing – but knowing and stopping were quite different animals.

There was due deference to be considered. He was a shit, but a shit who was king.

*

Relationships! It had all been so messy between Hammond and Charles of late; but how much more pickled had it become yesterday?

Hammond had recently discovered royal letters pinned on the wall behind the wall hangings – awaiting collection by Firebrace, it transpired. But he'd found them by chance rather than intelligence, as he searched for another – and very particular – jewel: Charles' agreement with the Scots. Everyone knew of it, but no

136

one could find it, and Hammond was determined not to appear the fool again.

'To break open my cabinet – and with such force!' complained Charles.

The force seemed only to add to the sacrilege.

'We must have no secrets from each other, your majesty.'

'For the good of the nation, a king must always have secrets, especially in his bedchamber! I do not inquire after your behaviour there.'

'I am not your prisoner; and I noted the cabinet was locked.'

'Of course it was locked! Is not your cabinet locked? I truly hope so.'

'A prisoner cannot have locked-away things, your majesty.'

Should the agreement be found, the king would be a damaged vessel indeed. But having smashed open his cabinet, Hammond had found nothing, apart from Charles' spiritual writings, which held no interest. And so the king's rage was pretend, and his mood relaxed, playful even. His good cheer sang of his relief at Hammond's failure . . . and ate at the soul of his gaoler. There and then, he decided to proceed further with this matter.

'And so I must search your person, your majesty.'

'I do not think so!'

Charles did not believe he would; surely he would not search the king's person?

'You give me no choice.'

He moved towards the king, who moved back, until stopped by the royal bed.

'No man touches the king!'

'Every prisoner must be searched. Now, please—'

Hammond reached forward, taking hold of the king's jacket; much inflamed, Charles pushed him back. When the colonel came forward again, Charles struck him with his fist, hitting Hammond's chin, a scuffed blow – but he would not stand for this invasion, he simply would not! If the king wished for a duel, then he had one, and full of fury, Hammond struck him back. He struck the king – and a harder blow as well, knocking the small figure backwards, on to the bed, like brothers playing.

Only one was a great deal stronger.

'Well,' said Charles, sitting on the side of the bed, dabbing at his lip, a little bloody. His face was marked in a way Hammond's was not, a swelling appearing.

'You struck me, your majesty.'

'I would like my cabinet mended and the lock returned, Colonel.' Hammond nodded. 'I believe it is the least you can do.'

'We can mend it, your majesty – but whether we can lock it again, I don't know.'

He knew his attempt to search the king's person had failed. It would not be possible now; any secrets in his pockets would remain there.

'I do forgive you, Robert,' said Charles as he stood up and brushed himself down. His lip was growing visibly. 'I know you act under the orders of careless men; so please receive my forgiveness for these violent acts. I forgive you, truly.'

Robert nodded and wished that he might retire tonight, and leave the island in the morning. And what if Charles returned to the throne, which surely he would? What future for Hammond then?

*

It was a victory for Charles, despite the sore lip. Hammond avoided him in the following days, and there were no more searches. Not that there was much of note to find; the agreement with the Scots had been smuggled out ten days before this altercation. But despite such happy circumstance, the king did not feel cheered: the new troops would stare at him with dead eyes, as one might gaze on someone of known disrepute, and he heard the army were once again finding unity of purpose . . . very bad news.

And then a message from London. It was brought to the island by the plain, fat man and left under the carpet by Firebrace. The king's son, the Duke of York, had managed to flee his imprisonment in St James's Palace, dressed as a girl, which was most inventive. And how gloriously humiliating for his captors! The boy had then been whisked away by agents of the émigré English court in Holland, and placed on a pincke which had stood for two weeks off

Gravesend ... so clearly a son with his father's spirit and his mother's skill in performance.

But there the celebration ended and the self-punishment began, for while the prince had escaped, he had not. His son had rather shown him up, he felt; he'd taken the glory on offer and left his father drifting towards futility and frustration. And when he next met Hammond, in need of someone to blame, he gave him a piece of the royal mind.

'You are grown very high since you came to the island, Hammond.'

'I did not seek this task, your majesty.'

'Perhaps you sought to be a pugilist instead?' Hammond looked sheepish. He was yet to reach an agreeable place within himself, concerning his action against the king; certainly he had not told it to anyone. 'And whether or not you sought it, Colonel, I believe you were rather pleased to be granted such a posting.'

'Such a posting, yes, but not such a prisoner.' Who would want Charles for a prisoner?

'A prisoner who will have the power of life and death over you one day,' said the king.

'The bowling green is ready, your majesty, and has been for a while. It waits only your royal skill.'

'Believe me, a bowling green will not save you.'

They'd started to build the green in February. It was an attempt to keep the king's mind on matters other than duplicity and escape – though it failed at present, if the London press was to be believed. The date of one rumoured escape plan had passed, with the king still confined, but the topic did not die, with Londoners reading of ever more imaginative plots, including the violent seizure of the castle (foreseen by Hammond in a vision) and his majesty carried away by attendants in a wheelbarrow. It was duly recommended by the reporter – for one cannot be too careful – that parliament order Vice-Admiral Rainsborough 'to stop, search and examine all wheelbarrows that shall presume to pass betwixt Dover and Calais and betwixt Southampton and the Isle of Wight'.

What could Hammond do? While London laughed, he interviewed Firebrace and a number of others, making things absolutely clear; but they said they knew of no escape plans and would most assuredly report them if they did.

He spoke privately with Firebrace. 'I believe we can trust one another,' he said.

'Indeed so, Colonel. I take no sides in this regrettable moment.'

'And you understand that the king must be kept here, for his own safety as much as anything else.'

'The king himself wishes to stay, so how could I disagree?'

'It's just that, well, you hear stories . . . I hear stories.'

'The inventions of the London press; I would pay no attention.'

Hammond smiled weakly and remained a man in the dark – in charge of a castle with a seeming life of its own.

*

'The king believes that his next escape shall succeed,' said Firebrace to Dowcett, whose shrug declared no interest. 'I have a letter from him.'

Yes, Firebrace received letters from the king now; surely the first seller of pig's livers in Swindon to do so? It was a shame his mother had not lived to hear of this. Though she probably would have said: 'And you wish me to be amazed?'

'Shall I read from it?' said Firebrace, eager.

'No,' said Dowcett. 'Oh, all right, then.' Firebrace deserved the pleasure.

'He says, "The n-n-n-narrowness of the window was the only impediment for m-m-my escape".' Firebrace caught his Scottish lilt surprisingly well, and the stammer.

'No – *he* was,' said Dowcett.

'All he needs, he says, is an instrument to remove the bar, "which I believe is not hard to get, for I have seen many of them – and so portable that a man might put them in his pocket. I think it is called the Great F-f-force or The Endless Screw".'

They both laughed.

'Is he talking about Mrs Whorwood?' said Dowcett, for there were rumours aplenty among the servants at Carisbrooke. 'I prefer them sweet and plump.'

'Abraham, you're married!'

'That doesn't mean I find them.'

140

'The king prefers them lean, it seems; and that's the end of it.'

'The king's end, certainly.'

Charles had also written to Captain Titus, one of the four con-servators, who now worked on his behalf. 'I pray you, think upon how I might remove the bar from my window, without noise and unperceived; and what time it will take me to do it.'

Firebrace had been active in the same cause: 'I have sent for files and aqua fortis from London, your majesty,' he said through the wall one evening.

'Can we trust our supplier?'

'He is a locksmith called Farmer in Bow Lane, and loyal to our cause.'

'Many say that.'

'He is recommended by Mrs Whorwood.'

'By Mrs Whorwood?'

'Yes, sire.' Firebrace knew he was home and dry.

'And what can he do, this Mr Farmer?'

'He can make us a saw to cut the bars asunder, and he offers aqua fortis besides.'

'We have his promise, yet these things, they are still not here.'

Charles always saw the problem as if the world was tilted against him.

'There has been a delay, your majesty; an unfortunate delay. Mrs Whorwood is doing her best.'

'And her best is very good.'

'So I hear, sire.'

'What do you hear?' Charles almost barked the words through the wall.

'Only that she is a most determined and resourceful lady, your majesty; nothing more is meant.'

His majesty seemed touchy and Firebrace was glad of the wall between them.

'She is an angel,' said Charles, calmed. 'Though I wonder if I'll I have time enough.'

Had Charles found a further problem? He had too much time to ruminate. He should play more bowls, but kept away from the alley, imagining he was punishing Hammond.

141

'Time enough for what, your majesty?'

'Time enough after I have supped and gone to bed, to remove the bar – the window bar.'

'There will be need for some preliminary endeavour.'

'I need an Endless Screw; then I will be well.'

*

Firebrace was confident of his plan for the king's escape ... a new plan, which did not need the screw.

'You change plans more often than I shit,' said Dowcett, which Firebrace took as a compliment to his quick thought.

The previous scheme, involving the window and the files, he'd been unsure about; he didn't trust the king with the prison bars. But remembering the Duke of York's successful escape dressed as a girl – much talked of in the London press – he imagined a different way, the way of disguise. And the healing evenings were the perfect setting.

These occurred every week. The sick came to the castle, loitered after supper, and if they were lucky the king touched them and made them well – in time. Healing was not always immediate, Firebrace had noticed. It was presumably the same with Christ. And some died before the healing took effect; this could also happen, due to age and other considerations. But such things mattered little, for here was an easy door out of the castle. All the king had to do was step through.

'It's simpler than you can imagine,' said Firebrace to his friend; he could call him that. 'All we require is a loyal man in the crowd of supplicants garishly dressed. This is the heart of the trick. People must notice him, talk of him, pass comment.'

'It does sound different,' said Dowcett, who gave encouragement with reluctance.

'Oh, it is different, Abraham, quite different from anything con-ceived before. And our character will wear a false beard – these can be obtained – and a periwig, a white cap, a blue coat, a pair of fustian drawers to come over his breeches, white cloth stockings, great shoes and an old broad hat.'

'Does the plan become saner in a while?'

142

'Patience! He will then step forward from the crowd and demand to be touched, when the king comes down for supper. He'll be hard to ignore.'

'Quite so.'

'And now for the trickery. After he is touched, he will be taken for a drinking session in the servants' quarters by myself – and perhaps you.'

'I am not involved, Firebrace.'

'You will wish you were, when the history books are written.'

'Truly, I won't. I prefer disaster from a distance.'

'I will hail this fellow as an old friend and ensure he is seen by as many people as possible.'

'The castle becomes a theatre.'

'Indeed, we become actors all – for an identical set of clothes will be hidden in the king's bedroom, and then the rest is simple. The king retires to his room after the meal, dresses up as the garish visitor, and on the signal – and with the cooperation of a trusted conservator on the door – he will arrive downstairs in the courtyard as the visitors are leaving. There he will merge with the crowd as they pass through the gate, and make his way to the meeting point, where the escape horses will be waiting.'

Firebrace wrote the details of the plan on a piece of paper which he left under the king's carpet. After reading the notes, the king declared that he thought it might work.

'I do much prefer the idea of disguise to removing the window bar,' he said, to Firebrace's delight.

The window had been much on the king's mind, and more particularly the bars, the files and the aqua fortis. He did not have experience or knowledge of these tools; but the disguise was different. With Henrietta, he used to dress up with great effect for the masques. He liked dressing up.

*

After supper, the king would enjoy conversation with the guests and the subject was generally religion; apart from ejaculation with Jane, it was the matter most dear to his heart. And there was more time these days, for since April, fourteen courses had been reduced

143

to ten, leaving additional space for debate after meals, with young Mr Troughton, his adversary tonight. Troughton was Hammond's chaplain, an Independent in his theology and therefore quite beyond the pale for Charles, who argued with elegant force for the Anglican settlement and the Book of Common Prayer.

'I would most certainly not have burned Cranmer,' he explained when asked. 'Though it took him to heaven sooner, so perhaps he gained?'

More and more, Charles contemplated his own mortality, and with the time captivity brings, composed meditations on the theme.

'I would have burned him,' said Troughton, mischievously.

'And your reason?'

'He placed us in a mad-jacket, your majesty.'

'A mad-jacket?'

'The Book of Common Prayer is such a restraining thing – when our prayers to God should be free and unconstrained.'

Charles smiled at the idiot. 'I doubt God craves your unconstrained prayer, Mr Troughton – if your unconstrained speech is our yardstick.' That won him some laughter. 'Such rough and disordered words when compared to the beauty of Cranmer's.'

'If by rough you mean clean from the heart, then rough they may be, your majesty. But surely God likes the heart?'

'I believe he prefers order, Mr Troughton. Truly, the heart is a most dangerous place.'

And then suddenly the king had a sword in his hand, which no one had foreseen. He'd reached out and seized it from one of the officers in the room, and such was the panic that even Troughton was quietened. And Charles did look wild; this was the memory. Ever since his barber had been dismissed at the end of February (for postal crimes) he'd been growing his hair and beard. He trusted no one else with a sharp blade so close to his neck, where accidents can happen, and he now resembled John the Baptist emerging from the desert – a vagabond and a wild man ... and the more so with a sword in his hand.

'Your majesty!'

'This is no war. Kneel, Mr Parfitt!'

Mr Parfitt was one of the attendants, and terrified. Was he to have his head removed?

'Kneel, Mr Parfitt!'

Mr Parfitt found no support in the shocked circle, and slowly dropped to his knees. He felt he'd been a faithful subject, always faithful . . . and if he must die . . .

'As your king, I knight thee, Sir William Parfitt, knight of this realm.'

The sword touched each shoulder.

'Thank you, your honour . . . your highness.'

Mr Parfitt, the newest knight of the realm, had wet himself.

July 1648

Wood held the letter in his hand, with casual display.

'Do you know Jane Whorwood?' he asked.

They sat in Hammond's study, a large room of dark dressers and chairs and a space that could swallow a person; though it didn't swallow Wood.

'Not to my knowledge,' said Hammond.

'You would know if you knew her,' said the inquisitor. 'People tend to . . . especially men.' Hammond nodded. What was he talking about? 'She prefers to remain unknown – though she's well known to me.'

'I weary quickly of riddles, Mr Wood,' said Hammond. He did not warm to this man or trust him: one who never asked a question unless he knew the answer.

'Still a soldier, I see,' said Wood with a smile that chilled more than it cheered. A smile should warm rather than freeze, Hammond thought so. 'Yet here is no riddle, Colonel, just a woman to fear.'

Hammond mocked at the idea. 'To fear? And how is that to be imagined, Mr Wood? Does she sew people to death?'

'Read this,' said Wood, handing him the parchment.

Hammond held it steady in his hand. It was a letter from William Lilly, the odd astrologer fellow, to Wood and recorded a meeting with Mrs Whorwood. She'd apparently been seeking material assistance – aqua fortis, her primary need – for springing the king from captivity at Carisbrooke. Hammond felt ill.

'She's a close confidante of the king,' said Wood. 'Very close.'

'How close?'

'We hear Queen Henrietta applauds her royal support with one hand only.'

'And you believe she comes here?'

'I would say so.'

'You would say so.' How he hated this man. 'And do we know her appearance?'

Wood paused for effect. 'Jane Whorwood is a tall lady, slim build, oval face, red of hair and with a crevice or two in her smile. Have you seen her?'

'So many pass through,' said Hammond, knowing his answer was weak. It portrayed him as a man overwhelmed.

'That describes a lot of your guards, does it?'

He could be a shit, Wood.

'I will ask around, Mr Wood. I do my best here . . . amid my many duties.'

'Exceedingly loyal, this woman; a most busy operator on behalf of Charles.'

'I understand.'

'The most loyal of any woman in England in his present miseries.'

'You certainly speak her up, Mr Wood.'

'I speak no one up. I merely notice what occurs . . . someone has to.'

Such a shit.

'I do wonder, though, if you do not obsess a little too much about this woman?' ventured Hammond, emboldened by dislike.

'You think so?'

'I do, Mr Wood. I wonder if perhaps you are not a little jealous for her?' Wood offered nothing back and Hammond stumbled on. 'And really, what damage can a woman do? Apart from burn a few cakes?'

'They swive in the guardroom, Colonel, not fifty yards from where we sit – Charles and Jane.'

'They do?'

'She fucks with the king, a fact known by every dog in the street . . . except you, it seems'

*

The meeting with Wood had been difficult. He didn't care for the man; and to have his oversight exposed in such a manner! He'd definitely be speaking to Charles, who'd been allowed free access to the guardroom during the day, because, in his words, 'I find it a sweeter place to compose my spiritual thoughts.' This would be the end of such sweet composing.

But, though hard to conceive, he faced a darker encounter the following week, when he moved to dismiss his mother from her post in the kitchen. Hammond had not slept the night before, as he contemplated the horror. He had no choice, however; this was the plain fact, for she'd fallen out with everyone, which was her way. Two of his best staff were leaving due to her 'judging comments', and to incense matters further, Charles used her as a whipping stick, accusing Hammond of nepotism – when Robert had simply wanted a good kitchen for the king!

'One of my staff described you as a man under the thumb of his mother,' said Charles, as they walked one day in the courtyard. 'Which caused some mirth, I'm afraid.'

'I'm glad to entertain.' He felt hot inside his skin at the thought. He would sack the king's household in its entirety – and then who would be laughing?

'But while that was possible – that you do indeed remain under her thumb – I said to them, surely everyone has the right to look after their family, no matter what the cost to others? I did my best to support you, Colonel. Nepotism has always seemed like a most sensible conceit to me. I mean, if you have access to treasure, why not hand out trinkets to those you hold dear? Quite so.'

Hammond found this most unfair. He'd had no wish to employ his mother, really he hadn't, but had panicked at the king's arrival, fearing for the table; and his mother did know her way round a kitchen. This was necessity not nepotism, two quite different islands with much water in between. Could Charles not see this? But the king had not forgiven her for reducing the food, this was remembered. He would not let that go, and his snide remarks about nepotism had been the final straw. He must sack his mother.

Robert discovered her in the kitchen, lecturing Josiah, a new steward. Hammond had learned how to souse a pig when a boy in Chertsey; clearly Josiah had not.

'So after you've stuck the pig, Josiah, you let him bleed well, they must be quite drained. And then with scalding water and resin finely beaten, you take off the hair. Yes?'

'Yes, Mrs Hammond.'

'Are you listening?'

'Yes, Mrs Hammond.' He looked at her with the intensity of one not listening at all, the eyes trying to make up for the ears.

'I will be asking you at the end, young man! What do you use to take off the hair?' She'd ask now as well.

'Water and—'

'*Scalding* water.'

'Scalding water . . . and resin finely beaten.'

'All right. I've taught your thick skull something.'

'Er, Mother?' said Hammond.

She ignored him. 'And then you let him lie in cold water, turning frequently – frequently, mind – until he looks white, white as chalk, and then cut off his feet. Have you cut off pigs' feet before?'

'No, Mrs Hammond.'

'You haven't lived much, have you?'

'Er, Mother?' said Hammond again – but she ignored him again . . . wilfully, he thought.

'And then the big slit, we can do that together the first time – you slit him open, take out his innards and cut off his head. Hanged, drawn and quartered like all papists should be.'

This performance was clearly for Hammond.

'You then take the two sides asunder, like these, lay them in cold water, steep there for a day and a night, changing the water three times.' Was she trying to prove herself, put her value on display? Hammond felt uncomfortable at this determined instruction. It took him back. 'And then – and only then – you take out the bones, tying them as hard as possible in the fashion of a collar of brawn and wrap them in cloth – the whole head of the pig in another cloth – and boil in water, salt, cloves, mace, nutmeg and a little rosemary until tender. You can't hurry tender, Josiah.'

'No, Mrs Hammond.'

'What can't you hurry?'

'Tender, Mrs Hammond.'

Robert could see why she ended up doing everything herself. She had the manner of a teacher, but not the skill of encouragement.

149

'And then you let it cool, pouring over the liquor used to boil it, adding only some beer – good to add some beer – and the cooking is done. Not so hard, is it?'

'No, Mrs Hammond.' His body turned to go.

'And then the presenting.' Josiah turned back. 'You set the two collars in a dish garnished with salt – the head entire in the middle – and stick in two sprigs of rosemary in flower and serve with saucers of mustard. Now, I want you to repeat that to me, everything you've learned.'

'I wonder if I could have a word, Mother?'

Mrs Hammond looked up, as if to say, 'The lengths I go to!'

'Shall we walk a little?' he said, as Josiah melted away like butter in a pan.

'Josiah! I'll be coming to find you!' she called, but there was no reply from the kitchen shadows. Flustered, Mrs Hammond followed her son. 'This is not a good time,' she said. 'Too much to be doing.'

She always had too much to be doing.

'Is Josiah not the sharpest blade?' said Hammond.

'Blunt as a log and quite as soft.'

'He will thank you one day,' lied Hammond.

'They need telling, these young ones. I do my best.'

And suddenly they were out of the corridor gloom and in the bright sunlight of the courtyard, where some soldiery loitered and heavy-hooved horses were brushed down; the salty air stiffened their manes, which needed attention.

'So what's all this about, Robert?' she asked, blinking a little.

'It's not easy to say, Mother.'

'You look all pasty. You sit too much in your study.'

'You must return now to Chertsey,' he said.

He had chosen the courtyard for their meeting, not wishing to be trapped inside with such awkward words, and certainly not in the kitchen where who knows what would happen?

'Not while I have a job to do here,' she replied firmly, folding her arms, which was not a good sign. Folded arms were the draw-bridge raised.

'They miss you greatly, I am told . . . in Chertsey.'

'Nonsense. Who told you that?'

No one. 'It's what I hear.'

'I waste away for something to do in Chertsey. What does one do in Chertsey – apart from take a boat somewhere else? Whereas here I can keep an eye on you and ensure the proper running of the kitchen.'

'Quite. But you don't, do you?'

'I don't what?'

'You don't ensure the proper running of the kitchen.' It had to be said.

'What do you mean?'

'There have been, well, some difficulties with other members of the staff.'

'Wasters who didn't know the meaning of graft. You're better off without them. It's work they don't like!'

'But hard to replace on an island such as this. We miss them.'

'I don't miss them.'

'You cannot do it all alone, Mother.'

'I'll do it all alone if I have to. Wouldn't be the first time!'

The conversation had not started well. How would he raise the topic of quality? It did need to be raised.

'The king has always eaten well in his life,' he said.

'And so have you.'

'Indeed, Mother, I am most fortunate.'

'You certainly never went without.'

'Yet the king—'

'Has papist tastes.'

'This is not about religion, Mother. He simply asks me why we do not use the recipes of Lancelot de Casteau any more.'

'Because I've never heard of him and don't intend to start hearing now. We have quite enough English recipes to be getting along with.'

'The king has possession of his book, *Ouverture de Cuisine*.' His French felt awkward in his mother's presence. 'It includes recipes – rather fine recipes – for whipped cream and choux pastries, which he has previously enjoyed. His majesty misses those.'

'And you too, no doubt?'

'This is not about me.'

'It's always about you, Robert. You always were a little pig, eager with your snout.'

'Mother . . .' Now he was worried who could overhear.

'And I'll not cook French frippery. I don't think we fought a war to cook French frippery. We eat ham and peas in England, soused pig, and plum pudding. You always liked plum pudding before you acquired airs.'

'And still do like it. I have no airs.'

'But I won't cook that nonsense.'

'And that is why you must leave.' She looked at him in shock. 'I want you to leave Carisbrooke,' he said, glad to get it out, like the relief that follows a good vomit.

'You dismiss me?'

'I'm not dismissing you, Mother.'

'My son gives me the boot! Well, that's a fine thing, isn't it? A very strange thank you indeed!'

'You have given wonderful service—'

'Not wonderful enough, it seems; not French enough! I will be leaving the island this afternoon.'

'We'll need you for this evening.'

'Then write quickly to Lancelot de Casteau. Perhaps he's available.'

'He's dead, Mother.'

'And I wish I was, truly I do, accused like this. Goodbye, Robert.'

It hadn't gone well.

* *

'We must be grateful, Mr Wallace, that we do not live in the Russian lands,' said Jane, contemplating the Thames at low tide, all mud bank and green weed. She felt confident here. With Brome, she did not feel so; with Brome, she knew fear and constraint, as if she had nothing to raise against him. But here in London's bustling docklands, she knew neither. If anything it was Mr Wallace who twitched a little and drew nervously on his pipe, though it was his office in which they sat, lined with tide manuals, sea maps and account ledgers. 'Czar Alexis is not as kind as our dear king,' she added.

'No one could be,' said Wallace.

'He creates penalties for smoking now, apparently.' She noted his pipe. 'First offence is a whipping, a slit nose and transportation to the Siberian wastes.' Wallace winced. 'The second offence is execution, which makes a third offence unlikely. Russia is not the place for a pipe.'

Wallace smiled. 'I am ever grateful for the freedoms of this land, Mrs Whorwood. The gift of the king, of course.'

'Of course.'

She paused; and they sat.

'I trust you do not question my great love for his majesty?' He was not comfortable with this woman. He'd prefer to be dodging a customs official, his more common work – on the few occasions they wouldn't be bought.

'Love is an easy word to utter, Mr Wallace.'

'And a true one, Jane.' He would try familiarity. 'You of all people should know that . . . how in the past I have given most generously.' He knew why she was here.

'Indeed. But that's rather the issue: you speak of the past, Mr Wallace, when we live in the present.' Wallace choked a little. 'History may be a happy remembrance, but it pays no bills.'

'My love for the king is an evergreen,' he said, for he'd once written poetry at sea.

'But how would his majesty know?' asked Jane, pointedly.

'Know what?'

'That his subject's love is like an evergreen? What signifiers are there?'

'He can be assured of it!' said Mr Wallace confidently.

'I see. So I am to tell him of this evergreen on the Thames?'

'I would be honoured if you would do so, Mrs Whorwood, for I will never forsake the king. And now, if that is all—'

He made to rise, but Jane stayed in her chair.

'Yet you do forsake the king.'

'A strange saying!'

'You keep money that he needs.'

'You ask a great deal.'

153

'I ask for two hundred pounds to win over some guards at Carisbrooke, and you give me a story about your parents' funeral arrangements.'

'I believe the fifth commandment entreats us to honour our father and mother.'

'I had not expected a sermon, Mr Wallace, as we are three days short of the Sabbath. But since we speak of these things, I declare that I have never found much sense or mercy in that commandment.'

'Then you must understand those of us who do, Mrs Whorwood.'

'I understand one thing.'

'And what is that?'

'I understand your recent delight.'

'Oh?'

'The good news was passed to me by a keen watcher of the Thames traffic after Greenwich.'

'I find your intentions just a little opaque, Mrs Whorwood.'

'Really?'

'I struggle a little—'

'A ship and its sails are a most visible thing, Mr Wallace. A fine sight, without question, bursting with a favourable wind; but hard to hide, unless one arrives at night, of course, when cargoes can creep quietly in, waking no one – not even the customs controller. What is the excise duty on tobacco these days?'

'Not all my ships arrive by day, I grant you, but always for the best of reasons.'

He'd known Jane for many years, ever since her stepfather had worked for King James – Master of Stables in those days. Such an energetic girl, a fine horsewoman, of course, and so restless now in the new king's cause . . . running it, or so he'd heard. For no man could think as quickly as Jane, ride as hard – or care as little for anyone else. Jane thought only of the king.

And she was pretty in her way: a tall girl, not for everyone and married to an oaf of some dimensions – they could all pity her there. But more desperate these days in her manner, there was no doubt of that: thinner of face, less girlish charm, less high spirited, more pressing. God knows, it was not right for the king to languish thus, in such restraint at Carisbrooke. And yes, the tobacco trade

154

had served him well and would continue to do so, if Jane kept silent. He paid enough customs officials already; he could afford to buy a crooked castle guard.

'I would like to make a love-offering to his majesty,' he said.

'And what is love worth these days?'

'Let two hundred pounds be a small expression of my affection.'

'That is most generous, kind sir. Shall I collect it tomorrow?'

*

Hammond sat reading another ciphered letter from Derby House, spilling with news of further escape plans. Today's revelations included the 'plain fat man' again, who was significant but hard to identify, as that description took in half of England.

'The aqua fortis destined for the king was spilt on the road by way of accident,' said the report.

Hammond had enquired of the king about his interest in acid, but Charles had refused to help his enquiries, even denying it with mockery.

'If I wanted acid I would have bottled Ireton's spittle!'

But there was no acid anyway. The pot-holed roads of Dorset had seen to that. One must hope it was not carried on the lap.

'But yesterday, at about four o'clock,' said the Derby House memo, 'a plain fat man set out to carry to the king a hacker, which is a specialized instrument, with the purpose to make the king's two knives cut as saws; he will have these with him shortly. The time assigned for the king's escape is late June, though it may be sooner if the opportunity serves.'

So they were guessing about the time.

'The fat man intends to go first to a gentleman's house in Lewes, Sussex,' continued the report. 'He will then travel to Newport with the hacker and dispatches, and on Saturday morning – or about that time – Dowcett or Firebrace or possibly another will go out and meet him and bring it all to the king.'

Firebrace? It couldn't be Firebrace; they were friends, in a manner.

'Therefore, ensure they are searched on returning and all will appear,' said the letter.

It seemed clear enough, and Hammond was still pondering the news when that afternoon, another letter appeared, with certain amendments, saying the fat man would come only as far as Portsmouth; he wouldn't make it to Newport, apparently. From there, he would hand over his business to 'some fisherman or some other such person'.

Hammond leaned back in his chair, stretched out his arms and laughed. He laughed out loud in his dark study, the laugh of deep despair. What in God's name was he meant to do with that intelligence? Intelligence was the wrong word for such stupefying vagueness. How could he be expected to police Portsmouth when he couldn't even police his own castle? Who was the plain fat man – and if he'd changed his mind once, might he not change it again? Or lose weight?

The fact was, Hammond received new escape plans every day; another day, another plan, one scheme merging into another. Today a disguise, tomorrow a ladder up the wall, next week, a fire in the castle, using charcoal heaped outside the king's window! But which communication to believe? He feared the true one, because he wouldn't credit it when it came.

There was a knock on the door. A guard entered.

'There is a courier to see you, Colonel.'

'From whom?'

'The lieutenant-general.'

What did Cromwell have to say to him? It would not be cheering, that was for sure. It was likely some complaint or cloying request.

'I am busy,' he said.

He'd lost all sense of anchorage; too much fantasy passing his desk every day, with no idea what was real. Hallucination and truth so wore each other's clothes, he began to doubt his sanity.

'The courier demands an immediate interview,' said the guard.

Hammond watched his hopes of a quiet retirement pass briefly through the room, like a ghost who turned to gaze on him and laugh unkindly before melting into the wall.

'Is he plain and fat?' asked Hammond.

The guard hadn't considered the visitor. 'You wouldn't call him a handsome fellow,' he said, remembering his sour breath.

'And his girth?'

'Hasn't gone hungry of late, but I wouldn't name him as fat. Large.'

The guard thought of his uncle, who'd widened horribly in recent years due to constipation. The courier wasn't as big as his uncle.

'Show him in,' said Hammond. Long, tall, short or thin, he didn't care. He had dismissed his mother, returned her to Chertsey in the foulest of moods – so how could things worsen? This was the liberation of despair . . . and now a man dirty with travel stood before him, grey hair curling. He introduced himself as Job Weals, a physician from Kingston. He had a wispy voice and said he brought important information from Oliver Cromwell himself.

'Please continue,' said Hammond. He wouldn't ask him to sit or settle in.

'I wonder if I could have some hot water, Colonel Hammond?'

'Some hot water?'

'It has been a long journey and I feel a little faint.'

Hammond looked on him again. This was not the manner in which the general's couriers handled business, not in his experience. Cromwell's men were driven, urgent with God; they didn't take tea before the dispatch was delivered.

'I think we'll proceed with our business,' said Hammond.

'It concerns both your safety, sir – and more importantly, the safety of the king.'

'I see.' Hammond's heart sank a little. Not another escape plan?

'There are schemes afoot and we will need to act quickly,' continued the visitor.

'I shall be the judge of what we need to do, Mr Wells.'

'Weals.'

'Mr Weals.'

'Dr Weals.'

'Quite so. You are here to pass on the information.'

'There is a plan to seize the king and to kill you, Mr Hammond.'

'Kill me?' Now he was a target as well?

'Indeed. You will not survive this endeavour.' Dr Weals shook his head sadly at this revelation, like an undertaker at the grave. 'And it is to take place early tomorrow morning.'

'I see.'

'Hence my haste and our need to act on the matter. A fleet is off the island, with men on board, ready to land.'

Hammond was listening now. 'Go on.'

'People will come from the mainland as well, on the pretence of visiting a fair in Newport; this has been established. Beacons will be lit to raise local royalists from their slumbers. There are many such men on this island, Colonel.'

Hammond sat gauging the strength of the two opposing armies. He had eight hundred men at his command. What numbers was this man suggesting opposed him?

'Do you have numbers?'

'Numbers?'

'These royalist insurgents. Do you have information concerning their numbers?'

'We know only that it could be over two thousand, sir.'

That was a good number. 'And the lieutenant-general's orders?'

The courier paused. 'You will hand over the king to myself, sir, and I will deliver him to Major Lobb, who commands Portsmouth, as you know.'

'I hand the king over to you, Dr Weals?'

'Those are the orders, sir.'

The guard, who'd decided Sour Breath was mad, looked at Hammond with concern.

'And your authorization for this order?' asked Hammond.

'This message was too secret to be written down, sir.'

'Too secret to be written down or for any authorization to be carried?'

'Yes, sir. The roads are not safe, the king's men everywhere. So it was decided to make of it a verbal message, delivered to you alone.'

'Nothing written,' said Hammond to himself.

'But I do have written credentials to Major Lobb, sir, sewn into my waistcoat.'

'So let us see those.'

'I'm afraid my orders were that they were for the eyes of Major Lobb alone.'

'I insist on seeing them myself, Dr Weals, like a physician might examine a patient – if we are to proceed in this matter.'

'Sir, I urge you to set these events in motion. Remember the landing parties—'

That was enough. 'Dr Weals, you take me for a fool, which is not the best greeting.'

'Why, sir, I—'

'We shall investigate your person.'

The guard stepped forward, removed Weals' coat, and ripping open the cloth found only documents stolen from the Portsmouth to London staging post; unusual in Cromwell's couriers.

'And these?' asked Hammond, holding up the papers.

'I know not how they come to be with me. The lieutenant-general definitely said—'

Hammond indicated dismay but couldn't manage anger. 'Enough, Dr Weals – or whoever you are.'

The courier turned out to be a Jonathan Sykes from Hounslow, who may have needed a doctor but was no doctor himself. He quietly accepted that the show was at an end and bowed his head, which was jerked back with some brutality by the guard before he was led out.

*

Meanwhile the king was once more in favour of escape via the window.

'I do favour the window,' he said through the wall.

He had declared the idea of garish disguise at a royal healing to be too far-fetched, which disappointed Firebrace; but Charles was now keen on the window again. He felt he could do better this time, while acknowledging that the bars remained an obstacle. He had now received a large number of files, however, and gave one of them to the conservator Captain Titus, so he could test it out.

'I know not how filing can be done without much noise and time,' he said to the captain through his half-opened bedroom door. 'But if you can clear this doubt, I absolutely conceive this to be the best way.'

'I will consider this matter, your majesty.'

'I think we must do more than consider. I hear the axe has fallen for you here.'

This was true. They'd heard that morning that Captain Titus was to be escorted off the island shortly.

'I have been told I am leaving, sir, though a date has not been set.'

'Then you must begin work on the bars without delay . . . but in a quiet manner.'

There was indeed urgency, for it was not only Titus who was to be removed from the castle. Firebrace was also to go.

'Why they have picked on you two, I am at a loss to know.'

'Because we work for your escape, sire.'

'Indeed. But how do they know that?'

'I imagine the walls have eyes.'

They had been busy with escape plans. When he wasn't testing the file against the king's window bars, Titus was organizing a ship to cross the Solent and a relay of horses on the mainland. And then Firebrace had come up with another escape plan.

'We use the window on the back stairs,' he told the captain. 'This will mean the window bars can be dealt with by others before the event.'

'Thus not involving the king in their removal?' said Titus.

'It does seem wise,' said Firebrace.

Titus nodded. And again, Charles warmed to the idea. He preferred the window on the stairs to the window in his bedroom, and wrote his approval to Firebrace.

I do extremely well like your newest way, for if you can make me room enough to go out at the window you mention, I warrant you, by the grace of God, that I shall get down the hill and over the works well enough. But I pray thee – for my satisfaction – ensure I am given the full breadth of the window when the bar is taken away, that I may be sure not to lodge, as happened previously.

Firebrace was also concerned about the king 'lodging' again. He'd put on a little weight at Carisbrooke, his days consumed by

spiritual writing, which had made monks fat down the years. He'd
been cheered, though, to hear that two guards had taken a bribe
of £100 to look elsewhere as the king made his way to the back
stairs. Where did Mrs Whorwood find the money? A remarkable
woman . . . and he'd heard she was now in position on board a boat
in the Isle of Sheppey, ready to take the king to Holland.

The courier from London was the last piece in the jigsaw.

*

Jane was desperate.

She'd been imprisoned on board this ship for five weeks, ready
to depart. Five weeks on the Isle of Sheppey! It was time the king
was in France, and this boat – hired and cajoled at considerable
expense – would ferry him there. But where was he?

Mr Browne, the ship's master, had been as patient as any man
could be, really a very dear man. But ever since the navy went over
to parliament, no ship could dawdle for long on the coast, where
seagulls and suspicion flew free and nothing remained unnoticed.

'We sit most obvious on the water, madam,' said Mr Browne.

'I know how obvious we sit.'

'We cannot stay.'

'We have to stay. We must wait for the king.'

But they couldn't stay and she needed to know what delayed
the royal presence. She wrote a letter to Firebrace, who'd been
strangely quiet, as had the king. Were they unable to communicate?
Had their letters been seized? Or had hers? The delay and unknowing was making her ill.

*It is both my grief and my wonder that the king has not yet
appeared, when that is what he wills the most. What delays his
majesty? In the meantime, we sit very obvious on the water and
yesterday, our boat was searched by the intolerable Vice-Admiral
Rainsborough, a blood-stained republican.*

*I need hardly tell you of this unspeakable man. I do not judge –
but really! He is of the mad Ranter persuasion – those who believe
God is in every creature and quite against organized religion. He
told me this himself, he does not hide it – and asked me where*

I stood on the matter. I confess I could only laugh with a hysterical sound – which I hope was goodly cover. He may have thought me fit for Bedlam, and if he does, I'm glad. He also believes the king should be elected by common vote, Firebrace. We must return our king to the throne – or we'll have a Ranter there!

In the meantime, Rainsborough is brusque in his manner and asks why we do not sail. We claimed a contrary wind, though there is a kind south-westerly almost every day. Mr Browne does all he can to find cause for delay, with repairs to the hull invented daily. But Rainsborough sniffs around with republican malice and we need news about how things stand. We need good news.

And how true that was, for she didn't mention the oyster poisoning, which had laid her very low for these past ten days. Only now was she emerging from the lower decks, which had been her own privy hell. But forty-eight hours later, there was light: a courier arrived, with a message from the king via Captain Titus.

'Guard rotas changed. Sunday 28th is the day of our endeavour. We hope to be with you on the 29th.'

Jane's heart leapt on the Sheppey waters. This was it.

*

All was set fair for the king's escape; this was the view of Firebrace from his new accommodation in Portsmouth.

He had left Carisbrooke, but not the king's service. It was 11 on a starless night. what better omen could there be? The first relay of horses was ready at Titchfield on Southampton Water, a fishing boat quietly anchored in a private creek near Wootton Park, and a party of horsemen, with Edward Worsley in charge, were gathered near the castle to take him there.

Inside the castle, Abraham Dowcett, Clerk of the Kitchen, faced the moment of truth alone. He approached the king's bedchamber, down the dark corridor with its creaking boards, ready with his cord of silk, reckoned to be kinder than rope to the king's soft hands. He entered the king's bedchamber without a knock, as planned; it was his task to let the king down from his window. They had returned to the idea of using the bedroom window,

162

rather than the stairs, but all was prepared and nothing seen by Hammond. The files had done their work, leaving generous space for the king's frame. He was not a large man, and there was a considerable gap between the bars. Dowcett was to see him to the ground, then go down the back stairs and meet the king in the courtyard. From there, he would guide him to where the horses were waiting.

The king feigned sleep as Dowcett entered. Wise as a serpent, innocent as a dove, as he'd said to Dowcett, who had nodded without comprehension.

*

'What is it?' said Hammond with irritation. He'd been woken from a deep and unhappy sleep. He was dreaming of his sacked mother – the moment of the sacking, which troubled his dreams more than any duel or battle he'd fought.

'I have with me two guards with a story to tell,' said Rolphe.

'What story? What's going on? Is she here?'

'Who?'

'My mother. Is she here?'

'Are you awake, sir?' said Rolphe, wondering if the colonel was still in a dream.

'Is it about my mother?'

'It does not concern your mother, sir.'

'Quite.' Hammond was waking now. He was talking to Rolphe; he was awake now. 'I'm awake, Rolphe.'

But he was angry about the men in his doorway and Rolphe led them in. What was Rolphe doing bringing them here? He was definitely awake now.

'What's going on?'

'These men, sir – they have been paid to be slack in their duties tonight.'

'Who has been paid?'

'These guards.'

'Paid by whom?'

'By the king, Colonel.'

'And to what end?'

'The escape is tonight, sir.'

'The escape is tonight? Have you seen a plain fat man?'

*

The king was sitting in the window, where once there were bars, but he could see that matters were not right down below. Dowcett had fixed the cord and left the bedchamber, but had not reappeared in the courtyard – so where was he? And while Charles had managed to place his body some way through the window, he discerned more people than normal in the courtyard tonight; and still no sign of Dowcett.

'Dowcett?' he hissed from the window ledge.

Nothing . . . and he decided against further action; there were too many figures in the shadows below. Cautiously, he slowly withdrew himself back inside, inch by inch, but a task harder than expected, with his legs waving in the outside air for a little while, as he fell backwards, before recovering his balance. He then tumbled down inside, clinging on to a chair to break his fall but landing awkwardly. He gathered his soiled self, listened for voices, placed the bars back in the window as best he could and retired to his bed.

And he was lying awake, clothed for day and with sore arms and ribs, when there was a knock on the door. Before he could answer, Hammond was standing there, a silhouette in the passage-way candlelight. The king did not like the dark – though neither did he care much for the light on this occasion. Hammond bowed before going over to the window to inspect the bars, all askew. He touched one and it fell to the ground with a clatter and much dust.

'They appear to have suffered some wear,' he said, noting the effects of the files. He shook his head.

'How now, Mr Hammond?' says Charles. 'You wake me for what purpose?'

'I heard you were going away, your majesty.'

'I know nothing of that.'

'So I came to say farewell. Or perhaps to persuade you to stay. I hope I can.'

'I believe, Mr Hammond, I speak from my bed, rather than a horse.'

'Though you were recently dressed and in your window, your majesty. Your legs waved cheerily to us all. And I am told that your horse is still waiting.'

'If it is, I know not of it.'

'A sad day, your majesty.'

'Every day is sad, Mr Hammond.'

'Then we must hope sleep makes tomorrow a better day for us all.'

'Indeed, quite so.'

Hammond walked towards the door, and then turned. 'And perhaps saddest for you, your majesty, is that not even two hundred pounds can buy you the loyalty of your subjects now. What happened to our king?'

August 1648

'Rats and dry biscuits, Charles! And a malicious oyster.'

She had never before called him Charles, but she did so now as his fingers moved eagerly over her uncovered breasts. He thought more of the consolations of sex than escape these days. Fantasies of Jane ballooned in his head, spilling endlessly through his imagination and beyond.

'I am surrounded by fools,' he said, 'your good self excepted, my little princess, my dear sweet Jane.'

He greatly enjoyed the feel of her flesh on his cock as they lay on his bed.

'Five weeks in the Isle of Sheppey, waiting.'

'I did not receive your letter until late. Perhaps the courier chose to crawl the journey, not wishing to be seen; and then there was trouble with the files and one plan became another, each with a new difficulty. What Firebrace and Titus were doing, I have no idea. And Dowcett! Well . . .'

There was a short pause between them.

'Do you wish to escape?' Jane asked.

'Of course I wish to escape!'

'Are you sure?'

'Of course I'm sure! How could you—'

'That's all I need to know, your majesty,' she said, quietening his lips with her finger. 'We've just been unfortunate. You've done your best – I'm sure you have. Surrounded by fools, as you say . . .'

Though Firebrace, melting with frustration, saw it another way. He was quite clear about who was to blame, as he told Dowcett.

'Really, if it was anyone else!' he would say in his despair of the king's vacillation.

'I don't know why you bother,' said Dowcett, who'd visited him in Portsmouth on his half-day; he supposed he must miss him in some manner.

'Because he is the king, Dowcett, God's anointed one!'

'If you say so, Henry, though I don't smell God here myself – just a lecher much absorbed with his own self.'

But Jane trusted the king. They'd just been unfortunate and their luck would change, of course it would. And now they lay together in his room, the king's treasure aching.

'Your husband – he is still in Holland?' he asked, wishing to move matters away from Jane's five wretched weeks in Sheppey.

'Why do you ask, Charles?'

'I wonder that a man is fool enough to leave you for so long!'

'He's back in England,' she said quietly.

'He's back?' Charles pulled his body from her, as though the jilted partner now stood in the doorway with a sword in hand.

'Though still a fool. He's been back for a year.'

'A year?'

'Yes.'

'Oh! Yet still you—'

'What difference does that make to me?'

'Well—'

'He comes back and swives with his kitchen maid.'

'He does not ... miss you?'

'I wouldn't know. Apparently not; he does not say as much. And I don't miss him – though that might change if I had a pistol.'

Did Charles miss Henrietta? Of course he did, for they were very much in love. Jane merely served the king in her absence, though she served him well.

'And he does not know?' asked Charles.

'Know?'

'About our ... merriment.'

'How would he know?'

'Then I am glad. My cock shall enjoy you in secret.'

He was swollen and now quite desperate; he tried to move on top of her again.

'Firebrace knows,' she said.

'Firebrace?'

'He knows.'

167

Charles was not pleased but would calm himself. 'Henry is most discreet. Now—'

'Henry and I, we work together for your release.'

'I need only your cunny for my release today, Jane.'

He smiled naughtily and indulged himself quickly inside her, while she remembered feeling sorry for Charles, all those years ago.

At court, people had only ever spoken of young Henry; it was 'Henry this' and 'Henry that'. Always of Henry they spoke, his older and 'better' brother. No one spoke of Charles, or if they did, they spoke for mocking amusement. But when Charles was a sickly twelve and Henry eighteen, the better brother died of typhoid fever, and the shock was profound in the kingdom. Henry had such gifts, such presence. He was a leader of men, a friend of Sir Walter Raleigh and young Charles had adored him . . . though whether Henry adored Charles, there were doubts.

Jane had heard the rumours . . . rumours of cruel teasing by the older brother, a rather harsh Protestant, no question of that; and then the awful story of the bishop's hat. Was there a crueller story on earth? When Charles was nine years of age, so it went, Henry snatched the hat from a bishop and placed it on his young brother's head, telling him that when he became king, he would make Charles Archbishop of Canterbury, and then Charles would have a long robe to hide his weak rickety legs. Charles is said to have stamped on the cap before being dragged away, crying uncontrollably.

But this was how it had been at court, where she'd lived almost next door to the princes. Behind Maxwell's courtyard wall at Charing Cross were the Spring Gardens of St James's Palace, where the diminutive Charles played in his platform shoes. There were twelve years between them, but he'd always felt close, even through the wall. To others, though, he was the sick boy, always second best, and nothing changed when Henry died. If anything, the chasm in popular assumption widened; Henry grew and Charles lessened. Archbishop William Laud, a supposed friend, had not helped. He'd chosen to describe Charles as 'a mild and gracious prince who knew not how to be – or how to be made – great'. If that was meant as a kindly word, it rather failed.

168

So while others had cheered for Henry, Jane had always cheered for Charles, and still did. It was no crime to be mild and gracious; these were virtues that drew Jane in. So she would always help the lost soul who lay asleep on her now, his breathing deepening, a king made captive.

*

Hammond did not rush to break the seal.

A letter from Cromwell was a bad start to any day. He could expect exhortation of some sort: encouragement to hold fast or to clamp down or to do the honourable thing, which Hammond was trying to do, despite not knowing what it was. When did he last know the honourable path? Did he ever? And if he did, when did he lose sight of it? He needed to untangle his loyalties. It would help to know who he served these days.

And parliament was his master, surely? That was the plain fact; it was they who paid him, at least. But was money the root of loyalty? For he still felt allegiance to the king, as any subject must. Who could not be loyal to the one who wore the crown, to God's anointed one – even if he had punched him in the face? He tried not to dwell on that, though the scene returned at night.

But there were other memories: his soldiers' faces, for instance, as they buried their friends after battle. The bravery of these men surpassed all things, as did the lack of appreciation for their work; parliament had been mean and cheap in its treatment of the soldiers. Hammond had never known courage, camaraderie or purpose like he knew in the army. Once a soldier, always a soldier; maybe this was so.

And Oliver's letter, read by candlelight in the guardhouse, proved no exhortation but a lament, as wearily the poor man faced war again. Hammond was aware of the dire situation facing the country: royalist uprisings in Wales, Kent, Colchester and Pontefract were coinciding with the Scots marching south. A second civil war was breaking out in England, and Hammond knew by whose invitation.

In the face of so many enemies, the army had divided its strength. Cromwell went first to Wales and then marched north to face the Scots. There had been three days of prayer before the march began,

169

but without the usual fervour and excitement. There was confusion in their hearts: why had God given them another war to fight, when they had won the last? Had they displeased God? Was he testing them?

With the seal broken, Hammond read Cromwell's words.

Oliver Cromwell
Lieutenant-General in the Lord's Army

Preston
16 August 1648

Dear Robin, [he was the only man to name him thus] I pray that God will teach this nation, and those that are over us, what the mind of God may be in all this and what our duty is now.

Hammond knew Oliver to be a good man as long as he knew what his duty was; when he didn't know his duty, he acquired a depressive spirit.

Surely it is not that the poor godly people of this kingdom should still be made the object of wrath and anger? Nor that our God would have our necks under the yoke of bondage?

And amid the lament was rage – rage at this second war, this unnecessary war, caused by the king's busy letter-writing and smuggled agreements.

This is a more prodigious treason than any that has been perfected before. The former quarrel was that Englishmen might rule over one another. But this despicable war is to vassalize us to a foreign nation! This is quite different.

Yes, Scotland felt pretty foreign to Hammond as he read on:

I must put down my pen, dear Robin. We will engage them near Preston. Hamilton has been providentially slow in his advance; otherwise he might have been laughing in London by now. God delights in the stupidity of arrogant men and Hamilton is thus. I wish Fairfax were here, truly; we have always fought together, never alone – and I am an unworthy commander. But it is a battle we must win, and by God's grace we shall – we will not be ruled by the Scots! We will pray for rain and a dampening of the Scots powder, on which they rely greatly. Control and discipline, as you will remember, dear Robin – control and discipline.

And while I am away, keep hold of the king for us all; he has much to answer for. And I trust Firebrace is gone. I am told he is the master of every plan to free this dishonest monarch from captivity.

Remember me in the fight.

For once, Hammond felt pity for Oliver. He knew the fear of battle. And yes, Firebrace was gone; he had not proved the friend Hammond imagined.

*

The king was playing bowls on the new bowling green. He would have preferred tennis at Hampton Court and often said this to Hammond.

'I miss the tennis at Hampton Court.'

'Then perhaps you should have stayed there,' came the reply.

'And be murdered in my bed by army plotters? I hardly think so.'

'It is a bowling green scarce equalled in the kingdom, your majesty, yet you complain.'

'It is so-so, no more than reasonable and a little mossy; but the tennis court at Hampton Court, that was most enjoyable – no moss, as I recall.'

The green was placed, with some thought, beyond the castle's curtain wall, that the king might not be oppressed by his captivity, yet inside the outer defences, that he might not be tempted to leave it. The king could not freely move around as once he did. His long walks around the island lay in the past, in innocent times now lost. And in truth, he greatly enjoyed his bowls, though he liked also to complain. So when the weather allowed, bowls became part of his daily round and this afternoon he threw with Colonel Hammond and two of his conservators, Thomas Herbert and Anthony Mildmay.

'He seems well disposed to life,' said Herbert.

'He is writing his great literary work,' replied Mildmay. 'Hammond saw it on his desk.'

'A royal Shakespeare? I did not imagine.'

'He writes meditations rather than plays.'

'Oh?'

'Spiritual meditations.'

'Ah.'

'They mainly concern death, I'm told.'

'Not a matter for the summer, in my estimate,' said Herbert, made uncomfortable by this news. 'When our spirits should definitely lighten a little.'

But despite his dark compositions, the king was well disposed to life. With the arrival of five hundred new troops and security much tightened, post in and out of the castle had initially become difficult. But praise God, July had brought improvement. Captain Titus had managed to get a letter from Jane through to him and the king was thrilled, replying immediately. 'I know not whether my astonishment or joy were the greater!' he wrote.

The cause of the upturn in post was Sir William Hopkins, who lived in Newport. He had connections with an illiterate woman who emptied the king's stool daily. The removal of the royal waste was hardly a task for the guards – it had no pleasant airs – but for a woman who could not read it was a considerable honour.

'The new way of conveyance is safe and unsuspected,' Charles wrote to Firebrace. 'And not tied to particular days, for I shit every day. Wherefore I urge you to make much use of this woman.'

A local uprising by royalists on the island was considered at this time. But reinforcements at the castle made this a risk to the king's person, for they were proper soldiers now, rather than a gathering of the elderly and lame. And bold uprisings around the country had not delivered as the king had hoped. Cromwell had crushed the life out of South Wales while Fairfax dealt harshly with Colchester.

But hope lived on: he still had his suitors, eager to please. The Scottish army had crossed the border on 8 July, and these soldiers were his liberty now, while parliament was also back in the game, bless them. Ignoring Cromwell – and quite unaware of the Scots – they'd offered him a new treaty, and sent three commissioners to negotiate. Charles had only to keep them talking and wait for the Scots to come south. The future was bright.

'Ours is a most blessed nation!' he declared to his bowls partners. 'An army of twenty thousand resolute men in England, command of the high seas around us – why, we need fear no one, neither kingdoms abroad nor conspiracies at home! We shall live in the greatest peace and tranquillity of any nation in the world! I believe so.'

'It is perhaps the Scottish conspiracies we have most reason to fear, sire,' Hammond said.

'Ah, the Scots. I do not have a good opinion of that n-n-nation,' said Charles, in his gentle Scots voice.

Hammond's eyebrows rose by themselves and something stirred inside.

'There you and Cromwell agree, your majesty. They march against his army now, invading our land.'

'Do they?' said Charles, casually, having read just that morning of their advance. 'Perhaps they have simply heard the cry of the oppressed English, Mr Hammond. God knows, we need no more war.'

Charles shook his head sorrowfully, like a helpless old man, but Hammond's patience was stretched; for he was a soldier again at Naseby, alongside the lieutenant-general, shoulder to shoulder on the cavalry line, wading in the mud with his men, feeling the dull terror as battle lines were drawn and breakfast beer consumed, deadening beer, the knowledge of what lay ahead, of what was to come, bravado and fear, jokes and vomit, shouted commands, the grunt of engagement, gunshot and sword, exploding heads, the hollering of horses, severed limbs, skewered bodies, the shrieks of the wounded long into the night, the tempting flesh of the army whores . . .

'Traitors and cowards, those Scots,' said the king jovially. 'Expect no great fidelity from them, I think. Trust only the people of England who have risen on their own, I believe: South Wales, Colchester, Kent?'

'I believe they miss Christmas more than they miss your majesty,' said Hammond.

Charles smiled. Parliament had attempted to suppress Christmas, something Charles would never do. Maypoles, St George's Day,

Christmas and other 'heathen and seditious revels' had all been banned by those parliamentary fools and with much outcry. They'd attempted amends, in their dull Presbyterian way. They now offered 5 November as a public holiday instead: the Day of Redemption from papist despotism. Hallelujah!

But it was a weak Hallelujah! across the land, and forcing shopkeepers to work on Christmas Day had been a difficult task for the local constabularies. Bury St Edmunds and Ipswich were not alone in defiantly covering their towns in holly and ivy.

'And your own plans?' asked Hammond.

'My own plans?' said Charles, contemplating the bowl in his hand.

'Should the Scottish army come south, I mean.'

'Should the Scottish army defeat the army of Cromwell?'

'I wondered if you had made any particular plans ... in that eventuality?'

'My plan is to throw this bowl and win the game,' said Charles with a smile.

*

The battle of Preston was blood and mud in August; Hammond heard immediately from Cromwell's own hand. The victory was his, crushing and complete, aided by hour upon hour of a heavenly deluge which soaked the powder of the Scottish infantry. Two thousand Scots were killed and nine thousand captured, these were the bare facts ... after which Oliver set off north. He marched towards the wasps' nest that was Edinburgh – though less waspish now for their lack of an army. Cromwell had long had the perfidious Scots in his thoughts.

But the victor was neither well nor happy, this was clear. Despite a remarkable campaign – and Hammond understood its efficient power – Cromwell appeared more despairing, more depressive ... and more religious.

'He suffers a paralysed spirit,' noted Ireton after receiving a letter from his commander. Cromwell did not say this; he could not see it himself. But he wandered the north unsure of a great deal, clinging to the outworking of providence as his guiding light, and victory in battle was the clearest guide of all. He had won battles, so God was on his side – but what follows the battle? What government should then appear? The Lord must declare himself on the matter! In a letter to Fairfax, with the Book of Isaiah open before him, he celebrated 'the wonderful works of God, breaking the rod of the oppressor as in the day of Midian – not with garments much rolled in blood, but by the terror of the Lord who will yet save his people and confound his enemies as in that day'.

But when? It was not enough for God to confound them in war; he must confound them in peace as well ... or what meant anything?

And it was to Gideon he returned most often. Of all the Old Testament figures, he admired Gideon the most: the farmer called from the plough, just as Oliver himself had been; a man called to train, choose and lead the army of Israel. Gideon crushed the Midianites, executed their kings and then returned to his farm. Was Cromwell a latter-day Gideon? Was this who he was on earth?

He had held this scripture in his mind as the Scottish army crossed the border on 8 July to march on London, and it remained his scripture now: the only story that made sense of these difficult days.

Gideon crushed the Midianites; and he executed their kings.

*

'It was I, my lord.'

'You name yourself as the culprit, Miss Osborne?'

'Yes, my lord.'

'You wrote those words?'

'I am a most foolish maid. You must forgive me.'

Hammond played along, for she was an honourable woman, one with spirit – and handsome. She was the sort of woman he might marry one day; he thought this as they spoke.

'A foolish maid with the writing hand of a child,' he noted. 'Such as your young brother might possess, perhaps?'

'Robin? Robin would never write such a thing!'

'Really?'

'He thinks only of his father, who we're on the way to visit.'

'Is that so?'

175

'In Saint-Malo.'

'Then you have some travelling to do. And perhaps some rough water.'

Hammond sat behind his large desk, an experience that tasted good this morning. There was an authority about a desk, particularly a large one, that bestowed the like on its owner; this is what he felt. But with authority comes responsibility and he must now sort out the unfortunate wall-writing incident in Newport. On the wall of a Newport inn were words from the Old Testament Book of Esther: 'Haman was hanged on the gallows he had prepared for Mordechai.' And if one wished to understand its relevance, for 'Haman' read 'Hammond' and for 'Mordechai' read 'the king'.

He was familiar with the verse. Royalist pamphleteers – whose recent epithets for him included 'the baboon' and 'the ape-faced blood-mongerer' – had often aimed this particular line at him. And now here it was again, scrawled in chalk on the wall of a nearby inn. The soldiers had acted as best they could, accusing Robin Osborne, aged eleven, of the crime; and they had two eye-witnesses to support them. Hammond knew one thing for sure: the words had clearly not been written by the elegant Dorothy Osborne, who, one felt, would be kind to a wasp.

But what was he to do?

Let not these awkward times kiss farewell to chivalry, thought Hammond, for she was quite charming. He saw mainly men or women of the brutalized sort, so she was a pleasing sight.

'Then you must be on your way,' he said. 'To Saint-Malo.'

'Thank you, sir. We shall not be charged?'

'You shall not be charged, no.'

She claimed to have written the words herself, but one could hardly punish such a woman, even if one did believe her; and Hammond did not, for one moment.

'And do tell Robin to clean the chalk from his hands before leaving,' he said, rising from his seat.

*

Charles was told of Cromwell's victory at Preston, while playing bowls.

'I have good news, your majesty,' said Hammond, heartily.

'My release?'

'The Scots – they were defeated.' He spoke as the king was about to throw; the royal hand went limp and the bowl dropped to the ground. 'Our nation is safe from the untrustworthy Scots. Good news for us all!'

Charles sagged and was silent for a while. 'This is so, is it?' he asked, straightening a little.

'Soundly defeated at Preston, yes . . . grave losses in torrential rain. They'll not be visiting England again soon.'

Hammond did not spare him and Charles twitched a little.

'This is the worst news that ever came to England,' he said. 'Quite the worst news.'

Hammond disagreed. 'If the Scots had won, your majesty, they'd now control the thrones of both Scotland and England.'

'You are mistaken, Mr Hammond. I could have commanded them back with the motion of my hand.'

'Is that so?' Hammond was sneering. 'Oh, that the healing of this nation were so simple! And that your hand could be so trusted.'

But Charles was in despair and left the game shortly after. Without Scotland for the king there was no France for the king. The French foreign minister Mazarin had placed all hopes on the Scottish adventure, he'd made this plain. There would be no alliance now, which left Charles lonely.

He looked out to sea, aware he had only ingenuity and God on his side . . . and Jane.

September 1648

'My dear Jane says I must escape! Always she says it!'

'This is so, my lord,' she replied, stroking his nose. 'You must escape. Your dear seven-one-five is quite right – as always.'

'And I will escape, Jane, I will.'

'You say this – yet you stay.'

'I say it because I will! But at least kiss me first.'

They were alone again in his chamber, Jane having gained the trust of the stool lady. She'd arrived in his room while he took supper, and he'd returned with excitement upon her discovery.

'I hear Cromwell and Ireton conspire,' she said, pulling away a little. She did not at this moment wish to kiss the king. She was not angry with him, how could she be angry? But she had on occasion been disappointed with him of late. He'd become indecisive these past weeks and no one warmed to that in a man. He was no longer the sickly boy, after all; he was the king, and Jane did like to get things done. She'd worked hard to get things done.

'We are talking with parliament,' said Charles.

'And who are they now?'

'Who are they, Jane? Well, I believe they are the rulers of this land!'

'Really?'

'Or at least imagine themselves so.'

'And is that how Cromwell imagines them? He rages against you in parliament.'

'Cromwell?' He smirked. 'Cromwell is a farmer who speaks without thought! I don't think anyone in parliament listens to his rustic ranting. No, he will calm himself, he always does, and then he will knock on my door again with tears of contrition.'

But he was frustrated by Cromwell, by the constant reappearance of this man, this wart-nosed oik. Charles had believed his business with the upstart was over, having played him well and easily in the gardens at Hampton Court. Oliver was a man from the shires, a minor country gentleman temporarily lifted from obscurity, nothing more; and awed by a king. And that should have been that, and indeed would have been, if the Scots had proved trustworthy, and if the rain had not soaked their shot.

'I have spoken with him before,' said Charles cheerfully. 'We will negotiate. He likes a king. I will charm Oliver a little, now come and kiss—'

'Charles, I don't believe Cromwell will be communicating with you now.' Again she found herself pulling away from his advances.

'And how could you know that, dear Jane?' He asked with condescension, as master to pupil, as one wise in the affairs of men.

'He allows his hawk to fly.'

'His hawk? I never imagined him a hunting man.'

'Henry Ireton.'

'Ireton?'

'This is what I hear. He has become more busy of late, and he does not buzz for you, your majesty. He judges the monarchy unnecessary, burdensome and dangerous, these are his words, this is how he thinks now' – she must make him understand – 'and he will persuade Cromwell thus. You cannot negotiate now. There is no more talking to be done; you must flee this place.'

The king was undoing his breeches, hard inside his pants. He liked Ireton even less than Cromwell, a great deal less. But really, that could wait.

'I would like you to take me in your mouth, Jane. Can you do that for your king?'

Jane looked in his eyes and then at his desperate member, exposed like an angry child. 'If that is what you wish, your majesty.'

She knelt down to receive the king.

*

Wood sensed the different air, a change in mood; and the second war had done this.

After the first war, they'd thought the best, hoped that Charles was misled by evil counsellors, that if only his counsellors were

179

changed, then he would change. They were monarchists, after all, so it must be true.

But they did not believe this now. Wood saw the change: the rotten fruit was not the counsellors but the duplicitous king himself.

Henry Ireton was no Leveller, what with their attacks on property; he would never attack property law. But while a late arrival, he joined them now in their republican chants; he would not countenance further negotiation with the man of blood, as he explained at a late-night meeting of army grandees, beneath the low roof of the Nag's Head near Windsor.

'What has changed, gentlemen, might be numbered thus.'

'He has learned lists from the agitators,' muttered Wood to Ludlow, hand over his mouth. 'The agitators love to number their demands.'

'First, a second civil war,' said Ireton, eyes as bright as the candles. 'Second, the reduction of the Scots to nothing. Third, the clear duplicity of his majesty in all matters, including his current conversations with parliament, and fourth – and we learn of this now – his repeated attempts to escape custody. I believe those simple facts change – or perhaps merely confirm – a great deal.'

'And Oliver?' they asked. Those round the table wished to know what Cromwell felt about all this.

'As you know, the lieutenant-general is currently engaged in the siege of Pontefract,' replied Ireton. 'But yes, he agrees – of course he agrees. He rages against Charles for defying the judgement of providence, so clearly declared at Marston Moor, Naseby and now Preston.'

Ireton paused his narrative there, without revealing the hesitations of his father-in-law. Oliver himself did not believe that killing the king would help, for there were plenty of other Stuarts loitering in Holland and France, he said – so what benefit in killing Charles? This was his new concern; but it need not be made public at this table.

And in his absence, Ireton proceeded with business. The king needed moving from Carisbrooke; this must be achieved. But all eyes round the table wondered the same: would Hammond cooperate?

Meanwhile, the parliamentary delegation has turned up in Newport with high hopes.

Hopes are especially high as the army is far away, distracted in the north. Previous talks with the king had failed for various reasons: the king unwilling to move, and with a choice of offers before him. But there were no choices now, so surely he would listen?

So thought the delegation as they moved into their accommodation on the Isle of Wight; here was clearer air than London, and more seagulls. They would offer the same terms as before and the king would agree. The army would fume, scream and rant – hysterical bunch that they were. But they'd come to their senses, allow themselves to be calmed and then pensioned off. It was time for the Presbyterian solution. But they must act fast: rumours of an intervention by the army strengthened by the day.

Some called it a race for the king.

*

Anthony Wood

> *Newport*
> *10 September 1648*

Mr Cromwell,
I write from the Isle of Wight, where preparations are now being made in Newport for the negotiations. Parliament smells a changing wind, one more favourable to its cause – and raises its dull sails once again, seeing themselves as the king's only remaining friend.

Such is their present sense; and in the early hours of dawn, when all doubts arise, they greatly fear a trial of the king, which they've heard rumoured. Ireton mentions it openly to all who will listen. Are you aware of these circumstances?

To this end, parliament becomes busy in affairs at Carisbrooke and effects change there. They have instructed Colonel Hammond that the king's imprisonment be altered. He is allowed the return of his former staff, including both Firebrace, his escape officer, and Mrs Wheeler, his laundrywoman and post lady.

A house for the negotiations is being prepared and Sir William Hopkins has made his home available to his majesty, spending a small ransom on redecoration to make it fit for a king; he hopes, no doubt, for high office. Quarters have also been reserved at various inns for the parliamentary commissioners, with, I am told, £10,000 borrowed from the city of London to pay for it.

He has proved an expensive king down the years . . .

And should you be a-worrying for young Mr Hammond, then be at peace – he is suddenly a rich man, made so by parliament. He has been awarded a personal pension of £500 a year, while his army pay is doubled to £40 a week for the duration of the treaty; and on top of these payments, sufficient one might imagine, he is also offered £1000 in delinquency fines. No wonder his conscience is quiet and he displays much favour towards the treaty.

Do you know Newport? It is the main town on the island, a small but increasingly monied place, prosperous on the earnings from trade, fishing, leatherwork and brewing. Three thousand souls inhabit this town with the streets well made, their own paving and water mains newly laid. The innkeepers are happy, for there is good business to be had, the place heavy with royalists, who wish to drink their king back to the throne. They gather mainly in the George Inn, where they toast the monarch and start fights with the soldiers.

Expectations are mixed. Pamphlets in London speak of high hopes, but others prefer caution, less inclined to optimism. Sir John Oglander was particularly sceptical in my hearing: 'They tell us we shall have peace and the issue of blood will be stopped; fair weather and all things according to our heart's desire! Perhaps we shall also see water into wine?'

I note that Charles also expects nothing from these talks. A letter he sent to Sir William Hopkins included these sentiments:

'To deal freely with you, Sir William, I have no great hopes that much good will come of this gathering, because I do not believe those who come to treat will have power to debate, but only to propose. Therefore, imagine all dispositions exactly as they were before this talking began; and let no one be deceived by a mock treaty.'

He talks to bide his time, Oliver, while he makes other plans.
He eases himself from imprisonment at Carisbrooke, that is quite
plain. Hammond, deep in parliament's generous pocket, has agreed
to this, which will not please you. Charles himself swings between
the wily and the holy; between negotiator and martyr-in-waiting.
Did you know he was writing a spiritual book?
  I lay these facts before you.
  In your service,
  Anthony Wood

*

Charles' stay at Carisbrooke did appear to be at an end – sensed
first by the kitchen staff, when the deliveries of hashed pullet and
neat's tongues were stopped.

Plans were far advanced for his move to Newport, where he
would reside in the redecorated home of Sir William Hopkins.
On his final day at the castle, the king strolled on the bowling
green one last time. Nostalgic already for this grass, he took little
notice as the nine-year-old son of Howe, the master gunner at the
castle, marched past him with a toy sword. But when the boy then
marched back again, as if presenting arms, the king spoke.

'What are you going to do with that monstrous weapon, young
man?' He had never liked blades.

'Please, your majesty, I am going to defend you with it, from
all your enemies – for you are with violet.'

'With Violet?'

'That's what my father said.'

The boy's father had told him that the king was a great hero,
that they must all defend him, for the monarchy was inviolate. And
Charles was strangely moved; he patted him on the head and gave
him a blessing.

'I am going away from here now and do not expect to return.'

'Never?'

'I do not think so.'

'Where will you go, your majesty? For I will come with you.
I will be your bodyguard and fight at your side.'

'And a fine bodyguard you'd be!'

The boy was sure his father would be pleased. He would tell him what the king said.

'So where, your majesty?' He liked the king; he did not wish him to go.

'That we must wait and see, my young friend. We do not always know where we go.'

'Surely a king knows?'

Charles smiled, then reached to his neck and removed the gold ruby ring that held his cravat.

'I would like to give you something to remember me by,' he said, handing the ring to the boy.

'Thank you, your majesty! I will always remember you.'

And that made Charles happy, for he wished to be remembered. And while he was glad to leave Carisbrooke, he was sad also, for it had been a place both wretched and warm. He had known himself a king here, though sometimes a prisoner. He had remembered his youth here, though sometimes felt old. And he'd remained faithful to Henrietta, if sometimes with Jane.

He gave himself now to the martyr's path, for this was his chosen way; though he might escape.

*

On 6 September, the king moved to the house of Sir William Hopkins where the army guard around him was formally removed.

'You are a free man,' said Sir William, with great cheer.

'Not quite,' said Charles. 'Would I stay with you if I was free?'

He could see no offence in this remark; it was a simple fact. If he were free, he would be in Whitehall ... though matters were improved now. With horses laid on for his convenience, he was permitted to travel round the island as he wished during the negotiations. Parliament would woo their king, love him into agreement; though the king felt only estranged. Four dismal proposals sat before him and not one was new. He'd been avoiding these same issues for almost a year now and as he gazed on them he felt tired.

First, they asked that all royal proclamations against parliament might be withdrawn – well, perhaps this was possible. But the abolition of the episcopacy? England with no bishops? He would never do that. Kings and bishops were of one fabric. And neither would he grant them control of the militia; there was no compromise there either. The king should control the army. And finally there was Ireland. He would slow things, this was his plan, delay proceedings as much as he was able; he'd be generous in generalities but opaque over particulars. And to further the delay, he would arrive late every day for his meetings with the commissioners.

*

'The commissioners arrive at the meeting house at nine o'clock,' noted Wood. 'But the king does not appear until three, camped with his advisors, trying to devise new ways to save the bishops and himself.'

Hopkins at least knew the truth, for Charles himself had told him: 'Bishops lie at the heart of the church settlement, Mr Hopkins, and I will never accept their abolition; nor will I accept the establishment of the Presbyterian Directory of Worship in place of the Book of Common Prayer. If there is a duller book than their Directory of Worship, I have not encountered it.'

Though as one day became another, and one delay became another, some commissioners became restless. Mr Bulkeley, a resident on the island, reminded the king that the time set for the treaty was running out and there was still much to do.

'We have barely started, your majesty, yet our deadline draws near!'

'Consider this, Mr Bulkeley,' replied the king. 'Do you not think that this treaty – if truly it can be called such a thing – does not more resemble the affray in the comedy?'

'Which affray, your majesty?' He did not visit the theatre and had never seen a comedy.

'The affray where the man comes out and says: "There has been an affray and no affray!" And on being asked how that could be, he says, "Why, there have been three blows given and I received them all!"'

Bulkeley did not like self-pity in a man and stated the unstated. 'You are being offered your kingship back, your majesty.'

'But at what price, dear sir?'

'After the years we have endured, I would call the price reasonable.'

'But then you are the one delivering the blows, are you not?'

'The blows are soft.'

'Soft on your hands, perhaps.'

*

Charles continued to converse with his host Sir William. It was time to think again of escape and he wished Hopkins to organize it.

'I wish you to make arrangements for my escape,' he said.

'Do you have any particular plans, your majesty?'

He hoped the king had firm plans, given the ruinous cost of his stay in his house. The high honour of housing his majesty was over. Bankruptcy loomed and he would have Charles on the high seas tomorrow.

'We shall make use of my new situation, my new freedoms. I am not guarded as I was and can journey about the island. Such liberty will help us.'

'Of course, your majesty.'

'We shall meet on this matter again – but we cannot act soon enough.'

'Indeed.'

The king lowered his voice. 'I have heard that what is feasible now may not be so in a few days.'

'Then we must get you from this place at the first opportunity.'

'My nights are consumed with healing, of course. I am much needed.'

'Your escape to France,' said William, calling his majesty to focus.

'I will need a boat.'

'We have a boat in mind.'

'But where will it take me?'

'We will need a safe haven, and we work to that end presently.'

'And good tides and a necessary wind. I will need those.'

Charles was a fussy man to help, thought Sir William. Firebrace had not spoken falsely.

'Creation will smile on our needs,' said Hopkins.

'And I wonder if a pass from Hammond might be useful.'

186

'Your majesty?'

'Whether it might give us more time, to obtain a pass from Hammond to wander quite as I wish.'

'I do not think it timely to involve him in plans for escape.'

'He is quite on our side.'

'I would still encourage caution. He is paid by parliament, remember.'

'I will leave at night.'

'Of course, your majesty.'

'So when can we be ready? I cannot bear another sermon from Dr Turner.' Dr Turner was the new chaplain assigned to him.

'I have heard he lacks an interesting mouth, sire; so use his many words as a backdrop to your plans for liberty – a workroom in which to sharpen them.'

*

The following day, after a long session with the negotiators, Charles spoke again with Hopkins.

'We speak of our dear bishops.'

'Oh?'

'And I do relent a little.'

'You have agreed to parliament's demands?' Surely he hadn't?

'No. But I have promised them good news on the matter.'

'I see.'

'But your preparations must go on, Sir William – concerning the boat and—'

'Quite so, your majesty, but do keep them talking a while longer, while final arrangements are made.'

'I will be quite plain, Sir William: I do not find it easy to dissemble to these people.'

'You have wisely dissembled for many years, sire. We ask now only a few more days.'

'Yet now I dissemble to the point of conscience.'

'You dissemble for the kingdom, your majesty; that must be your view. Your conscience can sleep soundly.'

Charles nodded and then raised a further concern. 'Intelligence suggests they might break these talks.'

'Who might break these talks?'

'The army, Sir William; this is what I hear, that the army might do so. And I must not allow that. We must keep talking . . . but we do not have long.'

'Just a day or two, sire. All will be quite arranged in a day or two.'

Charles then gave him a look; he could not help but note the delay.

'I wonder if you work for the army, Sir William, the way you keep me waiting!'

'I do not work for the army, sire. On the contrary, I give you my home.' And all my savings, he might have added, having that morning seen the week's bill for victuals. 'You gave little warning, sire – so it has taken a little time. But two days and we shall be ready.'

'Good, good! I will give them further encouragement tomorrow. They shall strike me with their demands and I will say thank you and ask to be struck again!'

*

The following day, the king and Hopkins met again.

'I have made too many concessions,' said Charles, disconsolate.

'They are concessions only if they are honoured, your majesty.'

'I have just granted parliament control of the militia.'

'You move fast.'

'Or rather I gave hope of such control.'

'Mere words.'

'And most difficult and unsuitable words for a monarch. What a wretched script to endure!'

'Yet you are still alive, sire, with breath in your body, food on your table and those around to assist you in your endeavours.'

'But enough is enough.'

'What is enough?'

'I have decided about the bishops.'

'What have you decided?'

The king paused. 'I cannot pretend agreement there . . . really, I cannot.' There was a limit to his deceit, a clear line in the sand.

188

'I will grant them whatever they desire with the militia, but I will not risk the damnation of my soul.'

'They will like having the militia; this will cheer them. They will drink heartily tonight, imagining a great victory.'

'I gave them the militia today only that I might escape.'

'Of course.'

'Then get me under sail, Sir William, and on my way to the continent! A Dutch pincke would be most suitable; that's what I need. The Prince of Wales must bring the fleet from Holland.'

'That may not be possible, sire.'

Hopkins had failed to mention that this particular fleet was presently penned in by the parliamentary navy off the Dutch coast, that its sailors were mutinous for lack of pay, and that the prince himself was a sick man. They would not be arriving this month, or the next, to save the king, being quite unable to save themselves.

'I feel so alone!' said Charles, almost to himself.

Hopkins also failed to mention that he was.

*

There was a mood of manly excitement among the negotiators. Those around Hammond's table at Carisbrooke saw a new attitude in the king and fine food before their eyes, with capon, chicken with cardoons, mushrooms, artichokes and oysters steaming in their pots. And then the veal arrived, brought in with some showmanship by Josiah, the young steward, who had blossomed of late. Glorious days lie ahead, said both their bellies and the wine.

'They say it requires the same power of thought to organize a battle as a feast!' declared Hammond. There was much merriment at that. 'The battle line, so it may appear terrifying to the enemy, and the feast, to be pleasing to friends! To friends!'

'To friends!' they all shouted, with glasses raised.

'I really do believe he's seeing sense at last,' said one diner.

A Newport newsletter had set the tone that morning. 'In all probability,' it declared, 'there will be a happy agreement, his majesty being cheerful, inclinable to anything – though intense towards his own interests.'

'He does seem to be giving away with some ease,' said another. 'I did not imagine he'd be so docile with regard to the militia. I certainly remember him stickier in the past on that matter.'

'I can vouch for that,' said Hammond and he enjoyed the laughter. This might all be turning out rather well, he thought, sensing a growing stature for himself. Perhaps he was appreciated at last? He was certainly well paid, but appreciation was better still.

'Even the Venetian ambassador in London speaks of a speedy conclusion,' said another, recently arrived from the capital.

'We must hope the king is not merely a very good actor,' said a cautious voice.

There was shock around the table.

'If he was acting,' came a confident reply, 'he'd have given up on the episcopacy, and he has not yet managed that.'

'A sign of honest dealings, I agree.'

'And he'll relent on that matter in the end. What other choice does he have? To knock on the army's door? I'm not sure they'd answer!'

More laughter.

'So how's old Farmer Cromwell feeling today, Hammond?'

'He is besieging Pontefract on our behalf,' he replied, suddenly sober. 'No doubt that matter concentrates his mind.'

There was an awkward pause.

'The church is not negotiable for the king,' said another, keen to be away from Pontefract – and Cromwell. 'It is the divine order and he will not risk his soul over that.'

'We'll see. He might find the throne persuades his soul!'

Hammond drank some more. The king was free and so was he; he should feel happier.

*

'I'm holding out as long as I can,' said Charles with impatience. 'Long prayers and the bishops can detain us a while, but I cannot promise another week in this place. Where is the boat?'

Hopkins had promised one seven days ago. 'We are doing what we can, your majesty.'

'You are not doing anything!'

190

'I hear the treaty period has been extended for two weeks, your majesty.'

'They speak of this.'

'Which gives us more time.'

'Do we have a boatman?'

'We do, sire.'

'Reliable?'

'A Newport merchant called John Newland; we hope him reliable.'

'Hope?'

'We do not know him well; but Firebrace commends him and that is enough for me.'

'I cannot think of any man who would betray me.'

'Quite.' Sir William could imagine a few. 'But many soldiers remain on this island. They do not encircle you, but they loiter. We have to take account of them.'

Charles did press Sir William endlessly, when he himself had much on his plate. Or rather, the king had much on his plate and Sir William had to pay the cook and his large staff to put it there; things were really quite serious. He needed a loan to sustain his outlay.

'A boat is the sweetest way. I like that travel the best,' said Charles. 'Though if there is no boat, then some other way, for with each day passing there is more reason to hasten. I fear the business of Ireland will break all; so really, I must be gone this week.'

*

'The woman is here to see you, your majesty,' said Hopkins.

'Mrs Whorwood?'

'Yes, sire.'

'Is she safe?'

'Safe enough. She came as a servant, carrying material from the market. She awaits you now in the parlour, if that is your wish.'

If that is your wish . . . The words could not hide the judgement. Charles had been apart from Henrietta for some time, Sir William was aware; but that hardly made this canoodling a proper affair. The royalist cause was an honourable calling, not something seedy and shameful . . . and adultery in his own home? This had not been part of his invitation.

Sir William returned to Jane, who sat in the servants' quarters.

'Is this wise?' he asked plainly.

'I seek only to serve the king, sir, as I'm sure we all do.'

'Perhaps not in your particular manner.'

'You know nothing of my manner.'

'I know a little.' However reluctant one's ears, some things were impossible not to hear.

'While you have slept in your soft bed these past years, sir, I have travelled the wet roads of England in the king's cause.'

'And Henrietta's?'

'Our noble queen, who I serve also.'

'And this you believe?'

'I do for the king what Henrietta cannot do from over the sea.'

'The king is a Christian man—'

'Does not a Christian man have needs, sir?'

'He will see you now.'

Sir William felt quite nauseous; and all this, in his bankrupt house.

*

Oliver Cromwell
Lieutenant-General in the Lord's Army

Pontefract
16 November 1648

My dear Robin,
I greet you from Pontefract, where concerns have delayed me for the present. I celebrate with you the clear providences of God, so constant and unclouded, that have brought our land to the edge of peace once again. We see God's hand in all that transpires, at Marston Moor and Naseby in the first war; and now at Preston and Winwick in the second.

To this end, speaking soldier to soldier and Christian to Christian, I abjure you to take your orders from God's army not

192

parliament, who dissemble shamefully in the face of providence.
I hear that they now speak with the king in Newport? What
good will come of a treaty with a man against whom the Lord
has witnessed? This treaty is a ruinous, hypocritical agreement,
despised by God. And yet Henry tells me you allow the king free
access to it?

We are ever mindful of what transpires around you and
intimately informed. Parliament pursues this course because they
now fear the army more than the king. Yes, dear Robin, it has
come to this. In the mud, blood and rain of Preston, the army has
destroyed their Scottish foes, so now they skip more freely and
more gaily to Charles. It was Fairfax who sent you to Carisbrooke,
not parliament. Yet it appears it is your fashion to listen to them
rather than to your friends!

You refuse to imprison Charles, and instead allow this traitor
to wander free. Yet we know the king of old, and he has not much
changed. He will speak of compromise – honeyed words, words
I have heard myself and been finely seduced by. But in his heart,
as God knows, he will be dreaming of escape, planning his routes
to France, and this cannot be allowed.

If I were with you, dear Robin, I would plead in my person,
and weep for your kind understanding. But instead, I must
write, calling upon your conscience in this matter that these
providences, so mighty and clear in the firmament, might not
be in vain.

Henry joins me in these concerns and knows you will be strong
in this matter, no matter what gold is placed at your feet.

In the Lord's work,
Oliver

Hammond put the letter down with an almighty sigh. So 'Henry'
was concerned as well as Oliver? That was not good news. It
sounded like a threat, and it was a threat – but really, what could
he do? Not that Hammond ever called Ireton 'Henry'; he'd always
called him 'Ireton' and found him distant, even when life had been
a simpler path, with right and wrong a clearer choice.

For now, however, he was simply relieved to have the king out of his hands. He would not dwell on the promptings of his conscience. And anyway, why should he not be properly paid for the load he had carried all these months? It was hardly the thieves' gold Oliver implied.

'You have a visitor, sir,' said his steward, Malcolm, from the study doorway.

'A visitor? I expect no one.'

'Mr Ireton, sir.'

'Mr Ireton?' His body was in immediate revolt. 'You must tell him I am busy today.'

'Yes, sir.'

'I'm sure you have but a moment,' said Ireton, pushing past Malcolm who looked bemused.

'Leave us,' said Hammond.

'You heard the colonel,' said Malcolm.

'No, Malcolm – you can leave us,' said Hammond.

The door was closed behind Ireton as he looked around, survey-ing the room.

'A good nest you have here, Robert! And well funded, we hear.' Ireton smiled. 'Your finances dance – but does your conscience?'

*

The dispatch arrived by courier and was passed on to Sir William. He took the letter to his study, a sanctuary since the king's arrival. Upon his insistence, it remained the one room in the house, apart from his bedroom, free from the royal ensemble, though his opinion was constantly sought by one person or another. His home had become a corridor of strangers, hurrying about the king's business and giving William the bill. He closed the door, sat down behind his desk and pondered the missive. Noting the name on the envelope and the seal, he removed it with mixed feelings.

The letter was from Jane Whorwood, a recent visitor here.

Mrs Jane Whorwood
Gatherer of funds and helpful news for the king

London
24 November 1648

Dear Sir William,
I write grateful to have met you this past week in your fine house;
and feel ever bound to you in the cause of the king. On that we
can agree, and it is that cause I consider now.

I stay in London, having left Newport last week, and am with
good friends, also faithful to his majesty as you are yourself. But
I write with urgency concerning the great business, suggesting it
be completed at the earliest opportunity.

I hear rumours of a notable design on which both army and
parliament agree, wherein they propose to dispose of his majesty;
this is the dark tale we hear.

Fairfax has less influence these days – perhaps the wonderful
Lady Fairfax has scared them away from him – and in his place,
the devilish Ireton drives affairs. He forces a petition upon
parliament which they call a 'Remonstrance', demanding the trial
of the king. 'The king dishonours any treaty made,' they say.
'Instead, we demand that the capital and grand author of our
troubles, the person of the king, may be speedily brought to justice
for the treason, blood and mischief he is guilty of.'

You will understand the significance of such talk, and how
there could be no more dangerous words uttered in this distracted
kingdom. I hear that Cromwell, though absent in the north – and
may he rot there – supports this.

And so advice must change, for the danger is pressing. Until
this present time, the king's friends in the city have believed that
he should make every concession and clinch the treaty. They
have encouraged him in this course – though not I. But this
development shakes their argument to its roots. The king is a
fine talker but is the time for talking done?

If he will then betake himself to escape – and this must be
the way – let him do it on Thursday or Friday next, but by all
means out of some door and not from the top of the house by

195

ladders; for I have heard too much of that way talked of by
some near him.

In the king's noble cause,
Mrs Jane Whorwood

Sir William laid the letter down on his desk. He was doing his best, no one could do more; and he'd heard of no escape plan involving ladders. Who spoke to Jane Whorwood of ladders?

*

'So who do you serve now, Robert?'

Ireton was wandering the study, gazing admiringly on the furniture. Hammond remained behind his desk, strangely trapped.

'I serve the nation, as I hope you do.'

Ireton nodded. 'Like the king, you have become a lover of art, I see.'

Hammond had acquired one or two paintings during his stay. 'Decoration, Henry.'

'Do you discuss paintings, Robert? I mean, with his majesty. Perhaps the king has promised you some of his. He has a fine collection.'

'We talk of many things.'

Ireton nodded again. 'Our paths have not much crossed, Robert, different byways travelled – but I feel them crossing now.' So did Hammond. 'And the matter is this: we need assurances of your support.'

'I support a good settlement.'

'Don't we all?'

'And we work for one now.'

'So I hear, so I hear. And they pay well, do they – parliament? They reward you adequately?'

'They pay me my dues. It has not been an easy calling at Carisbrooke.'

Ireton pondered another painting, and then a map of the island, given to Hammond by the businessmen of Newport after one particularly merry evening at the castle.

'Fine work,' he said, 'fine work. So who are you, Robert? I don't know if I know you now.'

'You never knew me.' The polite conversation was over.

'I thought you a soldier.'

'And I thought you a king's man. You shouted for him at Putney.'

'Very good.' Ireton smiled as an assassin might when the blade goes in. 'We need your support, Robert; it would be easier, otherwise it will not fall well for you. You cannot hide behind your desk for ever . . . with your paintings.'

'I do not hide!' Robert was up and facing Ireton like a duellist. 'I hide from no one.'

Ireton stood still. 'We need your support, Robert, that's all I say. This treaty will not occur.'

'Get out.'

'I wish you well, both Oliver and I, we do; and we count on your support, Robert . . . in the coming days. We do look for your support.'

And then he left and Hammond collapsed behind his desk.

'Can I get you anything, sir?' asked Malcolm.

*

Jane met the reinstated Firebrace at his new lodgings in Newport. She had travelled from London with urgency.

'I do not see how the escape was not attempted,' said Jane. She would get straight to the point.

'It was not my failing, Mrs Whorwood,' said Firebrace. No one had worked harder for the king's freedom than he.

'I hardly think it was the king's!' said Jane.

It was most certainly the king's, but Henry must stay calm; Jane was becoming hysterical in her senses. He admired the woman, but he would not be blamed. He would simply say what had happened.

'I held intelligence with him on the matter and received commands to provide a barque at Hastings in readiness to carry him to France.'

'This was a command from the king?'

'Yes, it was, and very clear. I was also instructed to send horses again to Netley and to lay others between that place and my house, to the end that if the commissioners of parliament should insist upon such particulars in the treaty as his conscience and honour could not submit to, he might be supplied with all things necessary for his escape.'

'If he could get across the water.'

'He took this for granted, Mrs Whorwood, confident he could achieve this. He's had no great restraints laid upon his person in recent days.'

'So what restraints appeared?'

'No restraints, as far as I know; and all these matters were punctually observed, believe me.'

Why did he have to answer to her, anyway? Firebrace did wonder. She was the king's whore, not his queen.

'Yet the king is still here on the island.'

'Because his majesty informed me that his condition was one of great melancholy.'

'Great melancholy?' said Jane with dismay. This was no reason for delay.

'Some persons near to him, so it transpired, had refused to serve him in his escape.'

'What persons?'

Why had Sir William not allowed her to stay in Newport and arrange these things herself? Was Sir William himself to blame? There was blame to be laid somewhere.

'And so he let go of the plan,' said Firebrace.

'Let go of it?'

'He quite let go of it and gave the order to discharge the barque and horses that awaited him ... which, with much sadness, I did.'

'Thank you. You can go.'

'This is my home.'

'Yes – of course, I'm sorry.' She was beside herself.

'I did all I could, Mrs Whorwood. I have not withheld any part of myself in these endeavours.'

'I'm sure.'

She felt a malady overwhelming her. She saw everything of value washed away in a flood, and felt rage at the rising waters and the fools who had let them rise: those around the king who had let him down, betraying him in his needy hour, like Christ in Gethsemane.

*

The army council were struggling. They sat round a table at Windsor and drafted an order for the reimprisonment of the king at Carisbrooke; but they did so with Hammond on their mind. How would he receive the order? Was the former soldier still their friend?

It was a question much debated in the requisitioned manor house where they met, watched by a dog who seemed surprised to see them.

'I believe we can trust Major Rolphe to do the right thing,' said Ireton to the council. 'But can we trust Hammond in like manner?' Silence followed, though everyone had a view. 'He is much entertained by his paintings, I discover. And presently imagines parliament his master.'

Rolphe was solid in the army's cause. A shoemaker from Blackfriars, he was reckoned to have at least thirty more shoemakers in his company – so a troop well prepared for a march. And all of them Independents, aware that agreement between parliament and the king, should it occur, would make their manner of believing a crime.

So here was a loyalty Ireton could trust. 'Certainly Rolphe is no lover of parliament!' he said confidently. 'We have a friend there, a true-hearted Englishman.'

The irony was not lost on some in the room, for while Ireton warmly commended Rolphe on this occasion, in last year's Putney debates he had savaged the poor man, when Rolphe had argued for an extension of the franchise. Ireton's response then had been to name him an 'idiot destroyer of the nation's fabric'.

'When you need a man, you warm to him. Is that not so, Henry?'

*

The delicate mission of speaking with Hammond was given to Colonel Isaac Ewer.

Ewer was the army commander in Portsmouth, and formerly butler to the Barringtons at Swainston, a house not more than

199

three miles from Carisbrooke. So in a manner he was going home ... but not as he once was. He had left as a servant, but returned now as a colonel. He would be opening doors for no one; the castle would be opening its doors to him.

'You are to deliver two letters to Colonel Hammond,' said the army council in their instructions to Ewer. 'One – sealed – from General Fairfax. The other – unsealed – written by Henry Ireton. This second letter will be shown to Hammond first. It contains full and adequate explanation as to why his duty in this matter lies with the army rather than with parliament.'

This was quite plain to Colonel Ewer.

'You are to watch the governor closely as he reads,' continued the letter. 'If you discern in his face an attitude of agreement and acceptance, then you are to hand over to him a full set of orders from the army council, and instruct him to remain at his post.'

Hammond would surely agree?

'If, however, his spirit remains hardened against these arrangements, then you are to escort him, with any force necessary, to army headquarters here in Windsor and consult with Major Rolphe, who shall take charge of the castle. You may speak with any honest officers as you find to be faithful and secret.'

Colonel Isaac Ewer hoped that Hammond would be in agreement with the army's wishes, for a further delicacy to his mission existed. Ewer had been a lieutenant-colonel in Hammond's infantry regiment; Hammond had been his commander. But since Hammond's posting to Carisbrooke, Ewer had gained both promotion and influence at army headquarters and returned now as one who outranked his former commander; the subordinate had become master. How would Hammond handle this new scenery?

Ewer's mission was delicate indeed.

*

Hammond was furious.

Presented with due humility by Ewer, the island governor held Ireton's proposals in a quivering hand.

He'd greeted him warmly enough, for they'd been close in battle and no camaraderie equals this. Yet a distance fast formed between

200

them, all the starker for the closeness once known. They sat with Major Rolphe, impassive throughout, as Hammond's discomfort grew.

'Sir,' he said, wishing to be clear, 'you ask me to lock the king away again? Is that really your meaning?'

'That is the army's meaning,' said Ewer. 'And therefore ours.'

Hammond stood up, amazed; he could not stay seated.

'You ask me to return him to his hutch here at Carisbrooke, with guards all around?'

'We ask that you obey your commander, General Fairfax, yes.'

'And this is the command of Fairfax, is it? There's nothing of Ireton here?'

He spoke with a sceptical tone, but for Ewer this was a straightforward affair.

'Our general is Fairfax, the both of us.'

'But how, in all conscience, can I do this, Ewer — while parliament and king treaty together?'

'They have no authority to treaty together.'

'No authority? They are the rulers of this land!'

'They were so — and look where that rule has brought us. Distrust seeps through this nation like blood in a bandage. You will remember that.'

'But they've extended the conversation for another week in hope of success. There is optimism that an agreement may be found. And I am to deny them that week? Am I, at your bidding, to deny our nation that week?'

'You are asked to intrude upon a treaty that spells ruin for the honest and the faithful of this land. Our public differences, disturbances, miseries and wars are caused by a single fellow; and this fellow must now be caged and brought to justice.'

'And that is so easily done?'

'A good regiment behind you makes many things easy, Colonel. We were soldiers together, we understand these things.'

'No,' said Hammond quietly.

'No?'

'I say no to this scheme — and I will not alter in this.' He could not proceed in this affair, he was quite certain. 'To reach the place that you desire, a dark place, you must first climb over my conscience, for I serve parliament in this matter and will wait to hear from them. When they instruct me in this manner, then I will follow.'

Ewer stared at him with indifference: a comrade who had deserted; and the conversation done.

*

The king lay on his bed, though not at peace. He was listening to night-time gunfire across the street from Sir William's house – a troubling lullaby.

He had not bothered to undress, being in poor spirits, unable to eat the pickled oysters. And when sleep came, it brought only nightmare. He dreamed 'of certain and terrible visions and that a party of armed men had conspired together to bereave me of my life'. He asked who fired the guns.

'They are musketeers sent by Hammond,' said Firebrace, who had been cleaning his fireplace.

Hammond? A man who could no longer be trusted, it seemed; though really, he never could be, always a parliament lackey.

'And the cause?'

'Some faithful subjects, sire – faithful to yourself – have been told to leave the island, and they take offence at the idea.' Charles nodded. 'They took an oath, sire, "to live and die together, in prosecuting their design: to null and obstruct the army's power and to sacrifice their lives for the preservation of his majesty's royal person from the hands and protection of disloyal subjects".'

'They act well. No surrender.'

'Loyal subjects do not surrender, your majesty. They have no care for themselves.'

Hammond had soon discovered the house where the ringleaders met and sent in musketeers, which was when the shooting began ... and then the groans; the groans of war, and the dead carried away. The king at the window counted only five of Hammond's men dead, which somehow didn't seem enough.

Unfortunately, a small fire had then started in the house of the plotters – it was not a castle, after all, nor built for the rough ways of gunshot. The troops took advantage, forced their way into the building and dragged out the bloodied survivors, who were still blessing his majesty. A most moving scene ...

But the next day, parliament's commissioners left the island. The talking was over.

*

Hammond also left the island that morning, though not with the commissioners.

He set off by himself, along rough Dorset roads, and much stirred by recent developments. Since Ewer's arrival, quite appalling enough, he'd received a letter from Fairfax, which ordered him to present himself at Windsor. It also informed him – and this particularly grated – that Colonel Ewer would guard the king during Hammond's absence. He was to be secured in Carisbrooke Castle until parliament gave their answer to the army's demands.

Hammond left reluctantly, but felt honour-bound to obey his commander-in-chief. His wife, Lady Fairfax, had a mind of her own – a rather shrill lady by all accounts – but Hammond warmed to his general and rode now in obedience beneath a grey November sky. He'd made his feelings plain before leaving, however. He'd announced his intention of opposing Ewer by force, if necessary, and left the king in the charge of Major Rolphe rather than Ewer – with injunctions to resist any attempt to remove Charles from the island.

Whether he could trust the shoemaker Rolphe remained to be seen; but he could trust him more than the upstart Ewer, the former butler who had risen way above his station. It was time Hammond's voice was heard, and so he journeyed into a cold north wind towards Windsor.

*

The day was kept as a fast at the king's residence, which meant no meat (apart from fish) and fewer courses. And on this holy day, the king listened to Dr Ferne preach on Habakkuk 2.3: 'Though it tarry, wait for it, because it will surely come, it will not tarry.'

Whether this was good news for the king was not clear; it could be heard variously, as the rain began to spatter against the window.

And later, as darkness fell, he sat down to write to his son Charles, who he had not seen for three years. He wondered how things were with him: a distracted boy when young, a sensual lip, the ladies said . . . but not without courage. 'The corn is now in the ground,' he wrote. 'We expect the harvest. If the fruit be peace, we hope the God of peace will in time reduce all to truth and order again.'

His son was hardly a spiritual boy – but perhaps he could be made so? There was a loud knock on the door; it was Firebrace. Charles lowered his quill, unhappy at the disturbance, as the visitor spilt his fears.

'God almighty preserve your majesty, for I fear some ferocious attempt on your person!'

Calming him as best he could, Charles discovered his reasons. Firebrace had seen soldiers carrying pistols, loitering outside his quarters, and feared abduction.

'There is yet a door of hope open, your majesty,' said Firebrace. 'The night is dark and I can now safely bring you into the street and conduct you to your old friend Mr John Newland, who has a good boat ready – and a good heart to serve you.'

'Mr Newland again?'

'You can commit yourself to the mercy of the sea, where God will preserve your majesty.'

'I'm not sure a winter sea knows mercy, Firebrace.'

'Kinder than those villains,' he jerked with his thumb towards the street. 'I fear this night they will murder you.'

Charles explained that even if there was danger, he could not escape, as he had given his parole and must be true to his word, though Firebrace observed that his word had not stopped him planning escape before. Charles did not respond. He was listening, becoming aware of horses, the night movement of troops and cavalry. The king had received intimations of this: that tonight, a considerable army was arriving on the island, fresh troops appearing under darkness, which suggested some extraordinary design afoot.

'It must be a sizeable plan, that such a body of men is so privately landed with the wind howling and the rain falling fast.'

'And not a good plan, your majesty.'

The footsteps outside the door ceased. No longer were the soldiers passing, they were staying. Sentries had been placed outside the king's front door. There was a knock and Firebrace cautiously opened the door. It was Captain Edmund Cooke, and they were glad to see him. He was formerly of Hammond's regiment and now a messenger. He'd been sent by the king to Carisbrooke Castle to enquire after his present safety, and he now reported back, wet from his travels and drying by the king's fire. He had scattered the guards a little and now felt duty stirring.

'Suppose, sire, I should not only tell you that the army may very suddenly seize you – Major Rolphe merely says "not tonight" – but that horses await you and a boat at Cowes!'

He was excited by the thought, as was Firebrace.

'Then we are set!' said Firebrace, new plans forming. 'And how might we leave?'

Cooke said he had the password and saw no difficulty in his proposed scheme: to smuggle the king from this place. He asked the king concerning his resolve in this matter.

Silence.

'Your majesty?'

The king sat on the edge of his bed, head bowed.

'They have promised me and I have promised them,' he said. 'I will not break first.'

'I fear it will not be long,' said Cooke, hope draining from his face.

'What troubles you, Captain?' said the king. 'Tell me.'

'Sire?'

'Your face is not well.'

'Not well when I consider the greatness of your majesty's danger, and your unwillingness to avoid it.'

'Let me make us some food,' said Firebrace, who was at his wit's end.

'Food is the talk of defeat,' said the captain, 'the refuge of the prisoner.'

'And that is what I am, Cooke. I am the royal prisoner.' Spoken quietly. 'There is no boat for me now; we will rest.'

Firebrace and Cooke withdrew to their quarters and the king lay down once again. He had slept in more comfortable beds and wished for Jane beside him, that they might swive one last time. Henrietta would understand entirely, with only a little complaint. He removed his cravat but then stopped. He would remain dressed . . . but seek rest before the morning light and all it might expose.

*

'Are you Colonel Robert Hammond?' called out the horseman, approaching him.

Hammond was nearing Richmond and had first taken the speaker for a rascal, drawing his sword as he rode. He felt angry and fearless; the one made him the other.

'Who asks?' he said.

'I bring a message from the House of Lords, sir – sent this day and with much urgency.'

'The House of Lords?' His tone changed.

'Yes, sir.'

'And what is that message?'

'You are not to leave your post, sir.'

'But I have already left my post! Do I appear to be sitting in a castle?'

The messenger paused for a moment. 'Then you are to return to your post, sir. This is the wish of parliament.'

'And you have authority?' He did not wish for another Dr Weals.

'I have here the instructions, passed on under seal.'

The courier reached into his bag and withdrew some parchment. Hammond took it, broke the seal and read. It was clear that he must return to Carisbrooke; he was a man under orders and here was a higher call than Fairfax. He was a parliamentarian and these were the commands of the House of Lords, the highest court in the land. He would return to Carisbrooke and deal with Ewer.

'I thank you, sir – and you can tell your masters that I gladly obey. I will return to Carisbrooke to protect the king from all who might do him harm.'

And then a sound, a sound he knew – horsemen, approaching from behind, the sound of cavalry that had once scared the royalists, and now scared Hammond. He looked about to see Ewer and twenty of his troops.

'Get out of my way, Ewer,' he said.

'That is not possible, sir.'

'I must return to Carisbrooke, as ordered by the House of Lords.'

'There are no lords now, Colonel Hammond, just the Commons ... the common people.'

'The common people? Are you a Leveller now, Ewer?'

'And you will accompany me to Windsor.'

'I go to Carisbrooke.'

'Windsor, sir.'

'And if I do not?'

'You will accompany me to Windsor, sir. This is how it shall be.'

And the fire in his belly died, for Hammond was quite without choice; and in a short while, he was riding with Ewer and his troops, away from Carisbrooke and his command, never to return to the island or his custody of the king. It had been a strange care, and he remembered the date of its starting, 13 November 1647 ... and the day of its ending, this day of 29 November 1648.

'An unexpected year,' thought Hammond as they rode north with soldiers he'd once led, when life had been a simpler thing.

*

The knock came at six in the morning.

The king was unready, caught again in restless dreams of lame horses and boats unready for use or impossible to reach. It was violent knocking; he heard the door open – Sir William protesting at such intrusion, and so early. And then Anthony Mildmay appeared with armed support at the door of the dressing room. He said the king should come with them, that they must leave now.

'If I must,' said the king, as five soldiers entered his room without due respect, all most offensive. 'And on whose orders?'

'Army orders.'

Charles received the blow without apparent pain. 'And where am I to be taken?'

'To the castle.'

207

'Carisbrooke? I return to Carisbrooke?'

Hesitation before the answer. 'No, sir.'

He was disappointed. 'Then where? Does my new home have a name?'

There were whispers among the soldiers.

'We cannot say,' said one.

'Hurst, your honour,' said another. He'd never seen a king before. 'Hurst Castle.'

'Indeed?' Charles felt bereft. 'You could not have named a worse home, I think.'

Somehow Firebrace talked his way through the circle of guards and started asking the king if he would like some breakfast; he would prepare him some breakfast. But Mildmay waved him away. There was no time for breakfast, he said. They wished the king clear of the town before the streets filled.

'The king will have breakfast,' insisted Firebrace and disappeared to raise Hopkins' sleepy cooks. But the king could not wait; he was not allowed to wait. When Firebrace returned – with assurances of a meal being ready within half an hour – the king was being led down the stairs. Firebrace knelt to kiss his hand, but as the king paused the soldiers pushed him from behind and he stumbled forward.

'Go on, sir,' they said, as they aimed him through the front door and towards the waiting coach. The king climbed in and turned round to find Rolphe attempting to join him.

'It is not yet come to that!' he shouted. 'Get out!'

Rolphe withdrew, brushing himself down, and watched as the coach made its way through the sleeping streets of Newport, turning west on to the Yarmouth road: a nine-mile journey for the king, his last on the Isle of Wight. Yarmouth was the nearer port, nearer than Cowes and chosen for safety; no ships from the Solent could interfere in Yarmouth.

At Portsmouth, later that morning, Saunders, commander of the troops there, wrote to General Fairfax, and the courier was soon on his way: 'Our God has done his work for us, all things are quiet in the island, the king went without any opposition to Hurst Castle and is there now; your work is now before you.'

December 1648

'He vacillates, Elizabeth.'

Henry Ireton sat with his mother-in-law in the damp parlour in Drury Lane, a lonely home of late with no sharing of the bed. Above the crowded London roofs shone the weak afternoon sun; a little blessed the parlour floor through leaded windows.

'Light without warmth,' said Elizabeth; and Ireton smiled at the assault. He'd heard it said of him before. Oliver remained in the north, outside Pontefract where he laid siege. Elizabeth had last seen her husband in late July. It was now the start of December, with no sign of Advent, the season recently banned by the Presbyterians. 'He is perhaps less certain than you, Henry.'

She would defend her husband stoutly in his absence . . . and only there.

'He knows what he must do, Mother, but attempts not to do it.'

'He is fighting.'

'He is not fighting, Elizabeth – he's drifting. He has Lambert with him. Lambert could take care of the siege; it's Pontefract, not Rome. He averts his eyes and drifts.'

Elizabeth knew of Oliver's drifting. It was not a good sign.

'And what must he do?' she asked, as if Ireton was a know-all to be humoured.

'He must bring the king to trial.'

'That is your solution.'

'And yours as well.'

'Not mine, Henry. You will not name me in your disloyal band.'

Authority had to be respected. Elizabeth was quite clear on that.

'It is the only solution,' said Ireton. 'Since the king took this nation into another war. And that war has warped Oliver, broken him. He's a different man, Elizabeth, believe me. Lost . . . harder.'

Elizabeth would not admit that Henry was right, that her husband struggled as never before. She would not grant him this affirmation.

'But not yet as hard as you, I'd wager,' she said.

'I was unaware that you did.'

It was almost flirtatious, but Elizabeth would not be charmed. She had respect for her cold fish of a son-in-law, but he wasn't someone you liked ... though perhaps Bridget had feelings for him? They seemed an honourable couple, not gay in any manner but honourable enough. And Henry was not afraid to act, a trait that Elizabeth privately applauded. When the king and parliament had ignored the army's 'Remonstrance', Henry had removed the vague Colonel Hammond from his position as governor of the island. He had then taken the king – in the early hours, they said – and placed him in Hurst Castle. And in a short while, as he'd made plain, he would deal with parliament and conduct a 'most necessary purge'. Her husband may vacillate, but not Henry.

'Oliver tells me he seeks other ways,' she said.

'Other ways?'

'Ways other than a trial. He is a royalist, Henry, as are my children. We are all royalists here. You will not find any in this house who are anti-monarchical.'

It was true: Bridget and her siblings all favoured kings and queens. Ireton had to endure this division daily, even though it made no sense.

'A king who has twice dragged them and their father into the mud and blood of war?' There was a pause and Ireton looked out of the window, at everything and nothing. 'And yet still Oliver wishes to save him.' He spoke with a resigned manner, staring at his own incomprehension.

'For which he should be applauded,' said Elizabeth.

Ireton decided on another tack. 'He sent Denbigh to speak with Charles about abdication.'

'And perhaps that is the way now. I know Oliver thinks so.'

'It has always been his hope, that Charles will choose to abdicate, with one of his sons succeeding him on the throne.'

'It was my idea before his.' Elizabeth puffed herself a little. She had suggested it first to Oliver, which he sometimes forgot. Why do men forget who gave them their ideas? 'It would seem the right way forward,' she added, because there was a right and a wrong way for Elizabeth.

'Well, Denbigh is the king's friend, so who better to persuade him, you might imagine?'

'A good choice.'

'But Charles would not even see him,' said Ireton, in the manner of a trap closing.

'Oh.' This was news to her and she was disappointed. Charles should have seen Denbigh. Why would he not see Denbigh?

'He sent him away without an audience,' said Ireton. 'Humiliating for Denbigh, of course, but Charles is more stubborn than a stain and quite beyond saving. He never needed counsellors to mislead him; he misleads himself.' He drank his beer from the pewter cup and added: 'The only visitor the king has agreed to see is a woman called Jane Whorwood.'

He let the name hang in the air.

'And who is she?'

'An associate of the king.'

'An associate?'

'What other word is there?'

'I hope you do not imply—'

'I imply nothing.'

'Charles and Henrietta have always been most devoted. '

'Though apart for some while.'

'As I have been from Oliver. Does that mean—'

'It means that there is no more devoted husband in Christendom than your Oliver.'

'The king and Jane pray together, no doubt,' said Elizabeth. The alternative did not bear thinking about, really not. There was a pause. Ireton wondered if she wished him to leave, but she didn't.

'And so the king is to be tried?' she asked, with a tight jaw.

She wished to speak with Henry to clarify the situation. Oliver's letters spoke of God and his desire to be with her; but clarified little, invaded by every possibility, but convinced of none.

'That must be our path.'

'And executed?'

Everyone in London knew that there could not be one without the other.

'What options does he leave us?' said Ireton. 'He leaves us none. We cannot banish him and risk future invasion. Imprison him, and we provide ourselves with a hub for every spoke of discontent. And we can hardly put a new king on the throne while the old king lives. It is not like buying a second pair of shoes.'

*

An urgent knocking on the Strand front door, followed by a wordless climb up the stairs; and now she stood breathless in his work place of charts, chalk dust and geometry sets. Jane was straight down to business.

'I need a chart for the king – quickly.'

Lilly smiled, as to a child asking for a blue rose. 'I will not do you a chart for the king, Mrs Whorwood.'

'I have come for that reason, Mr Lilly. It's why I'm here.'

'Then you will be disappointed.'

'I cannot be disappointed, Mr Lilly. This must go well for me.' She was close to tears. William sighed.

'The king is beyond the stars now,' he said, quietly.

'Beyond the stars?' She put down her travel bag and with her fingers brushed down her lacy yellow dress, which to Lilly looked tired: a garment that once spoke of life and delight but worn out now with travel and the stains of life. 'How can anyone be beyond the stars?'

William Lilly cleared away his charts; it was the end of the day. Jane had arrived unannounced and in a fluster. Lilly was too tired to join her in her anxious state.

'The heavens speak of disposition, Mrs Whorwood.'

'I'm Jane, if you don't mind.'

'The disposition of the elements towards certain outcomes. The stars can speak of favourable times, but of themselves they cannot change the hearts of men.'

'Are the stars then quite dumb about his fate?'

'He goes from strength to weakness, Jane. He goes hastily to worse and then worser.'

'How can you say that?' She was shocked.

'How can I not? Many tides have come for the king, Jane, kind tides – but he has caught none of them.'

'The king should not need tides.'

'We all need tides.'

'The king needs loyal subjects!'

'The king needs friends.'

'He has friends! Good friends, friends who would do anything for his liberty and well-being.' There was no doubting of whom she spoke.

'You have become such a friend, I understand. Some wine?' His physic could do with some wine.

'You "understand"?' said Jane. She didn't want wine. 'What is that supposed to mean?'

'It means that here is a small island and your business with the king is well known.'

'To one with parliamentary ears, perhaps; to one collecting stories. Did you speak of my last visit to anyone?'

Lilly did not answer and a rage came over Jane – or a melancholy she'd never known. She felt unheard in the world, quite unheard. An abandoned king, left all alone; yet it was her own abandonment she felt most keenly.

'He is abandoned, Mr Lilly! Charles is like Christ in Gethsemane while his disciples sleep!'

'And who are you, Jane – Mary Magdalene?'

'I do this for Charles and Henrietta – always for Henrietta!'

'I do not require your reasons, Jane. I am not the confessor you need.'

*

Charles looked out to sea, a small figure silhouetted against a winter horizon.

Two large soldiers talked nearby. He had attempted conversation, the common touch on display; it was why his people loved him. But on this occasion, his subjects chose surly silence, as if he was of no matter, no longer a king. He'd heard the phrase 'man of blood' on their lips, which was hardly true – he was a man

213

of peace, always a man of peace, now cruelly exiled to a bleak outpost . . . the bleakest of all: Hurst Castle.

He knew its history for he was an intelligent man. Built by Henry VIII, it stood solidly at the seaward end of the shingle spit that snaked for a mile and a half beyond Milford-on-Sea – a coastal fortress protecting the westward approach to the Solent. But it made a better prison, a rough lodging house, with its tunnels, dungeons and distance from the world. On clear days, he could glimpse the Isle of Wight and the Needles, which he had now grown to miss. He stood here less than a mile from his former home, but in truth much further away.

And there was nothing to do. Beside this winter sea with its dangerous currents, Charles would watch ships pass, by way of entertainment and longing. He would like to sail east himself.

And looking to France, he thought of Henrietta and his family, and he wondered how they might help him now. Henrietta would be doing her best, he was sure of that, though she did fade in his memory a little, as people do with the passage of time . . . four years now since they'd said goodbye, and he'd ridden his horse along the coast until he could see her ship no more. He'd lost the sound of her voice first. How had she sounded? He loved her, of course; but the loved can fade, first from our minds, then from our hearts. This is how it is, Charles assured himself. Perhaps he would compose around that theme tonight in his spiritual writings. He had been allowed to keep his quills and parchment, and in the evenings, by candlelight, he wrote devotional words to strengthen the weak who would come after him.

He was encouraged to hear that he would soon be taken to Windsor, for Hurst was no place for a king. Perhaps negotiations could then resume, though there seemed little to talk about. They must see sense in the end, surely? Jane always said they'd see sense in the end and her words were relief for his spirit. Hurst Castle was a brief darkness, a passing shadow; one must presume light ahead, a hopeful dawn. He turned his eyes from the horizon, and, feeling the chill, began the walk back to his cell.

The soldiers followed, laughing about some matter or other.

*

At the other end of the country, Cromwell lay in a tent outside Pontefract.

It was a freezing sky but no cold kept him wakeful tonight – only a churning spirit. He was lodged, like a wet leaf in a drain; he shouldn't be here. He knew that Lambert could handle this siege. Lambert was competent; there was nothing that required Oliver to remain ... apart from his lack of decision. How could he return south when he did not know his mind? It had been a slow falling of snow, but now it lay thick across his mental path: a pilgrim lost. Circumstance had removed all signs from view. Where to go? He would rise now, in the dark, he would walk and he would talk, speak out loud in the cold air, speak to the stars, to those fine portals of light in the darkness.

'This I know,' he declared to the heavens, 'that I seek no vengeance on a fallen enemy; that is not my heart. You know that is not my heart! And the death of a king, this is no small matter, no careless act in this nation of royalists. And perhaps I am one of them, a royalist myself, I believe so ... though maybe there are other ways.' What was he saying? 'And I am in no mind to make a martyr out of a miscreant, which appears his desire. I think he pursues the martyr's mantle now. Do you not think so?' He paused for some response from the heavens. 'And we must consider reaction to such a killing, for reaction there will be. Can we withstand them all in their shock and fury: Presbyterians, French, Dutch and Scots? I tire of the fight; I am tired; I have fought too much and for too long ...

'Yet I know this. The Lord has witnessed against the king, this is most clear. Do you not see this? At Naseby and Preston, the Lord has made his will most evident. So surely the faithful must witness also? And perhaps a trial, lawfully undertaken, would be a lesson ... a lesson for all time against encroaching kings. I am not against masters, I am no scraggy Leveller! You know this. But they must be good masters, masters of substance, or else their rank and prerogative become a meaningless thing. Why reverence a brocaded puppet larded by a priest with oil? Kings have their place; but they must also know their place.'

215

A change passed through him . . . some strange forming of his soul . . . a moment of peace, unknown for a long while. He gazed again at the heavens, and his final words to the Yorkshire sky spoke themselves, spoke through him, unthought and surprising – but clear: 'What must be done, Oliver, must be done. Now is the time.'

He returned to his tent and lay down in sweet clarity until, beneath the stars in the Pontefract dark, Cromwell slipped into the sleep of the decided.

*

A few days later, after the rutted journey south, Oliver stood up to speak in parliament, a gathering smaller in number than the one he'd left. He noted the spare seats: all Ireton's work. The purge he had promised was duly delivered. All king-licking Presbyterians were gone; only true hearts remained in the chamber.

Wood had informed him of these events when he reached Cheshunt.

'It was yesterday that your son-in-law stripped parliament bare. I presume you knew?' Cromwell smiled. 'Then you must practise feigning surprise, Oliver. It is best you are not attached to this.'

Ireton had done his work. Made resilient in the matter by Ludlow, he'd given Colonel Pride his favourite task, the sort he enjoyed – wielding the sword of judgement, separating the sheep from the goats. He'd stood at the doorway of the Commons with a dour band of well-armed soldiery, and there, on the morning of 6 December, stopped from entering any treacherous members who had supported the hypocritical Treaty of Newport.

'How many MPs were turned away?' Oliver asked.

'Two hundred and thirty-one,' said Wood.

'Leaving two hundred and ten honest and godly souls to continue with business.'

'The leaflets are not kind, Oliver. They call it a "rump"; the arse of the Long Parliament.'

'Better a faithful arse than a treasonous head, Wood.'

And it was this rump that Cromwell addressed now, much stirred in his soul. After months of indecision – months spent in the wilderness of unknowing, seeking the face of the Lord – he now

216

knew what to do. And there was none keener to hear his intentions than his son-in-law, sitting four seats away.

'If any man, whatsoever,' declared Oliver, his hand closed around his sword butt – 'if any man whatsoever has carried on the design of deposing the king and disinheriting his posterity' – he looked around a little – 'or if any man has yet such a plan in mind,' and he looked around again, 'then I say this: he should be called the greatest traitor and rebel in the world! Yes, the greatest traitor!'

There were surprised faces around him; the godly were shocked and Ireton tense. Where was Oliver taking this matter now?

'But since the providence of God has cast this way upon us,' he continued, 'since the providence of God has made our path clear – and really, my friends, it could not be clearer – I cannot but submit this day to providence. I submit! Let providence reign! This king must face trial!'

'Hear, hear!' shouted the Long Parliament's rump.

So a trial there would be; a trial of the king, when such a thing was quite impossible.

January 1649

Charles returned to London, seven years after his leaving.

It had been a hasty departure back then, mobbed by a crowd of undesirables – tradesmen, apprentices and seamen, that sort, who'd displayed the rough badinage of alcohol and violence; truly a day when it seemed a treason to be sober. And such ill-language! Charles had not been harmed, not physically at least. But how unnecessary! he thought.

'Privilege of parliament! Privilege of parliament!' they had shouted, as if that meant anything at all. What about the privileges of the king? They seemed quite forgetful of those!

But in the face of such violence, it had been wise to consider his position. And a week later, they had left the capital and their Whitehall home, sitting in the cabin at the stern of the barge, Queen Henrietta on his arm. She had appeared quite fearless, of course.

'I do not give zem ze pleasure,' she'd said, looking straight at the jeering crowds. And she passed her courage to him as he glimpsed the gilded weathervanes of Whitehall Palace, before the boat turned westwards, alongside the abbey and then under the great east window of St Stephen's Chapel – the Commons' chamber and the source of so much woe.

But that was seven years ago. Since then he'd started and lost two wars, mislaid his marriage, lost his freedom, drifted from his children, lied and conspired, joined naughtily with Jane, failed to escape and disappointed all negotiators but the Scots. It might not appear glorious to earthly eyes; this was so. But it was glorious in heaven, for what else had been possible against the small-minded tyranny of the people? How were they all so blind to the vision of Rubens in the Banqueting Hall?

He was a little scared now, with no Henrietta to stiffen his resolve.

'But I will not give them the pleasure,' he said to himself from his new holding in the Westminster house of Thomas Cotton, who had vacated his home to allow for royal detention.

*

It was the morning of the trial and the commissioners were gathered in their warm winter finery. They met in the Painted Chamber at the back of the Great Hall and the mood was nervous. There were no nerves among the preachers, who called the day 'momentous' and the gateway to the new Jerusalem. But Jerusalem did not feel near. There was unease in the ranks, uncertainty about the nature of the proceedings and the legal grounds for what they were about to do.

'How do you put a king on trial? You might as well try and pluck the sun from the sky.' And this was a parliamentarian speaking.

Hugh Peters had delivered a sermon to the assembly. He didn't hold back; he never did. But it was reckoned more uplifting for him than for his congregation, who felt queasy and ill-disposed. They were to try a king, the Lord's anointed ... and none had done this before. And then, after a long prayer – similar in tone to the sermon – Charles was seen to be arriving, a little early, as though he wished to catch them out. They looked out of the window and felt unprepared. He was now walking with guards through the garden towards them, and they were not ready. Not one of the commissioners in their heart imagined themselves to be ready.

Cromwell spoke out: 'My masters, he is come, he is come. The king is come.' He was trying to calm them but only consternation spread. 'We see him draw near – a little early is better than late! And in our hearts, approach now the great work that our whole nation will be full of.' He stood on the plinth vacated by the preacher. 'Therefore I desire we resolve what answer we shall give the king when he comes before us.'

A sense of foreboding prevailed.

'I know this man. I have spoken with him a great deal. And the first question he will ask is this: by what authority as commissioners do we try him? This shall be his question.'

And that explained the foreboding, for there was no answer from those around; and where could such an answer be found? There was no ancient manual to consult, no precedent in any known law. And then Henry Marten, never short of a word, rose to his feet and spoke simply and confidently: 'In the name of the Commons in parliament assembled and of all the good people of England. That is the authority by which we speak!'

Silence . . . and then around him, the outbreak of relief.

The words had just come to him, as occasionally they do, formed and ready. His wife had said something similar as they'd parted that morning – very similar – but he had given her lines their final shape, and he now sat down in some exhilaration. He was pleased for himself and for the happiness around him – relief that was physical. Faces relaxed; tight stomachs were eased. They had an answer, as the king approached through the garden.

'We must use those words,' said John Bradshawe, who was to be president of this trial. 'Note them, please,' he added to one of his clerks. 'In the name of the Commons in parliament and, er, whatever followed.'

The king had now entered the building.

*

And here was the setting for the first and last trial of an English monarch: the Great Hall of Westminster! Such a court was a thing unknown and unheard of, created from nothing. But the traders' booths had been cleared away and their complaints quietened by buff-coated troopers – men made mean by war and now billeted at Whitehall. And with the sellers removed, the south end of the hall hosted a wooden platform, separated from the rest of the space by a barrier three feet high.

The hall itself had two gangways in the shape of a cross, separating the four quarters where the public would be squeezed on benches, or pressed up standing against the wall; this is how it would be when the gates opened. In more comfort (though not much) and higher up, would be those in the two small galleries above the platform, which looked down on the commissioners. The commissioners would be judge and jury in this affair, sitting on benches covered in scarlet cloth at the back of the platform, facing out from beneath the great south window.

In the front row of commissioners, in the middle, was the raised desk of the president, John Bradshawe. He had been plucked from legal obscurity (and some said incompetence) to preside over the trial, and no one's first choice. He'd merely been the first lawyer to say yes after many had declined. What sane man would preside over such an event as this? And Mr Bradshawe came prepared, wearing metal lining inside his hat for fear of attack; the good behaviour of the public could not be guaranteed today. Beneath him, as a thin wall between himself and the mob, the court clerks were seated, alongside the mace and sword of state.

And there was the king's seat – or was it a throne? At the edge of the dais, on the spectators' right, was a crimson velvet armchair for Charles. He would sit with his back to the body of spectators. There was no defence council ready on his behalf – for what defence could there be? And anyway, Charles was intent on presenting his own.

On the left of the stage was the door that led to St Stephen's Chapel where the Commons met in ever-decreasing numbers.

How would the day go?

*

Charles was led into the hall, stately in demeanour, between two guards. He liked a stage; he knew where he was on a stage. Relationships, he didn't understand at all. But a stage – with its distance and formality – he could manage well.

'He has lost his throne but not his majesty,' as one royalist hack would write on witnessing the king's entrance.

Charles was surprised that no audience was there; he had been told his trial would be public and earnestly hoped as much. He would like his people to be with him, to witness his calm defiance. And they would be allowed in ... but not yet. There was court business to be undertaken first. Charles, meanwhile, cut a small figure on the dais alongside his tall guards. Had they deliberately been chosen to dwarf him? The king wore a black hat which he would not remove, and this was the first source of trouble.

221

'The defendant will remove his hat,' said the clerk.

But the defendant would not remove his hat and explained his reasons. 'I believe the removal of my hat would be a mark of deference to the present authorities,' said Charles, patting it more firmly on to his skull. 'And there is no deference; no acknowledgement at all.'

'This goes well,' muttered Ireton.

The forty-nine-year-old defendant had a grey beard – greyer for the past year – and his face was drawn, haggard; though peacefully resigned. According to Jane Whorwood, he had looked thus since his Christmas spent at Windsor, where he was taken after three bleak weeks at Hurst Castle. 'From the worst castle to the best,' as he'd declared on leaving that hateful place.

It was there, so some said, that he put all pretence of negotiation aside and embraced the martyr's way, setting his face towards the cross. Charles the Martyr, this was his destiny, and there was some peace in that discovery . . . though another escape plan had been ready as he left Hurst Castle, organized by Jane and involving a well-regarded mare called Eager.

On his departure from Hurst, he was told a horse awaited him in Bagshot, 'the swiftest creature in England'.

'There is no faster horse in Christendom,' said the ciphered note from Jane, passed on to him by the cook. 'Others have failed you, but I will not!'

It was to be the king's final attempt to escape, and was to occur on the journey to Windsor. Charles was to slip the guard of Colonel Harrison and be away on this fastest of beasts, the horse they called Eager, waiting for him in Bagshot.

But the cool hand of providence conspired against him again; and the king's chaplain, Father Downe, passed on the sad news.

'The horse we had hoped for has gone lame, your majesty.'

'Lame? Is he a parliamentarian?'

The chaplain travelled with the king to give him the sacraments; and to help with plans for escape.

'We have news only that the horse is indisposed, your majesty.'

'Eager is indisposed.'

'Yes, sire.'

'Poorly named.'

'The Lord gives and the Lord takes away.'

'I believe I've seen more taking of late.'

'So we travel now to Windsor, sire . . . with no other excursion foreseen.'

'I see,' said Charles, as one in a trance. 'The horse has fallen lame.'

'Yes, sire.'

'The fastest horse in England.'

'No longer, your majesty.'

'You can leave me now.'

'If your majesty requires anything further—'

'You can leave me now.'

'Perhaps your majesty would like the comfort of the sacraments?'

'You can leave me now.'

And so it was that he'd arrived at Windsor on 23 December, with the same slow horse on which he'd started out, while Eager recuperated in Bagshot. The travel had not been unpleasant in itself; he had liked his escort, Colonel Harrison, which came as a surprise. At the journey's start, he'd imagined Harrison would murder him – he was in no doubt of this, for this butcher's son was an infamous republican. Indeed, it was he who had coined the unfortunate phrase 'man of blood', the most common army epithet for Charles.

Yet Charles had found him to be both courteous and correct as they travelled together. 'If he had not been a soldier,' said Charles, 'and if I had met him before all this, I should not have harboured an ill opinion of him.'

And, strangely, Harrison's face was the first he saw as he entered the Great Hall and looked across at the commissioners. He did not seek anyone's eye, but maybe he looked for a friend. Charles smiled at the colonel, remembering their conversations; Harrison nodded in return, perhaps a little shamed, for he was no friend to this tyrant who deserved only death. And the colonel had seen much death in his time, both on the battlefield and at home, where not one of his three children had survived infancy. Thomas Harrison knew the task of this court, and would not flinch from seeing it through.

Charles looked around for comfort. Was Jane here?

The president of the court, John Bradshawe, was reading the charges.

'Charles Stuart, you are arraigned in this manner and in this day in relation to your chief and prime responsibility for all the treasons, murders, ravages, burnings, spoils, desolations, damages and mischief to this nation – enacted by you from a wicked design to erect and uphold for yourself unlimited and tyrannical power, to rule according to your own desires and to overthrow the rights and liberties of the people of England.'

Charles laughed at the word 'treasons'. That seemed to him most amusing, that a king could somehow be accused of treason against his own person. Risible! And then came 'the moment', as Ireton later called it. It was the moment when all might have collapsed . . . and Ireton found himself squeezing Cromwell's hand in fear. And the moment occurred when the king tried to interrupt proceedings by reaching forward to touch the prosecutor, John Cook, with his cane.

'What's he doing?' whispered Henry as Charles leaned forward with his stick.

They then watched in shock as the silver tip of the cane fell off and rolled across the stage. There was silence in the hall, all eyes on the metal ball, now come to rest. The king responded first, indicating to the prosecutor that he should pick it up. And this was when Ireton squeezed his father-in-law's hand, hardly able to watch.

'Do not pick it up,' he said to himself seeing the dark panorama of possibility. If Cook picked up the silver tip, the king's trial would be over . . . and theirs would begin. Charles' authority would be established, the king in command again. Ireton could see it all, if Cook bent down now to assist the king.

'He will pick it up,' said Cromwell gloomily.

'Don't!' muttered Ireton under his breath . . . and he didn't. John Cook stayed standing, ignoring the king, his divinely appointed ruler. And so Charles had to get up from his chair and, bowing down, picked up the silver tip himself. There followed a large release of breath among the commissioners, and Ireton released Cromwell's hand.

'Thank God,' he said. The law had not bowed to Charles. He had bowed to the law; this was Henry's view. The man before them was no longer a ruler of men but a prisoner of the court.

'I swear he's never picked up anything in his life!' joked a soldier, for the moment had passed and all could proceed; and Cromwell would never mention the squeezing of his hand.

*

With the charges read, the president announced, with some pomp, that the public may now be allowed in: 'Let the nation in to see justice done!'

The large doors of the hall opened and there was a thunderous rush of folk, soldiers instantly pushed back. Like water hurtling over rocks, they surged forward, making for the benches, shouting and jostling with soldiers who held their lines as best they could. Above the commissioners, and behind, the galleries filled as well, gentlemen and ladies of substance taking their seats. Charles could not help but look around at the filling hall; these were his friends, his subjects – though never quite as close. His subjects felt unnaturally close, which was not the true order of things.

He turned back towards the commissioners and composed himself. And when the court returned to calm, like that before a performance, Charles spoke.

'The soldiers?' he asked theatrically. 'Are they here to make difficult my escape? Or perhaps to protect my judges from the people?'

There was uncomfortable movement among the commissioners and cautious laughter in the Great Hall, as the coughing quietened.

'Still glad of a public trial, Oliver?' asked Ireton.

It was the most miserable of winter days and the waiting crowd had been standing in the snow too long . . . and then another moment. Charles was asked by the clerk how he pleaded; he did not answer, staring ahead in silence. He was asked again and then again, but he would not say.

President Bradshawe intervened. 'How do you plead?' he asked. 'We will not ask again.'

But Charles had a question of his own: 'I plead with a question and the question is this: by what power am I called hither?'

'They have no power!' shouted a woman from the gallery. Heads turned sharply and Cromwell muttered something to Ireton.

'It's the Fairfax woman,' he said. 'Why was she allowed in?'

'It's a public trial,' said Ireton. 'I forget whose wish that was.'

Lady Fairfax was the wife of the army's commander-in-chief – but no friend of the army now.

'She was a friend once, was she not?' queried Ireton.

'A family friend who has forgotten her friendship,' replied Oliver. 'The last kind word I heard from her mouth was at your wedding, Henry.'

'It seems a long time ago. These days, she appears as Queen Fairfax and quite the ruler of their marriage.'

Her husband was not in attendance today, despite being called as a commissioner. He was skulking somewhere – or locked by his wife in the privy, for she delighted in his absence. When his name was called out, she had loudly declared: 'He has more wit than to be here!'

She needed quietening, that was clear, though who was to do it, less so.

And then Bradshawe, the president, replied to Charles, reading his lines from the clerk's notes. 'By what power are you called, Charles Stuart?' (He enjoyed speaking to the king in this way.) 'By the power of the Commons in parliament assembled and of all the good people of England.'

'That's a lie!' shouted Queen Fairfax.

'It is no lie,' declared Bradshawe.

Don't get into a conversation with the woman, thought Cromwell.

Lady Fairfax, shouting: 'Not half, not a quarter of the people of England are with you! This charge is made by rebels and traitors! No law could be found in the history of England by which a king can be tried—'

'Will the lady please quieten herself!?' Now Bradshawe was shouting.

'So they must ferret about and find a gentleman from Holland, named Isaac Dorislaus. Yes, it was a Dutchman who framed these charges! A foreigner!'

'Madam!' shouted Bradshawe, but Mrs Fairfax didn't care. She was standing now.

'Isaac Dorislaus is a lawyer with a fondness for antiquity, who lifts up a stone and finds under it an ancient Roman law which declares that a military body can legally overthrow a tyrant!'

'How does she know about Dorislaus?' asked Cromwell.

'How do you think?' replied his son-in-law. 'She shares a pillow with the general.'

'Antiquity is sometimes true, madam,' said Bradshawe, drawing gratefully on his legal background.

'Then why do the army not overthrow themselves? For they are the tyrants here!'

There was laughter in the hall and it was Charles who calmed them down ... which served only to make things worse.

'England has never been an elective kingdom,' he said quietly, wishing to approach the matter by another path. No one responded, Bradshawe still confused as to whether the trial had actually begun. So Charles continued: 'I am a monarch not by election but by inheritance.'

'Hear, hear!' shouted a lone voice.

'Thus to acknowledge a usurping authority, like the one before me this day, would be a betrayal of sacred trust. So I must ask again: by what authority – and by that I mean, by what lawful authority – am I here?'

He paused, pleased at their discomfort. Bradshawe had given his answer and found it rejected, and as he didn't have another, he looked across to Cromwell who glowered.

'For, as we know,' said Charles, surprisingly free from his stammer, 'there are many unlawful authorities in the world. Thieves and robbers gather by the highways, authorities in their way ... yet we elevate them not.' And now he smiled for a moment, before seriousness struck again. 'Remember I am your king, your lawful king. Remember that well.'

'God bless your majesty!' cried a voice from the hall.

Charles paused with pleasure. The clerk was aware that Charles had not yet made a plea concerning innocence or guilt, and that the court could not therefore legally proceed – though it was proceeding, in a manner, led by the defendant and his supporters.

'I say it again: remember I am your king, your lawful king.'

'God bless your majesty!'

A second and third voice now joined in.

'Why doesn't Bradshawe intervene?' asked Ireton of Cromwell; but Charles would not be stilled.

'What sins you bring on your heads this day, my friends, and what judgement upon this land – the judgement of God.'

'Preston was God's judgement!' shouted a gaunt-eyed soldier who Charles smiled at . . . and then ignored.

'So think well upon what you do in this place,' said Charles. 'Ponder the weight of this time, before you go from one sin to a greater sin. For one moment leads to another, and what is lost can never be reclaimed.'

'You're a man of blood!' called out the rough voice of another soldier, who had lost two brothers at Marston Moor. 'A traitor!'

'It is Cromwell who is the traitor!' replied Lady Fairfax in a loud voice. 'Him!'

She pointed down towards Cromwell, who didn't move. Had former friendship come to this? And as her taunting continued, encouraging grunts of support from the crowd, action was finally taken. Cromwell caught the eye of Colonel Bawdsley, formerly a drayman, who threatened to order his soldiers to shoot into the public gallery unless the lady chose silence.

'They will fire upon you and you shall be much bloodied!' he declared, hoping this would please his lieutenant-general. But Cromwell only sighed. The musket was accurate enough in war, where general slaughter was appropriate, but aimed at the gallery, a few commissioners would be sent sprawling as well – and they did not have any to spare. After some discussion with Lady Fairfax – giddy with the attention and with ten muskets now pointing towards her – she was persuaded to leave the courtroom, though not silently.

'Does truth make the air unclean here?' she enquired. 'Is that the reason I am hustled in this petulant manner? Long live the king! And I speak for us all. I speak for England. Long live the king!'

Robert Hammond watched Lady Fairfax leave; in his heart, he applauded.

He too sat in the gallery, a row back from the fiery soul, and while it was unseemly for a woman to speak in such a forward manner, who could disagree with the sentiments? He surveyed the scene below him and found it unutterably bleak: soldiers minding the aisles in a courtroom where only one outcome was possible. He had feared this, had always feared this, ever since Charles had arrived in his care on the island. Hammond had fought for parliament, and gladly so, but not for rule by soldiers. The line between deceit and honour was ever more obscure.

'We fought against misgovernment – we didn't fight against the king,' he'd said to Ireton during an unpleasant exchange at Windsor. They came face to face there after he was abducted by Ewer on the road.

'And what if the king is the misgovernment?' said Ireton.

'He was perhaps let down by his advisors,' said Hammond. 'Not well served—'

'Not well served?' interrupted Ireton. 'Who appointed his advisors? They did not appear pristine from the soil, Robert! If his advisors were fools, perhaps a fool appointed them!'

Hammond looked down on Ireton now and eased himself back a little, hiding his form, for he was a royalist today and would prefer no army eyes upon him. Ireton's gaze did rove a little, glancing up and around; Cromwell's stayed singly on the king. Though as Lady Fairfax was finally evicted from the court, Oliver glanced up and their eyes met. Hammond was the first to turn away.

*

Charles was buoyant as Lady Fairfax was removed, for he'd found Jane.

After some discreet scouring, he'd discovered her seated in the gallery near the despicable Hammond. Now, there was a disappointing man! But Jane was true: she'd said she would be here for the trial, that she'd never leave him. He nodded graciously towards her, with fond memories of the guardroom and elsewhere, though particularly the guardroom. She replied with a nervous smile, which covered a mind considering a thousand different sorrows and fresh plans for freedom.

But the king's buoyancy was mainly in consideration of the commissioners. He was aware that one hundred and thirty-five of them had been appointed for this trial, chosen from a supposed cross-section of English notability – landowners, MPs and army officers . . . those reckoned to have enough of Cromwell in their veins to behave. But here was the interest for Charles: as he looked around now, he could count no more than seventy before him. This left sixty-five absentees, which was intriguing; it suggested that even his enemies concurred with the illegality of this gathering. So perhaps there were more twists ahead, with Fairfax – thanks to his wife – now famously absent. He had beaten the king in battle, but refused to be his judge in peace.

And Charles was buoyed also by the support of the people, crammed in around him. He was their king, was still their king, his seat here a throne. He'd been too long away, he could see this now, and they needed him, for he held their lives together – unlike the cold soldiers: 'like blocks of ice in the thawing winter lake', he would write. But around him was the warm and swirling support of the people, allowed in without restriction, and many more left disappointed outside.

How they loved him.

*

The trial, though going badly, had not been hastily conceived.

'It must be public,' Cromwell had said in his Drury Lane parlour some weeks before. Ireton's face wasn't sure, but his father-in-law was convinced. 'There will be no secrecy here; everything is to be done in the light of day, as befits God's people. It will be a public trial!'

And surprisingly, Ludlow agreed. Edmund Ludlow – the cushion-beater – was republican and Baptist, fierce at both and a man with Leveller sympathies. He'd helped Ireton purge parliament and it was Henry who'd brought him to Drury Lane today. Ireton needed an antidote to Cromwell's meandering and Edmund was that man. With an insatiable aggression towards the king and his ways, he would make Oliver listen; and no one would harm cushions in Elizabeth's house.

'He sinned openly,' said Edmund, 'so he should be tried openly.' Oliver nodded, glad of his agreement. 'He must be sentenced and executed in the face of the world,' continued Ludlow, 'and not secretly made away with, by poisonings – or other more private deaths.'

'We must have the trial, that is all I say,' said Ireton, wearily. 'Whether in sunlight, candlelight or darkness, I care not greatly.'

'I know what must be done,' replied Oliver. He spoke firmly but quietly, lest Elizabeth hear. He wished she was sewing with the poor women of Southwark, but this was not such a day. She was somewhere around.

'Though I will say this about a public trial,' said Ireton, 'and it's a warning: you will not make friends by opening the courtroom doors.'

Edmund looked at him. 'Do we need friends?' he asked. 'After all, Henry, you've managed without them thus far.'

Edmund was Edmund and would be ignored.

'What do you mean, Henry?' asked Oliver.

'You will simply make friends for Charles; that is what a public trial will do. They will take his side. The military way looks good in battle – but never in court.'

'They will see him as a man who ignores providence, as a man of blood,' protested Cromwell.

'No, they won't, Oliver. If you weren't at the battle, you neither see the blood nor feel the providential message. They will gaze only on long-suffering Charles, small Charles, gentle Charles, martyr Charles, father Charles, kind holder of the nation's soul.'

Henry's mind moved quicker than Oliver's, the future a clearer place; less attached to cloying notions of unity and purpose, which so slowed Cromwell's way. They did not ride a popular tide, this was the fact that Ireton could see, and consequently, the less public involvement the better.

'Maybe he will still negotiate. There is time.'

231

Ireton raised his eyebrows in dismay. Oliver was slipping again, and Edmund duly intervened.

'Oliver, the king will die in negotiation with both heaven and hell, and a third party if he can find it – the representatives of purgatory perhaps. But he will never say yes ... and he will never say no.'

'Quite,' said Cromwell, a little chastened. 'But definitely a public hearing.'

Ireton would settle for that.

*

And so on the first day of the trial, the public flocked in freely. But Charles did not recognize the illegal court; it was quite absurd, and therefore he could not plead ... though he still had much to say, much that he would like to speak about.

First of all, he wanted to explain that a king could not be held accountable by earthly judges – it simply could not be – and also, that nothing lawful could be derived from a body politic that had cut itself in half and removed one part of its indivisible law-making sovereignty.

'The fine figure of parliament has recently become a mere rump,' as one flier put it. 'An arse that passes much wind!'

And three weeks previously, this 'rump' had declared its heretical hand by asserting that 'the people are, under God, the source of all just power'. Laughable hypocrisy! For while claiming to represent the people this same parliament had banned, detained and excluded many of its own representatives! Power was not given to 'the people' as they claimed, but to *some* people.

So here in the Great Hall, it seemed to Charles that it was he – and not army or parliament – who both protected and guarded the people's rights, a noble cause indeed. Charles felt hugely noble today and with much to speak about.

But while he thought these things, he was not allowed to say them ... and was angry. He was silenced by a nervy Bradshawe and was finally taken from the court at the end of a day of accusation.

The soldiers shouted, 'Justice! Justice!' as he was led away. Others shouted, 'God save the king!'

'Why do they say that?' asked Ireton, genuinely bemused.

232

*

The day had been a disaster.

'The day went badly for us,' admitted Cromwell.

'It matters not,' said Ireton – though it did, for he did not wish to appear the fool. 'It is mere talk without substance.'

'But we do not appear well from the talking, Henry.'

'As I say, it's mere talk. There is only one result, and we need not concern ourselves greatly with how we get there.'

'We need a firmer hand tomorrow,' said Cromwell. 'And a better day.'

But the following day was worse.

The hall was packed again and John Bradshawe returned with his metal hat, presiding yet not presiding – for it was Charles who was doing that. And once again, he refused to plead when asked. So had the trial begun?

'We ought to put rocks on his chest like we would with any other man who refused to plead,' ventured Harrison, who favoured practical solutions.

And Ireton had suggested to Bradshawe, before the day began, that he drop the insistence that the king must plead one way or the other; that the whole process gave unnecessary attention to the accused.

'You cannot but give attention to the accused,' said Bradshawe, drawing again on his legal experience. 'That is the purpose of a court.'

'It is not the purpose of this court,' said Ireton. 'Or not that manner of attention.'

'Then perhaps you should not allow the nation through the door to listen!' said Bradshawe. Ireton agreed, but what could he say? 'Lady Fairfax was right in her way. No one wants this to be so.'

Ireton looked at him unbelievingly . . . while Bradshawe pondered his feet.

'You are now for the king, Bradshawe?'

'I am not for the king and never will be!' declared Bradshawe. 'I will die proud of these times!'

'You sound like one with a fancy for the king.'

'I merely know this nation of ours.'

And he also knew his wife Molly, who begged him each morning to spare his majesty.

'How could you, John Bradshawe, declare the Lord's anointed one to be guilty?' This is what she said in a hundred different ways. To which John replied every time that he would do only what the Lord commanded; so Molly knew what was coming.

'Then we must hope for his stammer to return,' said Ireton. 'He will impress less then.'

'If God so wills.'

But God didn't will, and instead of recognizing the court with a plea, Charles once again took the moment for his own cause; and, he sensed, the cause of those seated behind him.

'It is not my case alone,' he said firmly. 'It is the freedom and liberty of all the good people of England.'

'Does anyone really believe him?' asked Cromwell.

'Dung attracts many flies,' said Ireton.

'And you may pretend what you will, Mr Bradshawe – and you pretend much,' declared Charles, 'but I stand more for their liberties than you.'

And then he stood and turned slightly towards the crowd . . . and felt their gasp of appreciation.

'The accused will face the court!' declared Bradshawe. But Charles continued without a change of stance. If anything, he now faced his people more squarely.

'For if power without law may make law – and alter the fundamental laws of the kingdom – then I do not know any subject of the realm who may be assured of his life; or anything he can call his own!'

There were murmurs of approval which soon turned to outrage, and it happened like this. Colonel Hewson, one of the commanders of the guards, now stepped up on to the stage and walked across to Charles. What was happening? He was taller than the king, towering over him. He spoke with disdain.

'You set your people at war to keep hold of the trinkets of power. You care neither for the lives nor for the possessions of your subjects!'

234

Before Charles could reply, the colonel spat in the king's face, the slobber hitting the royal left eye, which opened in shock and then closed.

Silence broke out in the Great Hall, the hush of shock.

'God has justice in store,' said Charles, wiping the soldier's drivel with his handkerchief and returning to his seat. 'Both for you and for me, my friend.'

'God has justice in store!' echoed a female voice from the gallery.

Charles recognized the voice and looked up to see Jane looking down. He offered the faintest of acknowledgements and hoped she would not declare her love; he would not want that here, as the spitting colonel climbed down from the stage and rejoined his men. He stood awkwardly with them, glaring at the audience. The crowd was stirred, none believing what they'd seen – the king spat upon – but concern was held in, with no obvious disturbance.

It was, however, the end of the day's proceedings. Things had scarcely begun, yet already they were reckoned too broken for mending.

'This court is no longer in session,' said John Bradshawe, unsure how now to proceed.

'So soon?' asked Charles.

Bradshawe hoped that Molly would not hear of the morning's events – though she would, for everyone would hear that a soldier had walked on stage, shouted at the king and then spat in his face.

'What has happened to England?' asked John Stafford, Hammond's neighbour in the gallery. 'That a subject gobs on his king!'

'Indeed,' said Hammond. 'Can disrespect find better form than that?' He would not mention the fist that had knocked his majesty over.

*

Bradshawe, Ludlow and a slightly drunk Marten insisted that Cromwell listen.

Their leader had been taking the air in St James's Park, walking through the slush and snow with Ireton. The trial was a shambles to this point, and if God was here he was a master of disguise. Was the trial a sin? Charles had suggested as much and Elizabeth was

235

angry in the kitchen; there was much on Oliver's mind. So his son-in-law was his companion these days – almost his guard, ensuring no voice favourable to the king found his ear.

'You fear I will say yes to the wrong person, Henry?'

And Henry smiled, though without joy. Oliver was a determined man but porous to the charm and pleading of another; Henry knew this . . . and therefore a danger to himself and the cause.

'As the king is guarded, so is Oliver!' joked Marten, as they approached the hunched couple. Soldiers walked not far away, mindful of royal assassins. There were rumours.

'May the Lord's work be done,' said Bradshawe, striding forward.

'Perhaps he will need less guarding after our news,' said Ludlow, who thought Bradshawe an idiot. But it was to him the prison guards reported, as president of the court, and so he must be the bearer of the revelation.

'The three witches approach,' said Oliver when he saw them, and began to shoo them away, as a man who wanted peace. But they insisted he listen, and when Oliver talked over Bradshawe, Ludlow intervened.

'He does not regret the killings,' said Ludlow, catching Ireton's eye.

'Who?' asked Cromwell.

'His majesty.'

'He spoke with you, Edmund?' There was mockery in Cromwell's tone, and perhaps a little jealousy, supposing it was true.

'He has been speaking with his guards,' said Ludlow. 'Those who endure him at night as we must during the day.'

'They sought me out,' said Bradshawe, wishing to reclaim the story. 'He does not speak with the court – but he speaks with his gaolers!'

'And he tells them he does not regret the killings he caused,' said Ludlow, wishing for absolute clarity in the chill London wind.

'He says this?' said Cromwell, whose disappointment was manifest.

'The guards speak truthfully, I believe,' said Bradshawe. 'They say the king and his conscience claim no regrets at all.'

'It is there in his attitude, Oliver,' said Henry. 'It should not surprise; we have known this.'

And they had known it, though still it surprised, to hear it spoken. They all sensed the darkness fall over their leader's demeanour.

'Then we must encourage regret,' he said. 'For regret is a most godly virtue. Let us now find ourselves a warming fire . . .'

*

For the following three days, the trial of the king continued, but in private.

'Private – but not secret,' said Oliver, still trying to reassure, for many felt uncomfortable with this change.

But a different spirit ruled them now, a harder spirit, with news of the prison guards' words spreading fast. Oliver's fury, evident to all, made short and forceful work of all legal quibbles and pained consciences. He could be so strong.

'The king tells his gaolers he regrets not one single death,' he'd say, 'whereas I regret them all!'

For Ireton, nothing had changed. He'd thought it the best way to proceed all along, and the first two days of the trial did little to change his mind. In private session, without Lady Fairfax and the defendant, there would be fewer interruptions. And did the unrepentant king deserve any better? If he refused to acknowledge the court, did the court need to acknowledge him?

'The king has cunning,' said Ludlow, 'but it is a silly cunning – one that loses him all his friends. My mother used to warn me against such behaviour. Silly cunning only makes a fool of you, Edmund, she'd say.'

Bradshawe reminded the private gathering of the charges against Charles: that he took up arms against parliament and invited foreign armies to invade England. And in the secrecy of their own company, evidence was easy to find on both counts, even if some army witnesses wondered whether it was truer to say that parliament had taken up arms against Charles. However, this attitude was not deemed helpful in the circumstances – it was certainly not a thought to offer the ferocious Lady Fairfax – and so the hearing continued without further regard for the matter.

The main point – as witness after witness established – was that the king had fought against the lawfully elected parliament. Who may or may not have started it was not pertinent at this present time.

And he'd certainly invited the Scots.

*

'Have we perhaps met before, madam?'

'I would not know, Mr Hammond.'

'Yet you know my name.'

'I know Satan's name – but have never met him, to my knowledge.'

'I hope I am not Satan, madam.'

She was a striking lady: something both hard and soft about her.

'But related perhaps – for you are Mr Hammond, once of Carisbrooke Castle.'

'I am. But—'

'Where you failed to protect the king in his time of need.'

They were talking as the gallery emptied, having been sitting close to each other.

'I protected the king better than any man!' he complained in a loud voice, which he then regretted and hushed. He did not want his past made present here; it would not be well received. 'No man could have done more for the king.'

'But perhaps a woman did.'

And then it came to him, with a flood of fear . . . the ginger hair.

'Might you be Mrs Whorwood?' he queried. He remembered the warnings – and the rumours.

'Maybe.'

'I think more than *maybe!*'

'A name is not an offence, as far as I know,' said Jane. 'Though who can be sure these days?'

Hammond would reassure her, pacify her. She appeared nervous in manner. 'Nothing is ordinary, I grant you, madam. These days are difficult.'

'Difficult?' He had clearly upset her. 'Our king is crucified by lies and you announce it as merely "difficult"?'

'Our king has my support, Mrs Whorwood, but he lied to me every day I knew him.' This woman needed pulling in a little.

'How can a king lie to one with no right to know his business? He does not keep you informed, for he is king and you a subject . . . a subject in the pocket of Cromwell.'

'How would you know anything about such things?' He was hurt by that jibe.

'Cromwell wrote you letters. He was like a weight on your back, like a rider on a horse, exhorting you to imprison the king more securely and to listen only to the army.'

This talk was too familiar. 'Letters are a private affair. I don't know how—'

'And you never read mine – or those of the king?' Hammond kept silence. 'And on occasion,' she added in amazement, 'the king found you searching his bedroom while you imagined him busy elsewhere . . . searching the bedroom of the king!'

Did she know about the punch? He hoped she did not. But then really, why did he even concern himself with these matters now? What could it change?

'I'm not against you, Mrs Whorwood, believe me.'

'But are you for me?'

'*For* you?'

'I think I am clear.'

He wished to be out of the courtroom, to wash himself of the second day of the trial. But this woman pressed him, and blocked him from the staircase. They were now alone in the gallery, all others gone.

'And what exactly would one who was for you, be *for*?'

'There is still time.' Now she was whispering.

'Time for what?'

'Do you believe the king should die?' she asked.

Hammond looked around for snooping ears. There were none as far as he could see, though still a loud commotion below him, as soldiers struggled to empty the hall.

'I am not in favour of such a thing,' he said, 'and for that reason, I – and many others – are not sitting with the commissioners.' He had made a stand, and at some personal risk. Did she not appreciate this? 'You are hardly the king's only—'

'Then join with those who would see him free!'

Hammond laughed. 'You imagine the king can be stolen from Whitehall, so soaked with soldiery?'

'We can take him in St James's Park.'

'Not so easily done.'

'We have a guard on our side. They will walk him there.'

'Go back to your family, Mrs Whorwood.'

She drew nearer to him; she was a striking woman.

'You could visit Charles, make him aware of the plans. Tell him of our designs, that we have a boat ready for France.'

'Another one? Every boat in England has been ready at one time or another.'

Her face came close. He saw the skin, rutted by childhood disease, the blue-grey eyes alive with a plan.

'This is our moment – if you will join us.'

'You must think of something else to do,' he said moving back, stumbling on a chair. 'Really you must. This can't—'

'We will do it without you.'

'Really?' Was that a threat? 'And if I inform on your mischief?'

'You do not have the courage, Mr Hammond. I've always known you for a coward.'

And then she was gone down the stairs, as if too busy to stay with one so dumb, so lacking in spirit; and Hammond stood alone in the gallery. Should he go after her?

*

On 27 January, Charles, king of England, was declared guilty of the charges laid against him.

In the quiet privacy of the Painted Chamber, the English monarch was declared 'a tyrant, traitor, murderer and public enemy to the commonwealth of England'. The following day, he was brought again to the Great Hall to hear the outcome of his trial. Not all wished for this, Henry included, but Cromwell was insistent that all must be public; that there must be nothing private about their royal dealings, nothing covered over.

'We do what we do in the light!' he said, though the clouds were dark that day.

The hall was packed once again as the commissioners made their entrance and took their scarlet seats, less comfortable than they looked. They settled nervously, aware of their decision and troubled by it – or some at least. How would events conspire? The crowd settled, more silent than on those first two days. Some commissioners feared they'd revolt, there in the hall, and murder them all. What could the soldiers do if such an action was taken?

'I would like to speak,' said Charles, from his seat on the stage.

'You will not speak,' replied John Bradshawe. He was wearing a scarlet robe but kept his metal hat, which he felt he might need today, particularly on his return home to Molly; for he knew what must be done, the Lord's will in the matter. Charles again demanded that he be heard, that he had something particular to say, hitherto unexpressed.

'You would do well to hear me,' he said.

'I think not.'

'For what I report is most material to the peace of the kingdom,' Charles added. 'Most material.'

There was a compelling insistence in his words, as if he now spoke the truth – and he won a response in the commissioners' ranks. This was what they had wanted to hear. Perhaps even now matters could be altered?

'Is he offering concessions?' said one.

'Has this stubborn little man finally seen sense?' said another.

Though most commonly expressed was the question: 'Does he mean abdication?' Many hoped he did.

Everyone was looking at Bradshawe, who was looking at Cromwell. John Downes, a row behind them, leaned forward in agreement with the king's request.

'I say we hear him on this matter,' he said.

John Downes was the MP for Arundel in Sussex. He was a man made rich from his dealings in confiscated royalist estates. He was also a close friend of Oliver Cromwell – though not today.

'What ails thee, John?' asked Cromwell witheringly.

'Only the sense that . . . that perhaps the king should be heard, Oliver?'

'And providence spat upon?'

'I hardly said that.'

'This man has not recognized this court and yet wishes to lecture us further?'

'Well . . .'

'Sit back, John, sit back. I have wrath to spare today.'

The commissioners ceased to confer with each other. Ireton looked at Downes, while Cromwell turned to Bradshawe, who turned down the king's request.

'You have not owned us as a court, neither have you removed your hat – therefore permission is refused.'

And so beneath Richard II's hammer-beam roof in the Great Hall of Westminster, the verdict was delivered by the president, John Bradshawe, 'that the king, for the crimes contained in the charge, should be carried back to the place from whence he came, and thence to the place of execution, where his head should be severed from his body'.

There was a communal gasp: the death of a king announced.

Some said, 'They are killing God's anointed one.'

'What sort of a day is this?' asked a commissioner to himself. He would not sign the warrant, he knew that now. He would slip away, avoid the task and he cared not for the consequences.

But suddenly Charles was calling out. 'I may speak after sentence, I may speak after sentence!' he claimed, with panic now in his voice. 'I may speak after the sentence!'

But he was taken away, surrounded by soldiers. Some said that he looked like Christ, this narrative growing in force. They'd reached down to lift him from his chair, but with a royal wave of the hand he insisted on standing alone 'without rude handling'. He protested as he left, though he did not shout, for kings do not shout.

'I am not suffered to speak after sentence?' he said, in exaggerated wonder. 'Is this to be believed? The king is not suffered to speak? Then imagine what justice other people may expect!'

News of the verdict spread through the streets and the first trestles were set up outside the Banqueting House in Whitehall. They would become the scaffold.

'Old sanctities mean nothing now,' remarked one observer.

'The people of England have spoken,' said another.

'This was not the work of the people,' said a third. 'It's the passion of the demented few!'

'The mandate is from heaven,' said another. 'What further mandate is needed?'

While young Samuel Pepys, absconding from St Paul's School to hear the outcome of the trial, told his friends that if he had to preach a sermon on the king, his text would be, 'The memory of the wicked shall rot.'

'You think he's wicked?'

'Of course he's wicked!'

'How can a king be wicked?'

'The larger the throne, the bigger the wickedness.'

While up the hill, in the square by the Charing Cross, the republican preacher Hugh Peters chose Isaiah 14.18–20 to capture the day: 'All the kings of the nations, even all of them, lie in glory, everyone in his own house. But thou art cast out of thy grave like an abominable branch, and as the raiment of those who are slain, thrust through with a sword, that go down to the stones of the pit; as a carcase trodden under foot. Thou shall not be joined with them in burial because thou hast destroyed thy land and slain thy people! The seed of evil doers shall never be renowned!'

Though inside the hall, Cromwell had another matter on his mind. The judges were trying to escape.

*

He had put soldiers on the doors to ensure no one left, as some commissioners had tried to do. Cromwell knew their game. They did not wish to put their name to the death warrant, did not desire to be named as regicides, fearing the consequences . . . and made discreet attempts to scuttle away and join the crowd.

'No one is to leave this hall, not until I give the order,' he said to the guards. He then returned to the crowded dais where a table, pen and ink had been set out. He was concerned – deeply concerned, as he surveyed the turbulent scene. It was clear that certain commissioners had already managed to exit before the signing. They had disappeared into the morning; some said as many as nine.

243

The killers of the king could ill afford to lose more. They needed the company.

'You know I have never been for a king – even a nice one,' said Henry Marten, with alcohol on his breath. 'One man is not wise enough to rule a whole nation. Do you not agree, Oliver?'

'Certainly not this one, Henry.'

'You know one who is?'

They leaned together over the table where the parchment was spread out, handwritten in iron gall ink: the death warrant of a king. It required their signatures before it could be given to the executioner; and when Henry Marten flicked ink at Cromwell, Cromwell – bullish and playful – flicked it back and Henry laughed, which some found inappropriate. But that was Henry for you – republican, drunkard and, according to Charles, 'an ugly rascal and whore-master'.

'Richard, you are loitering a little,' said Ireton to Ingoldsby, who hung back from the action.

Ireton was the last person he wished to see. 'Only waiting my turn,' replied Richard, wishing he were well away from this place.

'Definitely loitering, Richard, and looking like a fellow who wishes he were not here – which for an army man and Leveller seems strange.'

'Perhaps I wish there were another way.'

'I'm sure we all wish that, Richard, but events have made matters very clear, would you not say?'

This was Richard Ingoldsby's first day of attendance. He had refused any part in the king's trial until now and regretted his presence this morning. He would have left straightway after the sentencing, but got caught in conversation with Miles Corbet, of all people, and then, when he was free to leave, he'd been stopped by the soldiery at the door – a soldier stopped by soldiers.

'Come, Richard, it is for this that you fought,' said Ireton.

And with that he was escorted to the table, where Cromwell took hold of his hand and placed in it the quill.

'This parchment cries out for your hand, dear Richard,' said Cromwell with kindness, for this hesitant man was his cousin, whose politics Oliver trusted. His heart was true – just wavering a little. Oliver glanced down at the warrant as Richard inked the quill. He counted the signatures and seals . . . Bradshawe's the first name in the column, his own name third, and then moving down, Ludlow the thirtieth to sign, and drunk Marten at thirty-two on the list. Richard would be the thirty-fourth; they still needed more. Where was Isaac Ewer?

'There are fifty-nine commissioners on or around this platform,' said Ireton.

'Then we have clearly lost some from the trial.'

'We have lost nine from the trial, Oliver – and seventy-six from our first choosing.'

This was a painful number.

'The royalist cause is a muscular body in this land,' said Oliver.

'A dead hand has a firm grip.'

'And this death will make a breach, Henry, you know this? A rough breach in our land between army and country.'

Ireton heard the panic again, saw the hesitant eyes. 'Do you return to caution, Father, like a paralysed man on a ledge? Will I again need to persuade you?'

Oliver remembered the stars above Pontefract and gathered himself. 'There is no caution now,' he said. 'No caution, I am quite decided.'

'Good.'

'We must prosecute this matter with speed and strength – and I will ensure that it is done.' And then louder. 'I will ensure that it is done!' Some heads turned.

'I like your resolution,' said Ireton, relieved.

'We will cut off his royal head with the crown still on it, if we must!'

*

'The king is saved!'

Hammond looked confused.

'He has said he will not do it!' said Jane, full of rushing and excited thoughts. 'Have you not heard, Mr Hammond? That he quite refuses?'

'Quite refuses what? And who?'

245

Mrs Whorwood had discovered his lodgings and confronted him in much elation. She embodied urgency at his door – but would not be allowed in. She would stay outside; he would keep her there. How had she found him? And further, did he really wish to speak with her, having been called a coward, which rankled greatly? Robert Hammond was no coward.

'And if Young Gregory will not do it,' she said, oblivious to his thoughts, 'then no one will do it! We are saved! The king is saved!'

'You must slow a little, Mrs Whorwood ... and explain what you speak.'

She must slow a great deal. Hammond had been attempting some maintenance of the chimney and was still wiping soot from his hands and thoughts from his mind when he responded to the frenzied knocking on his door; she had a frenzied way of knocking.

'Brandon will not execute the king! He has said this.'

Richard Brandon was called 'Young Gregory' after his father, who had been the common hangman; like father, like son, Richard now wore the fatal cloak with pride. Or did he? For Brandon had been approached in secret to execute the king, but declared in public that he never would do such a thing. After all, he'd worked for Charles, he said; the king had employed him. He'd beheaded the Earl of Stafford on the king's orders. So how could he now kill his former employer – and the monarch at that?

'He said so publicly in an alehouse in Whitechapel,' explained Jane. 'He has said that he would not kill the king!' Here were new possibilities for delay and escape. Young Gregory would hardly lie about such a thing – not in Whitechapel, where he was born!

So Charles was safe for now, surely?

*

This was to be a public killing. They would erect the scaffold in the wide streets of Whitehall where a crowd could gather from Charing Cross down to Westminster. Cromwell and Ireton had disagreed about an open-door trial and Ireton felt vindicated; it had been a disaster. But both were persuaded of a public execution. As Ludlow had said, his sins had been public, so why not his end?

'Let as many as possible see the death of the king,' said Ireton.

Queen Elizabeth – who he so admired – had wished the murder of Mary Stuart to be kept out of public view, a secret undertaking. But times change, needs alter and neither Cromwell nor Henry saw the benefit of some private violence in a dark place.

'A public death does rather end his attempts at escape,' said Ireton.

'We must hope so,' said Oliver. 'Or truly he is the messiah.'

'And we do the right thing ... we do the right thing.' Was Henry now nervous? 'Pretended negotiation or plans for escape – the king knew only these two ways.'

A pause.

'I waited for God, Henry,' said Cromwell, feeling the need to explain. 'I waited only for God.'

'And he has spoken?'

'Indeed he has.'

Better late than never, thought Henry. 'And when was that?'

Cromwell wished to tell Henry of this, perhaps it would calm them both. 'He spoke one cold night in a field outside Pontefract.'

'As to the shepherds, glad tidings.'

'He gave me there a peace that had long eluded me, Henry – the peace that passes all understanding.' Ireton nodded. He did not mind how Cromwell came to his views, just that he stayed with them. 'And you?' said Oliver. 'How did the Lord speak with you on the matter?'

'Me?' How would he phrase this? 'He spoke earlier to me, Oliver – with the army at Windsor.'

'How so?'

It would not sound as pious as Oliver's story; but piety is not always calm.

'I was listening to Wood at the time. He reported on the king's invitation to the Scots to invade our land, while he smiled benignly at parliament. Wood showed me the king's words in a letter, poorly coded, and I thought: *What a shit!* It was a rage that passes all understanding – still is.'

Oliver took it surprisingly well. 'So we came by different paths to the same clearing.'

'Indeed, Oliver. My path was just a little quicker,' he said, without a smile.

Oliver felt better for having spoken of God with Henry; they did not speak much of faith.

'We do God's work in the light of day and without shame,' confirmed Cromwell. The execution of the king was not about revenge; but about God's work performed in the light.

So a scaffold was erected in the wide street of Whitehall.

*

His majesty's rooms were adequate. One's standards drop as imprisonment stretches, and after Hurst he was just glad of a curtain. But he could not forget, could not un-hear the truth that he had once lived and entertained in palaces. And as he pondered a drab picture on the wall – a poorly painted master and dog – the sense of loss almost overwhelmed him. How he missed his pictures, his own art collection, comprising rather finer works than this . . . it had all started in Spain, of course, inspired by his visit to the Madrid court in 1623. Different days – but he'd become a knowledgeable art collector; he liked to think so and people had said as much to him.

'Such taste, your majesty, such wonder on your walls!'

While in Spain, he'd sat for a sketch by the court favourite Velázquez – a picture he'd sadly mislaid in his recent travels – and acquired works there by Titian and Correggio, among others. And then on his return, and at some public expense, he'd commissioned Rubens' masterpiece on the ceiling of the Banqueting House, so near to him now. He hoped to see the work one more time; it would both comfort and inspire.

His art collection had grown considerably after he purchased the Duke of Mantua's paintings, which offered him Raphael, Caravaggio and Mantegna in their pomp. And from there it had simply carried on growing, for he was a civilized man who wished to civilize the nation, and so what better use of public funds than the acquisition of works by Bernini, Bruegel, da Vinci, Holbein and Tintoretto? These were improving things – not to mention the self-portraits by Dürer and Rembrandt. He didn't know how many paintings he possessed; you do not count such things, you simply gaze. He had perhaps not gazed enough. But he would give them now to his friends and family, that they might gaze ... and be civilized. Or perhaps there would be a royal gallery in his memory, where his collection might be displayed and his passion and taste recalled?

'Charles – a man of great taste,' they would say, and that was a pleasing thought.

But civilized times were now a fading light. Little by little, he'd travelled far from those days, though when he started the walk, he could not tell. And after Hurst Castle – a nadir of hospitality – these sparse rooms of containment were adequate. He spent Sunday in prayer, refusing to see friends, for the time left was too precious. He might die tomorrow; he wasn't sure, no one seemed sure. When would he die? You should know when you will die. He was told they had difficulty finding an executioner, which once might have pleased him, but did not do so today. He wished for a good axeman, experienced and the best, rather than some hastily discovered extra. Was not Brandon available? Brandon was competent, he'd seen him at work. Or at least heard of his work ... Charles had not liked to watch, particularly Stafford. How could he have watched that killing?

And now Charles was remembering again – too much time to remember – and the pain ever fresh: the execution of the Earl of Stafford, his dear friend. It was Brandon with the axe that day. Charles had never found peace since, not in a complete manner; regrets lingered in the flesh between his bones and none more virulent than this dark stain, permeating his physic. So, of course, this was God's judgement on him: a right and inevitable judgement for tossing his friend to the parliamentary hunt to save his royal self. Stafford had even been tried in the same hall as Charles, as though prophesying his royal betrayer's end.

And in the meantime, the banging and hammering outside, ceaseless to his ears, the noise becoming louder and quite intolerable. Charles complained to his guards.

'The builders make too much noise,' he said.

'Scaffolds do not build themselves,' came the cheerful reply, though after some discussion his gaolers took him and his dogs for a walk in St James's Park, where it was quieter and the construction of the scaffold less invasive.

*

'Have we found an executioner?' asked Oliver. They met in the upper room of a hostelry off Whitehall. Elizabeth had said they could not meet at Drury Lane, since she was talking to a man about the damp. This is what she said.

'I will do it myself, sir, if necessary.'

Oliver could well imagine Colonel Harrison with axe in hand; it was not so different from a sword, though you were more keenly watched at an execution than in battle, where each looked only to themselves and their survival.

'I trust it will not be necessary, Thomas, but your straight heart does you credit at a time when some have become enfeebled in the cause.'

'Brandon is clear that he will not do it and tells everyone so,' said Harrison. 'He finds himself the toast of Whitechapel!'

'An aspiration for us all,' said Cromwell.

'He says that he will not stoop so low as to kill his king. That is what he says. The common hangman finds this death too offensive!'

'Everyone draws their conscience with different lines,' said Oliver wearily.

'And this line is drawn in a sewer, Lieutenant-General – for here is the most reasonable death he will ever supervise.'

'Indeed.'

'Yet he will not do it!'

'Brandon will do it,' said Ireton, who had been sitting quiet, keeping his powder dry, as sometimes he did. Harrison found Ireton a cold fish – not really a soldier, and, lest anyone forget, a rude supporter of the king at Putney. In Harrison's mind, if Mr Ireton had now changed his tone, it was all about his own advancement.

'He has said that he will not,' replied Harrison.

'And when did the lackey Brandon become famous for the truth?' asked Henry.

'He has said plainly, he will not do it; that is all I say.' Harrison would not step down in this matter.

'He saves face, that is all.'

'We want it done well,' said Oliver, seeking peace between the two. 'A clean cut – not some wretch but a craftsman ... kind and clean, like the Frenchman who took Anne Boleyn.'

'Thirty pounds and the contents of the king's pockets,' said Henry.

'That is the offer to Brandon?'

'It is.'

'And you trust him, Henry?'

'He will be paid after his work, to ensure seemly behaviour. And he'll have an assistant on the scaffold – one known to you – to guide him if he falters in his commission.'

'One known to me?'

'Known to us all, Oliver.'

And now Oliver wondered: who?

*

On Monday, the day before his execution, Charles was in a gay mood. He was playful even with his guards, who preferred him morose.

'You must take special care of me today,' he said. 'For I meet with God shortly and will tell him about you all, about your ways and manners.'

'You'll answer only for yourself,' said Edward Hobbs, who had fought at both Naseby and Preston and limped now for his pains, the victim of a Scottish pistol invited south by Charles.

'And I shall delight to do so. I suspect my hearing will be more cheerful than those of recent days.' The guards looked at each other but Charles was rather pleased with himself. 'Yes, I believe I shall enjoy the cheerfulness of heaven; and I wish it for your faces today.'

Hobbs presumed that Charles would go to hell, for how would it be heaven, if this deceitful snake were there? And today, Charles allocated his possessions, for which he no longer had need. He informed Bishop Juxon, who had led him in morning prayer, that his dogs were to be sent to his wife, Henrietta, in France.

251

'She always loved them, even if she hasn't seen them for a while,' he said. 'They can become reacquainted. They will all like that.'

And a small casket of jewels was to be given to his children. It was all he presently had to offer, apart from some books – precious books on religion – which would go to friends . . . and maybe one or two to family. He heard that his daughter Elizabeth was a keen reader of theology, which encouraged him.

There was a knock on the door, which was unlocked by a guard and pushed open. Charles looked up, surprised. Standing in the doorway were his two youngest children: Elizabeth, aged thirteen, and little Henry, Duke of Gloucester, aged ten. They hesitated for a moment . . . so the king reached out towards them and they approached with a curtsey and a bow. It was over a year since they'd spoken, since he'd last seen them – and how they'd grown, become quite grown-up! And as surprise quietened, he wondered about his words. He wished to see them, most certainly, and would explain why he must die and what they must do. These were important matters.

'And how are we this day, my prince and princess?' he asked. 'I hope everyone is being kind?'

They nodded, as though to a stranger.

'Then that is good news.'

To Elizabeth, her father looked different: greyer, more weary . . . and thinner than when they had met at Syon House, a place of rare good memories.

'You look tired, Father. And ill.'

'I sleep variously and the food is not quite what your mother and I once knew. But I forgive the cooks, and I hope God will too.'

When held at Hampton Court, Charles had been allowed to see his children. They would meet at Syon House in Isleworth, the Duke of Northumberland's home, sometimes for one day, sometimes for two. They had been good times together, riding in the grounds and walking along the Thames by the Church of All Saints. But when he'd fled from Hampton, he'd fled also from his offspring; and his letters had become less frequent over the year, his mind taken up with other matters.

Charles looked at Bishop Juxon, who had remained in the room, smiling on this family scene. He asked the priest to leave.

'Leave, please, Bishop.'

'Your majesty?'

'Leave us.'

And he did, with a surprised rustle of robes. Charles then indicated to the guard in the doorway that he should also withdraw; after some hesitation he obeyed. The door closed and alone with his children, Charles spoke.

'We have not long, my darlings, not long. So you must listen well, for we'll not speak again. And if I am not sad – and I am not, not sad at all – then you must promise me that you will not be sad either. Can you follow your father in this way?'

'We can, Father,' said Elizabeth, the leader of the two and assured beyond her thirteen difficult years.

'Now, Elizabeth,' said Charles, 'I speak first with you and in awkward words.'

She did not wish to hear awkward words, for most of the words she had heard in her life had been so.

'Tomorrow I will die,' he said. 'I know that now; it is to be tomorrow, and I wish it to be so.' Elizabeth stared at him. 'But I do not want you to be in grief or torment, my princess, for I die a glorious death.' Elizabeth continued to stare – these words were nonsensical. 'I die for the laws and liberties of this land, you see. Do you understand? I die to protect the laws and liberties of this land.'

'Yes, Father,' she said before starting to sob, which was not what she wished at all, as she must look after her brother.

'You must not cry.'

'I see nothing glorious,' she said, anger rising inside. 'You are the king.'

Passed around from family to family since the end of the civil war – endured rather than cherished by her reluctant hosts – her father had been her safety, distant but sure. He would come for them one day; this she had always believed. Only now, that would not be so. Her belief was mistaken. He was to leave her again and for always, and there was no glory here.

'I die to maintain the true religion,' continued her father. 'That is, the Protestant religion. So you must read wisely.'

'I will so do, Father.'

She read a great deal and not always in English. She could read and write in Hebrew, Greek, Italian, Latin and French as well, and spiritual reading was her favourite.

'Bishop Andrewes' sermons are good,' continued her father. 'You will enjoy those; and Archbishop Laud's book against Fisher is strong against popery.'

Elizabeth nodded.

'We are not against Mary.' The girl looked confused. 'I mean the Virgin Mary – we are not against veneration.'

'No, Father.'

'But we do not pray to her; that is the parting with Rome. We do not ask her to intercede on our behalf. That doctrine is an accretion, not there in the early Church Fathers.'

'I have read the Fathers, Father.'

'And we must attend to our buildings. We must repair and beautify our churches. Presbyterians know nothing of this; they would speak psalms in a cowshed. But outward beauty speaks of inner zeal.'

'Yes, Father.'

'You look sad.'

'They say that you could save your life – if you agreed to the end of bishops.'

Charles paused.

'I will not save my life for their loss, Elizabeth – no, for that would be a price too high. It would be as if I ate the Eden apple all over again. Do you understand?' Elizabeth nodded. 'As for me, dear daughter, I am at peace.'

'I am happy for you, Father.' There was no peace inside her young body.

'I have forgiven all my enemies,' he explained, 'and I hope God will forgive them also. We cannot be sure of these things, but I hope he shall. And you must tell your mother, when you see her – and I am sure you will – you must tell her that my thoughts never strayed from her, not once; and that my love shall remain the same to the last, even to the falling axe.'

Elizabeth, crying, took herself to the window. Charles could hardly attend to her, for he now reached out to young Henry and pulled him on to his lap: a heavier boy these days.

'Sweetheart,' he said, 'they will cut off your father's head tomorrow – they will do this.'

Elizabeth yelped; Henry was wide-eyed.

'And then perhaps – this might be their plan – they will make a king of you. They may do this . . . a tame king is what they want, unlike me . . . one they can control.'

The young duke nodded, he wouldn't cry like his sister.

'But mark what I say, Henry: you must not be a king while your brothers Charles and James live. You understand?'

'I understand.' He didn't understand.

'For be sure of this: they will cut off your brothers' heads when they catch them; they will do this. And then cut off yours too at the last, for this is how they are. So I charge you: do not be made a king by them, you understand me? Do not be made a king.'

'I will be torn to pieces first,' declared the duke on the king's lap.

'Well, you speak most admirably!' said Charles, delighted at such spirit, and in so young a child. 'And so you must look to the welfare of your soul, keep your religion and fear God, who will provide you with all you need. But though you must forgive – we must all forgive – never trust. Never trust anyone, for all these people want is power for themselves; and no grieving, Henry, no sad eyes – for much happiness awaits us all in another kingdom!'

He looked across at his daughter and picked up a Bible.

'Elizabeth, come now, join us here and take this Bible as my gift to you, for you are a fine reader, I have been told.'

Elizabeth received the book as the door opened again and a guard entered. Charles looked up, disappointed at this interruption.

'And now you dear things must go, before more louts come and interrupt this family with their orders and their swords. That's no way to treat a Christian family, is it?' Elizabeth looked at him. 'Not at all, not at all. So give your father a kiss, for that is the finest gift this king could now receive; the finest gift by far.'

They kissed beneath the soldier's gaze and then the door was opened and without a look back – or only a brief one – Elizabeth and Henry left.

Charles asked to be left alone. It was time to open the king's case, take out the letters it held, and commit them to the flames.

These letters must not see tomorrow.

*

Cromwell's parlour seemed smaller tonight, with Ireton restless and Elizabeth sitting rather than serving. Together and separately, they pondered the morrow.

'Will the people riot?' asked Elizabeth. 'I imagine they will riot; they will be very angry.'

'Angrier even than you?'

'I am not angry, Oliver.'

'Anger creeps from your pores, dear wife, whether you name it or not. Your mood could sink a fleet.'

'You do what you do, I have always said.'

'I grant you, Mother, there are not many who wish him to die,' said Ireton. Elizabeth said nothing. She wouldn't be cajoled or lectured by Henry. 'But then those who wish him alive are not so plentiful either,' he added.

He drank a little ale. Bridget had taught him not to fear his mother-in-law and her locked-jaw silences.

'Perhaps they are frightened of the soldiery who chew tobacco and lean on their pikes around London,' Elizabeth said. 'Perhaps that is why they are quiet.'

'Or perhaps the English are in greater love with the idea of a king than with the king himself. He scarcely impresses as a man.'

'I am told he performed well at the trial.'

A short pause.

'Who told you?' asked Oliver.

'Everyone says it.'

'He had his moments,' said Ireton, 'as does any ship a-sinking.'

'I am told Mr Shakespeare might have written his lines.'

'That goes a little far,' said Henry.

256

'He played us all very well,' agreed Oliver. 'But then he does play people well; that makes him neither good nor right.'

'And his fine playing – it does him little service in the end,' added his son-in-law. 'He dies tomorrow. That's where his foolish cunning has brought him.'

There was further silence as the fire burned, a necessary warmth on this cold January night. Oliver threw another log into the hungry flame.

'It did win him friends, Henry,' said Oliver. 'The trial, I mean.'

'As I said it would. Though for myself, I would set life over friends. He'll not live long to enjoy his new coterie.'

'And in the long game?' said Oliver, looking gloomily down the years that lay ahead. 'His family – we cannot kill them all.'

'It is over for his family. They gather dust abroad.'

'Not his youngest two, Elizabeth and Henry,' said Elizabeth.

'His youngest are taught how things are. They have watched their father's foolishness at close hand and will not copy his mistakes.'

'Did they see him?' asked Elizabeth.

'Who?'

'His children. Did they see their father?'

'They saw him.'

'For how long?'

'Long enough. He did not have long to give them . . . too busy preparing for martyrdom.'

'Do you see good in anyone, Henry?' Elizabeth did find him exasperating sometimes.

'Where it exists.'

Elizabeth thought that the king had been a kinder father than she herself had known; though one mustn't think ill of the dead.

'He does care for them,' she said.

'If he cared for them, Mother, he would have stayed at Hampton Court; you know this.'

'He's seen more of his children than I've seen of mine,' said Oliver.

'That's because you fight,' said Elizabeth.

'So I am to blame?'

And then a knock at the door.

257

'You expect someone, Oliver?'

'No, but I will see.'

'Be careful,' said Elizabeth, who feared for her door tonight.

Cromwell peered through the window. 'The guards stand firm. It is only a woman.'

He lifted the latch in the small hallway, opened the door and stepped out into a dark Drury Lane.

'A lady to see you, sir,' said John Shanks of Cromwell's former cavalry regiment. 'Won't be turned away.'

'A name?'

'She wouldn't give her name.'

Cromwell looked into the fog as a tall, waif-like figure in a linen undercap pushed herself forward. Shanks made to restrain her, and a small scuffle ensued as Cromwell reached for his knife, but there was no need. She was holding her hands in the air, saying she came in peace.

'You come late for peace,' Cromwell said.

'The hour I cannot help.'

'So what brings you?'

'I come from the king.'

'From the king?'

'Yes. Or rather, for the king. I speak for him.'

'A royal mouthpiece.'

'He cannot die.'

Cromwell felt strangely vulnerable to this line. 'Do you have a name?' he asked.

'My name does not matter.'

'It matters to me. I wish to know the name of the king's mouthpiece and who I talk to now.'

'My name is Mrs Whorwood.' There was nothing now to lose.

'Mrs Whorwood from Holton Hall?'

'And if I am?'

So they met again; almost a ghost-like figure at Bridget's wedding, but no ghost now, her warm breath a thick cloud in the cold night air.

'Go back to your family, Mrs Whorwood. Go back to your children.'

'And that is all you can say?'

'They're kind words for one who so disdains me – and disturbs my home at night.'

'And tomorrow will be worse than disdain. Tomorrow will be judgement, for you'll have blood on your hands – royal blood!' She held out her hands, imagining blood, and the guard looked uncomfortable. 'You think it will help if I go home – home to my dog of a husband – when I have no home but the king's preservation?'

'Then tomorrow, madam, you will be homeless again.' He sounded surer than he felt.

'I walked past you at the siege of Oxford. I walked through your lines and into the city with the money that sent our dear Queen Henrietta to France.'

'Then you blessed us.'

'No, I cursed you. I always cursed you to the king.'

'The queen was not good for the king. She rather governed him, making her husband fresh enemies every day . . . and perhaps you have followed her in that.'

'I merely point him to those with a true heart.'

'And away from reconciliation and unity. We might have been friends, the king and I.'

'He called you "the farmer" and thought you dribbled in awe.'

'Goodnight, lady.'

He turned to go but she grabbed at his shoulder and he span round with force in his eyes, as though to hit her.

'There will be an uprising tomorrow,' she said, face close to face. 'And the king will be freed; this I know. Whitehall will riot and you'll be unable to control such numbers. Better to make plans for peace now.'

'Believe me, I tried.'

'He will not be executed. I know this – it is in the stars!'

Cromwell stepped back, the rage spent. 'You consult an astrologer? Hah! Believe me, the king executes himself, Mrs Whorwood; he insists upon it. The night sky can do little about that. And sadly – and this is grievous – you helped him down this dismal path, filling him with vacuous dreams.'

'I call it hope!'

'And I name it treason, for the dreams were just dreams, and they bent his mind against healing.'

'Tomorrow, it will be you in fear of your life.'

Cromwell smiled with sadness at her desperate words. 'And a soldier knows that feeling well. I have never forgotten it. I bid you goodnight, Mrs Whorwood.'

'And I bid you an eternity in hell!'

As the guard took hold of her he moved back inside.

'Do not harm her – but send her on her way,' he said, closing the door on Drury Lane.

'Who was that?' asked Elizabeth as he returned to the parlour, shaken.

'No one,' said Oliver. 'No one important.'

30 January 1649

The boys from Westminster School were locked in for the day. But pupils at St Paul's were there in Whitehall early – those with a heart for it – joining the milling crowd and eating 'execution pies', as the vendor had named them, though not all had an appetite. Young Pepys shocked his friends when he called this 'judgement day'.

'This is judgement day and we need to be near the front.'

'Will we see brimstone?'

'We will see blood, if we get near enough. When the head falls, it spurts out everywhere. It spurted everywhere with Stafford, they say.'

'Kings' blood is different.'

'How so?'

'It's a different colour!'

'And I say it's the same – it just spurts further and more royally!'

His guards walked Charles and his dogs across St James's Park at ten in the morning. He had always liked this park; he would walk here with Henrietta in the spring, particularly in the later and happier days, when she had stopped fighting her adopted nation. A good wife in many respects, they had grown together over time – and now suddenly, here was Jane seeking his attention. What was she doing here? What in God's name was the woman doing? He did not wish for this.

'Good morning, your majesty,' she said, curtseying.

'Good morning, Mrs Whorwood.'

Charles asked his guards if he might speak discreetly to her, explaining she was a poor woman whose family he once helped. They gave him a few yards' grace, not wishing to lose him now. But it was only a desperate woman and what harm could she do?

'You must leave me now, Mrs Whorwood,' he said with quiet insistence.

'There are two riders, Charles, and a spare horse across the way from here. Do you see them?'

Charles could see figures in the distance as he raised his eyes . . . a horse, waiting.

'I have no need of a horse.'

'This is your last chance, your majesty.'

'You must go home, Mrs Whorwood.'

'I have no home.'

'But I do not know you now. Do you hear me, seven-one-five?'

Her heart sang; his eyes shared a secret.

'I have kept the letters,' she said, smiling.

'I have burned all mine,' he said, casually. 'I burned them last night, watched them consumed by fire. You should follow my example. They are gone.'

'I understand, I understand.' She understood, of course she did. 'But your horses await you, your majesty. You will thank me when you are free; you must run now and all will be well.'

'It is my dear wife I think of as I walk,' he said accusingly.

'I think of her as well, your majesty!'

'I remember that she and I strolled here together and how great our love was, and I wish to remember her now.'

'Our most excellent queen.'

'And you intrude upon my remembering, Mrs Whorwood, so go back to your husband and leave me, please.'

'Once my name was Jane.'

'Different days, my dear, different days.' And then louder, 'I wish you well, Mrs Whorwood, and every blessing on your dear husband and family.'

She turned, walked away, stumbled a little and then her legs gave way. She fell to her knees in St James's Park and felt the cold soil through her fading dress. And then she arose, wiped her muddied palms and walked on, towards the waiting figures with the horse, no looking back . . . though she did look back, to see her king, her dear little boy . . .

*

It is 1.30 on the afternoon of the day of execution.

262

Charles is guided by two soldiers up the back stairs of the Banqueting House. He passes through the Great Hall where he and Henrietta Maria had danced beneath the Rubens ceiling. He looks up to enjoy it once more, but sees nothing; he cannot see the painting. The two tiers of huge oblong windows are boarded with crude carpentry and the light shut out. The painting cannot be seen, he is denied its final charm. Though he can imagine its colours here in the dark, imagine the scene, the infant Charles held high over England and Scotland ... and his father carried to heaven.

'Soon to join you, Father,' he says, crossing himself. Would it be a happy reacquaintance? There were, one must admit, a mixture of feelings.

But he'd grasped the issue of the soot; he'd been quite clear on that matter. Soot from the many lamps had begun to soil Rubens' colours – such a tragedy – and so he'd limited the number of events here. Festivities had been relocated. One must protect beauty, what else is kingship for?

And the gaiety in this place! He's now remembering the visit of Indah ben Abdullah, ambassador extraordinary from the Sultan of Morocco. He'd come to negotiate a trade agreement, and what a show that had been! His gifts to Charles had included four Barbary horses and two saddles plated with gold of the most exquisite workmanship, while he had returned to Africa with a coach lined with crimson velvet, gilded and painted with flowers – and a copy of Van Dyck's portraits of the king and queen.

Such days! Torchlight processions through London, vast crowds pressing for a view. And they pressed again today, though differently. He walked towards his death which some, like his daughter, felt needless. Yet how could he have accepted such restriction on his divine office? And what would his father have said at such submission, such bending in the wind? He died now that future monarchs might be quite free from the restraint of monkeys.

He looks around. Ahead of him lies the door through which he will step out on to the scaffold. He'll step through the leaded glass on to his final scene. And he listens ... and hears it. He hears the presence of people beyond those doors, he hears the crowd, both shouts and stillness. They have come for their king.

Only slowly does he become aware of a figure, stationary in the shadows, familiar in outline, rounder and taller than Charles, with an unfortunate nose. Oliver Cromwell has come to say goodbye, but Charles has no time for this, no time for the man. He enjoyed their conversations at Hampton Court well enough, but he has never regarded Farmer Oliver as more than a servant, more than someone to do his bidding.

'I am not aware we have anything to say to each other,' Charles says quietly. 'I cannot offer you absolution, if that is what you seek.'

But Cromwell only stares and Charles is unnerved. Is he to be killed here, in private?

'I would like to be left alone to say my prayers,' says Charles. He is angry at this intrusion.

'I doubt not your piety and fortitude,' says Cromwell, to the king's deep disdain. As if Charles is concerned over how this man considers him! 'But I have yet to master your majesty's failure to read a plain lesson – or your lack of candour, your passion for intrigue and your unshakeable obstinacy.'

Charles looks at him through the half-light as if to say, 'Are you quite done?'

'I would have you on the throne,' adds Cromwell, surprising himself.

Charles smiles. 'You disguise your wish well.'

'You would not allow it, of course.'

'Because you did not offer a throne, Mr Cromwell. Had you offered a throne, we might have walked together; but the army consumed you, ate you whole, wild men at arms.'

'Only after deceit ate you.'

'You offered me a kennel in which the dog sits tied.'

'If a kennel, a very fine one.'

'But I am the king, not a dog.'

There was a silence between them.

'I wish to pray,' says Charles.

'And what of responsibility, Charles? You take none? I bid you take some!'

Now Oliver is stirred, mindful of Charles' lack of regret.

'I will pray for your guilt,' says Charles, 'for I see it troubles you and makes you look quite ill. You look ill, Mr Cromwell. Now let me to my God . . . and my people.'

It is a royal dismissal. Charles kneels, bows his head, pauses for a moment and then turns back once again – because he wishes to know.

'Did Brandon agree?'

But the figure in the shadows is gone.

*

Charles emerged through the tall window on to the scaffold, just before the second chime. He was struck by the density of the crowd: something solid, a carpet of heads as far as the eye could scan. His loyal people, reaching out to him – though soldiers positioned in-between, a line four deep, forcing his subjects back . . . and removing them from his final words. Charles had never possessed a big voice.

'How is the king to address his people?' he asked the bishop, who stood like a statue in the cold.

'God will hear.'

'I had hoped my people might also hear.'

'You don't have any people,' said the masked figure of the assistant executioner. 'Not any more.'

The king was composed, wearing two shirts; this had been the advice.

'Wear two shirts, your majesty, lest a shiver be construed as fear.'

'I will have no fear. That is what Henrietta would advise.'

'Then wear two shirts, so appearance matches your spirit.'

Charles looked down and found the block for his head a little low. He asked the executioner if it could be raised, but it couldn't be raised, he was told. He learned this from the shake of the masked axeman's head.

'A flat stone might be laid beneath it – to raise it a little?'

But again the executioner shook his head. This was not the time for him to be altering the height of the block. He was used to the block this height. With a different height, the swing must be different, the angle changed, and there was no time to practise.

Was it Brandon behind the mask? Charles was wondering if it was Brandon. He couldn't tell, for he had never wished to notice the man until now. The executioner's assistant stood four yards away, watchful, though who he was watching was harder to say. It was possible he was watching the axe. When Boleyn was killed, the poor girl, they hid the sword beneath the straw to calm her; but not so here. The executioner leaned on his weapon, as though it were a stick for an old man.

Charles was allowed to give his speech, written on parchment – he had taken some care. No one could hear him, with the crowd pushed back, but he spoke as loud as he could and believed that God would help the listening of the crowd.

'God will take your words to their ears, your majesty,' said the bishop and so he began:

'I never did begin a war with the two houses of parliament,' he declared from the cold stage. 'I never did begin a war – and I call God to witness, to whom I must shortly make account – that I never did intend to encroach on their privileges.' There was deep quiet across London, as though the city heard every word. Maybe a miracle was occurring; some said this.

'Rather,' he continued, 'they began upon me, this is how it was. For you, the people of this land, truly I desire your liberty and freedom as much as anybody, whomsoever you may be. But this I must tell you plainly: your liberty and freedom consist in having a government and laws by which your life and your goods may be most your own. This I affirm. But it does not consist – and I say this plainly too – it does not consist in having a share in that government, for that is nothing pertaining to you. You are to enjoy government, rather than be the government. A subject and a sovereign are clean different things.'

'Yes – and one difference is that we'll still have our heads tonight,' muttered the executioner's assistant, who seemed a confident man on the scaffold, almost a man in charge. And there was something in the voice Charles recognized . . . but he would not be distracted by an oaf. He continued his address.

'And therefore, until they do that – I mean, until you are given that liberty by your government – you will never enjoy yourselves.

And it is for this that I stand here now. I stand here on this cold scaffold for your liberty.'

'A secret death is beginning to have its attractions,' said Ireton, who was also cold, standing in the shadows with his father-in-law, just inside the windows through which Charles had walked. Ireton was not a man for the public stage, just one to get matters done.

'It could have been otherwise, my dear subjects,' said Charles, looking for his line. He held his script in chilling hands, fingers struggling to hold the parchment still; it wobbled a little. 'If I had succumbed to an arbitrary way, by which all laws are changed according to the power of the sword – then I would not stand here now! I would be in the palace in Whitehall rather than on a scaffold in the street. But I bear no grudge, no grudge at all. And as I pray that God will forgive those who bring me to this place, I offer myself to you, my English subjects, as the martyr of the people! Here I die, this day, the martyr of the people!'

'I think that's as much flatulence as I can stomach in one afternoon,' said Ireton. He was finding this speech most trying.

Charles was stirred within but struck by the chill. There was no protection from the wind here; it smacked his face. He turned to the bishop, folded his speech faithfully delivered and gave it into his keeping.

'Good words, my lord Bishop?'

'Good words, your majesty.'

'So I go now to where no disturbance can be,' he said. 'Isn't that so?'

'You do, sire.'

'Death is not terrible to me. I bless my God. I am prepared.'

And to the executioner, he gave instructions: 'I shall say but very short prayers – and when I thrust out my hands . . .'

He asked the bishop for his cap, and having placed it delicately on his head, mindful of appearance, he asked the executioner, 'Does my hair trouble you?'

'It would be best beneath the cap, sire.'

'Let me,' said the bishop, leaning forward to help, as did the executioner. Together, they ensured the hair was tucked inside.

'I have a good cause and a gracious God on my side,' he said to the bishop, who replied, 'There is but one stage more, your majesty, which – though turbulent and troublesome – is a very short one.'

'Short indeed,' said Charles. 'A mere swing of the axe!'

'A short path, but one that will carry you a very great way. For it will carry you from earth to heaven; and there, sire, you shall find, to your great joy, the prize you hasten to – a crown of glory.'

The king added, 'I go from a corruptible to an incorruptible crown, do I not? To a place where no disturbance can be.'

He had lived with disturbance long enough.

'You exchange a temporal crown for one eternal, sire – a good exchange, I believe.'

Charles now turned to his executioner, still unsure: 'Is my hair well?'

'Your hair is well.'

He then took off his cloak, felt the freeze and removed the jewelled figure of St George from around his neck. He gave it to the bishop, who placed it in the same pocket as the folded speech, deep beneath his robes. Charles looked down at the block and said to the executioner: 'You must set it fast.'

'It is fast, sire. I have set it well, as sure as a rock.'

'It might have been a little higher.' He did wish it to be higher.

'It can be no higher, sire.'

'Are they always so low?'

'Always, sire.'

'You will give me a moment?'

'Yes, sire.'

'When I put out my hands this way, then . . .'

Charles indicated what he would do, and then, as he stood, spoke a few words to himself, his hands and eyes lifted up to the clear January sky. He now moved quickly, and stooping down, placed his neck upon the cold block – how had it come to this? – while putting stray hairs under his cap. He was not quite ready, and imagining too sudden a strike, said to the executioner, 'Wait for the sign. I will stretch out my hands.'

'I will wait for your hands, your majesty.'

'Thank you.'

Encouraged by his father, Brandon had practised as a child, decapitating cats and dogs. He had a steady hand and an unerring eye. His father had never said that, but he knew for himself. He'd never used more than one strike and he'd killed before large crowds, especially at Tower Hill – that blood-stained ground to the north-west of the Tower. It was mostly nobility that ended up there, after imprisonment in the Tower – rich people executed for 'being an inconvenience', as his father told him, but folk who could draw a crowd. One hundred thousand had watched him relieve Stafford of his head, that's what they said. And Archbishop Laud? Brandon had done him as well; another freezer in January and the old man in his robes, playing the priest to the last.

As his father told him, you forget the crowd: 'It's just you and 'im. So swing fast and straight, aim for the nape . . . and hope the bugger don't move.'

Charles stretched out his hands.

And in one movement, Brandon raised the axe and swung it down, straight and fast, aim for the nape – and the royal head left the body. A cascade of blood, a red drizzle; the crowd groaned – a shocked and communal exhalation. But Brandon felt only relief flood his body: a good job, well done, well executed, as they said. He passed the bloodied axe to his assistant, handle upwards. He then bent down, and with some difficulty picked up the rolling head from the stage and held it up before the people.

In his best Whitechapel drawl, he shouted: 'Be'old the 'ed of a traih – uh!'

That's what they had told him to say, so that's what he said. It wasn't his mind but theirs. Now the surge of the crowd, the soldiers at tipping point, managing with a struggle to hold them back, while Brandon put down the head, a pale bloody thing, and reached into the king's pockets. Thirty pounds plus the king's pockets was the fee. He drew forth a silk handkerchief and an orange stuck with cloves, which surprised him a little. He would get ten shillings for that from the right person, so best to keep it safe. These were his thoughts as the body of the king was lifted up in haste, placed in a coffin, covered with black velvet, and carried from the stage

269

back through the window from which he had emerged some ten minutes ago . . .

Ten minutes that Jane had been unable to watch, standing in the doorway of her childhood home, just three hundred yards from the dreadful scaffolding, but her eyes elsewhere . . .

*

Some from the crowd were allowed forward, through the wall of soldiers.

If they paid a shilling, they could climb up on to the stage and dip their hankies in the royal blood. A queue quickly formed, one of grief above fury. Most desired only its healing powers, to be stored if possible – for when would this happen again? He had healed in life, this was well known, and he would heal in death. One woman dipped her finger in the blood and then crossed her forehead with it; another appeared to place it on her lips, as if receiving the sacrament.

'God bless your majesty,' she said.

The executioner left the stage in haste, fearful for his life if he stayed. He followed the coffin back into the hall, where he collected his payment from his assistant.

'You pay me?' he said.

'I do, yes.'

'Unusual.'

'Today is unusual, my friend.'

'You too are an executioner?'

'A good job, Brandon; you killed a wrong 'un.'

'I killed a king.'

And now he trembled a little, his knee buckling in horror, and his foot twitched, like a dying man himself. Today he'd killed the monarch of England and was now a man on the run, and forever so, keeping silent to survive . . . but he could not keep silent from himself.

'There will be none who know?' he asked.

'I won't be telling.'

Brandon counted the coins with shaking hands, placed them in the sack with his executioner's outfit, bowed to his assistant – he wasn't sure why – and then slipped through a tradesmen's door, back on to the London streets and towards Whitechapel, by a roundabout way. He would not speak to any of this day, though he felt the whole city stare, every face seeming to know his deed.

His assistant cared less about secrecy, and returned to the scaffold hiding nothing, his mask removed as he talked with the soldiers.

'His blood makes them happy,' said one, as they watched the dippers in various states of hysteria.

'Certainly makes me happy,' replied the assistant executioner; 'all very healing.'

And he watched as the troops marched in opposite directions between Westminster and Charing Cross, dispersing people north and south; they were not staying here to cause trouble. And there was no trouble in London that day, in neither Whitehall nor any other district. The people of England watched the killing of the king and then went quietly home. But it would be a day he, Cornet Joyce, remembered. And he could have done it, if Brandon hadn't.

'I could have swung that axe,' he said to himself, as he stepped from the stage, already being dismantled. 'Joycey could have done it.'

Epilogue

A wood-turner called Nehemiah Wallington sat in the London suburb of Clerkenwell.

He'd made his way back from the execution with little difficulty. The promised disturbance had not occurred; there'd been no rage or riot. If anything, an air of politeness had suffused the streets, solidarity with the moment and those who had shared it. He'd been one of those forced up to the Charing Cross by soldiery, after which he'd turned right down the Strand, marvelling at the new houses appearing. How long before little Clerkenwell was consumed by this leviathan of a city?

But for all that he'd witnessed and all that he saw, Nehemiah had walked home with contentment in his bones, and now sat with his pipe, looking again at the last recorded words of his brother-in-law Gerard. Gerard had been murdered eight years ago, in 1641, by the Irish rebels – rebels supported by Charles. And shortly before his death, Gerard wrote this: 'If the sundry rumours prove true, that these godless rebels act with the king's commission, then surely the Lord will not suffer the king, nor his posterity, to reign.'

And so it had come to pass.

Wallington put down his pipe and gazed through his small window on the street below. It was like a Sabbath out there, like the Lord's day: quiet conversations and no trade, apart from the preachers and pie-sellers. He picked up a notebook and wet his quill. He was a keen recorder of events, a man of many notebooks. And in his book today, he wrote: '30 January 1649, King Charles beheaded on a scaffold at Whitehall.'

In himself, he was weary of politics and hardly for parliament or army any more. He'd once been enthused and certain, but no longer; he was for no one these days. Yet the killing of the king was just settlement, this was quite clear – both judgement and prophecy fulfilled.

'Rest in peace, Gerard,' he said, as he closed his little book. That was enough writing for today.

Author's notes

Charles I: No one could accuse Charles I of pandering to the public. In his endless twists, turns and deceits, he remained constant in one thing: the divinity of his appointment and the divine rights this gave him. Death made both a martyr and a saint out of Charles; his spiritual work *Eikon Basilke* became a bestseller and a spiritual classic for royalists.

His two youngest children, Princess Elizabeth and Henry, Duke of Gloucester, remained prisoners in England after his death. In August 1650 they were taken to Carisbrooke Castle where their father had been held. Elizabeth fell ill after being caught in the rain on the castle bowling green, built for her father's entertainment, and died in September 1650 aged fifteen. Henry continued in captivity until 1653 when he was allowed to join his family abroad. Charles' eldest son Charles returned to England from European exile in 1660, when the monarchy was restored to much cheering in the streets of London ... though the journaller Nehemiah Wallington will not have been pleased.

Colonel Robert Hammond was replaced as governor of the Isle of Wight by Colonel William Sydenham, whose watch would prove less interesting than that of his predecessor. Hammond disappears from view in the early years of the Commonwealth, after the king's execution. But perhaps surprisingly, given their differing views on the captivity of Charles, he and Cromwell appear to have remained on good terms. In August 1654, Cromwell – by this time Lord Protector – made him a member of the Irish Council. Hammond travelled to Dublin to take up his post but died of a fever there in October 1654.

Jane Whorwood suffered for her close relations to Charles, which became an embarrassment to all. The royalist cause wanted a martyr, not an adulterer, and so Jane found herself erased without mercy from the royal records. She returned home to Holton

Hall in 1651 after a brief imprisonment, but in 1657 Jane left home permanently, fearing for her life. Brome, her abusive husband, went on to become an MP.

Jane died in 1684 aged seventy-two. Concerning her support for the royalist cause (wholly unacknowledged during the Restoration period), she wrote: 'My travels, the variety of accidents (and especially dangers) more become a Romance than a letter.' Indeed.

Whorwood's significance has been overlooked, and it lay not in her presence at Henry Ireton's wedding. Her work for the king was tireless and remarkable, in both energy and inventiveness, and for many years her affair with the king was an under-reported secret. But she also had a role in his downfall. Like Henrietta Maria, she colluded with Charles in his stubborn belief that he could simply go on bluffing and eluding his parliamentary and army enemies. She offered him a parallel universe in which to scheme; but perhaps not one that touched reality.

Tragedy also touched her only son, Brome. On 5 September 1657, aged twenty-two, wishing to travel with a friend from Hampshire to the Isle of Wight, he 'did hire a vessel that was leaky, which sunk by the time they were halfway in their journey', and was drowned. Jane was buried at Holton Hall, with her husband Brome and his mistress, Katharine.

With the death of Charles, **Oliver Cromwell** became the single most powerful man in England. He went on to become Lord Protector in 1653, and proved a benevolent ruler to those who opposed him, never vindictive. (Unless you were Irish.) He was also a major player in the cause of religious toleration, particularly the Jews – though he did struggle to tolerate parliament. He was finally offered the crown by parliament in 1657. There was much in him that favoured acceptance, but he was concerned how it would sit with his army support and so declined.

He died the following year and was given a magnificent state funeral, but matters soon turned sour. Charles II, on his accession, had his body dug up and hanged at Tyburn. After hanging 'from morning till four in the afternoon' his body was cut down and the head placed on a twenty-foot spike above Westminster Hall. In 1685, a storm broke the pole holding Cromwell's head, after which it fell – literally – into the hands of private collectors and museums, until 25 March 1960, when it was buried at Sidney Sussex College in his homeland of Cambridge.

Elizabeth Cromwell was the daughter of Sir James Bourchier of Felsted in Essex, who was a wealthy London leather merchant. When Oliver married her, he was marrying into money he didn't have himself. Their marriage appears a warm one, evidenced in the caring letters Cromwell wrote to her while away on his military campaigns. The royalists hated her as an extension of her husband, accusing her of drunkenness, adultery and frugality. Only the third slander possessed any truth and Elizabeth would have regarded it as a compliment; she had no wish to emulate the spendthrift Henrietta Maria.

If Cromwell was ambitious – a matter for debate – Elizabeth was not. She was keen that her husband place one of Charles' sons on the throne, rather than himself. Her feelings on the matter were such that most of her offspring were royalists as well; there's no evidence for the charge that she was ambitious for her husband.

After the death of Oliver, she retired to Wales until things settled down, after which she returned to England, moving to the house of her son-in-law at Norborough in Northamptonshire, where she died in November 1665.

Henry Ireton: In 1647, amid heated exchanges at the Putney debates, the Levellers accused Ireton of servility to the king, denouncing his dealings with Charles as a betrayal of the soldiers and people of England. But after the second civil war, Ireton's disdain for the king was the single most powerful force in England. In the autumn of 1648, with Cromwell up north and Fairfax dithering, it was Ireton who set in motion events that led to the trial and execution of Charles.

He was appointed Lord-Deputy in Ireland by Cromwell during the Commonwealth, but, exhausted by military campaigns, he contracted a fever and died in Limerick, aged forty. His body was returned to England for a state funeral in Westminster Abbey, where a grand monument was raised in his memory. Many Puritans were offended at this extravagance and probably the austere Ireton would have agreed. The monument was destroyed after the Restoration, and Ireton's corpse was exhumed and hanged at Tyburn in 1661, along with the bodies of Cromwell and Bradshawe. His head was exhibited at Westminster for at least twenty-four years.

He had four children with Bridget, who all survived into adult life. On his death, Bridget married another one of Cromwell's officers and confidants, Charles Fleetwood.

William Lilly was a controversial character with powerful friends and enemies, a penniless northerner who walked south to fame and fortune. He attracted the attention of many MPs through Sir Bulstrode Whitelocke, to whom he dedicated his book *Christian Astrology*, published in 1647.

Christian Astrology is one of the classic texts for horary astrology, which either predicts future events or investigates hidden elements in current affairs, based on an astrological chart. Jane Whorwood went to him for advice concerning Charles' escape plans, as well as seeking information about the procurement of acid. She was either unaware of his political leanings or happy to ignore them.

When his first wife Ellen died, he remarried – but in this matter his astrological foresight failed him. He described his second wife, Jane, as 'of the nature of Mars'. The unhappy marriage lasted until her death in 1654, at which Lilly 'shed no tears'. His third marriage, to Ruth Needham, was the happiest of all, she being 'signified in my Nativity by Jupiter in Libra and ... so totally in her condition, to my great Comfort'.

After the Restoration, Lilly quickly fell from grace, his politics not helping his cause. He predicted the Great Fire of London in 1666; that may not have helped either, for some thought it made him a suspect in starting it.

Sir William Hopkins was bankrupted by his hospitality to Charles and his court during the Newport negotiations; in consequence, he had to sell his house and leave the island. He did not live to see the Restoration of the monarchy. His house later became a pub, the Sun Inn.

After his ceaseless attempts to free Charles from Carisbrooke, **Henry Firebrace** (a conflation of two characters in Charles' service) returned to a quieter life in the service of the Earl of Denbigh. After the restoration of the monarchy in 1660, Charles II made him Clerk of the Kitchen. In 1689 Henry retired to Stoke Golding, where he died in 1691 aged seventy-one.

John Bradshawe, despite remaining an ardent republican, fell out with Cromwell during the protectorate years. He disagreed with Cromwell's treatment of parliament and was therefore excluded as an MP, until his final year. He died in 1659 of malaria. On his deathbed he said that if called upon to try the king again he would be 'the first man in England to do it', despite his wife being unhappy with the idea. His dead body received the same treatment as those of Cromwell and Ireton at the Restoration.

Only two of the regicides were pardoned in the Restoration, one of whom was Richard Ingoldsby. Remarkably, Charles II chose to believe him when he said that Cromwell had forced his hand to sign. Others in our story were not so fortunate. Thomas Harrison, the preacher Hugh Peter and the prosecutor John Cook were all hanged, drawn and quartered. Isaac Ewer, another signatory, died in 1651 in Ireland.

Many regicides fled to Europe, where some of them were murdered. Edmund Ludlow was the last surviving regicide, dying in Vevey, Switzerland in 1692.

The following liberties have been taken with known history.

While Hammond, keen to improve his table, did employ his mother in the kitchens at Carisbrooke after the arrival of the king, there is no evidence that he sacked her. She was a staunch Independent, however, and may well have been less accommodating of the king than her son.

We do not know that Cromwell made contact with Charles after the trial, although it would be strongly in character to do so. There was no opponent or adversary he did not seek reconciliation with.

Equally, we are not certain that Jane made contact with Charles after the trial, but there is strong hearsay to suggest that a meeting did take place. It would not have been a meeting well recorded by royalists, for obvious reasons.

Jane's post-trial conversations with Hammond and Cromwell are also imagined.

The only fictitious character in this story is Anthony Wood, the spymaster.